1923

BITTER HERITAGE

BITTER HERITAGE

BY
MARGARET PEDLER

AUTHOR OF
THE HERMIT OF FAR END,
YESTERDAY'S HARVEST,
RED ASHES, ETC.

NEW YORK
GROSSET & DUNLAP
PUBLISHERS

CONTENTS

BITTER HERITAGE

PROLOGUE

I

THE room was very still and silent, so still that even the tiny cracklings of the logs burning evenly in the grate sounded obtrusively noisy. Through the windows the bright afternoon sunshine slanted in, running golden fingers along the mellow old bindings of the books which lined the walls, and flinging tremulous patches of light on the carpet as the branches of the tall trees in the square garden outside wavered in the breeze.

Gay, heartless sunlight glinting in mockingly through the windows. At least, so it seemed to the slip of a girl crouched on the hearth beside the fire. For four days the blinds had been lowered because, in an upper room of the great grey house, a man lay dead. And now that he had been carried to his last resting-place, and the blinds drawn up again, the sunlight flooded the study where he had been wont to sit, exactly as though nothing out of the ordinary had happened—as though no immense and terrible metamorphosis had taken place, snatching a man out of the familiar world he knew into the unknown beyond, and leaving the beloved child of his heart to face the ruin he had left behind him.

For it *was* ruin, unequivocal and hopeless. Only

this morning the lawyer had told her that—an old, dried-up stick of a man with a parchmenty skin and pepper-and-salt hair and a maddening precision of speech. She had wanted to scream aloud when in careful, measured phrases, as though he had been talking to a child, he had explained to her that her father had gambled madly with the money which the public had invested in his companies and had lost it all.

"There are a large number of people ruined in consequence," he added.

"I suppose that's why Dad killed himself," she had answered. "He was such a dear that it would have made him dreadfully unhappy to think that through his miscalculation he'd lost other people's money for them."

An expression of sheer amazement crossed the lawyer's face. "He was such a dear" were the last words he, or anyone with an inside knowledge of Quintin Lindris's financial methods, would have applied to him. The man had sailed very near the wind on several previous occasions and got away with it, but over this last deal with fate, when he had speculated heavily with the investors' money and lost the lot, he had come to utter shipwreck.

He had recognised the fact with that peculiar faculty for facing the best and worst of things which was inherent in him—there was only one thing in life Lindris had not been able to face—and he had met it with the cool determination and assurance that knows irrevocably when the game is up. Always he had lived secretly prepared for an emergency which might make life impossible, and, when the newspapers burst into big headlines announcing the huge swindle which would ruin hundreds of families, they also blared out the fact that Quintin Lindris had committed suicide. He had escaped arrest by a bare few moments. A dead body and an empty phial which had held poison were all that remained for the law to pass judgment on.

And yet to one woman—to this child-woman of seventeen—he had always been "such a dear!"

The old lawyer blinked his eyes. He and his father before him had seen three generations of the Lindris family come and go. Quintin, fifty-three when he rushed headlong out of life, had been the longest lived of them, and each and all had the same wild, gambling blood in their veins, the same moral twist which made them utterly reckless and unscrupulous over money, driven by a headlong passion for chance and hazard. Yet each of them had possessed a certain charm and likableness which those who came in contact with them could not but feel and acknowledge. And each had been well loved by women.

"I think it must have made him very unhappy if he had realised how you were going to be left," commented the old lawyer drily. "That is, if he had any conscience at all," he added mentally.

"I'm going to be very poor, I suppose?" said the girl indifferently. Nothing seemed to her to matter very much beyond the crushing fact that Lindris was dead—that she would never see him again.

The lawyer nodded.

"Yes, you're going to be very poor," he answered. But his "how you were going to be left" had privately envisaged much more than the mere circumstance of poverty. This child, overwhelmed with her grief for a father whom she had obviously adored and equally obviously idealised, had not yet grasped in the least the significance of the shame and disgrace which must henceforth attach to the name of Lindris.

Embezzlement, suicide—to her, so far, the dreadful facts had come only in the softened guise of a miscalculation—a mistake—and death. Who was going to enlighten her, to put the hideous, unvarnished truth before her in plain words? The lawyer shook his head. Not he. He hadn't the cruel courage to pluck from her everything that counted, outrage her love for her father, and strip her bare of honour and good repute —all the things that go to make life sweet and clean and wholesome. Time would do all that quickly enough. He would confine himself strictly to the state of her finances.

"I think," he suggested gently, "you will have to consider taking up some kind of remunerative work."

"Shall I?" She raised a pair of tragic eyes that looked almost preternaturally large in her small white face, hollowed by tears and sleepless nights.

"I'm afraid it will be necessary," he answered, flinching inwardly from the dull misery in those young eyes.

"But why? Have you forgotten Rex? We—were going to be married in a year. Dad didn't want me to marry before I was eighteen. But perhaps—now——" A faint, shy smile lightened her pinched little face, the first gleam, so far, of anything that had spoken, even distantly, of happiness. "I wired to him, you know. He's in Sicily, and I'm expecting him back this after

noon. He couldn't reach England in time for the"—
she paused and swallowed jerkily—"the funeral. . . .
It will be all right when he comes," she added, a note
of confidence in her voice.

She looked up at the old lawyer as though she expected to read immediate relief in his face, but his
expression of gravity and concern remained unaltered.

"It will be all right when Rex comes," she repeated.

"Will it?" He spoke doubtfully, with a curious
absence of conviction. She thought he was rather stupid
and slow at understanding. Her own confidence rose
to meet what she subconsciously sensed to be an attitude of distrust.

"Why, of course it will," she said, smiling upbraid-
ingly.

He gave his shoulders a shake.

"Well, I'm glad of that." Adding, with a sudden
belated kindliness: "Meanwhile, you'd better have a
few pounds in hand to go on with."

He laid two ten pound notes on the table.

"But—but I can't take *your* money," she objected
swiftly, pushing them back towards him. He picked
them up and thrust them into her hand, closing her
fingers round them with his own hard, bony ones.

"Pooh! I can repay myself out of your father's
estate when everything comes to be settled up. There'll
be enough for that," he lied. "And—and"—he went
on awkwardly—"if you're in any difficulty, you'd better let me know. After all, I'm—I'm the family lawyer,
you know."

He was gone, leaving her staring blankly at the two
crisp notes in her hand—a slight, forlorn little figure

in her short black frock, with the mocking sunlight dancing all about her.

II

After the old lawyer's departure, the hours dragged very slowly while she waited for the coming of Rex—Rex Dereham, the man to whom she was engaged. She was extraordinarily alone in the world, without any near relations of any kind, and now that her father was dead, Rex was all that was left to her. The knowledge that he was actually on his way to her—that with every moment he was drawing nearer—brought with it a wan sense of comfort. She wanted him badly—needed his man's strength to lean on, his love to uphold and help her through this unbelievable thing which had happened to her.

Even now she could hardly realise it, realise that the quick, eager, splendid comrade who had been her father had gone out of this world. He had always been so tremendously alive, so full of swift, bubbling-up vitality, that it seemed impossible he could be *dead*.

She had been only a child of seven when her mother died, and she had but a vague recollection of her—of a soft-voiced, fragile, rather beautiful person, who always smelt faintly and delicately of lilies of the valley. Then one day, this fraily lovely person had suddenly vanished out of her childish life—her nurse had told her that she had been "called to God," whatever that might mean—and ever after that she and her father had been all in all to each other.

She had understood nothing of the business side of his life. He had confided nothing. She only knew that sometimes for days together he would be terribly pre-occupied, wearing a tense, almost haggard look of strain on his face, while at others he would be in absurdly high spirits, like a boy let out of school. But, whenever he was not engrossed in business matters, he and she had been glorious playfellows—hunting together, motoring, yachting, travelling abroad, enjoying everything that the good gay world has to offer. The only grumbler was Miss Marchmont—"Montie," as they affectionately dubbed her—to whom the girl's education had been entrusted, and who was wont to lament that the one thing it seemed difficult to find time for was her pupil's studies. But Lindris and his daughter only laughed her complaints good-humouredly aside. They found time to be happy together, and that was all they cared about.

But now, face to face with a complete revolution of affairs, with the absence of money, of even sufficient money to live upon, brought suddenly before her by the lawyer's dry: "I think you will have to consider taking up some kind of work," the girl began to appreciate her total unpreparedness to perform any kind of remunerative work. Of course, it didn't really matter, she reflected, since she would never actually be obliged to earn her own living. Rex Dereham was very well off, and as his wife she would be safe from any need to go down into the labour market and cry her wares. But it was rather discouraging, a trifle humiliating, to realise how few saleable wares she possessed.

She played the piano moderately well, and sang in a girlish, wistful little pipe of a voice that was not without its own attractiveness. She could ride almost any horse you liked to put her on, drive a car, and help sail a boat. But, when all was said and done, none of these qualifications, either singly or collectively, possessed much marketable value. Why, she wasn't fit to apply even for the humble post of a nursery governess! A faint, rather dreary smile of self-mockery crossed her lips. And then the train of thought prompted by the old lawyer's suggestion was submerged by a despairing recollection of the initial cause of all this self-examination, of the lawyer's visit itself, and of that heart-broken telegram summoning Rex to return.

She did not cry. After that first numb twenty-four hours which had followed the discovery of Lindris's dead body, when it seemed as though no tears would ever come to relieve the dumb misery which closed like ice round her heart, she had at last broken down and cried so much that she felt now as though she could never cry again—as though she had shed all the tears of a lifetime. She sat crouched by the fire, still and motionless, staring bleakly into the flames, waiting in the cruelly sunlit room for Rex's coming.

At last the silence was broken by the sound of the house door opening and closing, then followed a man's quick, striding footsteps. Finally the door of the study swung back, and Rex himself, the dust of night and day travel still on his clothes, stood on the threshold. His face—clean-cut and a shade hard-looking for all its indisputable good looks—was somewhat haggard, as if he had not slept much upon the journey. His keen, light-gray eyes—it was in the eyes the hardness lay—

flashed over the girlish figure on the hearth with a swift, questioning scrutiny that seemed to hold some hidden anxiety.

In an instant she was on her feet and had sprung towards him.

"Rex—oh, Rex!" Like an overtired child she slipped into his arms and a small, tremulous sigh of utter relief fluttered from between her lips. "Oh, darling, I have wanted you so!"

For a moment Dereham held her in his embrace, but above her bent head his face wore a curiously conflicting expression. It was as though the man were nerving himself to some action from which he inwardly recoiled. At last he put her a little away from him.

"My dear girl, this is all very terrible." When he spoke, the intonation of his voice was so oddly stilted, so unaccustomed, that she looked up, startled. It might almost have been some mere acquaintance speaking, perfunctorily condoning with her.

"Very terrible," he repeated, a trifle more human warmth creeping involuntarily into his tones as his glance took in the marks of strain on the young face upturned to his.

"But it will be all right now—now you've come. Only—only Dad——" She broke off, and the clasp of her hands on his coat sleeve unconsciously tightened as she tried to control the sob that had climbed to her throat.

"Yes, yes, I know." He spoke soothingly. "You must have had a terrible time, all alone like that, poor child. I can't tell you how sorry I am. It is a trag-

edy———" He hesitated, then demanded abruptly:
"Have you seen the newspapers?"

She shook her head, a look of bewilderment on her
face.

"The newspapers? No, I've not seen them. I haven't
wanted to——read. But I don't think," she went on
doubtfully; "I don't think there've been any about."
As a matter of fact, Miss Marchmont had seen to that.
At the moment, the daily papers would not have made
pleasant reading for the daughter of Quintin Lindris.

Rex uttered an ejaculation, half impatient, half despairing.

"Then you don't know——you don't understand———"
She answered quickly.

"Oh yes, I do. I know Dad's lost all his money. But
——I've lost Dad. That's the only thing that really matters. Rex"——she paused and regarded him with a funny
little smile——"Rex, do you know you've never kissed
me yet?"

Half instinctively he bent to kiss her, then suddenly
drew back.

"I suppose I'm trying to get used to the new order
of things," he said.

"The new order of things?" she repeated curiously.
"What do you mean?"

"I mean——I shall have to get used to not kissing
you."

"But——but why?"

He hesitated. Pain and a certain obstinate determination fought for supremacy in his eyes and mouth.

"Well——I hate saying it!——but we can't very well
afford to marry now, can we?"

She glanced at him in frank surprise.

"Why, I always thought you were quite rich," she answered. "Not that I mind a bit, though, dear, if you're not," she added hastily, fearing she might have hurt him, given him a wrong impression of her meaning. Then, as he remained silent, she continued rather shyly: "Does that matter—our not being rich? Would you mind it—very much, Rex? I could be ever so economical. I'd learn to cook—Montie would help me at the beginning, I know."

"It isn't that. It's not a question of money." He spoke harshly—a harshness born of the fact that what he was about to do went badly against the grain. No decent man likes being driven by circumstances into playing a low-down game—if for no other reason than that it pricks his self-esteem to know that he hasn't the courage to play any other.

"Then if it isn't a matter of money, what is it?" asked the girl slowly. "I don't understand." For the first time a chill sense of fear, of apprehension of she knew not what, ran through her.

"No, that's just it!" he broke out with a kind of suppressed violence. "You don't understand. If you did, you'd know at once that any marriage between us was out of the question. Why hasn't that old fool of a lawyer—why hasn't Miss Marchmont *made* you understand? . . . God! I don't see why I should have to do it!"

She retreated a step from his side.

"Rex—what is it I must understand? Tell me, why can't we be married?"

She spoke very quietly, but with a certain insistence

that drove him at last into speech. Rough, disjointed speech, because he hated what he was doing, hated himself for doing it, and because, too, in his own fashion—a fashion that could not stand the crucible test—he loved the girl who stood listening to him with hands tightly clasped and eyes in which ignorance and non-comprehension were word by word transmuted into a sick, tortured realisation of shame and disgrace.

". . . your father . . . a company promoter . . . swindled everyone who had money in his rotten companies. He's ruined hundreds . . . hundreds." The phrases knocked disjointedly against her brain. And then: "There's a very ugly name for a man who speculates with other people's money. . . ."

"I see." Was it minutes or hours after Rex had finished that she found herself replying? She glanced curiously at the clock on the chimney-piece. Its hands pointed to a minute past three, and she remembered hearing it strike the hour whilst Rex was still talking. The sweet, silvery tones had clashed grotesquely against the word "suicide." So it was only a minute ago—a minute that seemed to hold an eternity. It had transformed her all at once from a girl into a woman.

"I see. And you don't want to marry me . . . any longer . . . because I'm the daughter of a—a swindler and a suicide?" She spoke slowly and laboriously, as if she found it difficult to enunciate her words.

"It isn't that I 'don't want.' I'd give the world to marry you. You know that." He made a sudden impulsive step towards her, his arms held out. But she backed away from him.

"Oh, don't pretend!" she said wearily. "There's no need for pretence—now."

"I'm not pretending," he asserted vehemently. "I love you. You know I love you. But you must see for yourself that I can't marry you. It wouldn't be fair to my people—to my mother and sisters——"

She checked him with a gesture.

"Oh, haven't you the pluck to stand by your decision instead of hiding behind your mother and sisters?" Her low voice shook with a passion of scorn. "At least, be honest and say that it's you yourself who want nothing to do with me—because my name is Lindris."

Her scorn roused him to justification. After all, his reason told him that there was some justification. And the knowledge that this was the last time he would ever see her, the realisation that they were going out of each other's lives—and hers was bound to be such a broken life henceforth—stirred the love he had for her to an unwonted tenderness and gentleness.

Despite her movement of recoil, of repugnance, he laid his hands on her shoulders and stood looking down at her with eyes that held a very real misery.

"I know it must seem like that to you. But you're not being quite fair to me——"

"Are you fair to me?" she interrupted bitterly.

"My dear, your father's put you in such a position that no one will ever be quite fair to you. Don't you see, we none of us stand alone? I *have* my mother and my sisters to consider. I can't put—forgive me—the daughter of a thief, of a swindler, in the place my mother's held. Or"—his voice dropped a little— "make her the mother of my children."

A sudden tremor ran through her body. He had struck to the very depths of her womanhood with that last sentence. But an instinctive pride helped her to hide her hurt.

"I don't think I should ever want to be the mother of your children," she said, with a delicate inflection on the word "your" that stung like the cut of a whip.

She slid out of his grasp.

"Now, will you go please?" she went on tonelessly. "I should like you to go."

She stood rigidly watching him as he crossed the room and passed through the doorway—a thin, erect, defiant young figure, straight and unyielding as a slender rod. It was only when the door closed behind him and his footsteps had receded into silence that she broke, crumpling up into a little heap upon the hearthrug, where he had found her.

The fire had burned low, but she made no effort to mend it, only crouched beside its dying embers, staring into them with blank, unseeing eyes.

She was envisaging a new world—a new world wherein no one would ever want her again, because she was the child of Quintin Lindris, because she bore his name and his blood ran in her veins. "The sins of the fathers . . ." It was true, then; they *were* visited upon the children. Even sins that were, perhaps, only mistakes. For still her loyalty to the father she had adored made her try to extenuate his fault.

During the hours that followed she went down into the darkest depths life had yet revealed to her. She felt utterly desolate and outcast. She supposed lepers must feel as she did. Neither man nor woman would ever want her to share their lives—Rex had shown her that. She was set apart, damned from the outset, handicapped from the very beginning of things.

But life had still to be lived, and presently the inherent courage of untried youth began to stir in her. She would make her own life, stand alone if needs be, and out of the conflict of her thoughts emerged one crystalline resolve, born of an innate sense of justice and fair-play and of her love for Quintin Lindris.

"If ever there's something big I can do for anyone to make up for all the people Dad has hurt, I'll do it."

CHAPTER I

A MORNING IN PARIS

BILLY RIVINGTON, resplendent in silk pyjamas that rather suggested a sunset at sea and a dressing-gown upon which Chinese dragons sported over an elaborately embroidered country, rapped smartly on the door of his mother's bedroom. A voice, tinged with hungry impatience, responded to his knock.

"*Entrez!*"

He poked a curly head, fair hair still wet and gleaming from his morning tub, round the door.

"No luck, Mim," he observed with a grin. "I'm not the *sommelier* with your brekkie, so you can take that look of joyful anticipation off your face."

Lady Bridget, who had sat up briskly in bed as the door opened, sank back disheartened once more against her pillows.

"Ugh! Then for goodness' sake ring again," she said. "I've already rung three times without producing any result."

Billy nodded as he pressed the bell-push firmly and continuously.

"I know. These Paris hotels are the limit."

Releasing the bell at last, he bent over and kissed his mother heartily. It was quite evident that these two

were on the best of terms—on those charming terms
of an equality of friendship which so often exist nowadays betwixt mothers and sons.

There was small facial resemblance between them,
however, although a quizzical lift of one dark eyebrow
a trifle higher than the other when Lady Bridget
smiled, repeated in Billy's light-brown ones, and a certain humorous twist of the mouth betrayed the link of
relationship. But Lady Bridget's keen dark eyes, grey,
waving, shingled hair—once black as a crow's wing—
and her straight, well-cut nose with the disarming little
bluntness at its tip that robbed it of all severity, were
the exact antithesis of Billy's pleasant freckled coun-
tenance with its nondescript nose, appealing, whimsical
green eyes, and its crop of fair to reddish hair.

His mother's good looks were an inheritance from
her grandfather, while Billy took his nice blonde ugli-
ness from the Honourable Dickie Rivington, to whom
her people had hastily married her off when she was
barely one and twenty in order to prevent her con-
tracting what they regarded as a *mésalliance*. Subse-
quently, she and Dickie had lived a pleasant and
unexciting existence together until the latter was
gathered prematurely to his fathers as the result of a
motor accident. Billy's appearance in the world had
been delayed until eleven years after the marriage, but
his mother was a very modern and vital fifty-three, so
that the difference in their ages had raised no barrier
of outlook between them.

"I've had a letter from Carol Mortimer," announced
Lady Bridget, while they still waited for the *café com-
plet,* which they were wont to take companionably to-

gether. "She's sent me the name of that dressmaker, Madame—Madame—let me see——" She picked up the letter and ran her eyes down the first page. "Madame Clémentine. We'll go there this morning. I must have some clothes."

Billy nodded.

"Having none," he replied gravely. "Do I come with you?"

"Of course. Unless you've anything else you want to do—see Barbara or anything?"

He shook his head.

"No. Barbara only has jam every other day. I mean, by the laws and ordinances laid down by Madame Duclaire, Barbara is only permitted to play about with me every other day. Tommy-rot, I call it," he wound up discontentedly.

"Well, you must remember she's with the Duclaires in a kind of job—giving English lessons in return for French and music," Lady Bridget reminded him. "And they can't be expected to forget that fact just because friends of hers are stopping in Paris."

"No, I suppose not," he agreed with reluctance. "Anyhow, it leaves me free to supervise your choice of frocks, Mim—Oh, praise be!" He broke off joyfully as a waiter entered carrying the breakfast tray. "Here's our *café* at last!"

Billy attended to his mother's wants, then, perching himself on the foot of her bed, proceeded to demolish large quantities of roll and butter and *pain grillé*, accompanied by steaming hot *café-au-lait*.

"By the way——" He paused with a piece of roll half-way towards his mouth. "How are things with

Carol and that miserable old devil of a husband of hers? Does she say anything?"

Lady Bridget's cheery face clouded over. Other people's troubles were very real to her, and when, as in this case, they were the troubles of someone for whom she had a great affection, she was apt to make them her own.

"She says so little that I'm afraid they're rather worse than usual," she answered unhappily. "It's a very short letter, just giving me Madame What's-her-name's address and a few items of local news. That's all. She never mentions Sir Francis."

"I wonder," said Billy meditatively, "what on earth possessed her to marry him! It certainly"——with a grin——"couldn't have been love at first sight, for a more unprepossessing, malicious-looking individual I've never encountered. I'm certain he's mad. Besides, he dopes."

"She made a ghastly mistake, poor girl," assented his mother. "And she's paid for it since every day of her life. I think it was a case of marrying for money. Someone told me that the Kenyons had hardly six-pence to bless themselves with at the time of Carol's marriage."

"Humph! Well, if I were a woman I'd much rather starve than marry Sir Francis," commented Billy gruffly. "I'd do *something* else, anyway. P'r'aps not starve, exactly——take up some job."

"Oh, my dear, if women knew beforehand all that marriage involves, quite a lot of them would 'do something else.' You see, so few men are fitted to be husbands——really nice, understanding husbands *de luxe*."

"Aren't you asking rather a good deal? You couldn't very well be a husband *de luxe* on a small salary, for instance, mother mine."

"Oh yes, you could. You couldn't live a *de luxe* life in material things, I grant you, but you could be a *de luxe* husband in all the other things that matter. And there's a whole heap of those other things, which only a few men realise. I do hope," continued Lady Bridget, regarding her offspring reflectively, "that I've brought you up to be a decent sort of husband, Billy."

"I hope so," he returned modestly. Adding, with a chuckle: "Barbara will probably tell you off one day if you haven't. That is, if ever you and the rector come to the conclusion that we've reached a sufficiently ripe old age to get engaged."

"Well, you haven't yet, anyway," retorted Lady Bridget in decided tones, although she knew perfectly well, in her heart of hearts, that the question of an engagement between her son and Barbara Fane would be bound to come up for judgment before very long, once the latter had returned from her year's study in Paris.

Billy grinned.

"Meanwhile, Mim, you'd better go on training me up in the way I should go. I imagine that taking an intelligent interest in his wife's clothes is one of the adjuncts of a model husband, so suppose we both dress and I'll toddle round with you to Madame Clémentine's."

"Quite a good suggestion." Lady Bridget nodded across at him approvingly, and, pushing aside the breakfast tray, prepared to get up. "I'll dress at once. Bundle off, Billy."

So Billy bundled off, to return later on discreetly clad in the very latest, and looking, for all his undeniable plainness, a thoroughly well-groomed and presentable specimen of youthful English manhood.

Half an hour later found him and his mother seated side by side in two of the luxuriously upholstered chairs which adorned the show-rooms of the Maison Clémentine, while an array of attractive mannequins, with figures like sylphs, paraded up and down before them, exhibiting the latest creations of fashion.

"That's a smart frock!" remarked Billy with sudden enthusiasm. Lady Bridget looked in the direction indicated and wondered shrewdly to herself whether it were the frock itself or the girl who wore it which had really attracted his attention. She was not particularly pretty, but in some odd fashion she stood out from amongst her sister mannequins. She was very slight—but then, they were all that, these girls, just like a cluster of slender, swaying reeds. Yet something singled her out from the rest—some indefinable little air of independence, a half-shy, half-disdainful turn of her small head as, in obedience to a gesture from Madame Clémentine, whose alert, business-like ears had caught Billy's approving comment, she advanced a few steps and posed this way and that in front of Lady Bridget, the better to show off the model frock she was wearing.

She was rather pale, with a pallor born of an indoor occupation and overheated atmospheres, and out of the delicate whiteness of her face looked a pair of hazel eyes, the irises flecked with tiny specks of darker brown which gave them an odd depth of colour.

Straight brows, narrow and well-defined, and a sensitive mouth that yet held a certain unmistakable determination in the way it closed, gave a distinctive individuality to the young face framed in its crop of russet hair.

"It has a beautiful line, this model—*parfait!*" declared Madame Clémentine enthusiastically, giving a caressing little touch to a fold of the frock the girl was wearing. "Madame can see for herself how it slenderises the figure."

Lady Bridget, candidly aware of the rather widehipped, well-corseted figure bequeathed to her by a Victorian mother, snorted.

"That young woman's figure doesn't require any 'slenderising'," she returned succinctly. "She's as thin as a rail, so what's the good of showing off frocks on her which are meant for *me?*"

Billy chuckled delightedly, but Madame Clémentine's limited understanding of English failed to grasp the true inwardness of Lady Bridget's comment. She was only aware that her prospective customer was finding some fault with the mannequin's figure—one of her best show-girls, too. She burst into a torrent of French, interspersed with broken bits of English, volubly explaining that she was not proposing to squeeze madame into that identical frock—*non, non, pas du tout,* but into one like it, with the same marvellous line, made to the measure of madame's own excellent and desirable proportions.

"But, don't you see," protested Lady Bridget, unimpressed, when the Frenchwoman paused for breath, "but, don't you see, I've got to imagine myself into that frock? Haven't you got a mannequin with a good stout serviceable figure who could really show me, more or less, what *I'd* look like in the frocks you're trying to sell me? Billy"——turning to the latter in desperation——"you tell her. If you can't speak French enough for that after all the lessons you've had with the rector at home, you ought to be ashamed of yourself!"

But Billy was rocking with silent mirth and made not the least attempt to facilitate matters. His mother shrugged her shoulders resignedly, then, detecting a suddenly suppressed smile on the face of the mannequin, she darted at her with sudden hope.

"Do you understand English?"

The girl's eyes twinkled.

"I *am* English," she answered demurely.

Lady Bridget heaved a sigh of relief.

"Thank goodness!" she ejaculated fervently. "Then perhaps you can make Madame Thingumy understand what I mean."

The girl nodded, and, turning to the Frenchwoman, addressed her in fluent French.

"Perhaps——Maria-Thérèse?" she suggested tentatively. "She is much bigger than I am. And there are those models, some in large sizes, which have just come in from Huguelin which might suit madame."

The dressmaker's face cleared. She found her young English employée very useful at times in interpreting the curious vagaries of her compatriots. She issued a few quick instructions, and very shortly garments of a more suitable style, exhibited by a show-girl of bigger build, were put on view.

Meanwhile, the English mannequin herself stood by, now and then bending forward to arrange the hang of a skirt drapery or twitch the collar of an opera-coat into place, or to murmur a *sotto voce* word of advice to Lady Bridget: "Don't have that. It won't suit you. Ask to see the 'Victorine' model, instead." In the intervals when her help was not required Billy exchanged a few desultory remarks with her.

"Don't you get fed up with trying on frocks?" he asked presently.

She shook her head.

"What would be the use? It's my job. What I *should* like——" She broke off abruptly, as though she had nearly betrayed herself into saying something that would have been better left unsaid.

"Yes?" he said inquiringly. "What would you like?"

She hesitated a moment, then bestowed a small, whimsical smile upon him.

"To *wear* frocks like these."

He nodded understandingly. The sheer femininity of her had rushed out in her answer, and he realised with a quick sympathy the hardship it must be to any girl who loved pretty clothes, and couldn't afford them, to be hourly putting on the most delightful frocks—for other people to choose from.

"You'd look topping in them, too," he declared heartily. "It's rotten bad luck on you."

She gave a low laugh.

"Oh, well, there are all kinds of jobs. I'd ever so much rather be a mannequin than sell goloshes, for instance! Comparisons are sometimes quite helpful instead of odious."

"Plucky little person," commented Billy to himself, as she turned away from him to adjust some detail in a cloak Lady Bridget was trying on at the moment.

When at last the latter's many purchases were completed, both she and Billy bade the mannequin a cheery good-bye.

"Thank you so much for your splendid help, my dear," said Lady Bridget kindly, patting her shoulder. "I don't know what I should have done without it—bought all the things I didn't want, I expect."

Then she sailed out of the room, escorted to the door by a beaming and gratified Madame Clémentine, and the girl heaved a brief sigh, feeling almost as though a couple of friends had taken their departure.

CHAPTER II

PROPHECY

MADAME CLÉMENTINE was almost purring with satisfaction when, after the Rivingtons had taken their departure, she reckoned up the sum total to which Lady Bridget's bill would amount, but to the English show-girl the shop seemed to have become all at once unaccountably dull and depressing. It was as if the sun had disappeared behind a cloud.

The remainder of her day was passed as usual, showing off frock after frock to the ordinary unimaginative run of customers, who apparently regarded her as no more than an animated lay figure and would, she reflected, have been immensely astonished, and probably rather offended, if she had suddenly given vent to a perfectly human desire to wear any of the beautiful gowns they contemplated buying.

The memory of Lady Bridget's visit lingered in her mind, and she was conscious of the little warm glow of pleasure which an unexpected encounter with nice people is prone to leave behind it. It even accompanied her home in the evening when she returned to the tiny, roof-high, two-roomed *appartement* she rented in the Rue Grise—a narrow, drab-looking side-street whose depressing appearance tallied only too accurately with its name. And it was not until she had cleared away and washed up her supper-things, and was sitting with mind and hands idle, that the inspiriting little glow began to fade, petering out under an almost inevitable reaction.

But for her circumstances—the lack of money which compelled her to earn her living as a mannequin at Maison Clémentine, she realised that she might have met and known as friends just such people as Lady Bridget and Billy. She had been born to something very different from this mean street in Paris where she lodged, and she looked back with a sick longing to the days when she would, as a matter of course, have met and mingled with people like the Rivingtons. They were her own kind, just as her fellow-mannequins, as Madame Clémentine herself, most emphatically were not.

It was not often that she allowed herself to look back or dwell upon the past. Generally she managed to keep her thoughts firmly fixed upon the present, and busied herself with the fulfilment of each day's tasks as they came along. But to-day, in spite of herself, those English clients of Madame Clémentine's, with their breezy, friendly attitude and what, for lack of a better word, she described to herself as their "niceness," had somehow contrived to upset the stoical fortitude to which she had schooled herself. She was conscious of a sudden bitter sense of rebellion against her lot.

How she hated it all! The daily journey to Maison Clémentine, on foot if fine, fighting for a seat in an omnibus if wet; the compulsion of fixed hours; the nerve-racking necessity of being always smiling and pleasant, always respectful and polite, no matter how tired she felt, nor how much she longed to sit down and rest instead of gliding about the showroom, displaying one lovely frock after another for the benefit of some rich woman who had more time and money on her hands than she knew what to do with. She loathed it all! In spite of herself, a few slow, scalding drops forced their way between her eyelids and trickled down her cheeks. With a rush of self-contempt she snatched out her handkerchief and mopped her eyes vigorously, mentally apostrophising herself as "a sickening little coward."

She had only just finished drying away the last persistent tear when a resonant rat-rat sounded on the door of her *appartement*. Giving her shoulders a small determined shake, she hastily tucked away a rather moist handkerchief and prepared to answer the imperative knock. As she threw open the door, from the ill-lit gloom of the landing outside came a rush of cold, mist-laden air, together with the sound of a gay voice greeting her in French.

"*Te voilà, ma petite* Herrick!—*À la bonne heure!* I wondered if I should find you at home this evening."

"Naturally I'm at home," she replied, in the same language. Adding with a smile: "My social engagements are not precisely overwhelming, you know."

"*Tant mieux.*" The new-comer, a laughing, dark-eyed young man with the words "art student" written all over him, snatched off the béret he was wearing and, bending his head, kissed her affectionately on both cheeks. "*Et comment ça va, chérie?*" he went on, as she drew him into the room and closed the door, shutting out the chilly mist that mounted from the well of the staircase.

She smiled unmirthfully.

"A trifle worse than usual, I think," she said. "I've been feeling about as cheerful as a November fog. But now you've come, I don't propose to go on grousing. I'll make you some coffee instead."

"I'll help," he responded cheerfully. "You make it while I fish out the cups and things."

With the sure knowledge of long habit, he marched over to a tall cupboard in the corner and began to take down the necessary crockery, while Herrick, whose spirits had already risen several degrees since the advent of her visitor, busied herself preparing the coffee.

Paul Breton, son of a French father and an English mother, was almost her only intimate friend in Paris. Meeting originally at a studio "rag" in the Latin Quarter, whither she had been taken by a fellow-mannequin who occasionally sat as a model to some of the students, they had struck up a queer, understanding friendship with each other, almost fraternal in its quality, yet with just that piquancy added to it which came from the fact that they were not actually brother and sister. "It's because you're half an Englishman that we hit it off so well," Herrick was wont to declare. And it is certain that few of the other students of the Latin Quarter would have understood the blending of spontaneous warm-heartedness and English reticence, of fervent camaraderie and coolly detached independence, which was Herrick.

"And now, what's the cause of this particular fit of the blues?" demanded Paul in good round English, as they sat down on either side of the stove to drink their coffee, a tin of biscuits conveniently on the floor between them. He spoke English equally as well as French, and he and Herrick were in the habit of dropping irrelevantly from one language into the other just as the spirit moved them.

"The original cause?"

He smiled.

"Of course."

"Two ever such nice English people who came into Madame Clémentine's this morning—a mother and son."

"*Eh bien,* if they were so nice, why have they produced such a depressing effect?"

"Why, because——"

"Because?" he repeated quizzically, as she paused.

"Oh, because, I think, they made me realise what life might have been if only Dad hadn't lost his money. I—I'm so cut off!" she burst out passionately. "Cut off from the sort of life I'd like to lead—from the sort of people I'd like to know."

Paul nodded.

"I know," he agreed. "Parents are very careless— no sense of responsibility. They dump you down in the world for their own amusement, bring you up expensively—and then lose their money. And *you* have to pay the piper. . . . I've been through just the same kind of thing, you know, *ma chérie.*"

"But at least you had genius—genius which will one day bring you all you want."

"I don't know about genius," he objected. "I can

paint a bit, certainly, and I suppose I'll get on some day."

"Of course you will. Whereas I——" she flung out her hands in a little despairing gesture of emptiness—"I've no abilities, no training, *nothing*—except a pretty figure to hang clothes on! I'm in a rut, and I shall have to stay in a rut all the days of my life."

"Oh no, you won't," he promised. "You'll marry me one day—when my 'genius' has materialised into houses and gardens and chairs and tables. And we'll live happily ever after."

Herrick shook her head.

"No, I sha'n't. I sha'n't ever marry anyone," she said soberly.

"Fiddlesticks! Of course you'll marry. Tell you what, I've got a pack of cards in my pocket, and I'll read your fortune for you."

Her eyes sparkled. There are very few people, cynical or incredulous though they may profess themselves, who are totally impervious to the thrill which comes of trying to peep into the future, that is, unless the spirit of youth is completely dead within them. And in Herrick that spirit was very much alive, although checked and kept under by circumstances.

"Oh, Paul, will you? Can you?"

"Of course I will. I'd do any old thing to make you feel a trifle more bucked with life in general than you are at the moment."

"I don't know whether it will do that. Whatever good fortune there is in store for me—if there *is* any —must be ever so far away."

"Pooh! You can't be sure of that. Still, as a tonic for the immediate present, I'll give a studio party one evening, if you like. Would that please you?"

She nodded.

"'M." She made a little affirmative sound of pleasure. "I love your studio rags."

"Very well, then, that's settled. The present being happily arranged, I'll now proceed to show you how rosy your future really is."

He produced from his pocket a pack of well-thumbed, grubby-looking cards, and, subtracting the queen of hearts from amongst them, laid it face upward on the table.

"There, that represents you. The queen of diamonds is too fair a lady and the queen of clubs too dark. You've medium colouring, so the queen of hearts is your personal card." He held out the remainder of the pack towards her. "Now, shuffle them, and cut three times," he commanded.

"You won't make things up, will you?" she stipulated. "Don't pretend I've got a 'rosy' future just to please me. Promise."

He drew his finger across his throat, his eyes laughing down at her.

"*Je te jure!* S'help me!"

Then he dragged forward a small table and began to lay out the cards.

"I'd no idea you told fortunes," she observed, watching the proceedings with interest.

"I've a great many gifts that you've not yet unearthed," he answered with mock gravity. "Actually, I'm a veritable mine of undiscovered talent."

Herrick giggled suddenly, and then was conscious of a flash of inner surprise and gratitude as she realised that Paul's cheery fooling had already actually succeeded in its object of driving away her depression. She no longer felt low-spirited, but found herself waiting eagerly to hear his divination of her cards.

"Well?" she said expectantly. "What do you see?"

"Don't hurry me," he returned judicially. "It's really—yes, your cards are really quite interesting."

He had dealt them into four packs of equal size and spread them out, face upwards, on the table, with the queen of hearts in the centre, and he now sat staring down at them with an unwonted look of concentration in his eyes.

"Yes," he said at last ruminatively, "it's evidently quite certain. It appears in every pack."

"What appears?"

"Why, that a great change is imminent in your life, my young friend."

"Then I hope it's a change for better and not for worse," she suggested.

"Certainly it's for better. You're going on a long journey——"

"Fortune-tellers always say that," she interrupted snubbily.

But Paul remained entirely unmoved.

"I can't help what fortune-tellers always say. I repeat: You're going on a journey, across the water. And I see you very shortly meeting quite a number of people——"

"At your studio rag, I suppose!" interpolated Herrick flippantly.

"Don't interrupt. These will be people you haven't met before. Then—oh yes, here comes the king of hearts. He arrives very unexpectedly on the scene, and, you being the queen of hearts, of course his coming affects you more than anything else. He wants to marry you. . . . H'm. . . ." He paused irresolutely, poking the cards about with an irritable forefinger.

"Something bad appearing?" queried Herrick. "Go on. Don't be afraid to tell me."

"Well, there *is* trouble of some kind ahead," he acknowledged, with reluctance. "Because the knave of hearts has pushed himself in between you and the king. Knaves are always up to mischief—the knave of hearts especially. You remember—he stole tarts. A bad fellow."

He gathered up the cards and handed them back to her.

"Shuffle again, will you? And cut twice."

Herrick complied, and once more he laid out the cards on the table and studied them frowningly.

"There he is again, that thief of a knave, between you and the nine of hearts—that's the card of good luck and happiness, the best card in the pack." He swept them up together again. "Shuffle once more, a third time for luck. And cut them once this time—only once."

She obeyed, and for the third time Paul dealt them out.

"Oh, damn! Now the nine of spades—the card of misfortune—is standing right between you and the nine of hearts. And that wretched knave is above the king—trying hard to overcome him."

"My cards are bad, then?" said Herrick in rather a flat voice. It seemed very absurd, because of course she didn't really believe in any kind of fortune-telling, yet the fact remained that she was aware of a distinct sinking in the region of her heart because her cards had turned out so unsatisfactorily.

Paul, too, seemed somewhat disconcerted. His usually laughing eyes held a look of mingled annoyance and regret.

"I'm terribly sorry," he said. "But the cards do show that, although there's luck of some sort coming, something stands just between you and happiness. At least, it does at present," he added, trying to infuse a dash of encouragement into his tones. "But that doesn't mean that it always will."

Herrick shook her head. Her small, sharply-angled face wore a curious pinched look.

"Yes, it does. And I know what it is," she said quietly. "It will always stand—just there. Between me and happiness."

CHAPTER III

A DEAD MAN'S LETTER

YES. All the things ordered by Milady Rivington are ready to be sent to her hotel. And I believe you are to take them to her."

"I?" Herrick stared in amazement at the fellow-mannequin who had just presented her with this piece of information.

"*Mais oui, toi,*" replied the girl, nodding. "I over-heard Madame Clémentine saying so to the *première*. *Et pourquoi pas?* I only wish they would give *me* the chance of going! It would be much more amusing than remaining here, showing off frocks all morning."

"I think you must be mistaken," returned Herrick, and went composedly on her way upstairs to take off the frock which she had just been showing to some customers who were even then leaving the shop.

As the street door swung to behind them, Madame Clémentine's shrill voice, calling upon her to come back, arrested her midway on the staircase, and she obediently retraced her footsteps.

"*Ecoutez,* 'Errique," began the Frenchwoman, when the girl reached her side, "it is the affair of Milady Rivington. She has sent a telephone message desiring that her frocks shall be delivered this morning, and she asks also that you shall take them to her."

It was an unusual request for any customer to make. A dressmaker can occupy the time of specially chosen mannequins in more profitable ways than by employing them as errand-girls, and Herrick waited for the torrent of indignation which Lady Bridget's petition was certain to call forth. To her astonishment, however, Madame Clémentine continued with the utmost amiability:

"C'était le fils de milady lui-même qui m'a téléphoné. C'est un beau garçon, celui-là. Et d'une politesse! It was a veritable surprise to me that an Englishman could be so altogether *gentil.* Charming—but charming!"

Herrick, with a small amused smile, reflected that Billy must have been putting forth his most beguiling efforts over the 'phone in order to propitiate Madame Clémentine and obtain her agreement to his mother's request.

"It seems milady is very anxious that you yourself should take her frocks," pursued the dressmaker. "It is not usual, I know, but it is a little favour which *monsieur* has asked on her behalf. And she has bought a great many things, so, if it pleases her——" She shrugged her shoulders and regarded Herrick expectantly.

"I will go, madame, of course," returned the girl quietly.

The other nodded.

"Entendu, alors. You had better take a taxi and start at once." She moved away, pausing only to toss a final instruction over her shoulder: "And be sure to show milady how to put on that Huguelin cloak of

brocade. She has not the least idea how to wear her clothes."

Herrick felt inwardly rather excited as, a few minutes later, she drove away from the Maison Clémentine surrounded by several large cardboard dress-boxes containing Lady Bridget's new purchases. But outwardly she was perfectly composed when she presented herself at the hotel, and something in her manner—some intrinsic little touch of dignity—impelled even the gold-braided and brass-buttoned Cerberus at the door to an unwonted civility—and that, notwithstanding the multitude of cardboard boxes which betrayed her lowly position in the social world.

Arrived at the Rivingtons' rooms, she received a characteristically warm welcome from Lady Bridget, who forthwith plunged into an orgy of trying on the contents of the dress-boxes, Billy meanwhile standing by and delivering himself of appropriate masculine comment. It was not until over an hour had elapsed that Lady Bridget desisted and glanced exhaustedly towards the clock, whose hands pointed to half-past twelve.

"Thank goodness that's the last one!" she exclaimed in tones of heartfelt relief, as she disembarrassed herself of the Huguelin cloak. "But they're all wonderful. Tell Madame Clémentine I'm very pleased with everything. And now, I'm simply famishing for my lunch."

"I should imagine mademoiselle is, too," remarked Billy, with a kindly glance at the girl's rather white face.

"I'm sure she is. Why not stay and have lunch with

us?" suggested his mother hospitably. "That would be delightful. Billy, ring and tell them to serve *déjeuner* for three."

But Herrick arrested him with a hasty gesture as he was making his way towards the bell.

"No, no, please don't ring; I mustn't stop for *déjeuner*," she said. "It's very kind indeed of you to have asked me," she went on, turning to her hostess with a shy smile, "but Madame Clémentine will be expecting me back."

Lady Bridget's face fell like that of a disappointed child. For some unknown reason she found the little English mannequin curiously attractive, and she had been charmed with the idea of keeping her to lunch.

"Oh, surely Madame Clémentine wouldn't mind?" she protested. "Billy, go and telephone to her and ask in your prettiest French if Miss——" She paused and glanced interrogatively towards Herrick.

"My name is Waylen," supplied the girl.

"Ask if Miss Waylen can remain."

Billy rose manfully to the occasion. Once more his gay, boyish voice travelled ingratiatingly over the wires, and Madame Clémentine, her face wreathed in smiles, purred volubly back into the mouth of the telephone.

"*Mais oui, mais oui, monsieur*. Assuredly, if it makes pleasure to Milady Rivington, *la petite* can remain for *déjeuner*. . . . And milady is satisfied of the gowns? That is good. *Au revoir, monsieur, au revoir.*"

"So *that's* all right," said Billy to himself, hanging up the receiver, and proceeded to his mother's rooms to announce that Herrick had received permission to remain.

The lunch which followed, served in the Rivingtons' private sitting-room, was a friendly, informal meal that carried Herrick right out of the ordinary, work-aday existence to which she had become accustomed, back into the world she had once known, a world wherein the thought of money, of the price of things —which seemed to permeate the very atmosphere at Maison Clémentine—receded into obscurity, leaving only the evidences of its actuality in beauty of flowers and napery and gleaming silver, and the smooth sim-plicity of perfect service.

And through it all, diffused like some delicate and subtle fragrance, Herrick was pleasantly conscious of the happy intimacy of the relations between mother and son. Very soon she found herself chattering away with Billy as if she had known him all her life, while Lady Bridget beamed on them both and joined in the jokes and laughter as naturally and wholeheartedly as though no gap of thirty years or so separated her from them. Once or twice some chance phrase brought back abruptly to the girl the recollection that this was only a glimpse into another world, that soon she would be returning to the drab monotony of her life at Maison Clémentine, but she thrust the thought away, deter-mined to enjoy to the full this brief leave of absence which fate had granted her.

When lunch was over, Billy excused himself on the ground of an engagement to call for Barbara Fane and take her out somewhere.

"She's the daughter of our rector at home," he explained to Herrick, "and is having rather a dud time just now with some people called Duclaire, learning French and music. So I act as a little ray of sunshine whenever she can get a few hours off. Madame Duclaire fondly imagines we're doing the churches and museums together," he wound up with an enjoyable grin.

Herrick smiled a thought wistfully in return. It must be so nice for this other girl, she reflected, for this Barbara Fane, whoever she might be, to have someone like Billy blow in every day or two and take her right out of what was apparently a somewhat uncongenial *milieu*. It would make even a dull life much easier to bear. She bade him good-bye, and then, seized with a sudden panicky fear lest she might be overstaying her welcome, she suggested that it was time she herself should be going.

But Lady Bridget vetoed the proposal firmly.

"Nonsense," she said. "Now you've Madame Clémentine's permission to remain, you may as well stay and keep me company a little longer. Why, we haven't even had our coffee, yet."

So Herrick laughed and yielded, only too glad of the excuse, and presently she and Lady Bridget were chatting together with the easy intimacy which springs up so quickly between two women who are alone and subconsciously aware that each is sympathetic to the other. Almost before she knew it, Herrick found that she was confiding the history of her daily life, its difficulties and loneliness, to this new acquaintance, whose characteristic outlook on things, a mixture of intuitive understanding and humorous philosophy, made her so easy to talk to.

Never before had the girl unburdened her heart to anyone so frankly. During recent years, since circumstances had forced her into playing a lone hand against fate, she had learned to keep her troubles to herself, to settle unaided the difficult problems which confront everyone, no matter how circumscribed their lives, at one time or another. Hitherto, no one had ever seemed particularly interested in the affairs of an unimportant person like herself, and all at once she paused, aghast at her own loquacity.

"But I must have been boring you terribly, prattling about myself like this," she said, scarlet with embarrassment. "Do please forgive me."

"You needn't apologise," smiled Lady Bridget reassuringly. "I love being allowed a peep behind the scenes into other people's lives—if they'll let me look." She was regarding the girl with a curious intentness. Once or twice before, as Herrick had recounted the simple history of her daily life, there had been the same look of puzzled scrutiny in her keen dark eyes. "Do you know," she went on suddenly, "you remind me extraordinarily of someone I once knew—only she was a very beautiful woman and you're not? But you've the same colouring, and your eyes have the same little specks of darker colour in them that hers had. She's dead, now," she added with a brief sigh.

Herrick was struck by her intonation. She felt that the dead woman must have counted in some way in Lady Bridget's life.

"Did you—care for her a great deal?" she asked gently.

A momentary flicker of amusement lit up the dark eyes opposite.

"No, my dear, I didn't," answered Lady Bridget drily. "I cared for her husband."

"Oh!" Herrick suppressed a small gasp of surprise. The older woman smiled outright.

"Does that shock you? Oh, my child, it needn't. He and I had cared for each other long before he met her—thirty years ago. Manlike," she added grimly, "he recovered from the attack. I only met him twice after his marriage to her." She paused, then went on musingly: "It's odd how a woman always idealises the first man she falls in love with—especially if she isn't allowed to marry him. My people wouldn't hear of my marrying this particular man. He was a bit wild— mad about cards and racing, anything with a gamble in it. The bigger the gamble the more he liked it. And he wasn't at all well-off. So they turned him down as a detrimental and tied me up with someone else as quickly as they could. . . . He made a terrible mess of things finally, and finished up by committing suicide —so perhaps it was just as well my father vetoed the affair. Poor Quintin!"

"*Quintin?*" Herrick flushed vividly, and glanced across at Lady Bridget with startled eyes.

"Yes, Quintin Lindris. You must have heard the name. It was unpleasantly well-known about three years ago when he swindled heaps of people out of their money by speculating with it. Don't you remember the case? The papers were full of it at the time."

"Yes, I remember it." There was a curious clipped brevity in the girl's tones which might have arrested Lady Bridget's attention but for the fact that her mind was, for the moment, intently fixed upon the happenings of the past.

"I always believe he never intended as much harm as he actually accomplished," she went on retrospectively. "He was a reckless gambler, and I'm sure he felt quite convinced that he *wouldn't* lose—but that everybody would get their money with interest in the end, while he would have made a big fortune. . . . He had a kiddy whom he simply worshipped—she was only five years old the last time I ever saw him—and I often wonder what happened to her when the smash came."

She paused, and Herrick felt that some kind of response was incumbent upon her.

"Perhaps she went abroad," she suggested, with an effort.

"Perhaps. I tried to trace her afterwards, but couldn't find out anything about her. She'd simply disappeared. There was always wild blood in the Lindrises—she wouldn't have much chance of going straight, poor little brat. I expect she went to the bad."

"Oh no, she didn't," returned Herrick impulsively. And in the same instant could have bitten her tongue out as she saw the sudden attentiveness that leapt into Lady Bridget's face.

"What do you mean? Do you know her? Have you ever met her?" she demanded eagerly. Then, as Herrick, at a loss how to answer, stared at her in mute 'dismay, her eyes fastened on the girlish face and slowly a look of comprehension, of awakening recognition, dawned in them. She leant forward in her chair and peered at the girl with searching intensity.

"Who—who are you?" she demanded, her voice shaken and uneven. Then, with a swift certainty of conviction, she said, "You're Quintin's daughter."

Herrick bent her head.

"Yes," she answered very low. "He was my father."

Unconsciously they had both risen to their feet and now stood facing each other, the girl's attitude a trifle shrinking, defensive, as though she dreaded the outcome of her confession.

But she need not have feared. There was a very soft light in Lady Bridget's eyes when she spoke again—a wistful softness that held all the tenderness and sweetness and sadness of a romance that has been long dead in the eyes of the world at large but has still lived on, secretly, in one woman's heart.

"Oh, my dear!" she said, her voice warm with the love that had never died. "To think that you are Quin's child—Quin's little daughter whom he loved so much!" She drew the girl into her arms and kissed her. "Thank God I've found you at last!" she went on, almost solemnly. "It was your father's last request to me—to take care of you."

She was silent a moment, recalling scraps of his last letter to her—a letter which only reached her after he had taken his bitter way out of life.

"Do you remember the kiddy?" he had written. ". . . She'll be left high and dry when I'm gone, with nary a soul in the world to look after her. . . . Will you, out of the kindness of that big heart of yours— for it was always a big heart, Bridget—give her a helping hand at the start? Somehow I know you will, and I'm going out secure in that knowledge."

And at last chance—or fate—had suddenly made it possible for her to carry out the last behest of the man she had loved. With a little inward prayer of gratitude, Lady Bridget sat down once more and drew Herrick into a chair beside her.

"And now, tell me everything," she said. "All that's happened to you since Quin died. You've called yourself Waylen, haven't you?"

"It's my name—I've a right to it. I was christened Herrick Waylen—and of course I couldn't use the name Lindris."

"No, of course not. But I never knew you had a second name. Quin only told me he'd called you Herrick."

"Most probably Dad had forgotten it himself," returned Herrick with a faint reminiscent smile. "He was quite absent-minded over things like that. I wonder he didn't forget to christen me at all."

The two women laughed softly together, with tender indulgence, over the idiosyncrasies of the man they had both loved, and understood, so well.

"It would have been just like him," acquiesced Lady Bridget. "Now go on, tell me everything."

So Herrick told her—how Rex Dereham, the man to whom she was engaged, had cried off when disgrace overtook her, how she was left practically penniless, and how, feeling that she must start a new life of her own altogether, she had run away and managed to get into France.

"I took an engagement as travelling companion to an old lady who was going there—a very tiresome old lady," she added, smiling at the remembrance, "who required two lady's-maids and a companion to push and pull her along through life. I'm afraid my references wouldn't have borne investigation—I wrote them myself! But I suppose the old lady liked the look of me, for she engaged me on the spot. I left her when she returned to England three months later, and went to Paris, and then I got my job with Madame Clémentine. And I've stayed with her ever since."

"You won't need to stay with her much longer," said Lady Bridget with decision.

Herrick regarded her doubtfully.

"I'm afraid I must," she returned. "You see, I've really no qualifications—except the kind required for a mannequin."

"As far as that goes, you've been a companion once before. You could be the same again."

"Oh no, thank you," said Herrick hastily. "I'd never take *that* job on again. I'd no freedom—I couldn't call my soul my own. At least I'm free now, out of working hours."

Lady Bridget smiled.

"I didn't mean 'a companion' quite in that sense. There are different ways of being a companion, you know. Well"—with a glance at the clock—"I expect you really ought to be going back now. I don't want to impose on Madame Clémentine's good nature. Besides, I want to think everything over—all that you've told me."

"You'll remember that I'm only—Herrick Waylen, won't you?" Herrick reminded her a little shyly.

"Of course I will. Your secret is quite safe with me. As a matter of fact, when you're twenty-one I should drop the 'Lindris' legally and make Waylen your real surname, if I were you. How old are you now?"

"Twenty. It's just three years ago since—since everything happened," said Herrick expressively.

"Well, then, in a year's time. There's some sort of abracadabra called 'by deed poll,' I believe, for giving yourself a new name if you don't happen to like the one you've got. Meanwhile, we'll forget everything except that you're just Herrick Waylen. Now, run away, my dear, and inveigle some more middle-aged folk like me into buying your pretty frocks."

She kissed her good-bye, then, putting her hand under the girl's chin, tilted her face up and looked down into it with a curious expression in her eyes— half admiration, half a kind of thankfulness.

"You've been a plucky little devil, my dear," she said, rather huskily. "I'm glad you stood up to things —and ran straight."

CHAPTER IV

LADY BRIDGET'S PROPOSAL

BILLY, would you like to have a sister?"

Lady Bridget fired off this somewhat surprising question at her son one morning a few days after Herrick's visit to the hotel. Billy looked up with a quizzical gleam in his green eyes.

"Why do you ask, Mim? Have you just found one under a gooseberry bush?"

A secret little smile curved her lips and she nodded an affirmative.

"Yes, I rather think I have," she answered.

"Then it isn't much use my saying yea or nay, is it?"

"You know better than that," she replied with directness. "However much I wanted to adopt a daughter, I shouldn't dream of doing it unless you felt you'd like to have a sister."

"Well," said Billy consideringly. "It would rather depend on the particular young woman you proposed adding to our family party. Who is she?"

Lady Bridget hesitated a moment, then said firmly:

"She's the English mannequin at Madame Clémentine's—Herrick Waylen."

"Phew-w-w!" Billy emitted a gasp of frank astonishment, and his mother hastened to explain.

"Let me tell you all about it. I couldn't think why, all the time, she reminded me so much of someone I once knew—the wife of a man who was"—if there was a hesitation in her voice it was so infinitesimal as to pass unnoticed—"who was at one time my greatest friend. And when she was here to lunch the other day I discovered that she was actually his daughter. . . . He died some years ago—died very poor, although at one time he had been an extremely rich man. And just before his death he wrote to me, as his oldest friend, asking me, in the name of our friendship, to look after his kiddy—the mother had died years before."

"But, if you were looking after her, how on earth did she come to be earning her living as a mannequin?" interjected Billy.

"I wasn't looking after her—that was just it. I made every inquiry at the time—tried all I could to find out where she was, and couldn't hear anything of her."

"She was in France, I suppose?"

"Yes. She'd obtained an engagement as travelling companion to an old lady, and when that came to an end, she went to Madame Clémentine."

Billy was silent for a minute or two. Then he said quietly:

"So you want to adopt Miss Waylen?"

"Yes. I want her to come and live with us—if you're willing. Not otherwise, Billy."

"Well, darling, you go ahead and do it, as far as I'm concerned. That is, if Miss Waylen is willing to be adopted," he added with a note of mild speculation in his voice.

Lady Bridget laughed rather ruefully.

"You've hit it, Billy. That's just exactly what I'm

afraid of. Herrick is a remarkably independent young woman. However, I shall try to persuade her—if you're really certain you'd like it, too?"

"Sure," said Billy quietly. Adding more lightly: "In fact, I can see myself adopting 'Herrick' as a sister *con amore.*"

But, as they had both felt disposed to fear, Herrick, when first approached on the matter, showed no particular inclination to be adopted. She had been let down once so badly by the man she had trusted that she was not over ready to trust anyone, man or woman, too easily again. Moreover, the independent spirit fostered by three years of standing alone against the world, of being the sole arbiter of her own destiny, made her reluctant to give her life over into another's keeping. "She shied away from the idea like a suspicious wild creature," his mother confided to Billy afterwards. But Lady Bridget possessed to an unusual degree the gift of understanding, and her sympathetic comprehension of Herrick's attitude went a long way towards solving the difficulty.

"I think I know just how you feel," she said. "And you mustn't imagine I want to rob you of your independence. We can arrange matters on a perfectly business-like footing, if you prefer it. I'll offer you the job of companion-secretary, and you'll have your own salary, and your own rooms in my house." Then, as she saw Herrick wavering, obviously influenced by the frank fairness of the proposal she had made, she continued eagerly:

"I loved your father, Herrick. Dickie—my husband —was a great dear, and we were very happy and good friends in our life together—only, a woman never really forgets the first man she loved, however fond she may grow to be of another man. . . . I never had the chance to make Quin happy, but I'd like to make his child happy—if she'll let me try," she added with a persuasive wistfulness that it was difficult to withstand.

"Come and give me a trial," continued Lady Bridget, with that irresistibly kindly, humorous smile of hers that made it next door to impossible to refuse her anything upon which she had set her heart. "If you don't like it at Windycroft, you shall be perfectly free to go away and start again on your own—only you shall have a real start in life the next time. That I'd promise you."

"Windycroft? What a delightful name. Is that where you live?" asked Herrick.

Lady Bridget nodded.

"Yes. St. Heriot is the village—a dear little place tucked down in the country, and Windycroft is about two miles distant from it. But I don't think you'd find it dull. We've lots of jolly friends living near—and London is within very easy reach. No, I really don't think you'd find it dull."

"I'm sure I shouldn't. I couldn't imagine anyone being dull—with you," said Herrick impulsively.

"Then don't you think you could give us a trial—Billy and me?"

Still the girl hesitated.

"Are you sure—*sure* that you want me?" she asked.

"Quite sure," answered Lady Bridget simply. "And Billy is quite sure, as well. We're only waiting"—with a laugh in her dark eyes—"for you to feel quite sure, too."

And at last Herrick surrendered. It was a big decision to make, but, once she had capitulated, the very fact began to give her a curiously new outlook on things. She would be no longer a bit of flotsam and jetsam, tossed about on the waves of life with no one knowing or caring how she fared. She would have people of her own, people to whom her happiness and well-being mattered, and above all, she herself would have someone to care for, some other object in life beyond just the enforced selfish necessity of finding food and clothes and lodging. Lady Bridget's joyful acceptance of her surrender showed her very clearly that she was needed, that she could contribute to someone else's happiness—which is, after all, one of the best and happiest things in the world to know.

"Oh, my dear, I can't tell you how glad I am you have decided to come to us," Lady Bridget had said, when Herrick had finally yielded to her persuasions. "I've always longed to have a daughter of my own, and Providence only saw fit to send me a son—though I wouldn't be without Billy for the whole world," she added hastily. "But I did so want a daughter as well, and the next best thing to having one of my actual own is to have Quin's." Her voice deepened to a great tenderness. "He must have been very happy when you came. I remember, once, years ago, he told me that he thought it must be the most wonderful thing in the world to have a child of one's own. If things had been different——"

She broke off, but instinctively Herrick divined the

thought of which the utterance had been so suddenly checked—that if only Lady Bridget had been allowed to marry the man she loved, she, and not another woman, might have been the mother of this child of his. And Herrick's own thoughts went even further. If her father had had Lady Bridget beside him, partnering him through life, how different that life and its tragic ending might have been! Her wise, sane judgment would have steered him clear of difficulties, toughened his moral fibre, and his very love for her would have given him different ideals to strive after.

Still, all that was past, finished with. What remained was that she and Lady Bridget were invisibly linked together by their love for the man who was dead. And, deep down in her heart, Herrick registered a vow that Lady Bridget should never regret asking her to live with her, that in every way in which it was possible she would try to fill the place of the longed-for daughter who had never materialised.

It was settled that she should return to England with the Rivingtons in about a fortnight. "That will give you time to pick up a few frocks and oddments," as Lady Bridget observed. And it also enabled Herrick to set her small affairs in order before leaving France.

Madame Clémentine was garrulously overwhelmed at the turn of events. She was *chagrinée, désolée* at the idea of losing her *chère petite 'Errique*. She regarded her as her best mannequin. as she now unexpectedly assured the girl, and she did not know what she should do without her. She even offered her a much higher salary, and a commission in addition, if she would only remain with her. But when finally she realised that nothing she could say or do would avail to alter things, that Herrick was being suddenly translated from the world of those who sell into the world of those who buy, like the true Frenchwoman she was, she seized upon the practical side of the matter and executed a complete volte-face, imploring her to buy all her clothes at the Maison Clémentine, where, as *mademoiselle* well know, she would find only materials of the finest quality combined with a *chic* that was indisputable! And, somewhat amused, Herrick agreed, since, now that it had actually come to the point of leaving, she found that she possessed quite a warm corner in her heart for the dress-shop where she had worked so long, and even for Madame Clémentine herself.

Lady Bridget was anxious that Herrick should join her at the hotel where she and Billy were staying, but, although she spent the greater part of each day with them, she begged to be allowed to go back to her little *appartement* in the Rue Grise at night.

"You see," she explained, "it's been home to me for so long that I'm feeling just the tiniest bit homesick at the thought of leaving it."

And somehow Lady Bridget seemed to understand, for she said no more about her stopping at the hotel, but just sent Billy back with her in the evenings to see her safely to the door of the house where she lodged.

And so, occupied with one thing and another, her last two weeks in Paris seemed positively to fly by, and it was only a couple of days before the one actually fixed for her departure that she received a hasty scrawl from Paul Breton.

"Herrick, *ma très chère,*" he wrote. "I am *désolé* not to have been able to ask you to the studio before now, but I have been ill in bed. Very stupid on my part, just when I wanted to cheer you up, but *la grippe* is not to be denied. Please forgive me, and come to-morrow night, will you? I am asking all the usual crowd. Your devoted

PAUL.

"P.S.—I trust you have not yet taken that journey across the water which the cards predicted?"

And as she scribbled off an affirmative reply to the invitation, Herrick reflected, with a sudden thrill of surprise, that the first part of Paul's prophecy was already well on the way to fulfilment, since the day after to-morrow would find her actually "crossing the water" en route for England.

Would the rest of the fortune he had foretold for her from the cards come equally true? At the thought, a queer, involuntary shiver ran through her—a vague apprehension, a foreboding of she knew not what.

CHAPTER V

AN ADVENTURE IN THE NIGHT

IT HAD been a merry enough party in Paul's studio. Embryo musicians and singers and dancers mingled with the art students indigenous to the Quarter, and quite a lot of promiscuous talent was gathered together beneath the studio's high, sloping roof. Drifts of song and music, a turn volunteered by a couple of aspiring young exhibition dancers, and a supper of peculiar and surprising variety to which the guests had all contributed their quota, had combined to pass the hours until early morning very satisfactorily. And now the party was breaking up amid a gale of *"au 'voirs"* and *"à bientôts,"* punctuated by an occasional British sounding "So long, old thing."

"Mine will have to be—*adieu*," said Herrick rather sadly. She was conscious of a painful little tug at her heart at the realisation that this was the last, the very last, of these merry, go-as-you-please festivities in which she would be taking part. After all, life in Paris, despite its hard work and enforced economies, had had its compensations. "Next time you all meet, you'll have to 'turn down an empty glass' for me."

A general outcry of dismay greeted this announcement.

"*Mon dieu,* but why?"

"*Tu va te marier! C'est ça!*"

57

"Has Clémentine given you the sack?"

And from Paul a brief: "What's happened, Herrick?"

"I'm going to England," she answered him. "To-morrow. With the Rivingtons."

"To *live?*" he queried sharply. His boyish young face had gone rather white, and his eyes fastened on hers with a curious intensity.

"Yes, to live with them," she said. "That is, if I like it. Lady Bridget was a friend of my father's." And in a low voice she gave him a hasty summary of certain of the events which had led up to her impending departure for England.

"May I come and say good-bye to-morrow morning —as you don't go till after *déjeuner?*" he asked jerkily. Then, as she nodded assent, he snatched up a glass of wine and, holding it aloft, called out:

"Here's to our *chère petite Herrick. Bon voyage et bonne chance!*"

It was pluckily done, and an instantaneous chorus of good wishes drowned the queer husky note in his voice which not all his pluck could quite keep out of it.

Herrick felt a lump rising in her own throat as the warm-hearted young voices chorused eagerly round her, and she was glad when, after innumerable embraces and hand-kissings, she was at last out in the chill fogginess of the October night, walking briskly along in company with Lisette Legrand, whose way home lay for some distance in the same direction as her own.

They parted at the corner of the Rue Grise, the French girl voluble in her regrets that this should be the last time they would walk home together, and then, with a final wave of her hand, she disappeared into the fog. As she went, a church clock somewhere in the immediate neighbourhood struck three, and Herrick turned and made her way as quickly as possible towards her lodgings at No. 42.

The fog had thickened a little here, since the street ran downhill to the level of the river, but she could still see more or less clearly for some yards ahead as she walked on without slackening her pace. Nor did she feel at all nervous. The inhabitants of the Rue Grise, though poor, were in the main a respectable and law-abiding lot, and throughout the whole three years that Herrick had returned to No. 42, early or late, she had never experienced the slightest difficulty or unpleasantness. So that when a man's tall figure, blurred and indistinct through the fog, emerged into view a short distance ahead, she was conscious of no quickening of her pulses but marched steadily onward to meet him. He, too, like herself, was probably returning late—or rather, early—from some convivial gathering.

And then—it seemed to her that it all happened in a single instant—another figure sprang into view, shooting out like a menacing shadow from one of the hooded doorways, and leapt straight at the man she had first seen. Came a brief, abruptly stifled shout, then the two figures went down on the footpath together, the one who had sprung out from the darkness of the doorway on top.

Without stopping to question the wisdom or otherwise of such a proceeding, Herrick set off running towards them as fast as she could, her whole impetuous spirit roused to a perfect fury of indignation at the unfairness of the attack.

The two men were still struggling when she reached them, and it looked as if the man underneath were in a fair way to throw off his assailant. He had contrived to raise the upper part of his body from the ground and had twisted sideways, his right fist doubling for a blow. At that moment, however, his adversary's arm flew up, there came the flash of a knife, a groan, and his head and shoulders dropped suddenly and inertly back on to the pavement.

In the same instant, without the slightest hesitation, Herrick flung herself at the man with the knife, and so sudden and unexpected was her onslaught that it was jerked out of his fingers and went clattering noisily down into the gutter. In the next, she was beating on his face with her small clenched fists—thud, thud, thud, pounding at him recklessly.

"You beast! You beast!" she cried, and then, on a sudden inspiration, she screamed over her shoulder: "Come on! Come *quick!*"

The man, utterly taken by surprise and thinking, precisely as she had intended him to think, that she was not alone but that others would be coming up to join in the fray, abruptly turned tail and fled, scuttling into the enshrouding fog like a rabbit.

When he had gone, Herrick stood very still, feeling sick and shaken. For a moment everything seemed to be going round her, and she wondered vaguely if she was about to faint, then the smarting pain of her fingers, where her knuckles had struck against jaw and cheekbone, brought her back to vivid consciousness. She looked down at the man at her feet. He was lying very still—horribly still, and a sudden terror clutched at her heart. Was he dead—killed? What a ghastly predicament she would be in if he were—alone, at three o'clock in the morning in a Paris side-street, with a dead man!

Her first terrified impulse was to rush away and find instant refuge in the security of her own rooms, leaving the prone, motionless body where it lay, to be found by a *gendarme* or by the next passer-by. Then, with the thought that he might not be dead, after all, but hurt, she conquered that first feeling of recoil, and stooping, tried to roll the body over so that she could see the man's face, which lay hidden against his arm. Inadvertently she had laid her hand on his shoulder, and she withdrew it quickly as something warm and wet trickled across it. In the mist-blurred light of the street-lamp overhead she could see a brownish stain smeared across her fingers. She gave an involuntary shudder, then, setting her teeth, bent again over the wounded man. As she touched him once more, he uttered a groan, and, frightened though she was, she was conscious of a sudden immense relief in the knowledge that he was alive.

"Can you speak? Are you badly hurt?" she asked anxiously in French.

As though the sound of her voice recalled him to an instinctive sense of danger—to the danger that had menaced him before he lost consciousness—he raised his arm defensively. Then, as the pain of the injured limb shot through him, a muttered oath escaped him.

"Oh, damn!"

The unmistakable English of it gave Herrick a sudden feeling of reassurance. Here was a fellow-countryman in distress. She bent over him more confidently.

"Do let me help you. I'm afraid you're rather badly hurt," she said, speaking in her native tongue this time.

The man opened a pair of grey eyes and stared up at her.

"Hullo, who are you?" he muttered bewilderedly.

"I'm English, like you are," she answered. "Please let me help you. Can't you tell me where you are hurt?"

"It's my arm. That"—he swallowed an expletive—"that fellow jabbed a knife into me, I think."

She nodded.

"Yes, he did. It's lying in the gutter. Do you think you could stand if I helped you up?"

The owner of the grey eyes regarded the exceedingly slight young figure bent above him with a faint glint of amusement.

"Do you think you could manage it?"

"I'm stronger than I look," she asserted. She dropped on one knee beside him and slipped an arm underneath his shoulders. "Now, if you could put your sound arm round my neck——" she suggested. He obeyed, and a manful effort on her part, combined with a far more determined one on his than she knew, eventually sufficed to get him into a sitting posture.

He set his teeth for a moment as the movement jarred his injured arm. Then, forcing a smile:

"That was splendid," he said. "Give me a second's breather and we'll have another go. . . . That is, if you can?"

"Of course I can," she assured him. "Don't be afraid to lean on me. I'm really ever so strong."

Another struggle and at last he was standing beside her. His face was very white by the time this feat was accomplished, and he reeled a little.

"Lean on me," she urged again, drawing his arm round her shoulders and bracing her slim young body to withstand the weight. "There. Now, how d'you feel? Do you think you could walk a few steps?"

"I'm afraid I'm rather more than a few steps from my hotel," he said, with that gleam of underlying humour of which even the obvious pain he was in did not seem able to rob him.

"But I live close by," she answered impulsively. "That's where my *appartement* is"—pointing to a doorway only a few paces away. "If you can manage that little distance, I could bind up your arm for you."

"Oh, I can't possibly bother you," he protested. But he swayed unsteadily even as he spoke.

"Don't be silly," she said firmly. "Come along. Lean on my shoulder—it's only a very little way."

It was. But it seemed a very long way up the tall, narrow staircase to the top of the house where Herrick's *appartement* lay, and she often wondered afterwards how they ever compassed it. There were many pauses by the way, and many moments when she asked herself whether she had not attempted more than she could manage. But at last the slow, difficult climb was accomplished and the Englishman lurched into her little sitting-room and dropped nerveless into a chair. His eyes closed and she thought he had fainted.

She ran to the cupboard in the corner where she kept most of the small necessaries of life—from glass and crockery to groceries and an emergency bottle of brandy. Here everything remained still intact, notwithstanding her impending departure. In the adjoining bedroom her new trunks—the new trunks which Lady Bridget had bought for her—stood ready packed, strapped, and labelled, but her bits of furniture and a few odd household stores she proposed leaving behind her as a last gift to the fat, good-humoured old *concierge* and his wife, who, in their own way, had always helped to smooth things for her ever since she had first pitched her solitary small camp in the Rue Grise. And a French *concierge* has it in his power to make the path of the tenants in his building either a particularly thorny one or the very opposite, according to his disposition.

"There, drink that," she said, holding a glass of neat brandy to the Englishman's white lips. He obeyed, and, as the raw spirit trickled down his throat, a little colour came back into his face. He opened his eyes once more, and made an effort to sit up.

"I say . . . I'm being an infernal nuisance," he muttered apologetically.

"Nonsense," she retorted. "Don't try to move yet. Just rest quietly in that chair while I get some hot water and bathe your arm for you. It's been bleeding rather a lot," she added, casting a dismayed glance at the red stain which had spread over his coat sleeve.

She moved softly and quickly about the room, filling a kettle and putting it on to boil, and unearthing some odd pieces of linen which she tore into suitable strips for bandaging. When at last everything was in readiness, and a dose of disinfectant added to the waiting bowl of hot water, she came to his side and very carefully, with kind little hands that hated to hurt, helped him off with his coat, revealing a shirt sleeve soaked with blood which had flowed from a deepish flesh-wound in the upper part of his arm.

"I'm afraid I'll have to cut off your shirt sleeve," she suggested.

He nodded assent.

"I'm afraid you will," he agreed. "It's a most unprepossessing sight, isn't it? I'm terribly sorry you should have this to do."

"You needn't worry over that," she answered reassuringly. "I'm quite a good hand at first-aid."

"Are you? Where did you learn it?" he asked, encouraging her to talk while she bathed the ugly looking wound. He liked the sound of her voice. It was rather low-pitched and had a slight huskiness in it that gave it a kind of wistful attraction all its own. "Are you? Where did you learn it?"

"Oh, years ago—when I was quite young," she answered seriously.

An involuntary laugh escaped him.

"You're not a very great age now," he hazarded quizzically.

She remained grave.

"I feel ninety-nine some days."

"Then I'm afraid to-morrow—or rather, to-day—

will be one of those days, since playing the good Samaritan is robbing you of your fair share of sleep. . . . You won't be exactly blessing me a few hours hence."

She flashed him a sudden smile.

"Perhaps you'll be blessing me instead, to balance matters up."

"I shall indeed," he assured her. "Honestly, I don't know quite what would have happened but for your timely arrival on the scene. That infernal ruffian had me at a disadvantage. One doesn't expect to be knifed at any old moment when one is going placidly home to bed."

"The man was an Italian, I think," said Herrick. She had finished bathing the injured arm and was now binding it up skilfully with the strips of linen. "I suppose he was trying to snatch your pocket-book or something."

He regarded her with speculative eyes.

"You were a plucky little person to interfere," he remarked at last.

She flushed sensitively.

"I don't think there was much pluck about it," she answered hurriedly. "There wasn't really time to feel frightened." She fastened the end of the bandage with a safety-pin and regarded the result of her labours with considerable satisfaction. "There, I think that will carry you on until to-morrow, and then I should let a doctor see your arm, if I were you, just to be on the safe side."

"I shouldn't dream of letting a doctor interfere with your handiwork," he said gravely.

"A gash like that will have to be dressed every

day," she returned practically. "Now, let me help you on with your coat—I've sponged the sleeve." She suited the action to the word, assisting his coat on over the wounded arm with a gentle skill. Then, surveying him critically, she went on: "What about that bruise on the side of your face?"

"Is there a bruise?" He put his hand up and passed his fingers gingerly over his cheekbone. "It certainly does feel as if someone had biffed me one. I suppose I must have struck my face on the pavement when I fell."

The bruise was already turning black, a dark patch which had the effect of oddly emphasising the clear grey of his eyes. Rather weary-looking eyes they were, Herrick thought, with a hint of bitterness in them, as though tired of some of the things they had seen in life. In fact, the whole face, lean and dark beneath its dark brown hair, was somewhat cynical in expression when you came to examine it. There were deep lines scored on either side of the mouth, and the mouth itself closed in a line that was half sad, half bitter.

"Couldn't you bathe that bruise yourself while I make you a cup of soup?" suggested Herrick.

"Oh, good Lord! I can't let you do anything more for me," he objected, and made an effort to rise. But it was a somewhat unsteady effort, and it was obvious that he had not yet quite recovered from the effects of his encounter with the footpad. She pushed him gently back into his chair.

"Don't try to move yet," she said quickly. "You'll feel heaps better when you've had something to eat."

"But I can't impose on your kindness any longer.

If you'd just let me have another drink of brandy I'm sure I could get away all right," he protested.

"Soup—with a little brandy afterwards—and a dry biscuit," she maintained firmly. And set about preparing it. "Besides, I'm quite hungry myself," she added as an afterthought.

"Dinner for two, then," he yielded, with a smile. As he spoke, the church clock outside sounded four strident strokes. "And at four o'clock in the morning!" he commented. "You're not a very conventionally minded person, are you?"

Herrick paused a moment in her even stirring of the soup, which was now simmering in a saucepan above the flame of a methylated spirit burner. The Englishman's question had made her suddenly aware that, regarded from a conventional standpoint, his presence in her *appartement* was very open to criticism. In her eager desire to help, she had entirely lost sight of the fact that a properly brought up young woman does not, as a rule, entertain a total stranger of the sterner sex at four o'clock in the morning.

She laughed a little, then composedly resumed her stirring of the saucepan's contents.

"No," she admitted. "I suppose I'm not conventional. I've no need to be. I'm a free-lance, and it doesn't matter to anyone else what I do or don't do." But even as she spoke, it flashed curiously into her mind that in future what she did or left undone *would* matter to someone else—to Lady Bridget and to Billy, with whose lives her own would henceforth be interwoven. For a moment, however, she was still Herrick

Weylan, free-lance, of 42 Rue Grise. "So you see, there is no one to approve or disapprove of my early morning 'dinner-party.' "

"A man who cared for you might object," submitted the Englishman quietly.

"It would be rather stupid of him, in the circumstances. Don't you think so?"

"No, I don't," he returned, with sudden energy. "If I were he I should object very strongly. I should say that the other fellow—the 'other fellow' being me, in this instance!—ought to have damn well cleared out as soon as he was bandaged up."

"Oh, well, there doesn't happen to be 'a man who cares,' " she said lightly. "There never will be."

"How do you know that?" he demanded swiftly.

If she had been looking she would have seen a sudden glint in his keen grey eyes, like the waking to life of fire that has been smouldering beneath dead ashes. But she was preoccupied with the lid of a biscuit tin that obstinately refused to come off.

"How do you know that?" he repeated, taking the tin from her and removing the recalcitrant lid with the ease of muscular fingers.

"Well, if he did—care, it would make no difference," she said. Adding simply: "I shall never marry."

An expression of amusement crossed his face.

"Aren't you rather young to make such a sweeping assertion?"

She shook her head.

"Youth or age doesn't make any difference. Fate arranges these things for us—sometimes when we are quite young," she added, with an odd look of reminiscence in her eyes. "And you can't get away from fate."

"I don't altogether agree. In the main, we make our own fate."

"Oh, no." The reply came with the swiftness of deep-rooted conviction. "Some of us never have a chance of doing that. It's made for us by circumstances —by other people, by heredity."

He regarded her attentively. There was something about this slip of a girl, with her quaintly decided outlook on things, her warm-heartedness, her intrinsic courage and independence of spirit, which he found curiously arresting.

"Won't you be more explicit?" he said.

"Well——" She hesitated uncertainly, as though his question were a difficult one to answer. Then, her face clearing: "Oh yes, I can give you an instance of the kind of thing I mean. I—wasn't always poor. My father lost all his money very suddenly, and—and died just after. So I've had to earn my own living ever since, and that's meant quite a different life for me from the one I should normally have led if those things hadn't happened. Well, that's fate, isn't it?"

"It's rotten bad luck," he said heartily. "I know what it's like to be hard-up, too. I've nothing to grumble at now, thanks to a rich uncle who quarrelled violently with the family as long as he lived and then died suddenly and left me everything he had. But I did lose all my money at one time."

"So did I. Only I wasn't as lucky as you"——drily. "I never found it again."

"Perhaps you will, some day. Fate—you believe in fate, don't you? And so do I to a limited extent—has a wonderful way of evening up things."

She laughed.

"Couldn't *you* be a bit more explicit this time?"

He set down his empty cup on the table and stood up, looking down at her with a queer expression in his eyes, half quizzical, half something indefinable that sent her usually cool little pulses beating a shade more quickly than their wont.

"Certainly I can. It was bad luck for me being knocked down and knifed in the street—but fate has evened that up already."

A faint flush stole into her cheeks. There was little enough in the actual words themselves, but something in the quality of his voice as he uttered them gave them significance. He waited a moment, as though for her reply. Then, as none came, he continued: "I'm just realising the paucity of the English language. 'Thank you' is so ridiculously inadequate for all you've done for me."

"Oh, please———" The flush deepened in her cheeks. She hated being thanked for anything. "Anyone would have done as much."

He smiled.

"Do you think so? I fancy most women—and some men—would have made themselves scarce the moment they saw there was going to be trouble." He held out his hand, and, as her small fingers slid into it, he went on: "Anyway: Thank you, little Samaritan, for—everything. And I hope fate will pay you back what she owes you over to-night."

She felt the close grip of his fingers round hers, was tensely conscious for an instant of the odd, compelling glance of those keen grey eyes of his, then the door opened and shut and she heard his footsteps descending the narrow staircase outside. A moment later came the distant thud of the street door's closing.

CHAPTER VI

ACROSS THE WATER

IT WAS a very soft bed in which she was lying—as different as it could possibly be from the hard, lumpy one which had been her portion at No. 42 in the Rue Grise, and as Herrick lay snuggled into its springy, yielding softness she was conscious of a delicious sense of well-being. Even the smoothness of the sheet as it brushed her chin gave her a thrill of inward satisfaction, vividly recalling by the very force of contrast the coarse, though scrupulously clean, bed-linen to which the last three years had accustomed her.

She had been awakened by the entrance of a neat becapped and aproned maid, bringing her in a cup of morning tea with its accompaniment of wafer-thin bread-and-butter. It was a very long time since anyone had brought her morning tea. In Paris she had had to get up in the chilly dawn and make it for herself, and now, as she lay between the lavender-fragrant sheets and sipped it luxuriously, her thoughts dwelt curiously on the change which a short forty-eight hours had brought about.

Two mornings ago she had wakened in her tiny, sparsely furnished bedroom in the Rue Grise, wakened, as she reflected with a flash of humour, after a bare three hours of sleep—all that had been left of the night when the Englishman to whom she had played the part of good Samaritan had at last taken his way homeward. Across her mind the events of the last two days flitted like the unfolding of a cinema picture. First came a fleeting vision of the little group of friends who had gathered at the Gare du Nord to see her off; of Paul Breton's white young face as he thrust into her hands a huge sheaf of roses—roses which he could ill afford to buy and to find the price of which, she knew, he must have stinted himself of various dearly-loved small luxuries; of the tedious train run to Calais through miles of sodden, rain-swept country. Followed the brief "journey across water," and, later still, the bustle of arrival at Victoria. Then, after a night in London and a busy few hours' shopping the next morning, had come the final stage, the run down into the country through the early dusk of an autumn afternoon.

To Herricк, an exile from her own land for three long years, there had been something curiously comforting in the familiar dull hum of London's traffic—so utterly different from the shrill, strident noises of the Paris streets—and now and again the tears were not very far from her eyes when they rested on the twilit English countryside as the train bore the little travelling party of three homeward to St. Heriot.

By the time they arrived there it was too dark for her to glimpse much of the village, as the limousine which met them at the station sped swiftly through it and out on to the country road beyond, and the flare of the car's headlights served only to give her a vague, somewhat eerie impression of the long elm avenue which led up to Windycroft itself. But once within the latter's hospitable doors, she found herself surrounded by all the mellow beauty of an old English manor-house.

The hall, panelled and floored with oak, held a welcome in its very aspect. On the old-fashioned open hearth burned a huge log fire, its cheery flames sending long shafts of light flickering across the panelling and revealing the soft waxen sheen born of centuries of loving care. Here and there the regal scarlet and purple of fuchsias, or the yellow and pink and crimson of roses, glowed like tiny coloured lanterns against the dim brown background of ancient wood, while will-o'-the-wisp gleams of firelight glinted intermittently on old suits of armour glimmering in dusky corners beneath the gallery which ran above.

Herrick thought she should always remember that first glimpse of the hall at Windycroft. It was so utterly and essentially English, so like the old home in the country which had once been hers, and which, along with the tall grey house in London, had had to be sold when her father forfeited his right to any further possessions in this world. The queer inward thrill which it brought her made her realise how desperate had been the long ache of homesickness from which she had suffered in the past.

Perhaps Lady Bridget understood something of all that was passing in the girl's troubled mind, for she had suddenly drawn her into her arms and kissed her.

"Welcome home, daughter of mine," she had said. And there had been a quiet and very tender significance in her tones.

Those words had gone to bed with Herrick, a silver thread running through her thoughts as she fell asleep and when she woke again. She had been so long a stranger to the word "home," and all that it implied, that the idea of it filled her with a kind of incredulous wonder. And Lady Bridget so unmistakably wanted her to feel that Windycroft was home. There were kindly evidences of it in every detail of the delightful bedroom, with its adjoining sitting-room, which she had allocated for her use. And now, on this first morning after her arrival, even the weather seemed to be participating in giving her a welcome, for the sunlight was streaming in through the windows, and from the trees outside came intermittently the comfortable, home-like little chirruping of birds.

She finished her tea and then, springing out of bed, ran barefoot to the window and peered out with eager curiosity. Immediately below ran a flagged terrace, bordering smooth-shaven lawns, while to the right lay an old-world garden, its paths high-hedged with clipped yew of centuries' growth. Beyond again stretched a green sweep of parkland, broken by copse and wood, sloping down to a broad sheet of water which gleamed in the morning sunlight like a big silver shield.

Herrick drew a long breath. It was all so beautiful, so tranquilly beautiful, with that ordered, peaceful beauty of a place which has been loved and tended for generations. Her thoughts instinctively followed the trend suggested. Father to son, father to son, handed on from one to the other, and one day Billy in his turn would come into his inheritance and carry on the tradition and uphold the honour of the Rivingtons. Lucky, lucky Billy to have so goodly and so clean a heritage!

With a sharp sigh, she turned away from the window, involuntarily comparing his lot with her own. It must be so splendid to be facing life without a handicap, she reflected. Then, realising the utter futility of such comparison, she tried to push aside the memories which the thought had conjured up. At least, the last few weeks had brought her something new and very wonderful—shown her, through the medium of Lady Bridget, that she was not so much an outcast as, in the first shocked realisation of the meaning of disgrace, she had once believed herself to be. There was, at any rate, one woman in the world who, though knowing the whole history of the stock from which she sprang, had yet asked her to share her life—had trusted and believed in her.

She had made friends before, friends and acquaintances, but they had been friends and acquaintances who knew her only as Herrick Waylen—relationships built up on the unsatisfactory foundation of the false and difficult position into which circumstances had forced her. So that the knowledge that Lady Bridget had, open-eyed, offered her her friendship held its own peculiar comfort and stimulus; and now, as the contemplation of Billy's foursquare start in life challenged comparison with her own handicap, she made a determined effort not to dwell upon it. After all, there were plenty of other people in the world besides herself who had a skeleton in their private cupboards, and there was nothing to be gained by dragging out its dry bones and meditating upon them.

She gave herself a little mental and moral shake and turned her attention resolutely to the performance of her morning toilette, and by the time she had bathed and dressed she felt ready to face the world again with her customary philosophy.

CHAPTER VII

WINDYCROFT

BREAKFAST at Windycroft was a cheery kind of meal, served in the sunny morning-room, and with Lady Bridget and Billy chattering away light-heartedly, supplying her with bits of local information and thumbnail sketches of their neighbours, Herrick soon found herself forgetting the rather troubled thoughts with which she had begun the day. It was next to impossible to feel depressed in such an atmosphere, and when breakfast was over she assented readily to Billy's proposal that he should conduct her on a tour of inspection while his mother interviewed the housekeeper —"and generally lets 'em all know they've got to pull up their socks now she's home again," as he expressed it.

So they set off together, accompanied by his two dogs, hilarious at their master's return, their first visit being to the stables, where the men were busy grooming several good-looking hunters before taking them out to exercise.

"All fit and well, Larkin?" demanded Billy of the head groom, a wiry-looking little man, with a face like a wrinkled apple, who had supervised Billy's horsemanship from his earliest tumbles off his first pony to the time when there were few better riders across country.

"Yes, sir. Only waitin' to get a look at hounds, sir,"

answered the man, touching his hat. "There's no doing nothing with Flame here on a hunting day." He indicated a light-weight, breedy-looking chestnut mare with whom Herrick was making friends. "She knows when hounds are out as well as I do misself, and kicks up an almighty fuss in 'er box because she hasn't been allowed to go out with 'em while you and her ladyship 'ave bin away. It's time you was coming back, sir; you've missed all the cubbing this season. Does the young lady hunt?" he added, as he watched the chestnut, generally a rather nervous, suspicious creature with strangers, rubbing a soft velvet nose confidingly against the girl's arm.

"I used to," said Herrick, answering for herself. "But it's more than three years now since I've been on the back of a horse."

"That don't make a bit of diff'rence, miss," responded Larkin comfortably. "Once anyone rides well enough to follow 'ounds they never forgets 'ow it's done." He cast an appraising eye over Herrick's boyishly slender figure. "Flame would carry the young lady nicely, sir," he suggested tentatively to Billy.

The latter looked reflective.

"Yes," he agreed slowly. "Only the mare's rather a handful at times, Larkin, you know."

"A bit 'ot with 'ounds, sir, as you say. But she's a light mouth for all that—like a bit of silk it is—and I expect the young lady is a proper horsewoman."

"Are you, Herrick?" queried Billy, smiling.

Her eyes kindled with enthusiasm.

"Pretty fair," she admitted. "After all, I ought to be, seeing that I've ridden all my life."

"Right-o, then. Flame is yours to command. We were thinking of getting rid of her; she's not up to Mim's weight."

"Does Mim hunt, then?" inquired Herrick. During the time they had all three spent together in Paris she had fallen quite naturally into the use of Billy's affectionate little sobriquet for his mother—Lady Bridget, like all lovable people, being so essentially someone with whom formalities seemed out of place. "Does Mim hunt, then?"

He nodded.

"Yes. She generally rides that big black over there which one of the stable-lads is saddling now."

"And which do you hunt?"

"A couple of bays, full brothers. They're as like each other as two peas, so we christened them Romulus and Remus. Here they are," added Billy, leading the way to a couple of neighbouring horse-boxes over the doors of which protruded two nice brown heads, oddly similar except for the fact that a white blaze streaked the face of one of them.

"This is Romulus—the chap with the blaze," he pursued, pulling an apple out of his pocket and halving it. "That's absolutely the only difference between them in appearance. Romulus is a bit the faster of the two, though, in pace."

And Herrick, watching Romulus contentedly crunching up his half of the apple between his strong white teeth, never dreamed that a day might come when she would glimpse that sheer white blaze with eyes half blind with terror.

Presently they emerged from the stables into the

sunlight once more, and, strolling across the undulating parkland, came to the banks of the silvery lake
which she had seen gleaming up at her from the valley
when she had taken a first peep at her new surroundings from the bedroom window.

"Rather jolly, isn't it?" said Billy, with a kind of
awkward pride in his voice. Actually, he worshipped
every stick and stone of Windycroft, but he had a
queer masculine shyness of admitting it. "The lake's
a sort of half and half affair. The land on the opposite
side belongs to the Rectory, so we share the fishing
rights. You can just see the Rectory itself, through
that copse." He pointed to where the pinky yellow
stucco of a low, two-storied house showed betwixt the
trunks of the trees. "When I go over to mug up modern languages with the padre, I generally row across.
He's away just now. Overworked, so the parish rose
to the occasion and sent him off for a six week's holi-
day. Fane's a very decent sort," he added.

There was a hint of wistfulness in his glance as it
rested on the distant house between the trees, and
Herrick smiled a little to herself.

"He's the father of the 'Barbara' you used to go
and see in Paris, isn't he?" she said, a twinkle of mirth
in her eyes.

"Yes, he's Barbara's father." And something in the
boyish voice as he uttered the name, some instinctive,
quite unconscious note of tenderness, made her turn
quickly towards him, all the raillery gone from her
eyes, driven out by a sympathetic understanding.

"Then—it's serious, Billy?" she said.

"Quite—when Mim and the padre can be induced

to agree to it. They want us to wait until I'm twenty-five," he added gloomily.

"And how old are you now?"

"Twenty-one. But as no Rivington ever allows his son to inherit until he's twenty-five—they've all left that carefully in their wills for generations past—everybody seems to have overlooked the fact that I've already arrived at man's estate!" He kicked aside a twig with an irritable foot. "It's so absurd," he went on hotly, "stickling about whether you're two or three years older or younger! Barbara and I are quite old enough to know our own minds, and it's a jolly sight better to marry young than to marry wrong—like poor Carol Mortimer!"

"Yes," agreed Herrick. "I think it is. Mim told me about her. Sir Francis must be a rather dreadful person."

"He is," replied Billy heartily. "If he can possibly manage to interfere with her enjoyment of life or scotch anything she wants to do, he does it. And she's really such a dear. You'll like her, I know. Mortlake Hall, where they live, is a beautiful old place."

"I'm looking forward to meeting her," said Herrick simply. "I do hope it won't be long before I do."

"It might be this afternoon," he returned. "Whenever Mim's been away, Carol always rushes round to see her as soon as she gets back again—that is, unless old Mortimer has ordained that she shall do something else."

Apparently, however, on this occasion, "old Mortimer" had not—the actual reason being that he himself had been obliged to go into Tanborough, the neighbouring town, to interview his lawyer—for the early afternoon brought Lady Mortimer to Windycroft. She was accompanied by a big, hatchet-faced man who was ultimately introduced to Herrick as Mr. Beresford but whom everyone addressed familiarly and affectionately as Jem. He appeared to be about thirty-five, and although nature had omitted to endow him with anything in the way of good looks, there was a distinct quality of likeableness about him—a characteristic suggestion of latent strength in the beaky-nosed, square-jawed face, and something equally characteristic in the careless way his rather shabby, well-cut clothes hung on his loosely-knit figure.

An outdoor, man's man was Herrick's first impression; then, with a flash of insight, came the second thought—or one woman's man, and that the woman beside him. She could not have told what conveyed that unerring second impression to her mind, whether it was something quietly possessive in the way in which he helped Lady Mortimer off with the coat she was wearing, or whether it was merely the unconscious betrayal of eyes that could not hide their secret. But she was suddenly quite sure of it—sure that to this man and woman who had come together to Windycroft each represented the big thing—the thing that mattered—in the other's life. Even if she had had any doubts they would have been settled by the slight touch of self-consciousness, the almost nervous haste, with which Lady Mortimer rushed into explanation as soon as she had embraced Lady Bridget.

"Jem happened in after lunch to-day, so we thought

we'd come over to welcome you home, Mim darling," she said, pulling off her hat as she spoke. It was obvious that she was very much at home at Windycroft. "I hope we've not invaded you too soon?"

She was an unusually beautiful woman, slender, and with a kind of dryad grace about her that made her look younger than her actual thirty years. Mat gold hair—hair that was neither bobbed nor shingled but swathed closely to her small head—framed the delicately featured face, and when the momentary gaiety and warmth of welcome had faded out of her bluegrey eyes—more blue than grey—it left them rather wistful and appealing. Frightened, guarded eyes that seemed to look out on life like the eyes of a child that has been ill-used.

"Too soon?" repeated Lady Bridget. "Of course not. You and Jem both know better than that. Besides, I've got a surprise for you." She turned to Herrick, who, feeling a trifle conscious of being the only stranger, had retreated into the background whilst the first exchange of greetings was taking place, and, linking her arm affectionately in hers, pulled her forward. "I've brought back a daughter from Paris," she said triumphantly.

"Sounds highly improper, Mim," interpolated Billy. "You'd better explain, or Jem and Carol will be wondering if this is a late repentance."

"Don't be an idiot, Billy," rejoined his mother imperturbably. "Herrick is the daughter of a very old friend of mine," she continued to Lady Mortimer, "bequeathed to me in a last letter, and I've only just discovered her whereabouts. So now she's come to give us a trial, and if she likes us she's going to adopt us for keeps."

"Then I'm sure it will be for 'keeps,'" said Lady Mortimer, shaking hands with a frank friendliness that won Herrick's heart at once. "No one has ever been found yet who didn't love Mim—and put up with Billy," she added demurely.

It was astonishing how her face altered when she talked. The underlying sadness would be suddenly submerged in bubbling-up humour and light-heartedness, so that you forgot for a moment that secret fear which looked out of her eyes.

Presently Lady Bridget carried Jem Beresford off to advise her about some point regarding her poultry.

"I expect my man hasn't looked after them properly while I've been away," she said. "Anyhow, some of the young broods seem to be afflicted with a new disease. Do come and tell me what's wrong. Mr. Beresford is our great authority on poultry in this neighbourhood," she added explanatorily to Herrick. "What he doesn't know on the subject isn't worth mentioning."

Herrick, who had been laughing and talking away gaily with the big, friendly man, regarded him with mock dismay.

"Oh, help!" she exclaimed. "I'd no idea you were an Authority on anything, or I should have been much more respectful!"

"I'm not," he replied, smiling. "But as poultry-farming and violet-growing happen to represent quite a good proportion of my daily bread-and-butter, I've had to learn a little about them. That's all."

As soon as he and Billy had accompanied Lady Bridget out of the room, leaving Herrick and Carol alone together, the latter added a few more enlightening details.

"Jem doesn't really depend on his poultry-rearing," she said. "He's only taken it up because the doctors ordered him to live in the country. He was gassed in the war, and town atmospheres don't suit him. So he went in for poultry and violets—a quaint mixture, isn't it?—just as a hobby. But Jem couldn't do anything and not do it thoroughly, with all his heart and soul," she wound up with a smile. And Herrick acquiesced, adding mentally to herself: "Not even falling in love."

"He rents Two Ways Cottage"—Lady Mortimer was speaking again—"together with a small piece of land from my brother Mac. Did Mim tell you I had a brother, by the way? I expect so."

"Yes. You're twins, aren't you?"

The older woman nodded.

"Though any two people more unlike in looks you could hardly imagine."

"I think it must be terribly nice to have a twin sister or brother," said Herrick simply. "One would never feel lonely. You'd always feel you had someone who belonged to you in a rather special kind of way."

"You're quite right," answered Carol, with quiet conviction. "Sometimes I wonder what I should have done without Mac. He's been my sheet-anchor."

She paused, and Herrick could feel that she was hesitating on the brink of a confidence, almost ready to let her into the secret saddened places in her life instead of leaving it for time to reveal them—as it inevitably must. But precisely at this moment there came the sound of voices from the hall outside, a blur of pleased exclamation and greetings interchanged, and after a brief colloquy Lady Bridget re-entered the room, accompanied by a visitor, Jem Beresford and Billy bringing up the rear.

"Another arrival——" she began smilingly.

"Committee of welcome, bands and flags complete," put in Billy impertinently. "Let 'em all come."

"Here's your brother, Carol," went on Mim, ignoring him. "Herrick, let me introduce another of our neighbours, Mr. Kenyon."

Herrick looked across towards the new-comer, to find herself, with a sudden shock of surprise, face to face with the Englishman she had helped in Paris. For the fraction of a second there was a silence, while she was uncomfortably aware of the flush which dyed her face beneath his startled, sweeping glance of recognition—of recognition and something more, something that sent a disturbing little thrill tingling through her from head to foot. Then the familiar quizzical gleam relit itself in his grey eyes and he held out his hand.

"Why, it's my little Samaritan of the Rue Grise!" he exclaimed.

Lady Bridget looked from one to the other with some curiosity.

"Then you two have met before?" she said inquiringly.

"Yes—and it was a lucky thing for me we did," replied Kenyon. "Otherwise, at the present moment I should probably be lying in a French hospital—or awaiting decent burial! I was telling Carol this morning all about my final adventure in Paris."

His sister nodded assent.

"Though of course I never imagined that the lady to the rescue was Herrick," she said. "I may call you that, mayn't I?" she added, turning to Herrick. "I couldn't possibly think of you as 'Miss Waylen' now I know what you did for Mac. It was tremendously plucky of you to interfere."

"But what *did* she do?" demanded Billy, with exasperated curiosity. "Do remember that the rest of us are still in the dark."

"Yes. Tell us about the adventure, old man," subjoined Beresford. The tone of his voice, with its carelessly affectionate note of intimacy, indicated that he and Mac Kenyon were good friends in addition to—or rather, in spite of—being landlord and tenant.

So, while a couple of menservants moved quietly about the room, bringing in tea, Kenyon gave a brief description of the struggle in the Rue Grise, indicating his injured arm, still bandaged underneath his coat-sleeve. But he omitted to mention the length of his subsequent visit to No. 42.

Later on, when tea was well in progress, he contrived to seat himself next to Herrick, and addressed her under cover of the general buzz of talk.

"Fate's unexpectedly decent to us at times," he remarked conversationally. "She's let us meet again—which is really more than I deserve."

She glanced at him interrogatively.

"More than you deserve?" she repeated.

"Because I was fool enough to go off the other night

without asking the name of my good Samaritan," he returned, with a brief smile. "As a rule, fate doesn't overlook a slip like that. I might have had to look for you for years—and then never have found you again."

"That would have been a terrible loss," she answered, a note of mockery in her voice.

His glance flashed over her face.

"I should have regarded it so," he stated quietly.

And again Herrick was conscious of that odd feeling of inner disturbance which this man, whom she had only seen once before, seemed able to produce in her. Even while she went on talking to him, deliberately steering the conversation into less personal channels, she was subconsciously trying to combat this feeling. It was as though her spirit—the spirit of the free-lance—had sensed an approaching danger, danger of some infringement of its utter independence, of some unreckoned force that might some day thrust itself into her life.

"You must surely have left Paris almost immediately after we did," she remarked, for something to say.

"I did. Crossed yesterday, came down from town by the first train this morning, and went straight over to see Carol. You see"—explanatorily, as though to account for the promptness of that visit—"I've been away from St. Heriot for nearly a couple of months, roaming about the Continent with a friend who had crocked up in health and been ordered abroad. Carol and I are not often separated for as long as that," he added simply.

"You and she are tremendous pals, aren't you?" said Herrick, a thought wistfully. After all, a free-lance, whether by choice or compulsion—and, in her own case it had been originally a case of bitter enough compulsion—is debarred from the two most wonderful things in life, the only two things which money cannot buy—love and friendship. For you are no longer free when you have given either of these.

"Yes," answered Kenyon. "You see"—he hesitated a little—"I understand so much about Carol that no one else understands. There's never any chance of my misjudging her. I know just how splendid she is."

"He's been my sheet-anchor." Carol's words recurred sharply to her mind, seeming almost a corollary to those her brother had just uttered, and Herrick felt her interest in these two—these two who were bound together by that inexplicable, mysterious tie of twinship—quicken. Some link of deep mutual comprehension informed their thoughts towards each other, and once, earlier in the afternoon with the sister, and now again with the brother, Herrick had felt that she was on the verge of being admitted into that inner temple. And again, just as on the previous occasion, one of the little ordinary interruptions of daily life intervened to prevent it. The door of the sitting-room was thrown open and one of the menservants announced:

"Sir Francis Mortimer."

Very curious was the effect of these three words upon the roomful of people. It was as though a sudden chill wind had blown across a garden, robbing it of its sunshiny perfume and brightness. Involuntarily, Herrick's glance flew to Lady Mortimer's face. The gaiety and laughter had been suddenly wiped out of it. It wore a pinched look, like a flower nipped by the frost, and the haunting fear had leapt again to life in the lovely blue-grey eyes.

Meanwhile, Lady Bridget had risen and was greeting the new-comer with a certain punctilious cordiality —the kind of cordiality you extend to someone whom you do not like but whom, for certain reasons, you want to keep in as good a humour as possible. Good humour, in its literal sense, was the last quality to be hoped for from Sir Francis Mortimer, Herrick reflected, as Lady Bridget introduced him to her. He was a tall, angular man, somewhere in the fifties, who moved with a curious cat-like tread that gave her an unpleasant feeling of revulsion Even his handshake repelled her. The skin of his hand was as smooth and soft as a woman's, but when his thin bony fingers closed round her own she felt as though they had been encircled by the claw of a bird. His complexion was leaden, with sullen blue pouches underneath the cold, watchful eyes, and the long, thin-lipped mouth beneath the aquiline nose made her think of a bird of prey.

"You have chosen a very charming daughter," he said suavely, in answer to Lady Bridget's explanation of the new addition to her household. He shot a sudden unpleasantly significant glance in Billy's direction. "I presume your son—and heir"—with a slight emphasis on the latter word, impossible to misinterpret— "is equally as delighted as you are yourself."

Billy flushed scarlet—an awkward, boyish, furious scarlet, and his mother, hastily pinching his arm to check the angry retort which she could see was imminent, replied placidly:

"You are quite right, Sir Francis. I don't know which of us is the more delighted."

"How charming," he returned, shaking Billy's unwilling hand. "Charming. I congratulate you both. How d'you do, Kenyon?" he went on, turning to Mac. "I didn't know you were expected home yet. Come back to help me look after your sister, I suppose—he! he!" He gave a dry, cackling laugh. Then, fixing his eyes on Jem, he resumed in a tone of apparent surprise which yet held an underlying note of something else —something jeering and secretly triumphant: "And Mr. Beresford—and my wife. Both here, too, I see. Quite a gathering of new friends to welcome you, Miss Waylen."

"To welcome Lady Bridget, you mean," corrected Herrick curtly. She had conceived the most intense antipathy to the man, and as though he sensed it, and the cool young defiance which lay behind her brief rejoinder, he flashed a curious, speculative glance at her from beneath his pouching, wrinkled lids. Before he could make any answer, however, Carol, nervously strung up by his sudden appearance on the scene, rushed into unlucky speech.

"I didn't expect you would get back from Tanborough as early as this, Francis."

He turned upon her so swiftly that it resembled the remorseless pounce of a watchful cat.

"No, my dear, I'm sure you didn't," he replied silkily. "But, arriving earlier than you hoped, like a dutiful husband I have called to escort you home. The car is waiting." The last four words snapped out like a command.

"Oh, but surely you'll stay and have some tea, now that you are here," intervened Lady Bridget persuasively.

"Thank you, no. I can't give myself that pleasure. I have an important appointment with my agent."

It was evident that he had made up his mind to go, and to take his wife with him, so there was nothing for it but to submit, although Mim's kind heart ached as she bent forward to kiss Lady Mortimer's white face.

"Well, we'll all come to the door and see you off," she announced cheerfully. Then, as she and Carol walked on a little ahead of the others, she continued in a lower voice: "Don't look so scared, child. You've not committed a crime in coming over here."

"It's not that. He's been home"—there was no question as to which was the "he" to whom she referred. "He's been home and found out that Jem and I came here together. I'm not allowed to have any—friends," she added bitterly.

There was no time to say more. The big limousine was standing pulsing at the door. Sir Francis put his hand under his wife's arm and assisted her in with sardonic politeness, and they drove away, leaving Herrick with a last vivid impression of Carol's pale, frightened face peering out, framed in the woodwork of the window.

"Mim," she said, uneasily, as they turned back into the house together. "What was the matter? What does it all mean?"

"Tragedy, some day, I'm afraid."

And the crude brevity of Lady Bridget's answer seemed to hold some haunting prescience of the future.

CHAPTER VIII

NEW THREADS

IT WAS not often Herrick found herself alone, but this morning it chanced that Lady Bridget had gone into the village to visit one of her *protégées,* an old servant who had been invalided out of the staff at Windycroft, whilst Billy had disappeared in the direction of the garage.

At breakfast he had announced that Barbara Fane was expected home by the two-thirty train and that he proposed to drive the rector, who had returned to St. Heriot the previous day, down to the station to meet her.

"And you're to come, too," he had informed Herrick blithely, "to swell the reception party. I'll take the four-seater."

Soon afterwards he had departed with the intention of inspecting the car in question and had since remained conspicuous by his absence. From which Herrick concluded that some important detail of the car's interior anatomy must be requiring adjustment. If this were the case, she knew that the moment of Billy's return was extremely problematical, for he was never happier than when tinkering about with one or other of his cars. He was the happy possessor of a four-seater, a two-seater, and a motorcycle with side-car complete, and she had once told him that if fate had not ordained that he should be the heir to all the Rivingtons, she felt convinced he would have been a motor engineer. His reply had been illuminating.

"That's precisely what I should have liked to go in for," he had answered. "Only it would break Mim's heart if I didn't carry on with the old place. So I'm doomed to be a 'landowner,' worse luck! Still, I can always have a car as a hobby." And since then Herrick had realised that Billy's breezy acceptance of his lot in life had not been arrived at without an inner struggle.

She was thinking of this as she busied herself arranging the flowers which the head gardener had sent in that morning for the use of the house. This was one amongst the small duties she had taken upon herself very soon after her arrival at Windycroft.

"You know you promised me a 'job,'" she laughingly reminded Lady Bridget, when the latter protested. "And the very few letters you require writing aren't enough to keep idle hands out of mischief!"

So the care of Mim's most valuable china and of a collection of rare old silver, too precious to be entrusted to servants, had passed into her hands, together with another more pretentious piece of work, that of recataloguing the library.

Herrick had been too long a worker to be contented with an idle life. Moreover, as the days went on and added themselves to weeks, she found an ever increasing happiness in the accomplishment of the small tasks she had allocated to herself. They gave her a sense of "belonging," of being really and truly that daughter for whom Lady Bridget had so much longed, and to the girl who had been so suddenly pitchforked out into the world, cut adrift from all that meant home and people of her own, this new relationship was a very wonderful and happy one.

Her thoughts slipped back to that evening, six weeks ago, when a big closed car had whizzed her for the first time through the dusk-enshrouded village of St. Heriot—a stranger in a strange country. Now, every road and turning, every quaint thatched cottage and village shop was as familiar to her as the streets of Paris. In some ways, so quickly had the time sped by, it seemed almost incredible that she could have been at Windycroft six whole weeks, yet much had happened in the time, and it is by its fullness or emptiness that life must be measured. After all, existence is not merely a clockwork question of hours and minutes. It is the making of friendships, the pleasant little spells of everyday serenity, the interludes of vivid pleasure and happiness which count.

And all of these had gone to the building up of Herrick's first six weeks at Windycroft. The mutual liking betwixt herself and Carol Mortimer, which had sprung up at their very first meeting, had rapidly deepened into a great affection, and her sympathy for the woman who had the misfortune to be Sir Francis's wife was beyond measure. She knew now that all that Billy had told her of his tyranny, all that she herself had surmised, fell far short of the actual facts. When Carol's husband was at home he seemed to take a positive delight in curtailing her liberty, in thwarting her most innocent wishes, and in making her life generally a burden, and even in his absence she was never actually free from a maddening surveillance. She had confided this information to Herrick on one occasion when the latter was rejoicing over the fact that business matters had called Sir Francis to London for a couple of days.

"It makes no difference," Carol had declared bitterly. "Everything I do while he's away is always reported to him on his return—unless I'm desperately careful."

Herrick regarded her with dismay.

"By whom? You don't mean—you *can't* mean that the servants tell him what you do?" she exclaimed incredulously.

"No, no, not the indoor servants," answered Carol. Adding warmly: "They're all as loyal to me as they can be—particularly old Collins, the butler. But I'll tell you who does spy on me, and that's Humphreys, the second gardener."

"Are you sure?" asked Herrick, protestingly. It seemed to her too horrible to be true. She knew the man in question very well by sight—a fellow with a sullen, lowering type of face, not improved by a pronounced squint, and with one shoulder higher than the other. Now that she came to think of it, he *had* rather an odd, furtive way of being always about. She hardly ever remembered coming over to Mortlake without catching sight of him sometime or other, either slouching away between the trees as she came up the drive, or hovering round, presumably at work, in their vicinity, if she and Carol went out together.

"Are you *sure?*" she repeated.

"Quite sure. Do you remember that first day after

your arrival at Windycroft—when Jem and I came over to welcome Mim back?" Herrick nodded. "Well, Jem had called here for me and Humphreys, I know, saw us go down the drive together. He must have told my husband about it the moment he came back, and you know what happened afterwards. Francis came and fetched me away from Windycroft at once. I was enjoying myself, you see," she explained with a mirthless smile. "I'd suspected Humphreys of spying before that, but I wasn't sure till then. Now, of course, I'm on my guard about him. And so is Jem," she added, a sudden defiant brilliance in her eyes.

Herrick hesitated. Then, for by this time she felt their friendship justified it, she asked quietly:

"You and Jem Beresford—care for each other?"

Carol bent her head.

"Yes," she acknowledged. "You may as well know it. You couldn't be my friend without guessing sooner or later. But we know there can never be anything more between us except—just caring. We've faced the thing out. We've even discussed whether Jem should stay on at Two Ways Cottage or go away—leave the neighbourhood. . . . But we can't quite face that. We must see each other—sometimes—just as friends." She paused, then demanded abruptly: "Do you think we're wrong?"

For a moment Herrick made no answer. She had a swift inner vision of Carol as of some frail barque floating heedlessly on a quiet reach of water, whilst not far distant, unperceived and unreckoned with, swirling rapids eddied their way towards a dangerous whirlpool. Then, as she met the tragic questioning of the blue-grey eyes which searched her own, the vision vanished and she answered impulsively:

"No, of course I don't. The only wrong thing is that you ever married Sir Francis. What made you do it, Carol? Surely—you were never in love with him?"

The other smiled—a smile that held a bitter enough amusement at the question.

"Never," she said. "I married for money. Although I didn't want the money for myself. When my father died—he died very suddenly"—she paused, then went on hurriedly—"of—of heart-failure, we found ourselves left practically penniless. And mother was an invalid—used to all the ease and luxury an invalid requires." She halted again, as though she found it difficult to proceed.

"And so you married Sir Francis?" supplied Herrick swiftly.

Carol nodded.

"Yes, I married him, because he promised to settle an income on my mother if I did. And it seemed the only way out. Mac had got a job in an office, but he had never been trained for anything of that kind and could barely earn enough to keep himself. So I'd no choice. Francis had asked me to marry him several times before, but of course I'd always refused him. And he was very clever," she added cynically. "He didn't propose again until two months after my father's death—he gave us those two months in which to find out exactly what poverty meant."

Nothing could have been more typical of Sir Francis, thought Herrick, than that final touch—that sardonic waiting, like a furtive spider in his web, until the agony of seeing a sick mother suffering from lack of the bare necessities of life drove the woman he coveted into his arms.

"You were very brave," she said at last. "It was a splendid sacrifice to make, Carol."

"And a very useless one," returned the other bitterly. "Mother never recovered from the shock of father's death. She died six months after I was married."

It was easy enough, after Carol had confided the pitiful tragedy of her marriage, for Herrick to understand Mac's tremendous admiration for his sister. "I know just how splendid she is," he had told her that first afternoon at Windycroft, and since then, when they had been together, often by some small turn of phrase, some passing inference or comparison, she had gathered in how deep and unswerving estimation he held his sister.

And they had been together a great deal. Out hunting it was astonishing how frequently she found Mac Kenyon at her side, and, as it happened more often than not, when the day's run was over, that their way back lay in the same direction, it had become a pleasant habit for them to jog home side by side. Sometimes Billy was with them. But there were many occasions when, seeing Herrick safely companioned, he would join up with another group of hunting friends, and they two had ridden back, to all intents and purposes alone together, through the November dusk. And out of those leisurely saunters home, when they talked or were silent just as the spirit moved them, while Flame walked delicately, as a thoroughbred lady should, beside the big bay Mac bestrode, had grown a very pleasant comradeship—a comradeship which played a much bigger part in the happiness of this new life of hers in England than Herrick was aware.

Years ago she had put the idea of marriage, once and for all, so utterly outside her scheme of life that she did not realise that interwoven with this comradeship, as weft and warp are interwoven, was something deeper and more profoundly elemental than mere friendship. The only thing she did realise, was consciously aware of, was that whereas Rex Dereham had taught her a half contemptuous, half shrinking distrust of men, Mac was gradually leading her to readjust her ideas. Broad-minded and tolerant, there was one respect in which he was inflexible. "Disloyalty—a double game—is the only thing I can never forgive," he had said on one occasion. And over and over again, in the course of those intimate little talks they had together—which ran the gamut of most things from high heaven itself to modern jazz—she came to recognise the standard of loyalty and honour which permeated his thoughts—so stern a code that sometimes it almost frightened her. Once she had taxed him with it protestingly.

"Aren't you a rather harsh judge?" she said. "I think you expect almost too much of poor human nature."

"I've had my lesson—once—how people pay for crooked going," he had answered in a curiously hard tone. "No one requires two lessons such as I had."

The harsh brevity of his reply had left her wondering. Had Mac himself ever been guilty of something which could be called crooked—some weakness or disloyalty which had brought its own punishment and taught him finally a sterner code than that of most men? She could hardly believe he had. But that something had happened in his life, either to him or to someone intimately connected with him, which had crystallised a certain hardness and bitterness into his nature she was sure. And sometimes the thought struck her, with an almost overwhelming force, that perhaps, if he knew the whole truth about her—if he ever came to know that she was Herrick Lindris—it would mean a swift and certain ending to this new friendship which had come into her life.

It was not often that she thought of it. Usually the days were too well-filled for her to have many moments to spare for introspection. Only from time to time, if she happened to be alone—as now, while she awaited Billy's return from the garage—a little chill sense of fear would invade her heart. She tried to argue it away on the grounds that if Mim, who knew everything, could still trust and make a friend of her, surely Mac would not be less generous. A sigh escaped her. She wished unspeakably that she could be perfectly frank and candid about herself, that she had nothing to hide. Dad, to whom her happiness had meant so much, had probably never realised what a millstone he had hung about the neck of the one person he had loved best in the world. . . .

Came the sound of someone whistling gaily up the drive, breaking irresistibly across the wistful tenor of her thoughts, then striding footsteps through the hall, and a moment later Billy appeared, smilingly triumphant, in the doorway.

"The old bus is all right now," he announced cheerily. "Early lunch, and we leave at two o'clock sharp."

CHAPTER IX

THE RECTOR OF ST. HERIOT

BILLY buzzed the car along the road with the reckless confidence of youth, and within a very few minutes of leaving Windycroft he had braked her to a standstill at the Rectory door. The rector himself stood waiting beneath the old-fashioned, ivy-clad porch, and Herrick took an immediate liking to him as Billy performed an informal introduction between them.

"Latest addition to the family, padre—Miss Waylen. Only no one ever dreams of calling her anything but Herrick."

"It's rather early yet to ask for an extension of the privilege in my favour," said the rector smilingly, shaking hands. "But I shall hope to merit it before very long."

Anything less like the typical cleric than Fane could hardly be imagined. He was a big, long-limbed man, with a careless stoop of broad shoulders. A thatch of thick brown hair, usually more or less rumpled, crowned his lean, eager face, of which the most characteristic features were a pair of humorous grey-brown eyes, and a rather straight-lipped mouth that premised an odd combination of strength and sweetness. He was clad in a suit of well-worn tweeds, and looked, as Herrick reflected with inward satisfaction, just like any other human man. As a matter of fact, Fane never appeared in correct clerical attire except when actually conducting a service. "No one should live exclusively in uniform," he was wont to declare. "A parson in mufti has a far better chance of getting in touch with the black sheep of his flock. That blessed dog-collar's too stiff a fence for most of 'em to face."

He and Herrick sat together in the back seat of the car while Billy swept them off in the direction of the station and she found him as easy to talk to as an old friend.

"I guess you find our quiet little St. Heriot rather a change after Paris," he observed presently, and there was a very definite, though kindly query underlying the remark.

Her eyes met his frankly.

"Yes. But not quite in the way you mean. I wasn't having what's called a good time in Paris, you know. I was in a job there. As a matter of fact"—smiling—"I feel rather like Cinderella after she had been transplanted out of the kitchen."

Alec Fane took the explanation quite naturally.

"That's good. Then you won't get bored with us so easily."

Herrick laughed outright.

"No, I shan't get bored," she said. "When you've been cut off from friends—and from motoring and hunting and all the things you love best—for several years, and then a good fairy like Lady Bridget suddenly comes along and with a wave of her wand gives you them all back again, you don't get—bored."

The rector nodded understandingly. He had heard

quite a good deal, in letters from various people, concerning the advent of Mim's *protégée* from Paris, and he had wondered a little in secret whether Lady Bridget's warm heart might not have led her astray on this occasion. It was a far cry from the gay French capital —to St. Heriot! Would the plan work? Wasn't it a bit of a risk to throw Billy into the constant society of an independent young woman fresh from the forcing-house of Paris? And there was Barbara, too—Alec Fane's keen mind had been busy visualising all the possibilities that might result from the introduction of a frivolous, French imbued firebrand into the tranquillity of his little country parish. Visualising—not fearing them. His only real anxiety had been lest Lady Bridget might one day have to pay in such heartache as only a mother ever knows for her hospitality to this child of her dead friend.

But now that he had seen Herrick and talked with her, he realised that all his doubts had been groundless, and when the train bringing Barbara home pulled into the station, and he and Billy had greeted her, he made the two girls known to each other without any misgivings.

They presented a very complete contrast. Young as she was, there was a certain knowledge of the world in Herrick's face—knowledge that had been forced upon her through the happenings of the last three years—which was conspicuously absent from Barbara's round, innocent young visage, with its pansy-brown eyes and curving mouth flanked by childish dimples. Moreover, a trained sense of clothes and a certain finished grace of movement, product of the years spent as mannequin at Maison Clémentine, combined to set Herrick very far apart from the country parson's daughter, whose busy sojourn in the Duclaire household had been educational only in so far as music and the French language were concerned.

Barbara greeted her with a slight air of reserve, almost of suspicion, as though she were not quite certain that she was going to like the new-comer, and inwardly her spirits rose considerably when she found that she was to occupy the front seat of the car beside Billy—"just as usual," as she mentally told herself. Perhaps she felt some instinctive feminine fear of this other girl whom circumstances had suddenly thrust under the same roof that sheltered her beloved Billy. For Barbara was a very modest little person and had not even yet quite got over the amazing fact that Billy —to whom, as it appeared to her, the whole world of girls must be open—had singled her out for the bestowal of his affections.

Apparently the drive home reassured her, for her manner had completely thawed towards Herrick by the time they reached the Rectory, and the two were soon chattering together with the utmost friendliness. Presently the rector suggested that Herrick might like to come and look at a recent litter of pedigree spaniels which had been added to the Rectory kennels, and, suspecting the invitation to have been prompted by an indulgent wish to give Billy and Barbara a few minutes alone together, she assented with alacrity.

"I'm frankly mercenary about them," he acknowledged, as Herrick, having first made friends with the mother, lifted up one of the puppies in her arms, where, after one or two small protesting yelps, it settled down quite comfortably. "I breed them purely for profit. This is a comparatively poor living, you see, and the amount these youngsters bring me in enables me to give a helping hand very often when otherwise I should have to say 'no'—or else go begging round the parish. And I hate a begging parson," he added heartily.

"It means a good bit of work, doesn't it, looking after all these youngsters. How many have you altogether?"

He told her. Adding:

"Of course it's much easier for me when Barbara's at home. I can't rely on Janet, our maid-of-all-work, to feed them properly if I happen to be out. Her mind doesn't soar beyond bones and dog-biscuits, even for a sick puppy."

"You must be glad to have your daughter home again," commented Herrick.

"Yes. But"—with a rueful smile—"how long shall I be allowed to keep her, do you suppose?"

She smiled back at him a thought wistfully over the top of the puppy's silky head.

"I think she and Billy would be very happy together," she said. "And there isn't such a big lot of happiness about that one can afford to waste any, is there?"

The kindly grey-brown eyes flashed keenly over her face.

"You're rather young to have found that out already," he suggested.

She flushed a little.

"I don't think youth or age has much to do with it," she answered bluntly. "It's just fate."

He left it at that—Alec Fane had the rare gift of knowing when a wound was too sore to bear much handling—and they rejoined the others and a few minutes later Billy and Herrick had climbed back into the car and were speeding down the drive en route for Tanborough, where the former had some small commissions to execute for Lady Bridget.

Barbara and her father turned back into the Rectory arm in arm.

"Glad to have me back, padre?" she queried, as they entered his study, where a brisk, newly-lit fire was crackling in the grate.

He looked down at her with a quizzical smile.

"I've had my own way a good deal lately," he submitted teasingly.

She cast an amused glance round the room. The desk was littered with papers—bills and sermon notes and the manuscript sheets of an article on metaphysics jostling each other in indescribable confusion, while a dusty typewriter had been pushed aside to one corner where it balanced precariously near the edge. A vase of dead flowers adorned the chimneypiece, and the clock had stopped because no one had remembered to wind it.

"That's very evident," replied Barbara. "And when a man has his own way, it's the untidiest way imaginable. It looks as if this room had never been touched since I went away."

"It hasn't—since *I* went away," he affirmed eagerly.

"I gave Janet special instruction to leave everything just as it was till I came back again."

"She seems to have carried out your instructions to the very letter," observed Barbara grimly. She perched herself on her father's knee, and, exploring his pockets, unearthed a beloved old pipe and baccy pouch and proceeded to fill the former for him with the assurance of long experience. "There," she said, when finally the pipe was lit and drawing well, "I shall spoil you just for to-day. But to-morrow"—eyeing him firmly—"I and Janet will turn this room out. So you'd better make up your mind to go out and visit the sick and the sinners of the parish. Meanwhile, tell me all about Herrick Waylen."

Alec smiled a little.

"I can't tell you very much, can I? Seeing that I've only met her myself to-day for the first time."

"Billy says she's the daughter of an old friend of his mother's. It seems—funny, doesn't it, that Lady Bridget has never spoken of the daughter of an old friend like that, don't you think?"

The rector gazed musingly into the fire.

"Some old friendships don't bear talking about—when they're over," he said quietly. With the insight of a man who has suffered himself—for Alec Fane had been well-nigh heart-broken at the death of his wife, some ten years previously—he had recognised in Lady Bridget, beneath all her breezy philosophy and humour, that underlying sadness which lies hidden at the heart of either man or woman who has missed the way in love. And instinct told him that her action in adopting Herrick was no mere caprice, but hung linked to some chain that stretched into the past.

"Billy says that Lady Mortimer has made great friends with Herrick," said Barbara presently.

The rector smiled inwardly at the betraying frequency with which the words "Billy says" prefaced his daughter's observations.

"Does he? Well, goodness knows that poor little soul can do with all the friends Heaven sends her."

"All the same, it's rather disappointing for me," protested Barbara. "Herrick is nearer *my* age. Lady Mortimer is too old for her."

"Age has very little to do with friendship—within certain limits, kiddy. Besides, Herrick Waylen is—old in some ways. Older than her years, at any rate."

Barbara scrutinised her father consideringly.

"Yes, I think she is," she acknowledged, as though suddenly struck with the truth of his assertion. "You're very clever, padre dear, to understand so much about other people—what they're like inside, I mean. I wish I did, because I suppose that's what makes you so tolerant and—and nice."

He pinched her cheek.

"Don't wish that, my chicken. It's the last thing I should ever wish for you," he said. Adding rather sadly: "Tolerance and understanding are both the gifts of hard experience."

CHAPTER X

QUICKENING FIRES

I T'S almost as warm as if it were spring," remarked Herrick idly, as the car which was bearing her and Billy towards Tanborough sped along the broad country road. There was certainly some reason for her comment. Overhead stretched a faint blue sky, ruffled here and there with little fleecy white clouds while pale golden sunshine flickered across the pools of water lying in the road—left there by a heavy shower of rain the night before. The air was balmy, scented with the clean fragrance of the newly-washed earth.

"And within a couple of days we may be snowed under or frozen stiff," responded Billy pessimistically. "That's the kind of trick the English climate plays on you when you tempt it with a remark like that."

She laughed.

"Oh, well, except for the hunting, I shouldn't mind."

" 'Except for the hunting!' " he repeated in disgust. "And what's going to make up for hunting, I'd like to know?"

"Skating, perhaps," she suggested. "I should think you get pretty good ice on the lake at home, don't you?" It was odd how easily and happily now, the words "at home" came to her lips.

Billy nodded.

"Yes. Not so dusty," he admitted grudgingly. And then, relapsing into silence, he sent the car along at a speed that even the absence of traffic on the long, straight stretch of road hardly justified, since, in the country, there is never any certainty that a cow may not come ambling unexpectedly through the gateway of some adjoining field, or an old sow and her litter of piglets scatter themselves suddenly across the road.

"Billy, do steady down a bit," objected Herrick, as the car fairly leapt along. "You're really going too fast—and we're coming to a corner in a minute."

"Nonsense. We're all right," he answered. Nevertheless, he slowed down a trifle while they took the bend, gathering speed again as he perceived that there was nothing in sight when they had passed it.

And then, at the next turn in the road, it happened. The turn was a sharp one, and, as they swung round it, there was just a single instant before the impact in which Herrick had time to visualise the big grey car approaching and recognise Mac's lean dark face bent above its steering-wheel. And in that instant the stark, convulsive terror which overwhelmed her taught her all that had hitherto been hidden. She was conscious of no fear for herself in the inevitable smash which was coming. . . . Billy, as far as she was concerned, simply faded out of existence . . . her whole being was swamped in a wave of sheer, agonising fear for Mac.

Followed a tearing, splintering crash, the grind of brakes, and for one quivering, interminable second the car tilted horribly. Then it lurched back level again, and Herrick found herself staring past Billy straight into Mac's eyes as the two cars stood locked abreast.

"It was all my fault," declared Billy, while Kenyon slowly manœuvred his car free of the other, revealing a slightly bent grey wing on its off side.

"That's so," he answered briefly.

Billy climbed nimbly out of his seat to inspect the damage. The wing of his own car had crumpled up very completely under the impact of the heavier vehicle, and he stood regarding it with rueful eyes. In his estimation, a damage to one of his beloved cars was almost worse than a hurt to himself. Mac, who had by this time vacated his own driving-seat and joined him in the road, flashed him a glance of unmistakable anger.

"You're a damned careless young cub!" he said wrathfully. "If you want to go careering about the roads like a fool and taking corners on your wrong side, you've no business to ask Herrick to go with you."

"Well, she's not hurt," protested the other, in somewhat ruffled tones. Kenyon's taking him to task so sharply was totally unexpected and disconcerted him.

"It's no thanks to you that she isn't," retorted the elder man. "Another inch and your car would have turned turtle." He was rather white and his voice had roughened curiously.

Billy regarded him speculatively for a moment.

"I suppose it might have done," he acknowledged at last. "I'm awfully sorry, Herrick," he pursued, turning to her. "I'm afraid I *was* driving a bit fast."

Her inner relief was so immense that nothing else seemed to matter, and she smiled reassuringly into his crestfallen face.

"Just a bit, old thing. Still, as we've all come out of it alive and intact, you shall be let off with a warning this time."

"I'm terribly sorry about your wing, Mac," went on Billy, with honest regret in his voice.

"Oh, that's nothing." Kenyon dismissed the matter of the injury to his car carelessly enough. Then, after a pause, he continued: "You've come off very much the worse of the two. Why not run your car straight on into Tanborough—luckily she'll travel all right—and leave her there to be doctored up? You could get the six o'clock train back to St. Heriot, and I'll drive Herrick on to Windycroft. That is," he added, turning to her interrogatively, "unless you particularly wish to go into Tanborough?"

Her eyes fell beneath the searching glance he bent upon her and she answered hurriedly.

"Oh no. I was only going in to keep Billy company."

So matters were arranged on the lines he suggested, and presently she found herself gliding smoothly along beside him in the big grey car while Billy took his battered four-seater into Tanborough for repairs.

For some time they sped onward in silence, and Herrick was quite content that it should be like that. Those few anguished moments when death had hovered above the two converging cars had shown her her own heart—brought to her, in one blinding flash of illumination, the realisation that what she felt for Mac was not friendship, the easy good comradeship she had imagined it to be, but love—the kind of love which comes only once into a woman's life, and comes to stay, dimming all else. Love alone could have prompted that overmastering terror for his safety when she saw collision imminent, and now, as she sat silently at his side, her hands tightly clasped together, she felt shaken and bewildered by the revelation which had sprung out of the quickening fires of sudden danger.

"You all right, dear?"

Kenyon's voice came to her very quietly across her tense inner consciousness of him, and as he spoke he laid one hand over hers. She sat very still. The touch of that big strong hand covering both her own sent a queer tremulous thrill pulsing through her body, and there was something in Mac's voice, quiet though it was, that made her catch her breath. Something tenderly possessive. So might a man speak to the woman he loved and whom he knew loved him in return—in tones of which the tender solicitude "understood itself."

"Quite all right, thank you," she answered. The words sounded stilted, even distant, but they were all she could manage. She felt as though her heart were beating in her throat, and speech seemed almost an impossibility.

"That's good, then." Mac answered in a voice of supreme content, and she was conscious of a light pressure of the hand which covered hers before it was removed. After that he spoke no more until they were at the doors of Windycroft. Then, as she turned and half held out her hand, he smiled down at her.

"But I'm coming in," he said deliberately, and followed her composedly into the big panelled hall.

It was empty, lit only by the restless light of the flames which rose and fell from the big logs blazing on the hearth, and as they both instinctively made their way towards the fire it seemed as if the November dusk closed in behind them, plunging the remainder of the hall into shadow and shutting the man and woman together within a luminous circle of light. As Herrick's eyes nervously probed the twilight curtaining them round, she became all at once acutely conscious of her absolute aloneness with Mac. It seemed almost as if they two were in a little world of their own, cut off from all other, and she made a sudden, frightened, impulsive movement, as though to leave him. Instantly his arm shot out, barring her way.

"No, don't run away," he said, a note of tender amusement in his voice. "Herrick—darling—are you so afraid of love that you want to run away from it?"

She glanced up and for one quivering moment met the unmistakable demand in those grey, compelling eyes bent on her face. He must have read the unconscious answer in her own, for in the same instant his arms closed round her and he swept her up against his breast, kissing her with a fierce passion that almost took her breath away. And Herrick, surrendering, almost before she realised it, to the love that had so suddenly engulfed her, leaned against him, shaken to the depths of her being by the answering passion which had wakened to life within her.

Presently the close pressure of his arms relaxed, and he held her a little away from him.

"Six weeks have I been in love with you," he said whimsically, "ever since a certain night in Paris— wondering all the time whether I had a chance with you or not. And I believe it took that motor-crash to make you properly aware of my existence!"

"Well, I thought you were going to be killed," she answered with the utmost simplicity. "And—and then I realised how dreadful it would be if you were." She smiled at him rather tremulously, and he snatched her back into his arms.

"My beloved!" he said unsteadily. And once more he was kissing her with the imperious possessiveness born of those six weeks of uncertainty and suspense.

"Herrick! . . . Heart's dearest! . . . Say you love me. You haven't said it yet, and I want to hear it."

She looked up at him with eyes that glowed with a sweet and tender radiance.

"Need you hear it?" she said. "You *know* I love you." And for a little space after she had spoken they remained silent, close-held in each other's arms, wrapt in that first incredulous, bewildering joy of love given and returned.

It was Mac who broke the silence, broke it with the question that was bound to come sooner or later.

"How soon can we be married darling?"

"Married!" The word came almost gaspingly from her lips. She twisted round in his grasp and stared at him with startled, terrified eyes. Marriage! She hadn't thought of marriage. Why, she *couldn't* marry. Oh, she had been mad—swept, for a few moments, helplessly along by the irresistible, wonderful madness of love. And now, at the sound of the word "marriage,"

the bitterness of recollection, of harsh reality, had slashed across those dream moments like a flail, destroying them utterly.

"Yes—married," repeated Mac placidly. And into Herrick's mind flashed the strangeness of the fact that, of two people, the soul of the one may be undergoing the tortures of hell-fire while the other remains totally oblivious of the fact. "There's no reason why we shouldn't be married quite soon," he pursued. "I— and Greenwood—are both waiting for you."

Greenwood—Mac's home! And now he was thinking that soon it would be her home, too. She knew it so well—the long, low, creeper-clad house, with its red tiled roof, set just below the brow of a hill and looking, as the crow flies, towards Windycroft. . . . Just such a sweet, old-fashioned place as could be all of earth and heaven to two who loved!

Mac's voice, tenderly insistent, broke across her thoughts, and her vision of the old homestead scattered suddenly.

"Need we wait very long, my sweet—Greenwood and I?" he urged.

With a sudden vehement movement Herrick tore herself out of his arms.

"Yes," she said, speaking very fast and a trifle shrilly. "You'll have to wait—forever. Because— because I can't possibly marry you."

For an instant he stared at her blankly, too utterly amazed for speech, and Herrick, standing beside him with her hands clenched so tightly that the nails bit into the flesh, thought that never in the whole of life had a single moment seemed so long or so compact of agony. When at last he did speak, it was in tones of complete mystification.

"You can't marry me?" he repeated. "What do you mean? I don't understand you."

"Don't you?" Her voice was hard and emotionless. "I meant just exactly what I said, no more and no less: I can't marry you."

"But you haven't told me why. At least, I've the right to know your reason."

"Yes—I suppose you've the 'right.' All the same I can't give you a reason."

His eyes grew stormy. A curious fire seemed to light itself in their depths and smoulder there.

"You mean you refuse?"

She nodded, her face a white mask of denial.

"I refuse."

There was an ominous quiet about him. She felt as if she could almost see the working of his mind, knew the precise moment when bitter suspicion took the place of blank bewilderment—though of the nature of that suspicion she had no inkling.

"Perhaps I can guess the reason," he said at length slowly. "You've been merely fooling with me—amusing yourself at my expense—and now that the gullible fool has been gulled to the hilt, you're anxious to put an end to the game. Is that it? Is that your explanation?"

She listened to him with slowly widening eyes of horror. Obsessed by her own point of view, it had never dawned on her that her action could lend itself to such an interpretation until, with that chill ominous quiet which seemed to set them worlds apart, Mac had put it into so many words.

"No, *no!*" she whispered at last in a low, breathless voice of consternation. "Not that. Oh, Mac, how could you think it?"

"What else can I think?" he retorted implacably.

"Anything but that—anything. . . . You need never doubt my love for you," she went on simply. "Whatever happens, I shall always go on loving you."

There was something disarming in the sheer simplicity of her statement—disarming and convincing, and Mac softened in spite of himself.

"Then, if that's true," he said more gently, "tell me why you can't marry me? You must allow," he went on with a brief, ironical smile, "that that is not asking a very great deal."

She twisted her hands together. Her face had grown very pale and dark shadows had painted themselves beneath her eyes.

"No," she said in a low voice. "It's not. But—but still, I can't even tell you that. Don't you remember, that night in Paris, I told you I should never marry? Well, I meant it."

Mac stiffened again.

"Then why——"

She flashed his thought into words.

"Then why did I let you tell me that you cared? That's what you're asking, isn't it?"

He bent his head.

"Yes. Why did you?" he said sternly.

She shrank away from him. This was the Mac she was afraid of—the Mac whose inflexible code of loyalty and straight-dealing seemed to her to make no allowances for human frailty.

"Oh, Mac, can't you understand?" she exclaimed desperately. "It just *happened!* The accident—which made me know all suddenly that I cared—and then finding out that you cared, too. . . . And I never thought ahead, of—of marriage or anything, till you asked when we could be married."

It all came tumbling out so naturally, with a candour so unmistakable, that Kenyon's last distrust of her vanished. He took her hands in his.

"Then, darling, if that's so," he said tenderly, "can't you *try* to tell me why you won't marry me? There must be some foolish reason, and I expect, between us, we could scotch it. Let me help, won't you?"

She bent her head, laying her cheek for a moment against his hands. Then she lifted her face to his and her eyes were like bright, defiant stars.

"I'm not fit to marry anyone," she said, slowly and definitely. "I've bad blood in my veins. . . . If I married you, I should be sure to let you down sometime or other, and then you'd never forgive me. And I couldn't bear that."

"I think I could forgive you anything," he answered quietly. Adding, with a half-smile: "Do you imagine I'm going to accept anything so absurd as that rigmarole as a reason for our not getting married?"

"You must," she said vehemently. "You must."

"I won't. Look here, sweetheart, get this into your

head: Nothing in this world or the next is going to alter my love for you——"

"If you knew the truth it would," she interrupted passionately.

"Then *tell* me the truth!" he challenged. "Tell me the truth—and let me judge."

For a moment she stared at him with wide, haunted eyes. Memories from the past flooded over her like a dark tide. The voice of another man who had loved her sounded in her ears: *"The daughter of a swindler and a suicide . . . I can't make her the mother of my children."* That was the ultimate verdict. It had been Rex's verdict; it would be the verdict of every man.

She swung herself free of Kenyon's clasp.

"I *can't* tell you the truth," she said doggedly. "But you must believe that what I say is true. I shall never marry you or any other man."

The flames had died down on the hearth. Only a dull glow came from the smouldering logs, and in the faint light her face looked ghastly.

"You'd better go now," she said, almost in a whisper. "Will you—please?"

He hesitated. Then, as though he sensed that for the time being she could bear no more, he yielded.

"All right," he said. "I'll go—now. But some day I shall come back, Herrick. The past—*whatever it is*"—he emphasised the three words deliberately—"is not going to keep us apart always. . . . Till then, we'll go on being pals as usual."

"Oh, may we? . . . Will you?" she exclaimed brokenly.

He smiled.

"We certainly may—and will," he replied reassuringly.

Then she felt his arms about her, and in obedience to his unspoken demand, she lifted her face to his and gave him her lips. It was a farewell, she knew that in her heart—farewell to the man who, in other circumstances, might have been her lover, but who could never now be anything more than a friend.

CHAPTER XI

HALF A LOAF

BILLY stood gazing moodily out of the window, drumming with irritable fingers on the pane. A hard frost had set in a few days previously, putting a summary end to the hunting, and although by this time the ice was sufficiently strong to bear for skating, even that form of sport offered, in his eyes, a very poor substitute for a day with hounds. However, the only thing to do, in the circumstances, was to make the best of a bad job and take whatever goods the gods *did* provide, and he was at the present moment waiting to escort Herrick down to the lake.

The lake which lay between Windycroft and the Rectory provided quite the best stretch of ice in the district, and it was an understood thing that any friends and neighbours were welcome to come and skate there. Yesterday, being the first day upon which the ice had borne, Herrick and Billy, together with Barbara Fane, had had it pretty much to themselves, but this morning Billy could already discern from the window a few figures, black against the dull grey sheet of frozen water, skimming hither and thither.

Br-r-r, br-r-r, br-r-r! His fingers continued their interminable thrumming on the window until at last Lady Bridget, who was trying to write letters at a table by the fire, looked up and inquired resignedly:

"*Must* you do that, Bill?"

"Sorry, Mim." He desisted at once. "I think I feel rather like Flame this weather—Larkin tells me she nearly kicked her box to pieces this morning because the hounds passed by when they were exercising—and she knew it, of course."

"You're better off than Flame," commented Lady Bridget drily. "At least you get some skating when hunting's off the map."

He laughed.

"True for you, Mim. Still, give me hunting every time. I tell Herrick it's she who has brought on this confounded frost by bragging about the weather we were having—that day we went to meet Barbara at the station. It was simply tempting Providence! And the frost began the very next morning."

"The day you ran into Mac's car, you mean?"

"Yes." Billy swung round and regarded his mother with a half-humorous, half-rueful expression. "By the way, I thought I was being no end tactful and diplomatic on that occasion. Old Kenyon seemed so annoyed 'cos I'd nearly landed Herrick into a bad smash and so almighty keen on driving her home himself, that I fondly imagined there must be some particular reason. So I meekly toiled and moiled my solitary way into Tanborough, in order to give him his chance—and I'm blest if he took it, after all!"

A curious expression sprang into Lady Bridget's eyes—a look of sudden comprehension, as though she had just been supplied with the clue to something which had been puzzling her.

"How do you know he didn't take it?" she asked. Billy grinned broadly.

"I don't 'know,' of course," he answered. "I only assumed it because nothing's happened since—nothing of public interest, I mean, like the announcement of an engagement, for instance." He paused, then with a sudden twinkle in his green eyes, he added: "Perhaps Herrick turned him down! I never thought of that. Do you think that's the explanation?"

Lady Bridget shook her head at him.

"Run away, and don't cultivate a tendency to gossip, Billy," she replied non-committally. "I can't really see that anything has occurred which requires any special explanation."

But, notwithstanding the firmness with which she had nipped off the ends of Billy's sprouting curiosity, Mim herself had for several days been mentally searching for an explanation that would fit certain slight differences, both in Herrick and Mac Kenyon, which those discerning dark eyes of hers had not failed to perceive. The girl had been quieter than her wont, and once or twice she had appeared at breakfast with heavy shadows underneath her eyes, as though she and sleep had had very little to say to each other during the course of the previous night.

As far as Kenyon was concerned, he had "happened over" to Windycroft much less often than had been his custom latterly. Conceivably, of course, the infrequency of his visits might be attributed to the fact that there was no hunting—since a hunting day generally brought him in for a few minutes' chat after he had escorted Herrick back. But on the one or two occa-

sions when he had appeared Lady Bridget had de-
tected a certain controlled neutrality in his manner,
rather as though he were forcing himself to play a
part.

And she had been proportionately disappointed.
For Mim was far too true a woman to be devoid of
the match-making tendency, and Mac's expression,
when he had found himself brought unexpectedly face
to face with his "little Samaritan" the day after Herrick's arrival at Windycroft, had had its own significance to eyes as shrewd as Lady Bridget's.

It was a slender enough foundation, but one upon
which, in some feminine fashion of her own, she had
been unconsciously building up a castle of romance.
And now Billy's youthful frank comment, together
with her own awareness of some tangible change in the
relations between Mac and Herrick, had combined
to loosen the very keystone of the edifice.

She wondered whether they had quarrelled, or
whether, perhaps, Mac had not really been waiting
for the "chance" which Billy had so magnanimously
given him. Possibly, after all, she had been letting
her imagination run away with her and had miscon-
strued what was actually nothing more than a jolly
comradeship into something more far-reaching.

Just at that moment Herrick and Billy passed the
window on their way down to the lake, turning to
give her a cheery wave of their hands as they passed.
She watched them cross the park, tramping briskly
over the frosted grass, and now and again a gay
ripple of their laughter came wafted back to her ears
on the clear air. She smiled a trifle crookedly to her-

self; certainly, she reflected, modern man and maid very successfully avoided wearing their hearts upon their sleeves. . . .

"Mr. Beresford."

The voice of one of the menservants, and the simultaneous opening of the door, roused her sharply out of her musings to find Jem's tall, rather shabby figure standing on the threshold. He was carrying a basket which he tendered carefully as soon as he had shaken hands.

"Here's the setting of Wyandotte eggs which I promised you," he said. "I thought I'd bring them across at once. Have you got a good broody hen to put them under?"

Lady Bridget received the offering with eager, and equally careful, hands.

"Yes, I have. How nice of you to have brought them over, Jem! Thanks ever so much."

"I nearly popped a broody hen into another basket and brought her along, too," he vouchsafed, smiling, "in case you hadn't one at the moment."

"You dear!" Lady Bridget beamed at him. She could picture him so well marching stolidly over from Two Ways Cottage with a basket on either arm, totally oblivious of appearances as long as he was doing a friend a good turn. "Come with me, and we'll see these eggs safely settled in life, and then you must have a whisky and soda after your tramp—or a glass of sloe gin? Which shall it be?"

"Whisky and soda's good enough for the likes of me," averred Jem with a grin. And then, taking the eggs from her, he accompanied her out to the poultry yard, where the Wyandotte setting was satisfactorily disposed of.

"And how's your own poultry farm doing, Jem?" inquired Lady Bridget, when they had returned to the house and established themselves by the fire in the hall, Beresford with a whisky and soda at his elbow.

"Oh, simply humming along. It's nonsense people saying poultry farming doesn't pay. It pays all right if it's properly looked after—and as I've nothing else to do except look after mine it's paying jolly well. Why" — smiling broadly — "I've amassed enough money to settle down and get married on—in a modest way." And then, all at once, the smile left his face, as though it had been wiped off with a sponge, and he stared blankly at Lady Bridget, suddenly hit by the bitter irony of his own unthinking jest.

"But you never will?" she queried softly. "I suppose"—speaking with a shy urgency—"I suppose you couldn't—possibly, Jem, could you? You weren't meant for loneliness, you know. You'd be happier married, with kiddies of your own."

For a moment he stared into the fire, his plain, square-jawed face set like a mask.

"Think so?" he said at last jerkily. "Well, you're right. But there's only one woman in the world for me—and she can't be my woman. . . . You all know it, really. I don't see why I shouldn't put it into words —to you, Mim."

"I've guessed it," she admitted reluctantly. "But I thought—I hoped that perhaps—some day——"

He smiled at her rather as one might smile at a nice

child who was trying to comfort one in its shy, blundering child way.

"I might get to care for someone else? Is that what you thought?"

"Yes," she said simply.

He shook his head.

"No, Mim. There's no 'perhaps' of that kind in my life."

Somehow Lady Bridget knew then, once and for all, that there would never be any other woman for Jem but Carol. And she felt suddenly frightened.

"But it's all so useless," she said protestingly. "Sir Francis may live for years."

"He's good for another thirty-odd, I should say," assented Jem grimly. "I'm not counting on any dead man's shoes. You may rest assured of that."

"Then—then"—fearfully—"what *are* you counting on?"

"Counting on?" His voice had roughened a little. "I'm counting on half a loaf. On living near her— and just seeing her sometimes. . . . I once asked her to go away with me——"

"You asked her that? Oh, Jem!"

"Yes. I asked her, and she refused. God knows why. Her life must be absolute hell with that man. But she's got some reason—some stronger reason than the ones that usually hold a woman back. Only she won't tell me what it is."

"Thank God she's got it, anyway!" said Lady Bridget fervently. "For of one thing I'm sure: and that is, that if you *did* succeed in persuading Carol to leave her husband, he would never divorce her—never set her free to be your wife."

"You think not?" Beresford stared at her incredulously. "Oh, the man couldn't be such an unspeakable swine!"

"He could, and he would," she asserted, with decision. "He'd do it out of sheer deliberate cruelty—to punish her. I don't think any of you quite realise what Francis Mortimer is like. I've known him ever since I was first married and came to live here at Windycroft, and he's got more callous cruelty in his little finger than most people have in their whole bodies. I should imagine that, as a small boy, he probably took a fiendish delight in pulling off butterflies' legs and wings and watching the poor things wriggle."

"The brute!" growled Jem.

Lady Bridget nodded.

"Yes, he is a brute," she said. "And that's the reason I want you to be very careful not to do anything to infuriate him—for Carol's sake. He can't get at you. But he'll make *her* pay—always, for anything you both may do. Be discreet, Jem, even in small things. Do remember that."

"I'll remember. But"—with a slow, rueful smile—"it's a bit difficult at times."

"I'm sure it is," she said sympathetically.

Presently he rose to go, holding out his hand with a certain frank comradeliness that was characteristic of him.

"I think I'm glad you know—about Carol and me," he said, with an odd touch of boyishness. "If—

whatever happens, Mim, you'd always stand her friend?"

"Always, Jem. You know that," answered Lady Bridget, her eyes very steady. "But don't forget that 'no man liveth to himself alone.' And if—if ever you and Carol take the law into your own hands, remember you won't be the only ones who'll pay. You can't insulate yourself in this world, you know—like an electric wire. And other people would get hurt besides you two."

CHAPTER XII

VARIOUS PROBLEMS

THE cards show that something stands just between you and happiness."

Again and again since Mac had asked her to marry him had those words recurred bitterly to Herrick's mind. Her fortune, foretold by Paul Breton with no more serious motive than that of distracting her thoughts on a day when she had chanced to be in low spirits, had come uncannily true so far. And the thing that stood betwixt her and happiness, as she had told him at the time, would stand there always. She could never marry, and she could never tell the man she loved why she couldn't marry him.

Only on one occasion since the day she had given him her refusal had she and Mac been alone together for more than a few minutes. He had asked her then, once more, if she would give him her reason for refusing him.

"I can't," she had answered doggedly.

"You can't—now, you mean." He corrected her quietly. "One day you *will* tell me, and then you'll realise that it was no good and sufficient reason at all."

She shook her head.

"I shall never tell you," she said.

And in her inmost heart she knew that she never would. That would be the one thing she felt she could not bear—that Mac should ever know the truth concerning her parentage. To see his face change, to know that inwardly he recoiled from her, resented the fact that he loved her—just as Rex had resented it—would be beyond the limits of her endurance. At least, now, she could see him sometimes, meet him on the neutral ground of friendship, know the bitter sweetness of being with him. She was wronging no one in this. It was the same "half loaf" with which Jem Beresford was trying to content himself—with which so many men and women have to try to get through life.

Herrick faced the situation bravely, as once before she had faced a somewhat similar situation. Only the love which she had given Rex had been very different from the love she felt for Mac—as different as water is from wine. She had been little more than a child then, yielding the first sweet immature love of a very young girl in response to Rex's impetuous courtship. That love had died—died swiftly, killed by his treatment, as the first tender green shoots of a plant can be killed by a single winter's frost. It had left a scar in dying. But, nevertheless, it had died utterly. Whereas the love she had given Mac was a woman's love, a love that was interwoven with every fibre of her being, spiritual and physical, and she knew that the hurt of it would last as long as life.

Still, she did not propose to let it overwhelm her or to convert existence into one eternal book of lamentation. She had known for three years—ever since the day when Rex had thrust her out of his life—that she was as one set apart, cut off from love and the happiness love brings. That was her heritage, the burden

which her father's sin had fastened on her shoulders—
a sin for which she would always have to pay the price.
But, just as then she had refused to let it crush her,
had built up her own life in spite of it, so now, although the accident of love had befallen her, making
the price exacted a thousand-fold heavier than she had
dreamed of—a price which must be paid daily and
hourly in bitterest longing and unfulfilment—she still
faced life with characteristic pluck.

The nights were the worst—the nights when she
lay for hours staring into the dark with sleepless eyes,
or pacing restlessly up and down her bedroom. In the
daytime she could keep thought more or less at bay.
There was always some small job with which she
could busy herself in the house—her self-imposed task
of recataloguing the library alone provided her with
plenty of indoor occupation—and, although there
could be no hunting while the frost held, the swift
movement of skating, with the sting of the cold air
beating against her face, was a tonic in itself.

Herrick skated extremely well, and she spent many
hours on the lake, more often than not, alone, since
Billy had recommenced his studies with the rector, and
in consequence had considerably less free time at his
disposal. But at the moment it seemed as though solitude rather appealed to her than otherwise. A wooden
hut, warmed by a stove when required, stood on the
borders of the lake not far from the Windycroft boat-
house, and occasionally she would beg some sandwiches
from the cook and, lunching alone in the hut, remain
by herself on the lake for the better part of the day.

Lady Bridget, with her usual kindly wisdom, let

her go her own way without comment. Although the girl had not confided in her, she guessed that she was passing through some inner emotional stress, and gladly though she would have welcomed her confidence, she had no intention of trying to force it.

Now and again she would accompany her down to the lake—for Mim had been an expert skater in her younger days and could still "put up a very fair show," as Billy encouragingly assured her, and sometimes Jem Beresford or Mac would turn up and join them for an hour, and then, Lady Bridget was secretly pleased to observe, Herrick would seem to forget whatever it was that was weighing on her mind in the sheer physical enjoyment of the sport.

Carol, alone, never made one of the pleasant little skating parties. She had been firmly forbidden by her husband to adventure on the ice, even although Lady Bridget herself had taken her courage in both hands and interceded for her. Sir Francis, however, had no mind to pay a possible doctor's bill for the setting of broken legs or arms. Moreover, he considered a wife who could run about and wait upon him a far more desirable proposition than one who had temporarily incapacitated herself by a skating accident.

Carol's faintly uttered protest, on one occasion, to the effect that skating was such excellent exercise, had been quashed unequivocally.

"Walking is a far better exercise, my dear—and much less risky," affirmed her husband. "If I were a skater myself and could accompany you, it would be a different matter. I should see to it that you were careful."

Carol suppressed an involuntary smile at the vision which presented itself to her mind of Sir Francis's tall, angular black figure spread-eagling over the ice, and answered rather wistfully:

"Mac would look after me all right. I used to skate before we were married you know."

"What you did before you became my wife and what you do now are two very different things," responded Mortimer coldly. "I have no doubt your brother—or your friend, Mr. Beresford—would either of them be delighted to constitute himself your cicerone, but I do not wish it." As he uttered Jem's name he shot a swift, suspicious glance at her from under his pouched lids, and, despite herself, Carol felt a flush rising to her cheeks.

"I never mentioned Mr. Beresford," she burst out with her usual impulsive unwisdom. Her husband always seemed to have the faculty of driving her into saying the very thing that would have been best left unsaid.

He smiled sardonically.

"No. But I feel I interpreted your thought correctly," he answered.

For a moment Carol's self-control gave way. She could always feel the goad hidden beneath his smoothly spoken speeches, and that daily, hourly sense of being watched and spied upon, checked here and thwarted there, sometimes tried her nerves almost to breaking point.

"It seems to me you want me to have no friends!" she exclaimed a little wildly.

"On the contrary, I merely wish—and intend—

to have a decisive voice in their selection. And now, my dear, as the daily papers have come, I should be glad if you will read me the *Times* leading article."

So, outwardly submissive, although inwardly burning with a spirit of revolt, Carol had yielded, as indeed she always found herself compelled to yield, to her husband's dictation. But a day or two later, when he curtly informed her that he was going to London and should not be back until the following day, her inner rebellion translated itself into prompt action. From the window she watched the car which was taking him to the station speeding down the drive, and, as soon as it was safely out of sight, she flew to the telephone and, ringing up Windycroft, asked to speak to Herrick.

"That you, Herrick?" Her voice came bubbling along the wire in a little rush of happy and mutinous excitement. "Listen. *He's* gone away. For two whole days. So please ask me to lunch—and couldn't we have an hour or two on the lake together? My feet are simply tingling to skate once more!"

So strictly had Sir Francis kept watch and ward over his wife since the skating had begun that none of the little community of friends at St. Heriot had set eyes on her during the last ten days, excepting in church on Sunday. And after the service, as they had all stood chatting together at the lych-gate, prior to wending their several ways homeward, her husband had whisked her swiftly off into the Mortlake car before she had done more than exchange the barest of greetings with them. Hence, when Herrick heard Carol's voice, athrill like that of a girl unexpectedly released from school, she responded with whole-hearted enthusiasm.

"How perfectly splendid! I've been simply longing to have a heart-to-heart gossip with you. Look here, will you meet me down at the lake about twelve o'clock, and we'll have a picnic lunch together in the hut there? Mim and Billy have gone into Tanborough for the day—patronising the dentist and so on—so I shall be all alone."

The matter was speedily arranged, and Herrick hung up the receiver. But she did not immediately move away from the table on which the telephone stood. Instead, she stood hesitating, as though she were debating something in her mind. Finally, with a quick, impulsive movement she turned back, lifted down the receiver once more, and asked for a number. "Hullo! Hullo?" A man's voice sounded over the wire. Herrick spoke swiftly into the black mouth of the telephone.

"Is that you, Jem? . . . Sir Francis has gone up to town, and so Carol and I are going to celebrate by having a picnic lunch together in the lake hut. Would you like to come along and 'coffee' with us afterwards?"

Someone laughed softly at the other end of the wire.

"Should I not?"

"Then—about half-past one?"

"Half-past one it is. And, Herrick——"

"Yes?"

"You're a blessed little saint, my dear. That's all."

She smiled ruefully.

"I'm not quite sure whether I'm saint—or sinner," she said. And rang off.

There was a certain substratum of truth in her admission. If you had asked Herrick a short time ago —before that memorable day when Billy's careless driving had been fraught with such far-reaching consequences—whether it were acting wisely or unwisely to throw Jem and Carol together, she would have had no hesitation in declaring that it was altogether unwise and inexcusable. But then she had not known love as she knew it now, and the hopelessness of her own love affair had made her curiously tender and sympathetic towards the love affairs of other people. Jem and Carol were set apart exactly as much, as inevitably, as she and Mac. The barriers that separated them one from the other differed only in kind. And just as she knew that, for her, the mere sight of Mac, the sound of his voice, the touch of his hand, constituted all there was of real happiness in the whole world, so she knew that similar happiness for Carol and the man she loved lay only in the rare occasions when they could meet each other, secure from Sir Francis's lynx-eyed observation.

There could be no harm in their having an hour or so together, Herrick argued in her own mind. Carol herself had told her that she and Jem both recognised the fact that they were irrevocably divided, and, that being so, there was no possible danger in their snatching at the few happy, unspied-on moments which came their way.

So that it was with a light heart that she collected her skates, and a small lunch hamper packed in readiness by the cook, and made her way down to the lake. Carol was there, skimming over its frozen surface with the supple grace and assurance of an experienced performer, and she sped eagerly up to Herrick as soon as she caught sight of her.

"Isn't this glorious?" she exclaimed rapturously, as she embraced her. "I feel as if I had dropped ten years into the depths of the lake somewhere."

And indeed she looked it. The nervous, distrait expression had gone out of her eyes, leaving them clear and bright like a child's, the cold air had whipped a delicate flush into her cheeks, and her pretty mouth curved easily into happy laughter. Watching her, Herrick was conscious of a fresh surge of indignation and resentment against Sir Francis. It ought not to be possible for any man to take away, wipe out, a woman's youth and gaiety as he was able to do. This Carol, freed from the bondage he imposed on her, was a different creature—little more than a girl, for all her thirty years, and bubbling over with good spirits.

She fell in with the other's joyous mood and together the two skated about the lake and vied with each other in cutting figures on the ice until at last the pangs of hunger made them call a halt. They had lighted the stove in the hut beforehand, and a cosy warmth prevailed by the time they returned there for lunch and proceeded to unpack the hamper Herrick had brought with her.

"I'm sure I feel just like the maids do on their 'day out,' " declared Carol, munching sandwiches with enthusiasm. "Only they get one every week—and I don't."

"What about to-morrow?" suggested Herrick. "Couldn't you come down again?"

Carol shook her head regretfully.

"No," she said. "I daren't. Francis is coming home to-morrow, and of course he was careful not to give me the least hint as to the time he'd get back. He never does."

"But surely," submitted Herrick practically, "he will have to telephone or wire you what time to send the car to meet him at the station?"

"Oh dear, no! He might walk back from St. Heriot —he's a terribly good walker, you know—or he might elect to come by express to Tanborough and hire a car from there." Carol's face had sobered and the customary look of strain was once more visible in her eyes. "That's what is so unnerving—so—so wearing. I never know where he is or for how long I shall be free. Sometimes, when I think he's safely shut up for an hour or so in his study with Rawlings—that's his estate agent, you know—I suddenly meet him stalking about the garden, and find that he has been watching me for quite a long time."

"I don't know how you bear it!" burst out Herrick indignantly.

"I sometimes feel as if I *can't* bear it—any longer," acknowledged Carol with exceeding bitterness. "If it weren't for Mac, I think I should do something desperate."

"For Mac?"

"Yes. You see, it would simply break his heart if I did—what I'm sometimes tempted to do. And I care for him too much to do anything that would hurt him like that. Being a twin complicates life rather," she went on, with a faint enigmatic smile that was half sad, half humorous. "You can't act quite independently if you're a twin. Mac and I are so much more to each other than an ordinary brother and sister."

"Still, I don't see——" began Herrick.

"Don't you?" Again that faint, incalculable smile. "Well, supposing I did decide to do something definite and final, to—to leave Francis——"

"He'd get over it," broke in Herrick contemptuously. "It would only be his pride and selfishness that would be hurt. And you'd be much happier."

"No. It would be *my* pride that would be hurt—mine and Mac's. So I shouldn't really be happy."

"Your pride?"

"Yes," answered Carol. "You see, my marriage wasn't just like any other ordinary marriage. I told you, I married Francis simply and solely for money. It was a definite bargain between us," she explained flatly. "I gave him myself, and in return he undertook to make my mother an allowance—to be fair, it was a thoroughly generous allowance—as long as she lived. She didn't live long," she added with a sigh. "Only six months, but at least those six months were made as easy for her as money could possibly make them. . . . *Now* do you understand how I'm tied? Francis carried out his part of the bargain. I can't do anything else but carry out mine."

For a few moments Herrick made no answer. Regarded from that aspect, from the standpoint of the honest fulfilment of a compact made, she could see how hopelessly and inevitably Carol was bound. Nothing but death, the death of Sir Francis, could release her.

"And—is that—what Mac thinks, too?" she asked at last, guessing full well what the answer would be.

Carol nodded.

"Yes. His point of view is that it's a question of honour—that it would be utterly dishonourable of me if I failed to keep my side of the bargain. Oh!"—wearily. "We've thrashed it all out. I know what Mac thinks—and I know that if I left Francis, I should lose Mac. Honour—straight-dealing is a fetish with him. He would sacrifice anything and everything to it."

"Even his sister," commented Herrick rather bitterly, as the realisation swept over her more strongly than ever that, if Mac knew the truth about herself, knew whose child she was, not all his love for her could find them a way to happiness. He would give her up, sacrifice her, precisely as Rex had done, just as now he himself was sacrificing all his sister's happiness to a stern ideal of honour. Men were very ready to sacrifice their womenkind, she reflected, with a touch of cynicism.

"I wonder," she pursued, "if the circumstances were reversed, if Mac's own happiness were involved, would he still think the same?"

"I'm sure of it." Carol's reply came quite quietly, uttered with a steadfast belief that was unshakable. "I'm his sister, I know," she went on with a little deprecating smile, "and so I oughtn't to be his trumpeter, but Mac is one of the straightest people on the face of the earth. He simply couldn't do a crooked thing, and he's so fond of me that I think it would half kill him if I did. There's only one person in the world who counts more with him than I do," she added, looking at Herrick with a sudden directness. Then, abruptly, she asked: "Tell me, why have you refused him?"

"He told you?" exclaimed Herrick, flushing scarlet.

"No, *no!*" The other answered hastily. "I guessed it. Twins have a curious insight into what hurts each other, you know. Is it quite impossible? Don't you think you might grow to care for him?" she continued rather wistfully. "I should so love Mac to be happy. And you'd make the darlingest sister!" she wound up impulsively.

Herrick smiled in spite of herself. There was something disarmingly spontaneous and warm-hearted about Carol's special pleading. Then the smile faded.

"It's quite impossible—quite," she said at last, with a note of finality in her voice.

Carol looked at her curiously. There was a further question in her eyes, but it never reached her lips. Intuitively she sensed the pain behind the reticence of Herrick's brief rejoinder, and sensitively refrained from probing any deeper.

"Life's very difficult sometimes," was all she said, with a sigh. "Very difficult—and puzzling."

Herrick sprang up and began to busy herself making coffee.

"Yes," she answered bluntly. "It is—damnably

difficult. The only thing is to take it as it comes and get on with it." And in that she had unconsciously enunciated the whole philosophy of life—and not such a bad one, either—which the last three years had taught her.

CHAPTER XIII

PLAYING WITH FIRE

A CHEERFUL rat-tat sounded on the hut door, then the latch was lifted and Jem Beresford's big figure, skates slung over his shoulder, appeared on the threshold. He paused to stamp some frozen snow off his boots before coming in.

"I seem to have timed my arrival remarkably well," he observed, smiling, as Herrick relinquished the coffee-pot to shake hands with him.

Then his glance leapt eagerly past her to where Carol had half-risen from her seat by the stove, a startled flush dyeing her cheeks. If ever a man's eyes said "Darling!" Jem's did at that moment, but all his lips uttered was a perfectly commonplace: "Hullo, Carol!"

Her hand slid into his, and, as he held it for just a moment longer than was absolutely necessary, she turned to Herrick a shade nervously. His unexpected appearance seemed to have disconcerted her a little.

"You never told me Jem was coming," she said.

Herrick's attention was apparently concentrated on the coffee she was at that moment pouring out.

"Didn't I?" she answered carelessly, handing a cup to Carol as she spoke. "Oh, well, we've been so busy talking, haven't we?"

"It must have been a very serious conversation,"

commented Jem, struck by an unwonted sense of gravity which still lingered in the atmosphere. "You're both looking rather glum. Have you been squabbling?"

Herrick's mouth twitched.

"Not exactly," she replied drily. "On the contrary, we've been hard at work agreeing with each other. Here's your coffee, Jem; taste it and see if it's as you like it."

Beresford obeyed before he returned to the charge.

"Exactly right, thanks. Well, then, if a mere man may inquire, what have you both been agreeing about so cordially?"

"Do you really want to know?" asked Herrick.

"Yes, please, if I may." A little pinched look in Carol's face, as though she were suddenly afraid of something, worried him, and he wondered if the two girls had been discussing any fresh trouble or difficulty that had arisen to threaten the woman he loved and of which he was in ignorance.

"Well, then, if you must know, we've been discussing Life—with a capital L," said Herrick randomly. "And we came to the conclusion that it's so complicated it ought to be published with a key."

Jem looked relieved.

"Oh, is that all?" he returned. "Well, we most of us come to that conclusion sooner or later."

"I wish things were simpler—and no key required," remarked Carol wistfully.

He flashed a sudden glance at her and seemed about to make some swift rejoinder. Then he checked himself abruptly, his mouth closing in a straight, hard line. When he spoke again, it was on totally impersonal matters, deliberately diverting the conversation to some recent incidental happenings of the neighbourhood.

"How's the ice to-day?" he inquired presently. "It struck me as I came along that it seemed to be thawing a bit."

"You'd better go out and try it," answered Herrick promptly. "And take Carol with you. I'm going to wash up the coffee things."

"I'll help," volunteered Carol.

Herrick shook her head decidedly.

"No, you won't. Remember, it's your 'day out,' " she added smilingly.

A few minutes later she was left in undisputed possession of the hut, while Jem and Carol were skimming hand in hand over the gleaming stretch of ice. Carol's face still wore a faint expression of anxiety.

"Jem, did you know I was coming down to the lake this morning?" she asked, when at last they came to a halt. "Or was it just an accident, your turning up here to-day?"

Beresford looked down at her with some amusement.

"Accidents don't happen as luckily as that, in my experience," he replied gaily. "No, the *dea ex machina* was Herrick. She rang me up—and invited me to coffee."

"Oh!"

His hand closed more tightly round the slender one that lay within its big palm.

"You're not angry?" he asked.

She smiled, suddenly and sweetly.

"Ridiculous person! How could I be—angry?

No, it's not that. But—I'm a little frightened, I think."

"Why?"

"Oh, because it seems rather as if I'd committed all the sins in the Decalogue in one fell swoop! You see, skating is taboo, and *you*—really—are taboo, and I feel as though some dreadful punishment will overtake me. If—if that awful man Humphreys could see us——"

"But he can't," said Jem reassuringly. "You're quite safe here from his gimlet eyes, confound him. And I'll see you home—through the woods, so that you won't need to cross the garden or the drive at all. My dear," he went on, a note of rising passion in his voice, "we *must* see each other alone now and then. We're hurting no one—robbing no one by an occasional hour or two together. If Mortimer cared for you, it might be different, perhaps——"

"He has certain rights——" began Carol, thinking of that irrevocable bargain she had made—of the compact which must shackle her for life.

"Rights be damned!" broke in Jem savagely. "The only right a man has over a woman is the right to love and serve her. And I wish to God you'd give it to me —let me take care of you and look after you. I swear you should never forget it, Carol—my dear, my dear!" His eyes burned down into hers. His control— that iron control of his which had enabled him to play the friend so long—was gradually slipping under the strain.

"Oh, hush!" She laid her free hand swiftly across his mouth. "Jem, you promised never to ask me that again. You mustn't, dear, you mustn't," she urged, a little desperately. "Because it's so hard to keep on saying 'no' when everything that's me wants to say 'yes.'" She turned to him appealingly. "Oh, Jem, do help me —don't make it more difficult," she pleaded. "Do still be—my friend."

He set his teeth, slowly releasing his hold of her, and for a moment there was a tense silence while he fought down the fierce desire of all that was man and lover in him.

"Al right," he said at last, his voice hard with the compulsion he was putting upon himself. "All right— you needn't be afraid. I shall never take you, unless you want to come. But if ever you do come to me, no power on earth shall make me let you go again!"

"I shall never come," she said quietly; "I couldn't. You don't understand . . . there could never be any happiness for us if I did. Sometimes I think Mac is right when he says we ought not to meet—that you ought to go away from here."

"Does he say that?" Jem gave a short laugh. "If ever Mac himself knows what it is to care for a woman he'll find out that it's not so easy to 'go away.'"

"'If ever'!" Carol looked at him with a faint feminine indulgence in her eyes. "Haven't you seen— haven't you guessed? Oh"—her lips curving into rather a wan little smile—"I think you must be very blind."

"Haven't I guessed—what? You don't mean that old Mac——"

She nodded at him.

"That's just what I do mean."

Jem regarded her doubtfully. Then, all at once, a look of understanding illumined his face.

"Is it—Herrick?" he demanded.

"Yes. Herrick."

He smiled.

"Then that's why she understands things so well, bless her! When's the engagement going to be announced? There are no two people I'd congratulate more sincerely. She and Mac are made for each other——"

"Oh, stop, stop!" cried Carol, half laughing in spite of herself. "You're jumping to conclusions. No engagement will be announced because—because there isn't going to be one."

"What!" Jem's jaw dropped. "You don't mean that she's turned him down?" His own affection for Kenyon was so unqualified that it hardly seemed to him credible that any woman the latter had fallen in love with could fail to respond.

Carol lifted a pair of troubled blue eyes to his face.

"I don't know. I can't quite make out what has happened between them. I know—I can feel that Mac isn't happy, and it worries me."

"Don't worry, dear. Probably it will all come right in the long run. At least"—with a note of rather bitter envy in his voice—"they're neither of them tied up to anyone else. Hullo!" He broke off with an exclamation of surprise and gestured towards the border of the lake where a man's solitary figure had just come into view, striding along with head bent as though engrossed in thought. "There *is* Mac, of all people—exactly as we were speaking of him."

Jem sent his voice ringing over the ice in a welcoming shout and, with a brief start, as if jerked abruptly out of the very depths of abstraction, Kenyon looked up in response. A curious expression flitted across his face as he perceived whose were the two figures which had wheeled round and were now approaching him, an expression that was half spontaneous pleasure, half a species of dubious astonishment.

"And what's the meaning of this?" he asked, smiling down at his sister when they all had exchanged greetings. "Have the laws of the Medes and Persians as regards skating been revoked?"

"Oh, no." There was a glint of mischief in Carol's eyes as she answered. "In the absence of the law-giver they've been temporarily disregarded. That's all."

Mac's face took on a look of gravity.

"Not altogether wise, is it?" he said slowly.

She shrugged her shoulders. The rebellious mood of the morning, which had prompted her to defy, for once, her husband's petty tyranny, reasserted itself.

"I really don't think I mind very much whether it's wise—or unwise," she said with a sudden irritable defiance. "I've enjoyed it, anyway."

The unwonted edge to her usually charming voice spoke to Mac eloquently enough of the frayed nerves which sharpened it, and he refrained from any further criticism. But in his own mind he knew very well that for his sister to be skating alone with Jem Beresford was, in the circumstances, the height of unwisdom, and the one sure way he saw of saving her from any consequent trouble, should Sir Francis come to hear of it, was by accompanying her back to Mortlake Hall himself. For some reason his brother-in-law invariably treated him with a species of unwilling civility which he was far from according to most people. Possibly he sensed a certain quiet strength in Kenyon's make-up against which his own evil moods would batter in vain. And if Carol returned home, having been obviously in her brother's care, Mac felt fairly certain that not even Sir Francis would attempt to find much fault— at least no fault of which he himself could not shoulder the blame and thus screen his sister from any possible wrath to come.

"Well, suppose you let me see you home now?" he suggested. "You've probably skated quite long enough to-day for anyone who's out of practice."

Before Carol could reply, Jem intervened, his face suddenly stormy.

"I'm seeing Carol home," he said bluntly.

The situation had reached an *impasse*. Without putting his reason into actual words—and that was clearly impossible—Mac was helpless to oppose the other man's decision. For a moment he was silent. Then:

"Oh, very well," he replied curtly. And vouchsafing only a brief nod he turned away and left them alone together.

He had been tramping in the direction of the hut, taking what was a short cut towards Greenwood through the Windycroft valley, when he had encountered his sister and Beresford, and now, as he resumed his way along the edge of the lake he felt thoroughly angry and exasperated with them both—an anger and exasperation which sprang from a deep-rooted anxiety.

With one exception, they were the two people he loved best in the world, and it seemed to him they were heading for disaster—disaster which he was powerless to avert.

There are few things that make for a more jagged state of nerves than the feeling of impotence—of impotence to influence and save people who show no disposition to be influenced and saved, particularly when they are people whose well-being counts for a great deal in one's own life, and, as Mac approached the hut, his mood had written itself unmistakably in his bent brows and grimly shut mouth.

Herrick, her domestic labours finished, was standing idly at the hut door, smoking a cigarette, and so absorbed was he in his thoughts that he had drawn almost level with her before he was aware of her presence. Then he looked up and saw her. For an instant his face cleared, and a sudden eager light of recognition rushed into his eyes. But, in the same breath, almost, it died out, as though some other thought had submerged that first instinctive gladness, to be replaced by a deepening expression of uncertainty, of brooding storm.

"I didn't know you were down here," he said abruptly.

Herrick regarded him with momentary surprise—it was so unlike Mac to be churlish in his manner. Then an explanation presented itself to her mind. He had rather avoided meeting her of late, and perhaps the unexpectedness of the *rencontre* had found him unprepared. Churlishness, in a man, not infrequently conceals a very different emotion—and every woman knows it. A small, gamin smile tilted the corners of her mouth.

"If you had, I suppose you would have taken another way home," she suggested lightly.

But the swift denial she anticipated did not come. Instead, he inquired in a tone of extreme displeasure:

"May I ask if it was by your arrangement that my sister is here this afternoon?"

Herrick stared at him with increasing astonishment, conscious of a rising sense of annoyance. She had, of course, no knowledge of the circumstances which had combined to drive him into what was obviously a mood of ill-suppressed fury, and his manner was certainly intolerable.

"By my 'arrangement'?" she said stiffly. "I'm afraid I don't quite understand you."

His face darkened.

"Then I'll make myself a little clearer. Was it you who planned that Carol should come here to skate— a thing you know her husband has forbidden—and that Beresford should come too, so that they could spend the day together in his absence?"

The indignant colour flared up into her face, then retreated, leaving her paler than her wont. Put thus, with the unmistakable implication contained in Mac's speech, the whole thing sounded horrible—like some sordid intrigue in which she had taken a leading part. She knew that nothing was really further from the truth, and yet she realised instantly how difficult it would be to explain matters—to make it clear to Mac how impulsively and naturally the whole thing had come about. In any case, for the moment, explanation was far enough away from her intention. She was much too angry with him for daring to suspect her of deliberately scheming or planning anything.

"I don't 'plan' things in the way you're insinuating," she replied haughtily. "And I think everything you have just said is in the worst possible taste."

"There are times when good or bad taste becomes relatively a matter of unimportance," he retorted grimly. "And you haven't answered my question."

Herrick's hazel eyes sparkled with sudden anger.

"Nor have I the remotest intention of answering it," she answered. "I think it was an impertinence your even asking it."

"Impertinence or not, I want an answer," he returned doggedly. "You know—you understand the circumstances as well as I do. And Carol is playing with fire. It's my job—and the job of anyone who is her friend—to prevent it. And apparently, you—whom I would have trusted through thick and thin—have been working against me in this."

"You mean—you *don't* trust me then?" Herrick's lips were rather white, and her slight young breast was rising and falling unevenly. She was hurt beyond measure that he should have so misunderstood her, jumped to the conclusion which he had obviously drawn, and the soreness of fierce resentment surged up above every other feeling, driving her onward into bitter speech. "Well, there's no reason why you should. I told you once that I'd bad blood in my veins, so I don't look at things from the high altitude you do." The words came pouring out in a reckless torrent of anger. "You're more domineering and—and priggish than anyone I've ever met, and we should certainly never have got on with each other for a week. So it's an extremely good thing we agreed not to marry."

She paused, every line of her slim, boyish figure instinct with defiance. Kenyon surveyed her curiously. With her outburst of anger his own seemed to have died down, and there was a remote, impenetrable expression in his eyes as he regarded her.

"Only we did not—'agree'—not to marry," he observed. "That decision was entirely one-sided."

Herrick shrugged her shoulders.

"Well, whatever I felt then, I feel it even more strongly now," she rejoined in a hard voice. Then, as though to indicate that the interview was at an end, she stooped, and, picking up her skates from where they were lying on the floor of the hut, proceeded to put them on.

Mac watched her in silence for a moment. He made no offer to help her. Probably he realised that any such offer would only have met with a curt refusal and considered it, therefore, not worth making.

"If I may advise," he said in a perfectly indifferent voice, "I suggest you should avoid the upper end of the lake. It is beginning to thaw very fast, and the ice always gives out there first."

"Thank you, I think I can judge quite well for myself," she answered, not lifting her eyes from the skate she was busy securing at the moment. "I happen to like the upper end of the lake. And, as I'm not your sister, I suppose I can please myself when—and where—I skate."

Kenyon made a sudden involuntary movement as

though he would very much like to take her by the shoulders and shake her. Then he checked himself abruptly clenching his hands as his arms fell to his sides. Without a word of farewell, he swung round on his heel and strode away.

CHAPTER XIV

THIN ICE

HERRICK stood watching Jem and Carol as, after bidding her good-bye, they set off together for Mortlake Hall. None of the three had made more than a passing reference to Mac's unexpected appearance on the scene. Perhaps neither Carol nor Beresford had taken in the full import of the angry abruptness with which he had left them to their own devices. Much as they loved each other, and in spite of intermittent moments when Jem, man-like, rebelled bitterly against the sacrifice demanded, they were honestly trying to play the game, steadfastly resisting the temptation to snatch their happiness at no matter what cost, and their very consciousness of this helped to blind them to the dangers which Mac, as onlooker, could envisage only too clearly.

As far as Herrick was concerned she had no intention of retailing her own interview with him to anyone. For one thing, she was feeling too indignant, too resentful of the injustice of his surmise—and inwardly, too hurt—to wish to speak of it. But, beyond that, she realised that his censure would only add to Carol's burden, tarnishing the memory of the few hours' unexpected freedom and happiness which to-day had brought her with an ugly significance as of something preconcerted and designedly surreptitious.

Actually, nothing could have been farther from the essential truth of the matter. The whole impromptu situation had arisen out of a very natural impulse upon Carol's part—a sudden irresistible desire to take the rare chance of personal freedom offered by Sir Francis's absence and amuse herself, for once, just like anybody else—and by an eager, girlish impulse upon Herrick's part to give two people whom she knew to be unhappy the brief joy of being together for a little space. Out of all this, Mac, driven by anxiety and apprehension, had conjectured something motived and premeditated, and Herrick could see how difficult, in spite of the innocence of everyone concerned, it would be to correct this impression and straighten matters out. So she held her peace and let Jem and Carol take their way home in ignorance of the quarrel which had occurred betwixt herself and Mac, waving a cheerful valedictory hand to them as they looked back before disappearing round a bend in the woodland path they were following.

There was still another hour's daylight left before the early December dusk would drive her indoors, and, left in sole possession of the lake, she proceeded to work off in sheer physical exertion some of the vexation of soul which tormented her. There was storm in her heart, a chaotic mingling of pain and anger and resentment, and the rapid sweeping movement of her reckless progress over the black sheet of ice helped to thrust it temporarily aside. Hither and thither she flew, now flashing along at breakneck speed, now essaying complicated figures of which the very difficulty and daring seemed in harmony with the turmoil of her spirit.

The air, not quite so sharp as earlier in the day but with a certain warning dampness in its breath, cooled her burning cheeks, and her absolute solitariness on that wide stretch of frozen water, with the lonely, leafless trees at its edge stretching naked arms to a leaden sky whence a pale wintry moon peered down, gave her a strange sense of exultation. For the moment she felt as though she had escaped from the world and all its miserable mistakes—from love, and the cruelty of anger and the blind misunderstandings. and censure of friends, from all the things that have power to hurt so bitterly—escaped into a region where she was utterly untrammelled by the conflicting claims which life and the people amongst whom it has to be lived seem always destined to make. Subconsciously she knew she would have to go back to it, that it was waiting for her round the corner, as it were, but for the time being the glorious sense of complete solitude, the sheer physical rapture of swift, rhythmic movement as she fled over the ice, pervaded all her being.

And then, all at once, she became aware that she was no longer alone, and the knowledge brought her abruptly back to earth. A man's figure was standing some distance away on the farther bank of the lake, and for an instant, with a sudden glad leap of the heart, she thought it was Mac who stood there—Mac, come back to bridge over the quarrel and misunderstanding of the afternoon. But a second glance revealed her mistake. The man on the bank was about Mac's height, but there the resemblance ended. He was watching her very intently—had probably been watching her for some minutes, she reflected hostilely.

At any rate, she decided, the free entertainment she had been giving him—of what, although she hardly realised it, had been a really brilliant performance on the ice—should cease immediately.

She swung round and skimmed away in the opposite direction, towards the upper end of the lake. A fugitive recollection of Kenyon's advice, "I suggest you should avoid the upper end," flashed through her mind, but, instead of serving to check her progress, it merely acted as an incentive to proceed in that particular direction. The contrariness of human nature asserted itself—why *should* she be guided by Mac's recommendations, Mac, who had found such bitter fault with her? The very fact that he had put one specific part of the lake out of bounds, so to speak, gave her a kind of wayward delight in making it her objective.

At its farthest point the big sheet of water was comparatively shallow, varying from two to four feet deep at the utmost, and broken a few yards from the bank by a diminutive island on which a few scraggy bushes and a solitary tree put up a bid for existence. In front of the island the ice was spattered here and there with an occasional hummock of earth, crowned by straggling clumps of grass.

Fixing her eyes on the distant island, Herrick sped along. As she flashed forward, she thought she heard someone shouting, but she did not look round. It was probably the shepherd calling to his dog as he made his evening rounds of the sheep which pastured in the park. On she went. The surface of the ice was no longer dry; it gleamed wetly beneath her feet, and now and again the blades of her skates cut a slight jagged ridge as they passed over it. But, bent on achieving her object, she paid no attention to this. The spirit of "little girl" defiance which had prompted her to disregard Kenyon's advice was bubbling up in her. She would just circle the island and then return to the hut and take off her skates and go home. If—when— she and Mac were friends again she would chaff him about the solemn warning he had uttered and its entire superfluousness.

The ice grew rougher as she approached the island. Once or twice she stumbled and almost fell over a twig or tuft of rushes embedded in it. Then, all at once, with a splintering, rending crack, it gave way, and Herrick found herself plunged into the bitter, freezing water. She wasn't frightened, for she could feel the slimy mud of the lake bed underneath her feet. The water itself barely reached her waist, but the shock of its agonising cold drove a scream from her lips. It was not until she tried to extricate herself that she began to comprehend the real danger which threatened her—the danger of that numbing, almost stupefying cold which seemed to grip her body like a paralysing hand.

Stumbling and floundering, she strove to climb out of the hole into which she had fallen, only to find that all her efforts were perfectly futile. Everywhere the rotten ice broke away under pressure, and when she clutched at a clump of rushes they snapped off in her hand. Once she thought she had succeeded. Her legs still trailed in the water, but she had partially dragged herself on to some ice which appeared sounder than most of that which surrounded her, and the upper part of her body and her arms were stretched prone on its surface as she tried to edge her way back to safety. Then, with a grinding crash, that portion of the ice, too, gave way, and she found herself flung down on to her knees in the water. She was half benumbed with the intense cold as she staggered up again. Her limbs ached with it. Desperately she tried to call for help, but her voice, like the rest of her body, seemed frozen, and only a faint, uncertain cry issued from her throat.

It died away into the bleak, desolate silence of the frost-bound lake, and suddenly she was conscious of fear, definite, actual fear—the fear of death. It seemed ludicrous to think of dying—dying in four feet of water, but, if there were no escape from this ice-ringed hole into which she had fallen, the bitter cold would soon still the warm young life within her. And then, out of the chill, blank silence against which her cry for help had broken, came an answer.

"Hold on! I'm coming!"

In the same instant she discerned a man running towards her along the bank, covering the few remaining yards which still separated him from her with long, swift, eager strides. It was the solitary watcher whom she had seen half an hour ago, observing her from the side of the lake.

CHAPTER XV

A. STRANGER TO THE RESCUE

THE man speeding to Herrick's help drew level, crossed the frozen surface which intervened between the bank and the jagged hole in which she still struggled, and pulled up a few feet away, where the ice was sound.

"Take care!" she managed to call out, as he came to a halt. "The ice is rotten here."

He flashed a quick glance over her.

"So it seems," he answered, a flicker of humour in his voice. "Still——" He looked round, rapidly summing up the possibilities of the situation. Then, with incredible swiftness, he made a leaping stride on to a couple of hummocks of earth, tufted with frost-bitten grass and no bigger than stepping-stones, which protruded through the ice. For a second he rocked dangerously, then balanced himself, planting his feet firmly. Bending forward, he held out his arms.

"Now lean towards me," he said.

She hesitated, realising that he proposed lifting her clean out of the water, and doubting his ability.

"You can never do it," she protested.

"Quick! Do what I say!" he ordered sharply.

This time she obeyed the imperative command without demur, and, stumbling forward, leaned towards him. A moment later his arms, pliant and strong like steel, closed round her and drew her up out of the icy water.

"Clasp your hands behind my neck."

Again she obeyed, and felt him gather her up close against him as though she were a child. He paused and looked down at her with an amused smile.

"What a bit of a thing it is!" he said, as if struck by the lightness of the slender body which he held. "Now for it!"

Followed once more that long, leaping stride, this time from the crumbling hummock back on to the firm ice beyond it, a moment's breathless uncertainty, then a blessed sense of safety. With the consciousness of solid ice underfoot, Herrick made a tentative effort to slide out of her rescuer's embrace.

"No. Stay where you are," he said. "It's only a few yards to the bank. I won't let you fall," he added, a throb of amusement in his voice.

She yielded passively. Indeed, she was too spent to struggle—numb and helpless with the cold. When finally they reached the bank and he let her slip gently to the ground, she staggered and would have fallen but for his arm which still supported her. She clung to it with both hands.

"I—I can't stand," she said, her teeth chattering. She felt utterly wretched. Her wet clothes were clinging to her body, little rivulets of muddy water trickling down them and falling with a miserable plop, plop, on to the ground where she was standing, and she was shivering in every limb. "I'm sorry—so sorry," she faltered forlornly.

"You needn't be." He did not appear very sympathetic, this unknown deliverer, but he was at least prompt and practical. "Sit down," he continued, "and let me take your skates off."

This he proceeded to do in the most business-like fashion. Then, out of his overcoat pocket he produced a brandy flask, and, drawing off the lower half of its silver casing, which served as a cup, he filled it to the brim with the spirit and held it out to her.

"Now, drink that. It'll make you feel better. and save you from catching cold—if anything will."

She shook her head wearily. She felt too tired, too numb to make even the effort to drink. A curious languor was stealing over her. Everything round her seemed to be growing hazy and indefinite. The figure of the man beside her appeared no more than a vague murky shadow. She was only conscious of being cold —terribly cold, and even that sensation was gradually becoming blurred and indistinct.

"Drink it up. At once. Do you hear?"

Across the fog that was slowly closing round her the voice smote sharply, with an authority that pierced its way even through the clouds that were rolling up about her. She felt the silver rim of the cup against her lips . . . an arm behind her shoulders. . . .

"Drink this," repeated the same imperative voice as before.

And because, to her wavering consciousness, it seemed the easiest thing to give in and comply, she opened her mouth and drank.

The raw spirit ran down her throat like fire. She choked and gasped as she swallowed it. But it brought

her back from the nebulous grey world into which she
had been sinking and sent the blood pulsing through
her veins once more.

"That's better." The man kneeling beside her on the
frost-bitten turf surveyed her with a faint smile. His
face was very near her own as he knelt there, and
Herrick, beginning to revive, was struck by the extreme blueness of his eyes. Dangerous, dare-devil eyes
they were, shaded by rather long black lashes which
masked their deviltry with a certain disarming look of
appeal.

He partially refilled the cup with brandy and held it
out to her again.

"Just a little drop," he urged persuasively, as she
shook her head.

"I shall be drunk if I take any more," she objected.

"I think not," he said, smiling more broadly. "Anyway, we'll risk it."

Again she found herself obeying him. It passed
fugitively through her mind that he was the kind of
man whom it was easier to obey than to resist. There
was a certain dominant quality about him that it was
difficult to withstand. Not that he conveyed in the least
the impression of the cave-man type, addicted to
bludgeoning his way through life. But there was a
certain gay imperiousness about him—a sort of un-
arguable assurance that he was going to get his own
way.

When she had drunk the brandy he proceeded to
screw up the flask and replace it in his pocket. Then
he helped her to her feet.

"Can you stand all right now?" he asked. "Good."

He stripped off his overcoat. "Wrap this round you——"

"Oh, no, no!" she protested. "I'm all right. Please keep it."

He took not the slightest notice of her protest, but proceeded to help her into the coat exactly as though she had never spoken.

"Now," he said, looking down at her with an amused glint in his eyes, "do you mind telling me where you live? The sooner you get home and out of those wet clothes the better."

"Up there," she answered, with a wave of her hand across the park. "At Windycroft."

"Then to Windycroft we go," he rejoined briefly.

He did not vouchsafe any information as to whether he knew the place or not—had ever been under its hospitable roof. But it was obvious that he was acquainted with the way there, for he set off in the right direction without further question.

He walked briskly, and Herrick, her legs aching abominably, found it hard work to keep pace with him. A stumble and the faint cry of dismay which it drew from her lips checked him abruptly.

"Am I going too fast for you?" he said. His blue eyes twinkled as he went on. "True. I'd forgotten you took quite a lot of exercise trying to get out of that confounded hole you made in the ice. Still, the faster you walk, the better for you."

He slipped his arm under hers and they started again, and this time, helped by his support and by the impetus of the long, striding walk of the man beside her, she made better progress. Nevertheless, she was thankful to see the lights of Windycroft at last winking through the trees.

Billy and his mother just returned from Tanborough, were having tea together in the hall when they entered.

"What—why, Herrick——" Lady Bridget jumped up and stood staring in amazement at the somewhat quaint figure the girl presented in the masculine overcoat she was wearing. "And you, Gair"—her glance taking in Herrick's companion, who, it was apparent, was an old acquaintance. "Whatever has happened?" she demanded quickly, as she realised that something untoward had taken place. "Has there been an accident?"

The man addressed as Gair hastily explained the circumstances.

"Oh, you poor child!" exclaimed Mim, taking immediate possession of Herrick. "Come along upstairs. A hot bath and bed for you at once. Billy, look after Gair till I come down again."

With the utmost promptitude she swept Herrick off, leaving the two men together.

"What'll you have, Severn? Tea, or something stronger?" asked Billy, when his mother and Herrick had disappeared upstairs. "I should say that a hot whisky was indicated," he added, with a grin.

Gair Severn nodded.

"Thanks," he said. "I think it is."

The lighted hall revealed him to be a tall, slenderly built man, some thirty-two years of age, hardly conveying the impression of the actual physical strength he had evinced in accomplishing Herrick's rescue. But for all his light build there was a certain wiriness about him, a supple force that reminded one of tempered steel. His face was somewhat thin, clean-cut as a cameo, and under the gleam of the electric lights his thick, waveless black hair shone sleek and smooth like satin.

"I suppose you only came down from town this afternoon?" said Billy presently, when the visitor had been supplied with a hot drink and a cigarette, and was seated on the opposite side of the wide hearth, his damp clothes steaming a little in the warmth. "The padre and Barbara said nothing about expecting you when I was over at the Rectory yesterday."

A fleeting glimmer of amusement crossed Severn's face.

"They wouldn't," he replied drily. "I dropped down on them quite in the light of a pleasant surprise."

Billy nodded non-committally. He did not particularly care for Severn, and the latter's advent at the Rectory was always signally unwelcome, as far as he personally was concerned, since it meant that Barbara's time would be rather more taken up than usual.

Half-brother of Alec Fane, whose mother had married a second time, and twelve years his junior, Gair Severn was as unlike the rector as he could possibly be. The only resemblance between them lay in the possession of a certain unmistakable quality of charm, and perhaps it was their very dissimilarity which bound the two half-brothers together in an odd kind of friendship. From Gair's earliest childhood Alec had always bestowed a species of protective, elder-brotherly affection upon him, and since the death of the younger man's parents he had been in the habit of coming down to stay at the Rectory whenever he felt so inclined.

From a material point of view fate had differentiated markedly between the two half-brothers. Alec had nothing in the world to depend upon except what the St. Heriot living brought him, whereas Gair had inherited from his father far more money than was good for him—and hence enjoyed all the popularity and spoiling which, in these post-war days, inevitably fall to the lot of any wealthy and not too unattractive bachelor in London. It must be admitted, however, that he would have been whole heartedly generous over money matters to his less fortunate stepbrother if the latter would have permitted it. But Alec declined to accept from him any form of personal pecuniary help. "No, Gair, old son," he would say, with a whimsical smile. "Leave me my liberty to tell you off when you need it—which is more often than not! If you want to salve your conscience for being so disgustingly well endowed with this world's goods, there's my Village Pension Fund, my plan for a public library and entertainment hall, my bursary scheme to pay for special training for any girl or boy showing special talent— Oh! I can relieve you of your money in a dozen different ways." And the argument would end in a substantial benefit to one or other of the rector's deep-laid schemes for improving the lot of his poorer parishioners, since, whatever Gair Severn's faults, lack of generosity could not be numbered amongst them.

"And now," he observed, setting down his glass and regarding Billy's non-committal face with a slightly quizzical expression, "enlighten my ignorance. Who is the attractive young person I've just saved from a watery grave?"

"Her name is Waylen—Herrick Waylen. She's the daughter of an old friend of Mim's."

"Staying long with you?"

"She's living with us. Mim has—sort of—adopted her," answered Billy briefly.

In some odd boyish way he resented Severn's airily detached inquiries, although he was fain to acknowledge that they were a natural corollary to the afternoon's occurrences. There was something about the older man which invariably had the power to annoy him. Possibly it was due to a certain youthful feeling that there was something a shade patronising in Severn's debonair assurance. Or it might be the result of a chronic inner exasperation with the man who had, on numberless occasions during his visit to the Rectory, assumed a prior right to Barbara's companionship if it happened to please him at the moment so to do, dismissing Billy himself from the scene of action with a few careless, arrogant words that, fume inwardly though he might, the boy had not sufficient skill to parry.

Always, if the two were left alone together, there was a slight sense of friction in the atmosphere, and Billy rose with an inward sigh of relief when Lady Bridget re-entered the hall and joined them once more.

"Severn wants to have Herrick explained to him, Mim," he vouchsafed bluntly. "I'm sure you'll do it much better than I shall." And with a lukewarm "So long, Severn," he took himself off.

"How is she?" inquired Gair, when Mim had filled in the spaces which Billy's terse description of the circumstances of Herrick's advent had left blank. "She was in that ice-cold water quite long enough, I should say."

"I think—I hope she'll be all right," answered Lady Bridget. "Anyway. I've sent for the doctor just to be on the safe side. What a mercy you happened to be there, Gair! Otherwise she'd probably have died before anyone went near her."

"Yes. A hole in the ice is confoundedly difficult to get out of."

"How did you come to be on the spot at the psychological moment? I'd no idea you were down at the Rectory."

"I'd only arrived there from town half an hour before, and strolled down to take a look at the lake just in time to help Miss Waylen out of it. It was beginning to thaw, and when I saw her making straight for the upper end—where the ice always gives first— I shouted to her to stop. I suppose she didn't hear me. So I bolted after her, but of course I was merely on foot, and on skates she out-distanced me easily, and I only got up to her in the nick of time."

"Well, thank God you did!" said Mim fervently, her eyes suspiciously bright. "If anything had happened to Herrick, I think it would have broken my heart. She's the dearest and most lovable girl in the world."

A queer gleam showed itself in Severn's eyes.

"I'm inclined to agree with you," he said deliberately.

There was so much significance in his tone that Lady Bridget glanced at him with a sudden astonished questioning in her face.

"Gair!" she exclaimed in a startled voice. "Do you mean—what do you mean?"

"I mean—just what you are thinking I mean," he replied composedly.

"But it's ridiculous! You can't have fallen in love at first sight—especially with anyone who was dripping wet and looking their very worst!" she objected, half laughing.

Severn regarded her with perfect gravity.

"It doesn't seem likely, does it?" he agreed, unmoved. "All the same, I think it's happened."

Mim's reply was intercepted by the arrival of the doctor, and, bidding her good-bye, Gair forthwith took his departure. Half an hour's quick walking brought him to the Rectory, where he discovered Barbara kneeling by the fire toasting scones in preparation for a late tea.

"Dad and I had just decided not to wait for you any longer," she said, shaking a reproving brown head at him.

She and her father's half-brother had always been very good friends. No formalities of "uncle" and "niece" had ever been allowed to intervene between them, and they were practically on the terms of indulgent elder brother and young sister.

Severn explained the cause of his tardy appearance, his account of Herrick's adventure on the ice creating genuine horror in his listener's warm young heart.

"Evidently," he commented, as Barbara's little

ejaculations of dismay and sympathy punctuated his recital, "evidently Miss Waylen has established herself very firmly in the hearts of St. Heriot."

"I should think she has," she replied with characteristic fervour. "No one could help being fond of Herrick."

"Far be it from me to contradict you, fair niece. My only complaint is that neither you nor Alec informed me you had such a charmer living in the neighbourhood."

"Or I suppose you would have been down to pay us a visit long before now?" she suggested impertinently.

"Naturally."

There was an undercurrent of gravity beneath his bantering tones, and Barbara glanced at him with suddenly apprehensive eyes. Much as she liked him, she retained no illusions about him.

"She's far too good for you, Gair," she said with promptitude. "Besides, Mac Kenyon's in love with her." And then could have bitten her tongue out, knowing full well that she had said the very thing calculated to fire Severn to greater keenness. The merest hint of opposition was invariably sufficient to crystallise his determination into something as inflexible as granite.

His mouth twisted ironically as he surveyed the flush of annoyance which had risen to her cheeks.

"That so?" he drawled. "Then it's damned unlucky for Kenyon."

CHAPTER XVI

IN THE BLUE PARLOUR

"IT'S been such a happy day, Jem," said Carol.

The little speech broke very simply across the silence which had fallen between them. They were sitting together by the fire, tea and hot muffins long since a thing of the past, and now Jem was contentedly smoking, while Carol, hands clasped round her slender knees, had been gazing thoughtfully into the flames as they leapt and curled about the logs, now and then flinging upward a spray of tiny golden sparks which would lie twinkling for a moment at the back of the fireplace before they quivered out into nothingness.

The walk home, from the lake back to Mortlake Hall by the way of the fields and woods which lay between, had been accomplished without misadventure, and when finally Carol and Jem let themselves into the house by a side door, secure from any observation from the gardens, they laughed softly together like a couple of children playing at being conspirators. And then a third conspirator had come along and joined his forces to theirs—old Collins, the butler, who worshipped the ground Carol walked on and would have quitted Sir Francis's service gladly at any moment but for his devotion to his young mistress.

There was a slow kindly gleam in the old man's

eyes as they rested on her bright face, aglow from her recent exercise in the open air—and from something more fundamental, some inner spring of happiness which had sent the blood dancing through her veins and lit a soft radiance in her eyes. But Collins's manner was perfect—impassively detached and blank, as though no pulsing human emotions could ever shake him out of his composure.

"Where will you have tea served, my lady?" he had asked respectfully.

Carol paused. She had had no intentions at all concerning tea. She had meant to say good-bye to Jem and let him go home through the woods again, and then—oh, perhaps a cup of tea sent up on a tray to her room while she rested and let her thoughts dwell on the brief happiness which the day had brought her.

And now here was Collins quietly assuming that she and the man with her would be having tea together, a normal course of things that in the case of any other afternoon visitor, masculine or feminine, except Jem, she would have followed. It was a temptation of the devil—although anything less like the devil than the respectable, grey-haired old butler could hardly be imagined.

She hesitated, and was lost. There was no really truly reason why she and Jem shouldn't prolong the pleasure of each other's company a little while. They both knew the utter honesty of their intent . . . Sir Francis was away . . . this little time of being together would probably have to last them for weeks, possibly months.

Carol had spoken with sudden reckless impetuosity.

"Oh, serve tea in the Blue Parlour, Collins," she said.

And so, in the quaint six-sided room, with its tapestried walls, dim and blue and faded with time, they had had tea, and had talked or been silent together as only people who really love and understand each other can do. And the summing up of it all lay in Carol's: "It's been such a happy day, Jem."

As she spoke, she lifted her eyes—child's eyes now, soft and shining—to his face. With an abrupt movement he tossed his cigarette into the fire.

"I wish to God you could have all happy days," he said, his voice not quite level.

She laughed a little.

"Now you're asking for too much. I don't think anybody has that. Do you?"

"No, I suppose they haven't. But worries and troubles which can be shared are very different from the ones you've got to carry alone. If there were any prospect—in the future——" He broke off, then resumed: "If he would only try to make you happy, I could stand it better. It's knowing that *your* life is so difficult which makes things seem sometimes unendurable. For me—after all, I've got my freedom. I can work, and play if I want to, and see you sometimes. That makes my lot possible—no worse than the lot of many another man. . . . But your life is different. You're like a prisoner, a slave, almost. It's—oh, it's damnable!"

Carol was silent. She could not contradict him. Her life *was* almost unbearable—a slavery of mind and body to a man from whom she shrank in every sensi-

tive fibre of her being. No one but herself could ever
guess all that that slavery entailed. What she had
once confided to Herrick, that she had several times
refused to marry Sir Francis, was true, and it seemed
as though now, when at last circumstances had combined to drive her into his arms, he was secretly
determined to make her pay for the bitterness and
humiliation of those refusals.

It almost appeared as though Jem had read the
thoughts which were passing through her mind, for,
when next he spoke, it was even more vehemently than
before.

"If you were to tell the truth, I expect your life is
sheer hell. Only you won't say—you cover it up, screen
him. So that one can only guess from how he behaves
to you in public what he puts you through in private.
If you would only say, Carol——"

"I can't," she replied with quiet decision. "I can't
say anything."

"Because you're too proud!"

"Perhaps I am—too proud. Sometimes one's pride
is the only thing left to hang on to." She turned to
him with a faint smile—a smile that was far sadder
than any tears. "So don't try to take away my poor
little rag of pride, Jem."

"Forgive me," he said in a stifled voice, and there
was so much of pain in it that impulsively she held out
her hand to him. He took it and held it closely in his
for a few moments.

"Carol," he said at last, in a low, shaken tone.
"Will you let me ask you one question—tell me one
thing?"

"What is it?" she returned gently.

"It's a thing that may hurt that pride of yours to answer. That's why I've never asked it before. But it's tortured me many a time—not knowing. And to-day I feel as if I can't go on any longer without knowing the truth about it."

For a little while she made no answer. There was a look of apprehension in her eyes—an instinctive shrinking, as though she feared what the question he would ask might be. At length she seemed to summon up her courage to reply.

"Ask your question, Jem," she said.

"And you will answer it—truthfully?"

She bent her head.

"I will answer it truthfully."

"Then tell me, does that devil—does Mortimer, has he ever used physical violence towards you?"

She caught her breath sharply—he could hear the sharp little sibilant sound of it. A quick, shamed flush ran up under her skin. Nevertheless, there seemed to be a certain relief in her eyes at the form his question had taken.

"No," she said quietly. "No. Never."

The tension in Jem's face relaxed.

"Thank God for that!" he muttered hoarsely.

She regarded him curiously. How funny men were! Jem, she could see, was relieved, infinitely relieved, to know that her husband had never actually struck her. And yet, in her own mind, she was not at all sure that she couldn't better have borne, more easily forgiven, the honest violence of a blow than the form of super-refined mental and moral torture of which Sir Francis was such a past master.

"So you see, there are ameliorations to every lot," she went on lightly, a touch of unwonted irony in her voice. "At least, Francis hasn't taken to wife-beating yet. But, of course"—banteringly—"he may yet adopt the idea if he finds he can't keep me sufficiently in subjection by other means."

"If he ever does——" began Jem stormily.

But that sentence was destined never to be finished, for precisely as he spoke, the door of the Blue Parlour opened and the thin, angular figure of Sir Francis himself appeared on the threshold.

For an instant there was a silence, a stillness in the room so utter, so abrupt, that it was as if some unseen agency had suddenly bereft its three occupants of life, transfixing them where they sat or stood into voiceless, motionless lay-figures. Then came the whispering sound of an indrawn breath from Carol, as though she were about to speak—softer than any whisper, yet it seemed almost to shrill across that dreadful silence.

"I thought you were in London," she stammered, mistakenly as usual. Those cold eyes of Sir Francis's malevolently directed at her from beneath the wrinkled lids, like a vulture's, which overhung them, invariably seemed to paralyse her mental faculties, to draw from her the very thing he desired her to say, and not in the least what she herself wanted or intended to.

"That is perfectly apparent," he answered, advancing into the room with that queer, cat-like tread of his which reminded one of an animal ready to spring—to

spring when it has tortured and played with its victim
long enough. "But, fortunately"—with sarcastic emphasis—"my business in town was completed sooner
than I anticipated, so that I was able to catch an afternoon train back. It is, I perceive, an equally pleasant
surprise to you."

By this time Beresford had risen and was holding
out his hand.

"How d'you do, Sir Francis?" he said, contriving
successfully to override the tension of the moment
and greet his unwilling host with customary civility.
"We haven't met for some time."

"We have not," replied Mortimer, neglecting to see
the outstretched hand. He fixed his eye on Jem with a
malignant stare. "Are you here at my invitation—or at
my wife's, by the way? One is apt to overlook these
little details."

"I'm afraid I can only claim to be a chance visitor,"
returned Jem, hoping to make matters easier for Carol.
But by this time she had recovered her poise, and with
it the courage with which she occasionally dared to
defy her husband, and she refused to accept the shelter
offered.

"Mr. Beresford is here at my invitation," she said,
with a certain dignity.

Sir Francis's eyes snapped.

"Then, in that case, my dear, I must request you
for the future to abstain from issuing invitations to
every Tom, Dick, and Harry in the neighbourhood."

Carol flushed scarlet.

"For the present, however, please remember that
Mr. Beresford is our guest," she retorted swiftly.

Her husband smiled unpleasantly.

"*Your* guest, my dear Carol. Not mine. There is —quite a difference," he said silkily.

"I'm sorry my presence is so unwelcome——" began Beresford stiffly.

"It is. Most unwelcome," Sir Francis assured him. "I should be glad if you will remember that in future."

Jem's eyes blazed. His right hand had clenched itself unconsciously, and Carol realised that his self-control was rapidly deserting him. One or two more thrusts from Sir Francis's poisoned rapier of a tongue and he would see red, forget the other man's age, and knock him down. Her mind envisioned in a flash the consequences of any scene of violence, here, now, betwixt her husband and this man who loved her—the morass of trouble and scandal which it would create. Jem, his temper cooled, would never be able to forgive himself the bitter harvest of one such maddened moment. She turned towards him swiftly.

"Go, Jem," she said urgently. "Go at once."

But he stood his ground stubbornly. Slow to anger, once roused, Jem's wrath seethed moltenly within him.

"I can't," he answered thickly. "I can't leave you like this."

"Pardon my making the suggestion," intervened Sir Francis in his smoothest accents—he might have been merely commenting on the weather, "but I can think of no one with whom my wife could be more suitably 'left' than with her husband."

Neither Beresford nor Carol took the slightest notice of the barbed speech. They had eyes only for each other.

"Please go, Jem," she repeated steadily.

"You want me to?"

"Yes. I wish it."

Slowly his hand unclenched and he gave a twist of his shoulders as though relaxing their tautened muscles.

"Very well," he said.

He attempted no farewell. One long, unswerving look passed between him and Carol, then he turned and left her alone with her husband.

CHAPTER XVII

CONSEQUENCES

A SHORT, sharp attack of illness followed Herrick's immersion in the lake. Prompt measures and good nursing saved her from actual pneumonia which the doctor had feared might be the consequence, but, nevertheless, it was a somewhat frail and shaken Herrick who was finally allowed to sit up in her room for the first time soon after Christmas Day. Billy's merry face assumed a preternaturally grave and troubled aspect when, shepherded by Lady Bridget, he marched upstairs to pay a brief visit to the invalid.

"Great Scott!" he blurted out in honest dismay. "Ten days in bed *has* played you up, old thing, and no mistake."

Herrick smiled in spite of herself.

"Do I look such a sight, then?" she asked. "How tactless of you to remark upon it, Billy!"

"Don't be silly," he replied bluffly. "Of course you don't look a sight. But you've—you've shrunk, somehow, I think."

Certainly her face appeared very small against its background of velvet cushion. Its angles had sharpened a little, and the slight hollowness of her cheeks made her charming hazel eyes, with the tiny black specks flecking their golden-brown, look bigger than usual.

"She is a bit thinner," agreed Lady Bridget. "But we'll soon put that right now she's out of bed."

"It was rotten of you to fall through the ice on the very last day of the skating," chided Billy severely. "You've gone and missed several jolly good days with hounds, crocking up like this."

"Yes, it was very silly of me," assented Herrick meekly. A private recollection of a certain warning uttered—and disregarded—was responsible for this unwonted humbleness of spirit. "Tell me all about the hunting, Billy," she added, beguiling him diplomatically away from the subject of her accident.

He needed no second invitation, and soon her eyes were sparkling over his graphic account of the "top-hole runs" which appeared to have been a conspicuous feature of the hunting days she had missed.

"Just my luck to be out of it all!" she groaned. Then, flushing sensitively: "Oh, what a selfish pig I am, Mim, only thinking of myself when you've missed it all, too, while you've been nursing me."

Lady Bridget smiled across at her reassuringly.

"Well, my dear, as you know, I don't go out with hounds very often," she answered tranquilly. "At a liberal estimate I've only missed a couple of days. And I'll survive that, I think, without a heart-break. I'm too thankful to see you well on the road to recovery to grumble at anything else," she added, smiling.

"I've ridden Flame a time or two," vouchsafed Billy presently, "just to keep her from getting above herself, but she's a bit of a devil to deal with."

"She's always all right with me," affirmed Herrick.

"She and I understand one another—so I suppose I must be a bit of a devil, too."

"More than likely," he assented with a grin. "Incidentally," he went on, "I've bought a new gee—nothing to look at, but the pluckiest little rat of a horse I've ever ridden—baulks at nothing. I believe if I set him at a house he'd try to get over it!"

"You extravagant boy! You don't need another," protested Herrick. "At least, not this season."

"Yes, I do. I've sold Romulus—Kenyon's bought him. One of his own animals dropped dead in the stable the other day, and that left him rather in the lurch. So, as I'd seen the Rat, I agreed to let him have Romulus."

A faint flush stole up under Herrick's skin, and she quietly ignored the mention of Kenyon's name.

"You're becoming quite a horse-dealer, Billy," was all she said, banteringly. And soon afterwards Lady Bridget shoo'd him off downstairs again lest the invalid should get over-tired.

There were plenty of callers to see Herrick during the next few days, and one of the first among them was Gair Severn. He arrived with a sheaf of flowers —filched from the Rectory hothouses—and a calm assurance of his welcome that rather amused her.

"You've been a long time recovering from your dip in the lake," he told her discontentedly, after they had chatted on more or less impersonal topics for some time. "I shall be outstaying my welcome at the Rectory if you don't hurry up and get well."

"I don't quite see the relation of the one thing to the other," she submitted mildly.

"Don't you?" His blue eyes raked her face, challenging in their gay deviltry, appealing in the disarming softness bestowed by their absurdly long lashes. "I should have thought it was evident to the meanest intelligence. Having been selected by fate to save you from premature extinction, I'm naturally waiting anxiously for the next move in the game."

"Are you? I don't suppose there'll be any 'next move.' Why should there be?"

"Don't be absurd," he said reprovingly. "Haven't you ever read any novels? You don't suppose fate introduces people to each other in that noticeable kind of fashion just for nothing? It's merely a first step of course."

"In what direction?" asked Herrick demurely. It rather entertained her to cross swords with this extremely self-confident young man.

He surveyed her in silence for a moment. Then:

"Do you really want to know?" he said coolly. "I could tell you, if you wish."

She shook her head.

"No, no, I won't trouble you," she returned hastily. "It might be"—with deliberate intention—"an unpleasant direction—one in which I shouldn't want to go."

"I'm afraid that wouldn't make the remotest difference," he replied. There was a calm conviction about the assertion that startled her a little. She was all at once aware of a certain tenacity of purpose that might lie behind this man's gay imperiousness of manner—of the possibility of a hidden, dogged strength in his make-up, backed by a headlong recklessness which would sweep from his path anything and everything that adversely crossed it. Against her will she was conscious of a faint, uneasy sense of apprehension, and it came as a welcome interruption when, just at this juncture, the door opened to admit two more visitors, Alec Fane and Barbara. As they entered, Severn bent towards her and said swiftly:

"Don't you believe me? You will—some day."

And not even the cheery presence of the rector and his daughter served to quite dispel the slight feeling of misgiving with which, somehow, Gair had managed to inspire her.

Nevertheless, she was fain to acknowledge that he made a most entertaining companion. With characteristic sang-froid he at once established himself as a daily visitor, and, in spite of his unconcealed arrogance, which invariably roused her to half amused, half irritated opposition, she found herself liking him and looking forward to his visits. He was so alive, so irrepressible, that his entrance into the sick-room produced much the same vitalising effect as a sea breeze, pungent with the tang of brine. And there was no gainsaying the charm even of that gay masterfulness of his, the more especially as he knew instinctively how to combine it with a certain protective solicitude in little things which appeals irresistibly to every woman.

Perhaps Herrick looked forward to his visits all the more because someone else evinced no disposition to visit her at all. Mac Kenyon, so Lady Bridget reported, had sent over on several occasions to inquire as to the invalid's progress, but he himself had remained conspicuous by his absence, and Herrick was inwardly bitterly hurt. Even though they *had* quarrelled that day on the ice, Mac need not have remained so obdurately unforgiving and unfriendly. The only explanation she could find lay in the subsequent happenings at Mortlake Hall. Carol had been over to see her and had told her of Sir Francis's unexpected return home and of its consequences.

"Of course," she had said drearily, "the whole thing was just a trap. He never intended to stay the night in London. And now Jem can't come to the house at all. If he did"—with a wan smile—"he wouldn't be admitted. I know Francis has given orders to that effect. That's one of his methods of punishing me—to humiliate me in the eyes of the servants."

And Herrick, seeking for an explanation of Mac's continued absence, inwardly decided that he had chosen to hold her responsible for all that had occurred and was manifesting his displeasure accordingly. The thought brought back all the bitter resentment she had felt on the actual day of their quarrel, and, since it nearly always happens that when a woman is angry and sore at heart with one man she is prone to be kinder than her wont—far kinder than she intends—to another, she had gone a long way on the road towards friendship with Gair Severn before she and Kenyon met again.

And then, one afternoon, without any warning, he was ushered into her little upstairs sitting-room, where Lady Bridget and Billy, together with Severn and the rector, had foregathered for tea. Inwardly Herrick thanked whatever gods there be that she was not—as she quite easily might have been—alone. The presence of other people, ignorant that any quarrel had taken place, helped to tide over the awkwardness of this first meeting, and under cover of the general conversation the sudden quietness which fell upon her passed unnoticed by all except one person. Severn, alert with the memory of Barbara's impulsive, "Besides, Mac's in love with her," did not fail to observe the slight self-consciousness which Kenyon's arrival produced, and he was also quick to note a certain betraying want of spontaneity in the manner of each of them towards the other. The key to the situation was missing, as far as he was concerned, but he was intuitive enough to recognise an underlying discord.

His own manner was as light-hearted and insouciant as ever, and, when the subject of Herrick's accident came under discussion, he described the whole occurrence for Kenyon's benefit with an air of proprietorship which the latter found exasperating to the last degree.

"It was lucky I was there," he wound up. "Those whom the gods love"—piously—"don't necessarily die young. Instead, they are permitted to rescue beautiful ladies from wet lakes. So I know the gods love me."

"Well, I suppose no man would have stood quietly by and watched a woman sink through the ice, whether the gods loved him or not," commented Kenyon, a slight note of acerbity in his voice.

"Naturally not," replied Gair delightedly. "But the general arrangements were so good! There was I"—waving his hand expressively—"on the spot at exactly the right moment, just like a hero in the

movies, brandy flask and all complete—thanks to my
valet, who'd shoved it in my pocket last thing because
it was such a beastly cold day."

"It might have happened to anyone else," returned
Mac disparagingly. "I was on the lake half an hour
earlier. So was Beresford, for that matter." For a
moment, involuntarily, his and Herrick's eyes met, to
fall apart again quickly and self-consciously.

"Of course it might," agreed Gair, unperturbed. He
was enjoying himself immensely. "I'm merely commenting on the fact that it happened to be *my* luck to
be there at the right moment."

"Oh, damn your luck!" burst out Kenyon irritably.

Lady Bridget went off into a gale of laughter.

"Really, you're both too absurd!" she exclaimed.
"Herrick, you'll positively have to provide oppor-
tunities for Billy and Jem and Mac to do the rescuing
stunt turn and turn about. Then they'll feel that all
men are equal."

And so, in the melting-pot of the general laugh
that followed, the covert hostility which had lurked
behind the jesting argument was momentarily submerged.

Soon afterwards Alec Fane rose to go.

"Well, I must be off," he said. "It's good to see
you looking more like yourself again, Herrick," he
went on, regarding her with a very kindly glance as
he shook hands. "At this rate, you'll be out in the
hunting-field in a few days." He turned to his half-
brother. "Come along, Gair. Too many visitors at a
time aren't good for our invalid. We shall be tiring
her out." And Severn, left with no choice in the

matter, had perforce to follow Alec's lead and make his farewells.

"We'll come down with you and see you safely off the premises," volunteered Mim. Very few visitors ever quitted the hospitable portals of Windycroft without their final glimpse being of Lady Bridget, standing at the top of the entrance steps, waving a cheery hand to speed them on their way. If any one of them did, you might have been quite sure that it was an unpleasant someone for whom even her capacious heart could find no place. Accordingly, she and Billy accompanied the two half-brothers downstairs, laughing and talking as they went.

Presently the sound of their voices died away, and a curious silence descended on the little room where Mac and Herrick, with all that lay between them of heart-burning and misunderstanding, had been suddenly left alone together.

A curious, waiting silence, palpitant with conflicting impulses and promptings. . . .

CHAPTER XVIII

AVOWAL

IT WAS Herrick who spoke first, contriving with a considerable effort to pitch her voice on a note of entire detachment.

"You were really a most unexpected visitor this afternoon," she observed, feeling that at all hazards the silence must be broken somehow.

Kenyon, who had remained standing after the others had left the room, staring absently into the fire, moved his position slightly. But he did not look at her. He was resting his elbow on the chimneypiece, his face shaded with his hand.

"Was I?" he said quietly. Then, with disconcerting abruptness: "Will you tell me why?"

This was carrying the war into the enemy's camp with a vengeance, and Herrick sparkled up into hostility.

"Oh, I wonder you condescended to come over and visit me, seeing that I fell into the lake because I disobeyed your orders," she said airily.

Beneath the shading hand a glint of amusement crossed his face.

"I wonder, too," he replied.

But he volunteered no explanation, and she fumed inwardly. He was leaving it all to her in the most detestable fashion, she reflected indignantly. From the couch on which she was lying she could not see his expression. If she had been able to she might have interpreted his silence differently.

"Well," she flung at him at last, defiantly. "Why *did* you come?"

He lifted his head from his hand, and his grey eyes held a rather weary look, like the eyes of a man who, though still fighting, sees only inevitable defeat ahead.

"I came," he said slowly, "to apologise."

"To apologise?" She faltered uncertainly. An apology was certainly the last thing she had been anticipating. He had not conveyed the idea of being in the least penitent.

"Yes. It was beastly of me to speak to you as I did that day on the lake. . . . I'd no right to. And I want you to forgive me. I haven't much place for excuses as a rule—although"—with a brief smile—"it's always much easier to find them for oneself than for other people—but perhaps I had a little more excuse than you knew for my damnable temper that day."

There was something curiously disarming in the quiet avowal of regret, and Herrick found her anger melting rapidly in spite of herself. She was even conscious of an awakening contrition for her own share in the quarrel. The bitter speeches had not been all on one side, by any manner of means. But she was feminine enough not to let her wrath appear to be too easily appeased.

"Couldn't I—know the excuse?" she asked.

He glanced at her in some surprise.

"Surely, by now, it's obvious enough, isn't it?" he

said. "The excuse, if you'll let it count as such, is my
wish to save Carol, if possible, from any added unhappiness."

A vision of Carol's face, ineffably sad at times, with
its frightened, guarded eyes, flitted across Herrick's
mind, spurring her to a sudden passionate anger.

"Why you ever *let* her marry that dreadful old
man, I can't think!" she burst out. And then was
shocked and horrified to observe the effect of her hasty
speech.

Mac's face changed—greyed slowly beneath the
lash of the scornfully uttered words. His whole frame
seemed to stiffen like that of a man under the knife.

"It's the bitterest regret of my life that I couldn't
prevent it," he answered. "For once, just when it
mattered most, I was utterly helpless. . . . I wonder
if you can realise what it means to a man to be helpless
to save a woman he loves from certain misery?"

The pain in his voice was so deep that Herrick
felt her heart contract. She remembered what Carol
had told her—that Mac had been practically penniless
at one time, drudging in an office for a mere weekly
pittance, and powerless to give his mother even the
actual necessaries her frail health demanded. So Carol
had to be sacrificed. . . .

"But even now, it often seems as if you were on
Sir Francis's side," she said doubtfully. "You don't
take Carol's part."

His face set itself implacably.

"I can't help what it seems. Carol made a bargain
and she must keep it. If she didn't, it would be un-

bearable. Our mother"——the words seemed dragged
from him——"our mother lived and died on Mortimer's
money, money bestowed upon a certain definite understanding, and if Carol fails to keep her share of that
bargain——then she lived and died on Mortimer's
charity."

"I see." Herrick spoke slowly, strickenly, under
her breath. She was beginning to envisage the whole
dreadfulness of the situation——its inevitability and
torment. "How——ghastly!"

"Can't you understand"——Mac went on as though
he had not heard that bleak whisper of dismay. "Can't
you understand that it's my very helplessness in the
matter which maddens me? If _I_ could have earned that
money——even by binding myself as Mortimer's slave
for life, I wouldn't have cared. But it was only Carol
who could make the bargain he required. . . . And
now, the bitterest gibe of fate is that I've more than
enough money for every need."

Herrick sat up suddenly on her couch, her eyes
shining.

"Well, then, pay him——pay him back the money he
allowed your mother," she exclaimed impulsively.
"And set Carol free to leave him."

He shook his head.

"Impossible. Mortimer didn't advance money——
to be repaid by money. You know, as well as I do,
that that would be baulking the contract."

"I suppose it would," she admitted, the light dying
out of her face as she recognised the hard truth of
what he said. "Oh, Mac, it's a terrible position!"

"Hellish. Sometimes even I feel tempted to say 'Go —go to Jem.' But it would only mean utter misery for Carol. Like me, she could never bear to think of our mother's having lived on Mortimer's money, unless he'd had his due return. That would torture her always. Nor," he went on gravely, "is she the type of woman to stand up against an irregular position— with all its disabilities. She's far too sensitive, too proud. . . ."

"But she and Jem could be married!" protested Herrick. "It would only mean waiting for a time. And then they could be happy—openly happy—together."

Kenyon regarded her in silence. There was a curious expression on his face. At last he spoke.

"Are you imagining for one moment that Mortimer would divorce her—set her free?"

"Why, of course."

"Then you were never more mistaken. That's the very last thing in the world he would ever do. His one remaining satisfaction in life, if Carol left him, would be the fact that he could punish her, decline to set her free, force her to live as no woman of her temperament could bear to live. Why"—his mouth twisted into a very bitter smile—"I believe it would be an actual inducement to him to try to live as long as possible." He fell silent once more. When he spoke again, it was very quietly, with a deep sadness in his voice.

"So now you see why Carol must be saved—even from herself. And why, that day on the lake, for the moment I regarded you as almost an enemy."

She flushed a little.

"I could never be your enemy, Mac," she said gently. "You know that."

It was as though she had touched some secret spring —jerked ajar the door of some hidden chamber in his heart. His expression altered.

"There's only one thing I want you to be to me," he said, almost roughly. "And you know what that is."

The clear hazel eyes met his unwaveringly.

"And that's the one thing I can never be," she said.

"You won't always say so."

"Always," she insisted steadily

He moved across from his place by the chimney-piece and sat down on the end of her couch He had not at all the look of a man who has just been refused for the second time by the woman he loves. Herrick felt instinctively that he was not accepting what she said, that she was opposing her will, her young determination, against a deep, quiet strength that was bigger and greater than anything she could bring to fight it. She would never convince Mac, never get him to yield to her decision. Always he would be waiting for her; his love . . . waiting for her. . . .

"Child"—he was speaking now with little passion but an unspeakable tenderness "Child, you don't understand what love is—what I mean when I say I love you. It doesn't only mean that I want you— though God knows I want you more than anything on earth!—but it means that I want to take care of you, shield you, lift the burden from your shoulders. I know there *is* a burden—let me help carry it."

"I can't," she said in a stifled voice, shaken to the depths of her by the knowledge that this love, ineffably tender and selfless, such love as is rarely offered to women, was hers for the taking. And she might not take it.

"Is it that you're afraid?" he went on with infinite gentleness. "Afraid of love? If it's that which holds you back, it need not do. I'll never ask you to give me anything you don't want to give—that you're not willing to give. If you'll come to me you shall be as free as you are now. And then some day—some day, I think you wouldn't be afraid any more."

She was silent, overwhelmed, touched to the core of her being. There was only one thing she could give him in return—the knowledge that her love for him was as complete, as passionate, as selfless as his own, that in loving she held nothing back. So, since courage and sincerity were part of her, she told him.

"It's not that, Mac," she said simply. The faint colour had deepened in her face, but the eyes she lifted to his were candid and unafraid. "I'm not—frightened of love. If it were possible, I would marry you to-morrow, if you wished it. And I wouldn't want to hold anything back—to give you only a part of myself. You see, I love you. . . . Only, dear, you must believe me. I *can't* marry—you, or anyone."

"Are you married?" he asked swiftly.

Her eyes widened.

"No. Oh, no."

"Then, some day you will marry—me," he asserted quietly. He bent over her, took her two hands in his, and kissed their palms. "I can wait—now I know that you love me as I love you. . . . Body and soul, beloved, in this world and the next, I love you."

CHAPTER XIX

ANOTHER KIND OF LOVE

CLOP! Clop! The hoofs of the horses made a soft, rhythmic, squelching sound on the sodden turf as Gair Severn and Herrick rode slowly homeward across the park at Windycroft. They were returning from one of the daily rides together which Gair, with that peculiar faculty of his for getting his own way, had contrived to inaugurate. Lady Bridget having declared that Herrick must on no account think of hunting again until she had essayed some riding of a less exhausting nature, he had promptly suggested himself as escort.

"She can't possibly be allowed to go out alone," he represented strategically to Lady Bridget. "She might turn faint or something. And, as old Alec is keeping Billy with his nose pretty firmly to the grindstone whenever it isn't a hunting day, you'd better let me and my brandy flask do duty."

"Larkin could go with her," Mim had answered with a perfectly grave face. "He's a very reliable man."

"And am I not a very reliable man?" demanded Gair. "After my recent efforts on the lake I should have thought my references would read: 'Sober and energetic, and trustworthy in all emergencies.' Herrick"—he appealed to her dramatically—"I ask you. Do you prefer me—or Larkin? Choose!"

"I'd much prefer to roam about by myself, thank you," replied Herrick with great promptitude.

But Lady Bridget shook her head.

"I don't think you must do that," she objected, smiling. "You're not very strong yet, you know."

"In that case, then, I'll choose the lesser evil," answered Herrick, with a small grimace. "Gair—and his brandy flask."

So it had been arranged, and for several days now she and Severn had ridden together regularly. Once they had encountered Kenyon, motoring over from Greenwood to Mortlake Hall, and his face had set itself like a mask when he perceived who was Herrick's companion. Probably, if he had given her the opportunity, she would have attempted some explanation, let him understand in the course of conversation how naturally it had come about that she and Gair were riding together. But Mac had merely lifted his hat and driven past them without slackening speed.

"I shall be in quite good form for hunting, I think, by the day of the meet at Windycroft," she observed, as Severn held open a gate for her to pass out of the park into the drive. "I'm not in the least tired this afternoon."

"Is there to be a meet there, then?"

She nodded.

"Yes, next Thursday. And Mim thinks that would be an appropriate moment for my first appearance on the scenes again."

"Which, being interpreted, I suppose means that she knows she'd have difficulty in keeping you at home if hounds were meeting at Windycroft?" said Gair, smiling.

She laughed outright.

"That's about it," she acknowledged.

By this time they had reached the house, and found Larkin waiting outside in readiness to take Herrick's horse. She turned tentatively to Gair.

"Will you come in?" she asked indifferently.

His eyes danced.

"Please—as you're so pressing." And he followed her into the firelit hall.

Lady Bridget had not yet returned from a round of calls she was paying that afternoon, so Herrick, who would much have preferred to get straight out of her riding kit into something negligently soft and silky and have a cup of tea sent up to her sitting-room, resigned herself to a *tête-à-tête* tea with Severn. She hoped he wouldn't stay long. Outdoors, when a touch on Flame's bridle could set yards betwixt them in an instant, and bring any conversation that displeased her to a summary conclusion, she did not mind his company. But of late a little fear of him, the same uneasy apprehension of his stubborn force of will which had fretted her earlier in their acquaintance, had grown and deepened in her mind. More than once, when they had been alone, she had felt this force assert itself, trying to dominate her, as unmistakably as Flame could feel her hand upon the reins, and the intimacy of a firelight talk *à deux* was the very last thing she desired.

She studiously directed the conversation into the

most commonplace channels, but it seemed as though
Gair must have divined her thoughts, for after oblig-
ingly following her lead for a few minutes, he suddenly
looked across at her with mirthful eyes and demanded:

"Why are you so almighty scared of me?"

She flushed scarlet.

"Scared? I'm not. Why should I be?"

"Couldn't say, I'm sure. But if you're not, why
this carefully stilted conversation—about things that
interest neither of us? Mrs. Somebody's cook having
run off without cooking the dinner, and the new litter
of pups at the Rectory, and Beresford's confounded
poultry—bah!"

Herrick folded her hands in mock resignation.

"I'm sorry my local gossip doesn't interest you," she
said demurely. "What would you like to talk about?"

He flashed her a swift glance that seemed to scorch
her like the sudden flaring of a flame.

"About you—and me," he said deliberately.

"Oh, no." With a mighty effort she contrived to
retain her sang-froid and answer him still in the same
tone of good-humoured mockery. "I don't consider
we should make at all an interesting topic of conversation—either individually or collectively. Think of
something else."

But he broke through her poor little defences with
a ruthless downrightness that admitted of no more
feinting or evasion.

"I don't want to think of anything else. *You*—
occupy the whole of my horizon at the present moment. When will you marry me, Herrick?"

The abrupt unexpectedness of the question took her

aback, and for a moment a rush of sheer panicky terror overcame her. Then, mustering up her courage, she said:

"When will I—*what?* You must be mad, Gair!"

"Never saner," he replied coolly. "Don't pretend to be surprised. You know, you must have known from the beginning that I wanted you—loved you." His voice had deepened. All at once his coolness had deserted him, and looking into his eyes she read there a leaping passion that made her shrink nervously away from him.

"Oh, please—please——" she began protestingly, raising her hand as though to ward him off.

In an instant she felt it grasped and held. He was on his feet and had pulled her up beside him. She struggled vainly to release herself.

"Let me go—let me go!" she exclaimed breathlessly, twisting her hand in his. But she might as well have tried to free it from a vice.

"No, I won't let you go!" he said. "I want you—oh, my God, how I want you!" With a sudden movement he flung his arm round her, crushing her to him, and bent his head to hers. She felt his breath on her face, and made a wild effort to push him from her, thrusting her free hand betwixt his mouth and hers. But he drew her arm down with an effortless strength that she was powerless to combat, and her face, ash-white, with wide, defiant eyes, and lips closed in a scarlet line of resistance, was at his mercy.

"Don't!" she gasped in a low voice of blazing anger. "Don't, Gair!"

But no word of hers could have checked him then.

He stooped his head and she felt his lips close down on hers, straining against them, kissing her with a burning passion that seemed to rob her of all strength. When finally he released her, she swayed a little and caught at a chair-back to steady herself. She looked white and shaken, like some flower beaten down by a tempest. But she had never lacked pluck. Recovering herself by a sheer effort of will, she faced him with a cold fury of contempt.

"I hope you're content—if it satisfies you to kiss a woman who has *loathed* it," she said. There was such concentrated disgust and scorn in her voice that it slashed across the storm of his passion like the cut of a whip-lash. Even Severn's indomitable arrogance winced under it. Fear, anger, pleading would have left him unmoved, but that scornful candour of physical distaste, of unmistakable recoil, pierced his armour.

"Content?" he said sullenly. "No, I shall never be content until you're my wife."

"Then I'm afraid you're destined to remain discontented," she replied. "For I shall never be your wife."

"You'll never be the wife of any other man," he retorted grimly. "I swear it."

All at once he smiled down at her with a gay challenge in his eyes.

"I never say things without meaning them, you know," he went on easily. "And I tell you, you'll never marry any other man. Do try to believe that."

The sudden passion which had mastered him ap-

peared to have spent itself. This was the old familiar
Gair, mockingly imperious and debonair, and Herrick
felt her poise returning.

"I can believe that quite easily," she retorted composedly. "Seeing that I've no intention of ever marrying anyone."

He threw back his head and laughed boyishly.

"Good intentions are made to be broken," he informed her confidently. "I'll help you to break that
one."

"No," she returned. "You won't." Her anger
against him was rapidly evaporating. It was impossible to remain actively incensed against Severn for
very long, and Herrick was not the first woman to
make the discovery.

"Don't be silly, Gair. Forget this—this foolishness
of to-day and let's go on being friends as we were
before."

He shook his head.

"I shall never forget—to-day," he said. "And I
haven't the slightest intention of allowing you to
forget it either."

"Oh!" She made a gesture of impatience. "You are
impossible!"

For an instant his blue eyes looked into hers with
a stark demand in them that there was no misunderstanding.

"No, I'm not," he said simply. "I'm a man in love.
That's all. And remember: I'm not taking 'no' for an
answer. I never shall. Some day—sooner or later—
you'll marry me."

And somehow that quietly spoken declaration impressed her more than all the passionate utterances which had preceded it—was to linger in her memory, imbuing her with an upsetting conviction—fight against it though she might—of the permanence of his determination, filling her with an indefinable fear of his reckless certainty of victory.

It was just at this opportune moment that Lady Bridget returned from her round of visits, and Herrick welcomed her arrival with an inward sigh of relief. She had begun to feel that if her *tête-à-tête* with Severn were prolonged much further, her nerve would give out. The elder woman cast a quick, scrutinising glance from the girl's face to that of the man beside her. The signs of recent tumult were clear enough to her discerning eyes, and when, a few minutes later, Severn proposed taking his departure, she made no effort to detain him. When he had gone, she sipped her tea in silence, regarding Herrick reflectively over the brim of her cup. Then, setting it down on the table beside her, she smiled.

"That's a very dangerous young man, my dear," she observed. "Take an old woman's advice, and don't play with fire."

Herrick gave a rather hard little laugh.

"I'm very safe from fire of that kind. I imagine it would soon cool down—as it did with Rex—if he knew who my father was."

Lady Bridget shook her head.

"There I fancy you're mistaken. If I know Gair —and I think I do know him pretty well—it wouldn't matter to him a row of pins whether the father of the woman he's in love with had been good, bad, or indifferent. . . . And he is in love with you."

A faint smile crossed Herrick's lips as she recalled the stormy scene just passed.

"He seems to think so," she admitted wryly.

"Then—unless you propose to marry him—look out for squalls! Gair's had too much his own way all through life to take a beating easily. Have you actually turned him down?"

"Of course I have—as I should turn down any man. You know quite well, Mim, that I can never marry."

"Why not?"

Herrick winced at the direct question. But if Lady Bridget observed it she took no notice. Having decided in her own mind that a certain wound she knew of required probing, she had no mind to be turned aside from her kindly purpose because the patient flinched.

"Why not?" she repeated, as Herrick made no answer.

The girl turned her head aside.

"You seem to have forgotten," she said at last, in a low voice, "whose daughter I am."

"And do you mean to tell me you've put the thought of marriage right outside your life—because of that?" asked Mim incredulously.

Herrick's glance came back to her face.

"Certainly I have," she said with spirit. "Rex showed me very clearly what men feel about marrying the daughter of a—a thief. . . . Those were the words he used—'a thief and a suicide.' "

"So that's the idea you've got into your head?" Lady Bridget considered a moment. "I don't think you need necessarily take Rex Dereham as entirely representative of his sex." She paused again, then went on deliberately: "Mac Kenyon is a very different type of man."

The rosy colour streamed into Herrick's face.

"Who—how did you——" She stammered off into silence.

"I guessed," said Mim, her eyes suddenly very soft and tender. "Oh, my dear, it wasn't very difficult to see how things were between you—if one has known what it is to be in love, and to be loved, oneself. . . . Tell me, has he asked you to marry him?"

"Yes."

"And you've refused him?"—gently.

"Yes. Not because . . . I didn't care. But because I did." In some way peculiarly her own Mim had broken down the barriers of her reserve, and she continued: "I couldn't marry Mac unless he knew the truth about me. And I can't tell him the truth. If I did," she added bitterly, "he wouldn't even *want* to marry me."

"I'm not so sure about that," replied Lady Bridget quietly. "Love is a very wonderful thing." Perhaps, unconsciously, she was giving voice to the wonderfulness of her own love for Quintin Lindris—a love which had triumphantly stood fast in spite of sin and shame and disaster.

"I don't think you've the right to assume that Mac would let what has happened in the past stand between you," she pursued earnestly. "Why not tell him—tell him the whole truth? And give him the chance—the chance, Herrick"——her voice glowed with eager aspiration——"of being big."

The girl shook her head.

"He might not take it," she said drily. "I've no illusions about men."

Lady Bridget smiled rather sadly.

"Very few of us have—about men in general, whatever we may pretend. But every woman has illusions about one man in particular—the man she loves."

"And pays for them afterwards," retorted Herrick. She had paid once, dearly, and just at the most impressionable time of her life, and the bitterness of it still lingered in her heart. "No, Mim dear, I can't tell Mac. I daren't risk losing—everything. I'd rather keep what I have . . . just his friendship. That's something."

Her lip quivered, and Lady Bridget felt her heart contract with a pang of overwhelming pity for this young life which seemed to have been destined to be marred from the very outset.

"Then don't tell him," she suggested impulsively. "There's no real reason why he need ever know. He's marrying you—not your father. And perhaps later on, when you've learnt to trust and lean on his love for you, you'll find it easy—so easy—to tell him the whole story."

"I couldn't do that. It wouldn't be playing the game," replied Herrick. "Perhaps—oh no, there's no way out, really."

"I'm sure you'll find a way some day, between you,"

answered Mim. Notwithstanding the experience life
had taught her—or was it, perhaps because of that
very experience?—she had an ineradicable belief in
human nature. "I wish I could help you. But I think
only time can do that."

CHAPTER XX

FLASHLIGHTS

THE rector's study was in an unusual state of grace —swept and garnished almost beyond recognition. He had quitted it an hour ago—rushing off, hatless, at the behest of an urgent message to visit a parishioner who was apparently dying—and Barbara had occupied the time since his departure in setting the room to rights. Billy had been helping—or hindering, whichever way you like to look at it—and now the final touch of freshly cut flowers in the vases had been added and the regeneration was complete.

"I think that's a very creditable performance," remarked Billy, casting a prideful glance round the room.

Barbara nodded approval.

"It's rather a transformation scene, isn't it?" she assented. "Really, Billy, my own"—regarding him with a rueful smile—"I think we shall have to give up all idea of ever being married. Padre's no more fit to be left alone than a child."

"Give up fiddlesticks!" he retorted, with more force than elegance. "That's just one of the things I wanted to talk to you about, old dear. I'm tired of this hole-and-corner business, and I propose we strike for the right to be engaged. That's the first step on the road towards matrimony at any rate."

"There's not much of the 'hole-and-corner' business about things, actually, though, is there?" she said, smiling. "Everybody really knows perfectly well about—us, don't they?"

Billy grinned.

"They'd be blind as bats if they didn't," he observed.

"And Lady Bridget and padre both approve, in their hearts," she went on.

"Exactly. And that's why their objecting to our being openly engaged is so absurd—so utterly unreasonable. They know it's a foregone conclusion that we *shall* be engaged ultimately, so why try to blink the fact?"

Her face softened. Intuitively she knew the real reason which lay at the back both of her father's and Lady Bridget's reluctance to consent to an engagement.

"That's just it, Billy. They do know it, and they know, too, that if we were engaged it's precisely what you said—the first step on the road to matrimony."

"What then?"

"Well, you silly old thing, they want to put off our being married as long as possible. You see, we're each of *us* all they've got—each of *them*. It's not 'unreasonableness.' It's just—love."

"I don't call that love. It's pure and simple selfishness," declared Billy, unconvinced.

Barbara gazed into the fire, her soft brown eyes unusually thoughtful.

"I think all love is selfish in a way," she said, at last, slowly. "At least, if it's selfishness to want the person you love with you. You see"—looking up at

him with a smile—"*we're* selfish that way. We want
to be together."

"Of course we do," returned Billy vigorously. "It's
only natural. After all, it's our turn now. The last
generation have had theirs, and they oughtn't to
grudge us ours. We can only live once—and we don't
want to wait till we're old before we begin."

She was silent. Billy had never talked like this
before. She didn't know that he had even thought
like it. He was usually so light-hearted, so ready to
take life as it came, apparently regarding it all as a
jolly, amusing sort of adventure. And now, underneath that surface insouciance, the urge of youth was
at work, rebelling against the assumed prerogative
of an older generation to dictate, making its demand
for an individual existence, seeking for freedom to
direct its own course.

"We don't want to wait until we're old before we
begin." The vehement utterance found its echo in
her own heart. With her, too, in spite of a nature
naturally pliant and unselfish, the desire to spread
her wings, to fulfil her own life, had been unconsciously
growing and deepening.

"And yet we can't begin by hurting people, Billy—
by hurting padre and Lady Bridget," she said unhappily. "Perhaps—if we wait a little longer—something will happen. They may even begin to think themselves that they're not being quite fair to us."

"Oh, the earth may suddenly stand still—or the
sun fall out of the sky! It's about as likely," growled
Billy, with frank unbelief. Yet something was going
to happen, and before very long—its impulse eman-

ating from the very last source he would have thought likely. "Oh, well," he pursued. "I suppose we must carry on for a bit longer. Only, if your 'something,' whatever it is, doesn't happen soon"—smiling in spite of himself—"I know I shall *burst!*"

Barbara laughed, relieved to see that, for the moment, at any rate, all danger of open revolt was tided over. She didn't, as she had said, want to begin their life together—the life that was to be so wonderful— by hurting other people.

"After all, old thing," she said consolingly, "we're not the only people whose affairs don't run smoothly. I could name one or two others in our own immediate neighbourhood."

"You mean poor old Beresford and Carol? Well, if you deliberately marry the wrong man, as Carol did, you're sure to have to pay the piper, sooner or later."

"Don't be idiotic, Billy. No one 'deliberately' marries the wrong man—or the wrong woman, either," affirmed Barbara sagely. "They do it by mistake, or are pushed into it by their families, or circumstances or something. And they never think it's going to turn out half as bad as it always does." She paused, then continued rather anxiously: "I only hope Mac and Herrick aren't going to make a muddle of things. People in love do seem to me to be aggravatingly stupid."

"As how, oh, most sapient young woman?" demanded Billy.

"I should have thought that was obvious—even to an undeveloped intellect like yours," she answered superiorly. "Mac's in love with Herrick, and Herrick's in love with Mac——"

"How do you know?" interrupted Billy.

She smiled across at him.

"I don't know *how* I know, but I just do know. So why don't they behave like sensible people and get engaged? I wish they would," she added in heart-felt tones.

"All in good time, my infant. You want to hurry matters too much."

"I think there's need for hurry in this case," she said soberly. "I've a feeling in my bones that Gair may upset things. He'll go any length to get his own way, you know. Incidentally, he's out riding with Herrick this afternoon."

Billy laughed.

"I must say he and old Mac are rather like two dogs manœuvring for the same bone," he observed.

Barbara's eyes held a look of concern.

"I know," she assented. "And I don't exactly envy the poor little bone."

"Who's the 'poor little bone' in question?" demanded a cheerful voice, and Alec Fane thrust a wind-ruffled head round the half-open door.

"Hullo, padre!" Barbara exclaimed in surprise. "I wasn't expecting you back as soon as this. Is poor old Cartright dead?" she continued on a more serious note.

"Not he!" returned Alec sturdily. "He's had a heart attack, that's all, and, as usual, thought he was going to peg out. So, also as usual, he sent for me to help him make his peace with Heaven. It appeared he had several things on his conscience that he wanted to get rid of—a few brace of birds poached off Kenyon's shoot, a small matter of a young lamb he'd pinched one night from Farmer Marvin's flock, and a bad beating which he gave his wife two days ago. He fancied they might all rather militate against him in the next world."

"I suppose he feels much better now he's got them off his chest," remarked Billy.

"Ever so much." Fane nodded humorously. "In fact, there's not the slightest doubt that he'll make a complete recovery and resume his pinching and poaching activities *con amore*. Then, in course of time, he'll have another heart attack and send for me so that he can unburden his conscience once again. Cartright has every intention of making the best of both worlds —like a good many other people. What about some tea, kiddy?" he went on, turning to Barbara. "It's thirsty work trying to convince people of the error of their ways."

She laughed and nodded.

"I'll go and get it," she said. "It's Janet's day out. You can come, too, Billy, and make the toast." She suited the action to the words, sweeping Billy off in her train and leaving her father to cogitate upon the peculiarities of human nature as evidenced by the Cartrights of this world. Followed, shortly, sounds of domestic activity issuing from the kitchen regions, and these finally materialised into the welcome appearance of fragrantly steaming tea and crisp hot-buttered toast.

"By the way, where's Gair?" asked the rector presently, when the golden pile of toast had considerably dwindled beneath the threefold attack on it. "Hasn't he come in yet?"

"No," answered Barbara. "He went up to Windy-croft after lunch to take Herrick out riding. We were only just speaking of him when you came in."

Her father smiled quizzically.

"Surely he wasn't the 'poor little bone' I heard you commiserating?"

Billy went off into a shout of laughter.

"Not likely, padre!" he answered mirthfully.

"No, Herrick was the bone," explained Barbara. "With Gair and Mac fighting for her."

"Oh!" After that first brief exclamation Fane was silent for a considerable time, his eyes profoundly contemplative.

"Dear me!" he observed at last, his brows wrinkling up whimsically. "I seem to have been curiously blind."

Barbara regarded him indulgently.

"Darling old thing, has it only just dawned on you that Mac's not going to have it all his way, if Gair can help it? I've known that ever since the day Herrick went through the ice and Gair pulled her out."

Alec nodded.

"Perhaps you're right," he admitted. And then adroitly turned the conversation. Mentally, he was reflecting upon how completely a preconceived idea that a certain definite thing is the case can blind you to the thought that any other thing is possible. No amount of pointers, no indications—which would have been clear as daylight to you but for that preconceived idea—make any impression. It is only when the other, unthought-of possibility is flashed before your mind that the signs and portents which you have ignored become suddenly of consequence, every detail falling into place with unmistakable significance, dovetailing like the scattered pieces of a jig-saw puzzle solved by a master hand.

Fane had perceived clearly enough that some sentiment more profound than friendship existed betwixt Mac and Herrick, and had rejoiced in the fact. He loved them both and could imagine no two people better suited to make each other's happiness. And so convinced was he that they were on the way to this, approaching it by gradual and natural stages, that his mind had not admitted the possibility of a *tertium quid* in the matter. And that the *tertium quid* should be his half-brother had been furthest from his thoughts.

But now, with the flashlight of Barbara's youthful discernment turned upon the subject, the whole circumstances took on another aspect, and details he had disregarded, small incidents which held their own significance, leaped to the forefront of his mind, each waving its own danger signal.

And since Alec Fane was a man who never put off till to-morrow what he thought should be done to-day, he took his own method of dealing with the matter that same evening. Barbara had gone to bed, leaving the two half-brothers alone, and for some time they sat by the fire in companionable silence, Alec puffing away at his beloved pipe, Gair with a whisky and soda at his elbow and a cigarette between his lips.

At length the rector took his pipe out of his mouth and looked thoughtfully into its glowing bowl.

"I hear there's to be a meet of hounds at Windycroft next Thursday," he remarked desultorily. "Shall you be here for it?"

"You bet I shall," responded Severn. He flashed one of his quick, charming smiles at his half-brother as he added: "That is, unless you kick me out before."

Alec returned the smile.

"That's not very likely, is it?" he said. "All the same," he went on with deliberation, "you're paying us a rather longer visit than usual, aren't you?"

Severn's body stiffened and he flung a look of sharp interrogation at the rector.

"Is that a hint?" he asked, with sudden haughtiness. "Am I outstaying my welcome?"

Alec shook his head and smiled.

"Of course not. You know that as well as I do. But, frankly, old man, I think your stopping down here any longer is—no good."

Gair's eyes narrowed a little.

"No good?" he repeated. "In what way?"

The other paused a moment before replying. Then he said quietly:

"It's a waste of powder and shot from your point of view. If I'm any judge, Herrick's heart had gone out of her keeping before you came here."

Severn's half-closed eyes gleamed wickedly beneath their lashes.

"Kenyon, I suppose you mean?" he drawled.

"Yes. Mac Kenyon."

"Then, if that's so, why the devil doesn't she marry him?"

The rector pulled at his pipe reflectively.

"Some feminine scruple, I imagine. Time will probably cure it."

Gair sprang suddenly to his feet, almost upsetting the small table beside his chair with the violence of his movement.

"Not if I can help it." He spoke in a set, determined tone that seemed to force its way between his teeth. "And I think I can."

"I fancy you over-rate your strength," returned Fane. "If, as I believe, Kenyon and Herrick are in love with one another, it's too late for you to try to win her."

"It's never too late to win any woman," retorted Severn. "At least," he added, with a spontaneous smile, "I've never found it so yet."

The rector frowned, resisting the engagingness of the smile with an effort.

"If you merely want to count Herrick in as one amongst a dozen other conquests," he began sharply, but Severn interrupted.

"I don't. I want to marry her," he said briefly.

"Have you told her so?" asked Fane.

"I have."

"And her answer?"

Gair shrugged his shoulders.

"An unvarnished and quite explicit refusal," he said.

"In that case, then, I don't think you've any option but to go straight back to town—and not wait for the Windycroft meet."

Severn regarded his elder brother with unqualified astonishment.

"And leave the coast clear for Kenyon?" he exclaimed. "Great Scott, Alec! What do you take me for? A fool?"

"No. But I understood you were in love," replied the rector mildly. "Genuinely in love this time."

"So I am. In that, at least, you're right. And that being so, I don't propose to efface myself and leave it all plain sailing for the other man. Look here, Alec, have you ever known me give up anything I really wanted?"

Fane met his eyes with a steady directness.

"It might be the better way of proving your love— if it is love," he said quietly.

"Oh, I know what you mean," scoffed Gair. "Give her up, do the Christian self-sacrificing stunt, and all that. Bah! You talk like a parson—tarred with the same brush, every one of you!"

Fane smiled.

"I rather think parsons can talk like men, sometimes, old chap," he said. "And think and feel like them, too. We're not a race apart, you know."

"Perhaps you're not. But as it's part of your job to go around picking out the mote in other people's eyes, you damned often overlook the beam in your own," retorted Gair pointedly.

There was so much significance in his tone that the rector sensed a definite accusation behind it.

"What do you mean by that?" he countered squarely. "I've had my tilt at you. It's only playing fair to let you have yours at me. What's the grouse, old man?"

"Well"—Severn still spoke heatedly, notwith-standing the disarming sincerity of the rector's ques-tion. "Well, what about young Billy and Barbara? You're getting your own way with them right enough —you and Lady Bridget. *They* want to be engaged; *you* don't want them to. It might"—with a palpable sneer—"be 'a better way of proving your love' to let 'em, poor young devils. But you don't look at a thing in that light when it applies to yourself. You cod your-self that they're too young, don't know their own minds, and so forth. But it isn't really that at all—and you know it. It's just selfishness, pure, unadulterated selfishness—because you and Lady Bridget don't want to part with the apples of your respective eyes. . . . So don't be a fool, Alec, a preaching fool. We *all* try to get our own way, if we're frank about the matter. And I'm going to try and get mine."

And with that he quitted the room and went up-stairs to bed, leaving Fane to envisage the mental and moral scenery brought into view by a much more cruel and heart-searching flashlight than the one Barbara had unwittingly wielded.

For long he sat there, alone by the dying embers of the fire, while fragments of Gair's hot-tempered arraignment reiterated themselves in his mind. . . . "*They* want to be engaged; *you* don't want them to." . . . "It's just selfishness—pure, unadulterated selfishness." . . . The accusation battered against his consciousness, and before the judgment bar of his own utter honesty, Alec was fain to acknowledge its truth. He—and Lady Bridget—loving this boy and girl as they did, purely and unselfishly in most things, in this were subjecting them to the stranglehold—the frustrating, stultifying stranglehold—of an older generation upon a younger.

It must end. They must be set at liberty. Slowly and painfully—for, as he had told Gair, "We're not a race apart"—Alec fought down his own will, his own desires in the matter, and the very agony of the fight showed him how much of selfishness, of instinctive, unconscious taking thought for his own happiness had lain behind his refusal to sanction an engagement between his daughter and the man who loved her. But in the end he won, conquered the insistent demands of the fatherhood within him.

And at last, his decision taken, he, too, climbed the winding Rectory staircase and went to bed. Tomorrow, he would go and see Lady Bridget, and with his own hands help to place the first of those stepping-stones which would take Barbara away from him and set her free to live her own life.

CHAPTER XXI

LONG ODDS

CLOUDY skies and a light moisture lying on leaf and grass predicted a good hunting morning when finally the day of the Windycroft meet came round. A pleasant sense of bustle prevailed in the house. Servants hurried hither and thither, and a cheery crowd of hunters had gathered in the great panelled hall. Here an ancient refectory table had been spread with appetising plates of sandwiches and sausage-rolls, while glasses and gold-foiled bottles, decanters and old-fashioned goblets, gleamed and twinkled invitingly in the fugitive sunlight.

From outside came the stamping of impatient feet as the horses waited unwillingly in charge of grooms until their respective riders, busy regaling themselves with the store of good things provided within, should choose to reappear, while every now and then came the sharp crack of a hunting-crop, as the Whips kept this or that hound from straying or quarrelling with his neighbour, or the clatter of smartly trotting hoofs as a late-comer rode up the drive.

No meet of the season was more popular than the one at Windycroft, and the members of the hunt had turned out in full force. Even Sir Francis had decided to grace the occasion with his presence, much to Carol's delight—as the number of hunting days which fell to her share was always measured by her husband's inclinations, since she was never allowed to hunt unless he accompanied her.

Perhaps the announcement of the engagement between the rector's daughter and the heir to Windycroft had contributed to the large attendance at the meet to-day. For the "something" which Barbara had been vaguely hoping for had materialised at last. Alec Fane had paid his projected visit to Lady Bridget, and out of a long and rather wistful conversation between the two old friends had emerged permission for the young people to become engaged. The news had flown through the neighbourhood, as news always will fly in a country district, and the occasion of the meet at Windycroft had been made an opportunity for tendering congratulations. So that there was much laughter and gaiety this morning in the grave old raftered hall, healths were drunk, and a buzz of good wishes and friendly teasing filled the air.

Barbara, who had driven over in the Rectory ponytrap with her father, moved about with a shy radiance in her brown eyes, the colour coming and going delightfully in her pretty face as first one and then another wished her luck and happiness, while Billy's obvious pride and joy in the glorious culmination of his hopes were mingled with an unusual and very charming tenderness of manner towards his mother, as though his boyish soul sensed something of the bitterness of the sacrifice she was making for him and wanted to comfort and reassure her.

To more than one person that day the moment of tendering their good wishes brought an inward pang of envy. The shy, tranquil joy which irradiated Barbara's young face could not but remind both Herrick and Carol sharply of the high wall which stood betwixt them and any like happiness, and a very solid substratum of truth underlay Mac's quietly uttered: "I think you're an uncommonly lucky young devil, Billy." As, equally, Jem Beresford's smiling: "You've got us all beat for sheer, undiluted good luck, my son, and I hope you're duly grateful to Providence."

However, all things come to an end in course of time, both painful and pleasurable, and presently the topic of the new engagement gave place to the real business of the day, and people began trooping out of the house in search of their respective mounts. Lady Bridget, who proposed remaining at home on this occasion, thanks to a slightly sprained knee, had invited the rector and Barbara to keep her company and lunch with her, and the trio of stay-behinds came out on to the top of the steps to watch the exodus of hounds and hunters. A few minutes later the M.F.H. rode off at the head of his pack, the Whips trotting behind and cracking their long-lashed hunting-crops to drive a recalcitrant hound or two into line, while the whole hunt came straggling along in their wake, laughing and talking as they went.

Herrick found herself riding between Jem Beresford and Billy, who was mounted on his new purchase, the Rat.

"He's not exactly a beauty, Billy," she remarked, casting an appraising eye over the little beast's eweneck and bony frame, adorned by a tail which reminded one irresistibly of a worn-out bottle-brush.

"Beauty's only skin-deep," replied Billy sententiously. "You wait till you see him go. I'd back him to beat almost anything in the field to-day, except perhaps Romulus himself." He threw a glance to where, riding ahead with Carol, Mac bestrode the big bay horse with the white blaze which had once had its home in the Windycroft stables.

"And I'd back Flame to beat the two of you," Herrick defied him, smilingly, as she laid a soothing hand on the arched chestnut neck in front of her. The mare was very much on tiptoe this morning, her first day out with hounds for a fortnight, prancing excitedly on her four shining black feet and shying coquettishly at every shadow. She pulled eagerly at her bit, and it required all Herrick's good horsemanship and patience to persuade her to behave like a lady and keep her place in the long file of hounds and horses as they trotted down the avenue. She seemed to resent the fact that anyone or anything should precede her, and tossed her head restively when the restraining hand on her bridle prevented her from dashing ahead.

Jem Beresford regarded her critically.

"Your man's giving that mare too much corn," he observed quietly. "She's a bit above herself to-day."

Billy glanced at the impatient chestnut.

"Yes, confound him! That's Larkin's fault. He overfeeds his horses, and then when you get 'em out into the hunting-field they're all over the place like squibs."

"Oh well," said Herrick comfortably, "she'll be able to let off steam when we find a fox. A few ploughed fields will soon reduce her to order."

The opportunity to let off steam came before very long. Flame fidgeted pettishly while hounds cast about in vain in a small wood, but presently a big brake, hardly ever known in the history of the hunt to have been drawn blank, yielded a strong young fox, and to the clamorous baying of hounds and raucous shouts of "Gone away!" the whole hunt streamed in pursuit. Scent was excellent, and soon hounds were running mute and fast, the field stringing out behind them into a long, broken line as the headlong pace found out the respective weaknesses of man and horse.

Flame was well in the van, flashing along like a red-gold streak, and Herrick revelled in the sheer joy of their speed together, of the air rushing past her, soft and moist and fresh with the dew of morning, and of that racing, unflagging pack of hounds ahead.

It was a splendid thirty-minute run, and they finished up with a kill in the open not a quarter of a mile away from the broad acres of Greenwood. For the moment it sufficed to tranquillise Flame's spirits, and she was glad to take a breather whilst hounds cast about for a fresh fox. They were unlucky, however, and the wait prolonged itself into a wearying, unfruitful hour or so. Hounds drew several coverts unsuccessfully, while the members of the hunt walked their horses about and tried to while away the time in conversation. Presently the sun came out, and people began to look glum, prophesying that the rest of the day would be blank, and one or two drifted off homeward, impatient at the lengthy interval.

Flame shared the general dissatisfaction and began

flinging up her head restlessly, fighting her bit and
pawing the ground as Herrick's light, firm hand restrained her. Severn rode across to where the little
tussle betwixt horse and rider was going on.

"The sooner hounds find again, the better for you,"
he remarked. "That mare of yours hasn't had enough
exercise lately. How long is it since you rode her, I
wonder? . . . Not since the last time we were out
together, I suppose?"

Herrick flushed under the quizzical glance he threw
at her. With characteristic audacity, he had inquired
over the 'phone, the very day after she had declined to
marry him, at what hour she would care to go out
riding, receiving in return a curt refusal to ride with
him at all. But apparently the latter had failed to
impress him with any sense of his own shortcomings—
the stormy scene which had taken place between them
having left him entirely undismayed—and Herrick
felt irritably aware of her inability to break through
his guard of arrogant self-sufficiency.

"The mare has been exercised all right, even if I
haven't ridden her myself," she answered him coldly.

"All the same, if you want a thing done well, do it
yourself," he returned. "Incidentally, there was no
valid reason why you should have refused to ride with
me—the next day."

"Do you think not? I'm afraid I don't agree with
you."

"Well"—Severn spoke consideringly—"the fact
that you're ultimately going to marry a man seems to
me rather a reason for than against riding with him."

"Only the reason you've mentioned doesn't exist at all in this case—either for or against," she said sharply.

At this moment Flame, who had been sidling impatiently to and fro, created a diversion by going straight up in the air on her hindlegs, and it was a minute or two before Herrick could reduce her to order again.

"I wish to goodness they'd find a fox," she said, when peace was temporarily restored.

"I don't," replied Gair calmly. "I'm enjoying myself. You've avoided me so persistently for the last two or three days that it's a refreshing novelty to find myself in your company again."

"I'm sorry I can't return the compliment."

He smiled with unruffled amiability.

"I don't think that really matters. I've always understood that a little aversion—to begin with—is an excellent augury for a happy married life. Sort of promise of spring, you know."

"Oh, stand still!" Herrick apostrophised Flame angrily, her increasing annoyance with Severn making her irritable with the fidgeting horse. Unconsciously she jerked the bridle, bringing the bit sharply against the mare's soft lips, and, incensed beyond measure, the animal plunged, then reared again, her forefeet pawing the air. With a swift movement Herrick lifted her arm and brought her crop down smartly between the chestnut's ears, and, at the same moment, the hounds found and gave tongue vociferously. The combination of the two things was too much for the high-strung, mettlesome mare. She sprang

forward with a bound, and the next moment she had
bolted.

For the first few seconds of that wild rush Herrick
hardly realised what had happened. It was only
when she found the usually yielding mouth completely
oblivious to her hands upon the bridle that she recognised the danger. The mare was utterly out of hand,
beyond any control of hers. Behind her, vaguely, she
heard a clamour of shouts and cries, mingled with
the deep baying of the hounds. Then, as the chestnut
dashed on, increasing the distance from the coverts
they had been drawing, these sounds died away, and
she was conscious of nothing except the thundering
hoofs that raced beneath her and the shrieking of the
wind in her ears as they tore along. Luckily, for some
distance ahead, the way lay clear and unobstructed—a
broad, undulating strip of moorland running between
hedged and cultivated fields and patched with clumps
of gorse and bramble thickets. But, farther on, the
stretch of moorland terminated abruptly in an un-
fenced twelve-foot drop into an intersecting road.
Herrick remembered this with a sudden paralysing
feeling of blank horror. Somehow she must check the
headlong pace of the maddened animal she rode before
they reached that drop. If not, even as they fled along,
she could vision the inevitable end . . . the flying,
whirlwind rush to the very edge, the blind leap into
space . . . then the sickening crash of horse and rider
as they hurtled down on to the road below. . . .

She strained at the reins, tugging at them with her
whole strength. Then she tried to saw the bit against
the mare's mouth, but she had gripped it well between

her teeth and galloped on like a mad thing. Herrick might as well have tried to stem a torrent with a straw for all the effect she could produce. Hopeless, now, of pulling up the runaway, she still held on, with aching arms and hands grown numb with the terrible strain, hearing only the ceaseless thud of the chestnut's flying hoofs. And then, all at once, she became conscious of a double beat, of other hoofs battering in the rear. She dared not look round. If she had, she would have seen Severn, bent low over his saddle, galloping in pursuit, urging his horse along with hands and voice and remorseless spurred heel to an almost incredible speed. It was a wellnigh hopeless task—to outride a runaway. Yet the big long-striding thoroughbred Gair bestrode was slowly but surely gaining on the shorter-paced little mare. There was the remotest chance—the one odd chance in a million —that he might come up with her in time. Few men would have attempted it, judging it utterly useless, but Gair was a man who took chances, even remote ones. And there was just the barest possibility that he might yet save the woman in front of him from the unthinkable death to which she was being carried.

Flame heard those pursuing hoofs as well as her rider, and Herrick felt her make an effort to increase her speed. But terror was already driving her along to the last ounce of pace she possessed—she had reached her limit. And so the race went on, with the sun shining and the wind blowing, and no sound at all save the thud of those frenzied hoofs, no sign of human life except a girl, now almost rocking in her saddle, and a man with set face, bent low over his

horse's withers and urging him along with every force
of mind and will and body that was his.

. . . And then suddenly, precipitated into the
green blur ahead which she instinctively knew to be
still moorland, Herrick's straining eyes perceived
something else—something big and dark that was
rushing towards her. For the fraction of a second
she thought her sight had played her false, shown
her a mirage of something that did not exist—that
could not be. Then her vision cleared and she knew
for a certainty that it was Mac, galloping towards
her almost at right angles. Nearer, nearer he came
. . . she could see the white blaze streaking the face
of the big bay horse he rode. In another moment he
had swerved and was galloping beside her, riding
level. She heard his voice, but she was too dazed,
too spent to grasp the sense of what he said. But she
knew his hand was on Flame's bridle, iron strong,
jerking the bit from those clenched teeth . . . felt
the mad speed slacken . . . sober gradually to an
even pace. The landscape steadied, the trees and
hedges, which had been flying past her, rocked slowly
like a pendulum run down. The world seem to stand
suddenly still. . . .

Mac leapt to the ground.

"You're all right. I've got you." His words came
to her clearly this time, as she almost fell out of the
saddle into his arms, dizzy and inert, and stood leaning against him, gasping for breath and helpless to
stand upright without support.

In the same moment Severn reached them and
pulled his horse to a standstill. Mac, still encircling

Herrick with one arm, tossed him the reins of the other two sweating, trembling horses.

"Take these brutes!" he commanded sharply. And for an instant the two men stood glaring hostilely at each other, Severn with his lips twisted in a baulked snarl of fury, Mac with an unconscious light of triumph in his eyes—the triumph of the man who is winning against long odds.

CHAPTER XXII

A DOUBLE CONFESSION

"MY GOD, Herrick! I thought it was all up with you."

Jem Beresford's voice shook a trifle in spite of himself, and his ugly hatchet face had gone pale beneath its customary tan. A very real friendship had grown up betwixt him and Herrick, and the sight of her being swept helplessly along towards that twelve-foot drop had filled him with horror. He had been amongst the first to reach her when those of the field who had witnessed the runaway had come hurrying up to inquire if all was well.

Mac, who was still supporting Herrick with his arm, regarded him with some astonishment. A man who is in love with a woman never seems to imagine that any other man—always excepting, of course, a possible rival—can be to any great extent preoccupied with her. Friendship for her, uncomplicated by love, being completely off the map in so far as he himself is concerned, he is apt to discount it in regard to another man. So that Mac received a slight shock of surprise on perceiving how much Herrick's recent danger had affected Jem Beresford. It was very slight. His attention focused on the urgencies of the moment, it hardly more than knocked at the door of his consciousness and vanished almost immediately. But it was to come back again later on, barbed like a dart, and rankle in a wound already festering. For the moment, however, Mac merely glanced curiously at the other man's blanched face.

"You certainly do look a bit white about the gills, Beresford," he remarked. Then, collectively addressing the little group of people who had gathered round, he continued: "Anyone got a flask about them? I left mine behind this morning."

A flask was speedily forthcoming, and when she had swallowed some brandy a faint colour began to steal fugitively back into Herrick's face.

"I shall be all right directly," she declared rather gaspingly, for her heart was still throbbing painfully in her side. "I feel"—she tried to smile—"I feel as if I'd no breath left in my body."

"I don't suppose you have—much," commented Severn grimly. "You weren't exactly in training for a gallop of that description."

"Bring her into my cottage," suggested Jem. "It's only a field away and she can rest there a bit."

"Right." Mac signified approval. "We'll carry her between us. Will you look after the horses, Severn?"

Gair nodded, and stood sullenly watching the other two men as they linked their hands together to form a kind of chair and moved off, carrying Herrick between them, across the meadow which was all that separated them from Two Ways Cottage. A groom, who had been amongst the small crowd which had collected, followed behind, leading Jem's horse. The remainder of the group melted away in search of the hounds, and presently Severn, too, remounted his horse and rode off, leading the chestnut—now a very weary and subdued-looking quadruped—and Romulus with him.

It did not take many minutes to reach the cottage, which stood between the meadow and a branch turning off that identical road into which, but for Mac's intervention, Herrick must have been hurled. The side-road in question was little more than a farm-track, bumpy and uneven, and terminated in a roughly paved court that fronted the cottage. Another similar track on the opposite side of the solitary little dwelling led away directly from the back entrance, ultimately debouching on to one of the main roads, and it was this peculiarity which had given the place its name of Two Ways Cottage. There existed a local superstition amongst the village folk that the cottage was unlucky, because it looked in two diametrically opposite directions. But Jem had scouted the notion and lived there very happily and comfortably, served by Joe Westcott, an odd-job man who helped him with the garden and poultry and looked after his pony and trap, and by an old family servant who had once been his nurse and who fairly worshipped the ground he walked on.

She it was who came bustling to the cottage door as Kenyon and Beresford arrived on the threshold with their burden.

"Oh, my dear life!" she exclaimed, throwing up her hands as she caught sight of Herrick's white face. "Has the young lady been hurt, sir?"

"No, she's not hurt, Muffet," explained Jem. "But she's just had a very narrow escape from being killed. Her horse ran away with her."

"Oh, my dear life!" repeated Mrs. Muffet. "She must be all shaken up like, poor young thing. Bring her in at once, Master Jem, and let me put her on the couch with a hot-water bottle to her feet."

Jem nodded.

"That's the idea, exactly," he said. "She's dead beat, and we want her to rest here a bit."

In a few minutes Herrick was comfortably tucked up on a couch, thankful indeed for the softness of its cushions to her weary muscles and for the warmth of the hot-water bottle at her feet. Reaction had set in and she was almost shivering with cold and weakness.

"A glass of hot milk, with a drop of something in it, would do her good," said Mrs. Muffet. "Make her sleep, maybe." And forthwith bustled away to get it.

Presently Kenyon drew Jem out of the room into the tiny hall.

"Look here, Beresford," he said. "Your horse is waiting outside. There's no need for you to stay here any longer. I and that excellent Mrs. Muffet of yours will look after Herrick, and when she's rested I'll motor her back to Windycroft."

Jem hesitated. It seemed rather churlish to go off and rejoin the hunt, after what had occurred, yet he could make a pretty good guess that, when Herrick had recovered a little, she and Mac would be quite ready to dispense with any third person's company.

"With any luck you should pick up the hounds quite soon, if you start at once, and get another good run before the day's out," pursued Kenyon.

"Sure you don't mind? Isn't there anything else I can do?" asked Jem.

"Nothing at all," Mac assured him.

"All right, then. I'll be getting along. And I'll tell Muffet to have some lunch ready for you both presently. So long, old chap." And a few minutes later came the sound of his horse's hoofs as he cantered back across the meadow.

Meanwhile Herrick had obediently drunk the hot milk "with a drop of something in it" which Mrs. Muffet had brought her, and now lay with closed eyes, too utterly worn out to concern herself about anything that was going on around her. She was still looking rather white, and her face was shadowed with fatigue, when Mac stole quietly back into the room and seated himself near the couch on which she lay. Once the heavy lids lifted and she met his glance, in her eyes the vague interrogation of someone only half-cognisant of her surroundings. A slight involuntary shudder shook her slender frame, reflex of those terrifying moments through which she had passed.

"You're all right, dear," said Mac soothingly. "Perfectly safe now. Shut your eyes and go to sleep again."

She closed her eyes obediently, subconsciously reassured, and before very long she had fallen into a tranquil slumber.

It was over an hour before she awoke to find him still there, sitting silently beside her, keeping vigil. Hardly aware of what she was doing, she held out her hand towards him as a half-awakened child might

do. There was something innocently appealing in the
instinctive gesture. With a stifled exclamation Mac
caught the outstretched hand and held it between
both his.

"Herrick . . . my beloved!" he muttered unsteadily.

The sound of his voice recalled her to full consciousness, and she drew her hand sharply away and sat
up, looking at him with startled, apprehensive eyes,
a nervous shrinking in her whole attitude. For a moment he did not speak, but a look of resolution came
into his face. It was as if, all at once, he had thrust
the uncertainties and demurrings of the past behind
him—would have no more of them. Perhaps Herrick
sensed his determination, for she gave a little cry of
protest, smothered almost before its utterance by his
lips on hers. She sprang up from the couch as though
to escape, but in the same moment his arms enfolded
her and he held her against his breast with a quiet
strength that there was no resisting.

"No, dearest of all," he said, as he felt her struggle
faintly in his hold. "Don't try to fight against things
any longer. It's no use. I'm never going to let you go
again. Instead"—smiling down at her with a tender
mockery—"we're going to be married and live happily ever after."

"Oh, but, Mac, we can't!" she protested. "I've told
you . . . and nothing is altered. The same reason still
exists——"

"Well, we'll have that reason out, and scotch it
once and for all. You've told me"—still regarding
her with that gently quizzical smile—"that you're not

married—you've no secret husband stowed away in prison or a lunatic asylum—and that being so, there's nothing in this world can stand between you and me."

"There is. I've told you about it before."

He shook his head.

"You've told me nothing, sweet. That's just the trouble. But this time you're going to tell me." Beneath all his tenderness she could feel the strength of his determination—an unwavering resolve to know the truth, and her heart sank.

"I can't. . . . I can't, Mac," she declared breathlessly. "It could do no good. You must believe me when I tell you there *is* something which must separate us."

"I'm afraid I don't believe it, darling. Don't you see, in the long run, it must depend on ourselves—on you and me—whether we *allow* anything to come between us. Let me hear what it is—this bugaboo you're so afraid of. And you'll find it's nothing that need keep us apart."

She made no answer, only a look of mingled fear and misery grew in her eyes.

"I'm still waiting to be told," he said, after a minute or two's silence, and there was a quiet persistency in his grave voice against which she was beginning to feel it useless to fight. She might as well try to pit her strength against a rock. Her body twisted with a little writhing movement of despair.

"No . . . *no!* Won't you let me off, Mac? Please don't make me tell you," she implored him.

But he was inexorable.

"You must," he insisted. "Dear, we can't go on as

we are. It isn't bearable. I'm fighting something vague and intangible all the time. I must know what I'm up against."

"Very well, then, if you *must* know." Slowly but quite deliberately she unclasped his arms from about her and faced him. "One of my parents did something once . . . that I'm ashamed of," she said, speaking in a low, difficult voice. "Not just a little thing—I don't mean that. But something disgraceful—utterly bad. Something that you would be the first to condemn . . . that everybody would condemn. . . . Oh, it's—it's horrible to feel ashamed of one of your parents!" she exclaimed, smiting her hands together. Then, with an agonised rush of entreaty: "Don't ask me to tell you what it was, Mac . . . I—I can't do that."

The halting, painful confession was over, and she stood in front of him with bent head, her hands hanging clasped before her, like someone awaiting judgment—judgment and punishment.

Mac laid his own hands on her shoulders a moment.

"Thank you, dear, for telling me," he said gently. "And my answer to all this is: That I don't care what your parents did—either or both of them. I'm not wanting to marry them; I want to marry *you*. Nor am I going to ask you what it was—I don't want to know. All I want to know, sweetheart, is do you love me enough to marry me—love and trust me enough?"

She lifted her downbent head. The colour, which had ebbed from her face while she forced herself to make that hated confession, was coming slowly back into her cheeks.

"I love and trust you absolutely," she said simply. "It isn't that. I don't think you've understood, even yet, Mac. I'm the child of my parents, their blood is mine, and, as I've told you before, it's bad blood. Some day, the same weakness—wickedness—may come out in me, and I shan't be able to help it. Don't you see, it's *that* I'm afraid of?"

"I'm not," said Mac. "I'm not afraid"—smiling a little—"of any weakness or wickedness suddenly showing itself in you. I've never seen a sign of it yet. Listen, dearest," he continued, as her face still remained troubled. "I'm going to tell you something—swop confession for confession, and perhaps, then, you'll feel differently about it all." He paused, as if trying to decide how he should tell her, then went on quietly: "No one's parents are perfect, and some are very far from it. My own father was only saved by circumstances from committing suicide."

A tremor ran through her. Suicide—one of the very shadows which had helped to darken her own life!

"He had been very—unwise—over money matters." Kenyon was speaking again, choosing his words carefully. "It was through that we were ruined—lost everything. And when he realised what he had done, how much unhappiness he had brought upon my mother and the whole family, he hadn't the courage to face life any longer. Actually, he died of heart failure, brought on by the shock of his losses, but he was found in his study, dead, with a loaded revolver on his desk beside him, and there is no possible doubt, from a half-finished letter which he must have been writing at the very moment death came to him, that he intended to shoot himself."

"He had been—unwise—over money matters." Unwise! How many sins and mistakes that kindly word is often made to cover! In a moment Herrick's mind had leaped to the conclusion that Mac's father had made a failure of his life much in the same way her own father had done. It was amazing. Amazing—and terrible. But it yet held a curious, unspeakable comfort for her—it was like a bond—a sad and sorry one enough, in all truth, but still a bond—betwixt herself and the man she loved.

For a few minutes after he had ceased speaking they were both silent. Herrick's thoughts were crowding thick and fast upon each other, and his had gone back to that day of sudden grief and calamity when he had walked casually into his father's study on some unimportant errand, to find him huddled in his chair —dead. His hand, from which the pen had fallen, had dropped inertly across a sheet of half-scribbled notepaper in front of him, and the westering sunlight flickered redly along the barrel of a revolver lying a little to one side on the desk in readiness to help him out of life.

"I can't face it," ran that last letter which Mac's father had written to him. "So I'm taking the only way out. Son, try not to think of me as a coward, and do whatever you can for your mother and Carol. I'm played out, finished. I should only be a drag on the wheel, so——"

The letter had broken off here, and the elder Kenyon

had died where he sat, of heart failure, by a merciful dispensation which had sent Death to free him from a burden that was heavier than he could bear.

Mac jerked himself out of these thoughts of the past back into the present again.

"So you see, beloved," he resumed quietly, "it was only by good luck that my father wasn't a suicide. Does that make any difference to you or to your love for me—the fact that he was a suicide in all but actual fact, in intention and in cowardice?"

"Of course it doesn't."

"Then why should you think that anything one of your parents may or may not have done should make any difference to me, if the same kind of thing, reversed, doesn't influence you?"

"But I'm a woman. Men are—different," she said slowly, the memory of Rex Dereham keen and bitter in her mind.

"Are they? Well, then, I must be the exception which proves the rule. For I think you and I are very much alike. We neither of us care what the other's father or mother may have done. So that seems a good foundation on which to build together. Herrick"—he held out his arms to her—"will you come to me—now?"

For one last moment she still hesitated, frightened to take the happiness which was waiting for her. Then, swept by a rush of utter trust and confidence, she went to him, and their lips met in a first perfect kiss, unmarred, unshadowed by any doubt or fear.

CHAPTER XXIII

FOREBODING

ALWAYS, the first days of an engagement between two who love each other are enveloped in an aureole of golden light, a mystic radiance which, long afterwards, even when everything else may have grown stale and commonplace, or when doubt and distrust have entered in to destroy, still lingers in the memory —the vision vouchsafed of the miracle of love. And to Herrick the days which immediately followed her engagement to Mac Kenyon were days of enchantment—aglow with an upspringing of joy that seemed all the more wonderful and vital by contrast with the darkness and hopelessness which had preceded it.

There was a happiness that almost hurt, so poignant was it, in the realisation that the shadow which had lain across her life during the last three years, compelling her to feel an outcast from the world, had at last been lifted—made of no account. And the manifest delight with which the news of her engagement was greeted by the little group of friends who had become warp and weft of her life at St. Heriot served but to add a further joy.

"What did I advise you?" demanded Lady Bridget, in happy triumph. "To tell Mac the truth. I knew you'd find him big enough and fine enough to disregard it."

252

"I didn't tell him everything, though," confessed Herrick. "He didn't even want to know what it was that Dad had done—so I never told him."

"He was quite right not to ask," asserted Mim. "There's never any good accomplished by digging up the dead bones of the past and looking at them. I think," she added, with one of those sudden smiles of hers which irradiated her face as a flash of sunshine might illumine a quiet landscape, "I think I'm very pleased with Mac—even although, of course, it means that I shall lose you before long."

"You'll never lose me, Mim," declared Herrick earnestly. "I should never let myself get lost—from you. Greenwood isn't very far away, and I shall be over here as often as ever you'll let me come." Impulsively she flung her arms round the older woman's neck. "Why, Mim, I owe you everything in the world —even meeting Mac. Do you think I could ever—forget?"

"No, I don't think you would, dear child." Lady Bridget brushed her hand quickly across her eyes and went on teasingly, as though to cover some deeper emotion that threatened to overflow. "But I flatly decline to take any responsibility for Mac! You picked him up in Paris—very literally."

Carol's pleasure in the engagement between her brother and Herrick was yet another added joy. She seemed almost to forget her own troubles for the moment in frank rejoicing over her brother's happiness, and both Billy and Barbara jokingly preened themselves on the fact that they had set an excellent example which others were now following, the former asserting that there was certain to be a third engagement announced before long, since things invariably happened in threes.

There was only one person to whom the news brought anything but satisfaction, and that was inevitably Gair Severn. On the day following that of the Windycroft meet, he had quitted St. Heriot by an early train to stay with friends who had offered him a couple of days' hunting in another district, and it was therefore not until his return that he learned what had taken place. Barbara, outwardly composed although inwardly slightly nervous as to how he might receive the news, had been his informant. His unruffled demeanour, however, served to reassure her, and the curious whiteness that crept round his mouth passed unnoticed by her.

"That so?" he observed coolly, when she had confided the facts. "There seems to be quite a plethora of engagements in the neighbourhood. If only old Mortimer would see fit to shuffle off this mortal coil, I suppose we should hear of yet another one."

"Oh, Gair!" Barbara tried to look appropriately shocked, but as Severn had only expressed in words what was everybody's inward thought, she was not particularly successful.

"Oh, Barbara!" he mimicked. "Don't try to be a plaster saint, my dear; it doesn't suit you. As for Mortimer, he'll probably dope himself out of this world sooner or later—only he's a tough old bird and I'm afraid poor Carol will find it'll be later rather than sooner."

Barbara's innocent eyes grew round.

"Do you really think Sir Francis takes drugs?" she asked in somewhat awestruck tones. "Billy always swears he does, but I never believed it."

"And I never doubted it. A man doesn't have that leaden skin of his—and his moods—for nothing."

"Carol never says anything about it," observed Barbara doubtfully.

"She wouldn't. One very rarely talks about the things that matter most."

And with that he turned away abruptly and swung out of the room, leaving her to wonder whether, after all, Herrick's engagement was one of the things that "mattered most" to Gair, and if that was the reason why he hadn't talked about it.

Herrick herself was not left long in doubt upon the subject. He joined her by the lake, whither she had been tempted for a stroll that same afternoon by a burst of warm sunshine—one of those brief foretastes of spring which sometimes follow a soft rain even in January. She reflected, afterwards, that since the particular part of the lakeside where she was walking happened to be visible from one of the Rectory windows, he had probably seen her there and deliberately followed her.

He greeted her conventionally enough, but there was a restless brilliance in his eyes which warned her that the composure of his manner was only a veneer and liable to crack at any moment.

"And how are you after your exciting experience of last Thursday?" he inquired politely, as he turned and fell into step beside her.

She tried to answer him as naturally as possible,

despite her intuitive feeling that a somewhat stormy undercurrent lurked beneath his surface calmness.

"Oh, quite all right, thanks. I was rather stiff the next day—and so was poor Flame! But we've both recovered now."

"Flame, of course, merely met her due deserts and paid the penalty for exceeding the speed limit," said Gair. "All things considered, you had a very lucky escape."

"I had, indeed," she replied fervently. Then, with a trace of nervousness in her manner, she continued: "Gair, I want to thank you for——"

"Failing to overtake you?" he said, with sudden harshness. "Don't. It's only success that counts, you know. Keep bouquets for Kenyon, who reached you in time."

There was so much bitterness in his voice that she was touched to a quick sympathy.

"I wish you wouldn't speak—or even think—like that, Gair," she said simply. "It counts just as much that you *tried* to help me."

"Does it?"—jeeringly. "Well, the fact remains that Kenyon has received the due reward of virtue—or success, whichever you like to call it."

"Reward?"

"Yes, reward. Haven't you promised to marry him?"

She nodded.

"We're engaged, if that's what you mean. But"—with a small, involuntary smile—"it wasn't in consequence of his coming to my rescue."

"Still, that supplied a jumping-off place, didn't it?"

he retorted, always with that same gibing note in his voice.

"I think it would have—happened, anyhow," she said softly, thinking of the steady light in Mac's grey eyes when he had said: "Dear, we can't go on as we are—it isn't bearable."

"Well, it's unfortunate that it *has* happened," replied Severn grimly. "It's made a bigger mess of things for me to put straight."

Herrick stole a fugitive glance at his face. The veneer of politeness had cracked very completely now, and there was a dare-devil gleam in his eyes which she had seen before and which sent a stab of apprehension through her. Nevertheless, she didn't propose to let him guess that she was afraid.

"You're rather difficult to understand, aren't you?" she said, forcing herself to speak lightly. "Am I to take this as your particular method of offering your congratulations?"

"No, you're not," he returned bluntly. By this time their way had led them into a small wood, and he came to an abrupt standstill beneath the trees. Involuntarily she paused beside him. "I don't propose to congratulate you at all," he went on. "It would be a sheer waste of time." He smiled down at her, half mockingly, half caressingly. "You silly dear! Do you suppose for one moment that I'm going to let Kenyon run off with the woman I want myself?"

Herrick's small head went up defiantly.

"I don't see how you can very well prevent it," she said. "You can't force people into marrying you nowadays, thank goodness!"

"Can't you? I'm not so sure about that." Severn's eyes grew meditative. "There are ways—if one chose to think about it, I imagine. But I don't want to force you. Herrick, don't be a little fool. Give yourself to me—you're the only woman in the world that matters, as far as I'm concerned. The only woman"—with a brief laugh—"I've ever wanted to—marry."

The swift indignant colour stained her cheeks scarlet. While he spoke, her slender figure had tautened like that of someone with muscles braced against a storm. Her glance met his squarely.

"And you are the very last man in the world I would dream of marrying," she said, with a quiet, incisive coolness that drove at him far harder than any more vehement protest would have done.

It seemed to snap some link of self-control within the man beside her. With a sudden swift movement— so swift that she could not evade it—he bent forward and caught her up into his arms. For an instant she felt his eyes blazing down at her, was strickenly, terrifying conscious of her utter aloneness with him in the sheltering aloofness of the little wood, then his mouth sought hers, crushing her lips beneath his own with kisses that bruised and hurt, while the flame of his passion swept over her like a scorching wind from the desert. When at last he took his mouth from hers, she almost reeled in his grasp.

"Do you understand what I mean now?" he said hoarsely. His face was white, grown suddenly haggard, and something savage and unleashed looked at her out of it. "That's how I love you—want you! Do you think—now—that I'll ever let another man take you?"

She struggled against him, but his arms held her fast.

"Let me go—let me go, Gair," she said breathlessly, twisting and turning as she fought to release herself.

"Let you go—to Mac Kenyon?" he returned derisively. "Swear that you'll marry me—not Kenyon—and I'll let you go. Not otherwise."

All at once, at the sound of Mac's name, that terrible, frightening feeling of being alone with Severn seemed to leave her. She would never be alone in the world any more, never again have to fight life single-handed. For the future it would always be she and Mac—together! Her courage returned, and she ceased to struggle. Standing unresistingly in Severn's grasp, she bent her head back so that she could meet his eyes with the cool bravery of her own.

"Then I'm afraid we shall have to stay here indefinitely," she said, her voice edged with a gentle contempt. "For I assure you, Gair, I've every intention of marrying Mac and none whatever of marrying you. . . . We seem to have reached an *impasse*, don't we?"

For an instant he wavered, stung by the flick of derision in her tones. Then his grip relaxed, although he still held her lightly.

"You're rather a plucky little devil, aren't you?" he said, with a mixture of amusement and reluctant admiration.

"Thank you," she replied demurely. She felt that

she was winning—for the moment, anyway. "And now, may I go home, please?"

Suddenly he laughed.

"Yes, you may go," he said. "But you needn't think you've won. I've never been defeated yet." His eyes met hers, and she knew that they were not the eyes of a man who was easily defeated. The temporary flash of amusement had died out of them, replaced by the old familiar arrogance—reckless and unconquerable.

"Don't forget, Herrick. I never give up—never. And you'll marry *me*—not Kenyon or any other man."

And even though he released her as he spoke, standing aside with a half-mocking bow for her to pass, she was conscious, as she made her way homeward, of this man's indomitable will power as of some menacing shadow that still lay across her path. A nebulous foreboding weighed her down. She told herself that as long as she and Mac believed and trusted in each other, Gair could have no power to hurt them. But, in spite of herself, his last words beat persistently in her mind, ominous as the mutter of distant thunder: "You'll marry *me*—*not* Kenyon or any other man."

CHAPTER XXIV

POINTS OF VIEW

THE following day Severn quitted the Rectory abruptly and returned to London, and, as far as Herrick was concerned, his departure added considerably to her happiness and peace of mind. That secret, undefined fear of him which had found lodgment somewhere in her consciousness did not altogether leave her, but with his absence from St. Heriot it retreated into the background of her thoughts, only emerging spasmodically to give her a little jolt of uneasiness, as who should say: "Don't forget I'm still here!" Nevertheless, it was unquestionably a great relief to her to feel that the possibility of a chance encounter with him at any odd moment was removed, and, with the sense of freedom which this knowledge brought, she was able more completely to enjoy her new-found happiness.

Mac had the wonderful faculty of combining lover and friend which is so rare to find amongst men. Too often the demandingness of the lover almost swamps everything else, and although it is sweet to a woman to be made to feel his need of her, to respond to those glowing moments when love and life seem to be fused together into a single glorious significance, she also longs for the cheery, everyday kind of happiness which

two good comrades find in each other's company—
in the interchange of thoughts and ideas, the laughter
which springs from a like fount of humour, the ability
to be young and childish, and "play" together.

And all these things Herrick found in the man she
was learning to know ever better and better as the
weeks slipped by. There were profounder deeps in
his nature than she had guessed, an idealty of thought
that harmonised with her own secret ideals, a sense
of loyalty that now no longer seemed to her stern
and unbending, but something very splendid in its fine
discrimination. And, with it all, there was that quick
sense of humour which goes farther than anything else
to grease the wheels of existence and make them run
smoothly. He would be such a wonderful fellow way-
farer to journey through life with, she thought to herself sometimes with a little inward thrill at the sheer
marvel and poignancy of the happiness which had
come to her, and then would register a vow in her
inmost soul that whatever of good her love could bring
into his life, it should be his. She had no means of
guessing then at what a bitter cost that vow would
one day claim fulfilment, nor on how hard a road the
supreme altruism of love would set her footsteps.

The only cloud which shadowed her horizon at the
moment was the knowledge that Carol's life was gradually becoming more and more irksome and difficult
to bear. She complained very little—least of all to
Herrick, and the latter suspected that she refrained
out of an unselfish wish not to intrude her own troubles
on another's happiness. But she was losing her spirits
—those fugitive gay good spirits that not even Sir

Francis's tyranny had hitherto been able to quench, and in her eyes, which had lost their childishness, dwelt an expression of conflict and uncertainty, as of some-one who was always thinking what to do, which way to turn—wrestling secretly in spirit.

One day when this gradual change in Carol had been occupying her thoughts for some time, Herrick mentioned it to Kenyon. She and Lady Bridget had been lunching with him at Greenwood, and afterwards Lady Bridget had departed to the village, bent on some philanthropic errand, leaving Mac and Herrick to roam about the house and gardens, planning certain alterations they proposed to make. It was one of their principal amusements in life just at this time—deciding upon the various improvements which could be accomplished there. They would make enthusiastic plans, suggestion crowding upon suggestion from one or other of them, sketches would be drawn and colour schemes discussed, and then they would joyously scrap their ideas and begin all over again. They were like a couple of children about it. It was a lovely game, and, as Lady Bridget remarked, "kept them good and quiet for hours at a time." And ultimately, out of the hotch-potch of ardent schemes, something delectably individ-ual and characteristic—the something that turns a house into a home and "grounds" into a garden—would assuredly emerge.

They had been good-humouredly disputing over the best position for a rose pergola, and the question being at last satisfactorily settled, the ensuing pause in the eager flow of Herrick's thoughts had been suddenly filled with the recollection of Carol's affairs. She had once wanted a rose pergola erected in a particular situation at Mortlake, and Sir Francis had naturally and inevitably decided to have it placed somewhere else— with the result that the roses bloomed in vain. No one ever walked there; its green-clad arches had been based on too much bitterness. It was the memory of this episode, recounted to her on one occasion by Carol, which diverted Herrick's thoughts into a new channel.

"Mac," she said, as they stood together in the garden, bright with March sunlight, "haven't you noticed a great difference in Carol lately? She's grown so much quieter than usual. Sort of preoccupied."

He nodded, a sudden look of gravity in his eyes.

"Yes," he said briefly. "I've noticed it." Adding after a moment: "Perhaps, when Jem has actually gone away, she'll find things a bit easier."

Herrick turned and regarded him with blank astonishment.

" 'When Jem's gone away'!" she repeated. "Gone where? What do you mean?"

"Didn't you know? I thought Carol had told you. He's practically decided to leave St. Heriot—at any rate for a time—going abroad probably."

"Leaving St. Heriot! But—oh Mac!"—with profound dismay. "That would mean the end of everything for Carol. I don't think she'd be able to bear her life at all if Jem went away."

Kenyon looked thoughtful.

"On the contrary I think she may find it much more bearable—once the first wrench is over. The present arrangement is asking too much of human nature. If a man and woman care for each other as they do, then, in the circumstances, they're better apart, cut off from ever seeing each other at all."

"Yet you didn't seem in any hurry to cut yourself off from ever seeing me again," hazarded Herrick, with a smile.

He smiled back.

"No, because you were free, and there was always the chance things might come right for me. There's none for Jem." His face grew grave again. "There's only one thing for him to do—cut it out. Quit."

Herrick's heart sank. In a way, she could see the force of Mac's stern ultimatum. Yet her love and sympathy for Carol made her realise with a desperate, overwhelming pity all that the latter must be going through, all that she must be fighting against, now that it had come to the actual parting of the ways. It was not in the least surprising that she was showing signs of strain.

Herrick glanced at Kenyon curiously. Did he realise it, too, she wondered? All the grief and pain involved in that brief verdict: "Cut it out. Quit." But she could glean nothing from his face.

"I'm not quite sure that you're right," she said, ponderingly, at last. "I think—I'm afraid Carol is getting to the end of her tether."

His expression remained impenetrable.

"I hope not," was all he said.

She was silent for a few minutes. Then:

"I think you're always very hard on Carol," she burst out suddenly in a puzzled voice. "Although you're not a hard person ordinarily, Mac. You were— wonderful—to me over those past things which I thought were going to spoil my life for always. And yet, as regards Carol——"

"The two are quite different," he interrupted quietly. "In the one case—in Carol's—she made a choice, a bargain if you like to call it so, and she must abide by it. In the other, you, being the transparently honest little soul that you are, refused to marry me until you'd told me all about those 'past things.' In fact, you were really giving me *my choice*—as to whether"—smiling—"I'd risk marrying anyone with such a sticky past. And having chosen, of course, *I* shall have to abide by it, however badly you may develop."

He was laughing down at her openly now, but, instead of responding to his banter, she was conscious of a sudden inward qualm of apprehension.

"That's just what I'm always afraid of," she answered seriously. "Supposing I *did* develop badly!"

"Well, I should have to stand the racket, if you did. Like Carol, I've made my choice."

"I wonder if you would," she said slowly. "You see, if I turned out all wrong it would ruin your life."

"It certainly would. But even if it did, that would be no excuse for me to shirk my responsibilities—run away from them. I should have gone into it with my eyes open, so if I had to pay the reckoning—I should just pay, and that would be the end of it."

Herrick was silent. Somehow, she knew that he was speaking the truth. Whatever happened, whatever of calamity might result, once they were man and wife, Mac would accept it and dree out his weird no matter what the cost. The thought frightened her. Supposing

—supposing by any awful chance she were ever severely tempted in any way, and fell, as her father's inherent weakness had made him fall? Mac would pay, as he had just said he would, for the rest of his life, would stand by her, sharing disgrace, or scandal, or whatever might ensue.

"Oh, Mac, I do wonder if we've done right!" she exclaimed in distress. "Supposing I ever failed you?"

"I'm not going to suppose anything so ridiculous," he replied placidly. "Why should you, most dear and foolish person?"

She did not answer him. Instead, she put another question.

"Don't you believe in heredity, then?"

He took her by the shoulders and gave her a gentle shake.

"Now, look here, you've got to put all that kind of nonsense out of your mind, beloved. You're too honest —too sound to the very core—to be afraid of anything your parents may have done. A man isn't necessarily a drunkard because his father was one. In fact, the knowledge of his father's weakness should be a safeguard. He knows what he's up against."

"Yes, in regard to just that one particular temptation," assented Herrick. "You may be right in that. But he must have inherited a certain weakness of character—a want of balance, in some way, which might perhaps develop in another direction in the son."

"We've all inherited certain weaknesses—if not from our immediate forbears, then from *their* forbears," said Kenyon. "And we've also inherited certain finenesses and strength. We're very composite—a mixture of the qualities of many generations. And as I see it, our particular job in life is to develop the good side of our inheritance and jump firmly on the bad one."

"Do you think we can—do that?"

"I'm sure of it," he said quietly. "If it weren't I shouldn't believe in God."

And so it was with a very comforted and tranquillised spirit that Herrick went to bed that night. Perhaps it was true, after all, true that you could overcome a bad strain in your blood. Even—her face glowed suddenly in the shrouding darkness—overcome it in your children, because, knowing the possible danger, you were on guard against it—could hand them on a torch that burned more strongly and with a clearer, purer flame because you had tended it.

CHAPTER XXV

TWO WAYS COTTAGE

WELL, it means the side-car, then, that's all."

Billy spoke resignedly. He had just received a telegram informing him that a fox-terrier pup he had purchased was being sent to St. Heriot by train and would arrive there at nine o'clock that very evening, and he had proposed motoring to the station, accompanied by Herrick, to fetch the dog home. And now the chauffeur had come up to the house to impart the news that when he had driven Lady Bridget that afternoon he had found something amiss with the two-seater, and that its interior was at the moment more or less resolved into its component parts on the garage floor.

"I didn't suspect you'd be wanting the car this evening, sir," the man explained, "so I was giving it a thorough overhauling."

"I didn't expect I'd want it myself," replied Billy. "Oh, well, we'll use the side-car. You don't mind, do you, Herrick?" he added, turning to her. There was nothing else for it, as they both knew, since the four-seater was away being repainted.

"Of course I don't," she answered. "I can manage with the puppy on my lap all right—provided it isn't a very excitable little beast. Wouldn't it be awful,

269

though," she went on with some concern, "if, appalled by your driving, it suddenly leapt out into the road?"

"It would be dead," replied Billy tersely. "As a matter of fact, though, it's too young to go leaping in and out of cars. It'll have been sent along in a basket, and all you'll have to do is to hang on to the basket."

Herrick looked somewhat relieved. The idea of swinging along in the side-car, trying to restrain a lively young dog from hurling itself into the roadway, had not precisely commended itself to her.

An hour or two later, after a somewhat hurried and informal dinner, they bade Lady Bridget good-bye and set off on their errand.

"Drive carefully, Billy," his mother cautioned rather anxiously.

Billy kissed her.

"Of course I will, Mim," he said good-humouredly. "You needn't be a bit afraid. I'll drive most circumspectly. So long, old darling." And with a final wave of his hand, he bustled Herrick out of the room and into the waiting side-car.

"You all right?" he asked, as, having tucked a rug well round her and fastened the apron, he mounted the motor-bike.

"Quite."

"Right away, then!"

They sped swiftly down the avenue and out on to the road, but they had not covered more than a mile of the way before Billy found himself compelled to drive much more circumspectly than he had anticipated. A light mist hung on the air, thickening here and there into patches of actual fog, and it became necessary to proceed slowly and with caution. Now and again he swore softly, fearing they would be too late at the station to receive the puppy immediately on its arrival.

"And then," as he remarked bitterly, "some fool porter will probably have dumped the poor little beggar out on to the platform and left him there, catching his death of cold."

Fortunately, the way rose presently in a gradual ascent, so that, as they climbed, they found they were leaving the mist behind them, and very soon they were slipping along a stretch of level road and making up for lost time. Just as they approached the station they overtook a rather shabby-looking dog-cart, driven by a man who sat hunched up in an awkward heap on the box-seat, jerking the reins and clucking at the cob he drove like some farmer's lout. Herrick glanced curiously at him as the lights of the motor-bike flashed momentarily over the unkempt turn-out, then uttered a little cry of astonishment.

"Why, that's Humphreys—Sir Francis's squiffy-eyed gardener, driving the old dog-cart which Carol never uses now," she said.

"P'r'aps Mortimer's made him a present of it," suggested Billy, as they whizzed along.

She laughed.

"Not very likely! Sir Francis doesn't give away much."

"Then I expect the man's going to the station to fetch home some flower-pots or plants or something," he amended. After which, the unexpected appearance of Humphreys passed out of both their minds.

Very soon the sparse light of the little country station twinkled into view, and such good speed had Billy made since they had emerged from the fog that they had to wait a short time for the arrival of the train. Just as it was signalled, the dog-cart driven by Humphreys came into sight again, and, whipping up his horse, he pulled up outside the station a minute or two before the train ran in. With surprising agility, considering the awkwardness of his figure, the man sprang down from the high dog-cart, hitched the reins to a post, and made his way on to the platform, followed more leisurely by Billy.

The latter went straight to the guard's van in search of his puppy, losing sight of Humphreys immediately the train began to shed its human freight. It had been a big market day at Tanborough, and the small, ill-lit station platform was soon crowded with farmers and their wives, tradesfolk, servant girls and their attendant swains—all the miscellaneous country crowd which swarms into any neighbouring town on a market day—elbowing their way towards the exit. Here the inevitable delay of ticket collecting occurred, and Billy, the basket containing the puppy carefully shielded in the crook of his arm from any haphazard jolt, found himself momentarily wedged in a corner against a projecting piece of wall. From the other side of the projection came the sound of a sullen, growling voice pitched on a low, rather confidential tone.

"She's gone to Two Ways Cottage. And there's only 'two ways' for a woman that I see of—one with 'er rightful 'usband and t'other with some other man."

"You're quite sure?"

Billy gave a great start as he heard the answering voice, and the arm which held the basket jerked involuntarily against his side, drawing a pathetic squeak of expostulation from its interior.

"You're quite sure?"

It was the thin, disagreeable voice of Sir Francis Mortimer which asked the question, and Billy listened anxiously for the reply.

"Oh yes, I made sure right enough. She walked over there this afternoon, after tea-time, and I followed 'er. She 'asn't come back, so I thought I'd inquire of the kitchenmaid when I took in the vegetables, and sh'd 'eard as 'ow 'er ladyship 'ad left word she was dining with 'er brother."

"You've done well, Humphreys." Sir Francis was speaking again. "We'll drive there—to Two Ways Cottage—and see if she *is* 'dining with her brother.' "

Then the stream of people moved forward. They were passing the ticket collector more rapidly now, and two minutes later Billy had emerged into the station-yard, where the side-car waited, and deposited the basket containing the terrier pup in Herrick's arms.

"May I just open it and peep inside?" she asked eagerly.

"No, you mayn't," he returned gruffly. His young face looked unwontedly set and stern, pale beneath the yellow light of the street-lamp which flickered hard by. "Listen, Herrick," he went on quickly. "Something pretty ghastly's happened—or will happen if we don't prevent it."

In a few words he told her of the conversation he
had overheard between Sir Francis and Humphreys.

"So you see," he wound up, "old Mortimer means
catching her there—at Jem's cottage. And then the fat
will be in the fire and no mistake."

"It will, indeed," she agreed in tones of dismay. Her
own face had whitened as she grasped the full import
of what had occurred. "Let's start at once," she went
on urgently. "We must get to the cottage first, Billy,
whatever happens."

He nodded, almost flinging himself on to his machine, and soon they were rushing through the night
towards Two Ways Cottage, bent on saving Carol
from the consequences of her own indiscretion.

For a while all went well, and gradually the tense
anxiety which Herrick felt relaxed a little. She and
Billy would reach Jem's cottage long before Sir
Francis, fast though he might drive, could get there
in a horse-drawn vehicle, and Carol would make good
her escape before her husband arrived. It had been
terribly unwise of her to go to Two Ways Cottage, but
it was not difficult to divine how it had come about.
Sir Francis away—not expected back, probably, until
the next day, Jem leaving St. Heriot within the week,
and he and Carol unable to resist having this one
evening together—a few last hours in which to take
farewell. It was mad of them to have risked it, knowing Sir Francis's propensity for returning home un-
heralded—popping up where he was least expected
and least wanted.

"Oh, he is a fiend!" burst out Herrick indignantly,
as she and Billy buzzed along. "It's all diabolical 'cute-

ness on his part, letting Humphreys come to the station for him in that old dog-cart. No one, of course, would dream he was coming back—except Humphreys, who was in the secret and has evidently been told off to spy on Carol."

"Yes," agreed Billy heartily. "He's about the biggest old swine on the face of the earth. However, we needn't worry. We shall do him in the eye this time all right." He giggled suddenly. "He'll look rather a fool arriving post-haste at the cottage—outraged husband and all that—and finding Carol *not there!* He can't overtake us now. That's certain."

But unfortunately, when Fate is in a malign mood, there is very little that is certain, and a safety that seems assured may be suddenly transformed into unlooked-for danger. Not five minutes after Billy and Herrick had been chuckling confidently over the prospective discomfiture of Sir Francis their hopes received a sudden check. The road from the station to Two Ways Cottage ran through a strip of low-lying ground, and here they found their progress checked once more by a heavy ground mist which grew thicker and thicker as they descended into the valley, until it was almost like driving through an opaque white sea.

"Oh, confound everything!" muttered Billy furiously, as, their pace reduced to a mere crawl, they crept slowly onward, the headlight only adding to their difficulties and creating a confusing glare. "This is the very devil!"

Herrick bent forward anxiously in the side-car.

"Do try to keep in the middle of the road, Billy,"

she urged. "It's frightfully boggy at the sides, and
if we get stuck in the mud we shall have a dreadful
business to pull her out."

"I know," he answered. "That's just what I'm
afraid of. I can hardly see a thing, and the damn headlight makes it worse. Shall I switch it off till we're
through this?"

Hardly had he finished speaking when matters were
abruptly decided for him. Herrick felt the side-car
lurch, then jerk forward unevenly for a yard or so,
to the accompaniment of a squelching oozy sound of
mud sucking against the tyres, and finally stop dead.

"That's torn it!" ejaculated Billy, jumping off and
promptly sinking over his boots in mire. "Now we'll
have the job of our lives to get her out—and no time
to do it in, either."

"Can you manage it alone?" asked Herrick anxiously, as he pushed and pulled to drag the machine
out of the soft ground into which it had run.

Smothered curses and loud breathing, accompanied
by unproductive jerkings of the side-car, were the only
response, and finally she disembarrassed herself of rug
and apron and scrambled out to help, depositing the
basket containing the puppy on the seat meanwhile.

It was a longer job than they had anticipated to
pull the machine back on to the solid surface of the
road, but at length it was accomplished.

"There's only one thing for it now," said Herrick,
"I must walk in front and guide you till we're through
this patch of fog."

Billy demurred.

"At that rate, any slug of a horse would overtake

us," he protested unhappily. "We shall soon have old Mortimer on our heels."

But she persisted.

"He'll not be able to do more than a walking-pace through the mist, any more than we can. And we *daren't* risk another hold-up like that we've just had. You can make up time when we've cleared this belt of mist."

Reluctantly he assented. He was inwardly fuming with impatience over the time they had already lost, but he realised that her suggestion was the only practicable one. So the journey was recommenced at a snail's pace, with Herrick trudging pluckily along in front, calling instructions over her shoulder as she went, and the puppy, missing the warmth of her encircling arm and the rug which she had held cosily round his basket, whimpering pathetically from the side-car.

It was over at last. The mist thinned slowly as they emerged from the valley, and at length Billy pulled up to enable Herrick to resume her place. As she stepped into the side-car once more, there came to their ears the regular clop-clop of a horse's hoofs, sounding eerie and mysterious through the swathing fog behind them, and menacingly close.

"Good God! They've overtaken us!" exclaimed Billy hoarsely. He bent over his handlebars and the motor-bike shot forward.

On they went through the dusk-enfolded countryside, trees and hedges and an occasional slumbering cottage slipping past like sombre shadows as they sped along beneath a faintly starlit sky. Came a steep ascent, followed by what seemed an endless stretch of newly laid stones along the road and an enforced slackening of pace. Then a good surface once again, and at last they came to Greenwood, and, leaving the house on their right, took the road which led directly to Two Ways Cottage.

There were lights in the windows of the long, low house. Tenderly Herrick envisaged it, as they swept past, with its creeper-clad walls and genial red-tiled roof. She wondered what Mac would be doing at the moment. That he was at home, she felt sure, because an oblong of orange light from his study window glimmered friendly betwixt the trees. A little warm rush of feeling tingled through her veins. It was Mac's sister she and Billy were racing along to save, and they were actually helping Mac himself—sparing him the anxiety of ever knowing what a foolish risk she had run from the consequences of that foolishness.

For that the consequences would be very serious if Carol were discovered at Jem's cottage by her husband, Herrick did not doubt. However innocent he might believe his wife to be in his own heart, she knew instinctively that Sir Francis would deliberately put the worst construction on her folly, and henceforth make her pay for it to the uttermost limit.

At this juncture, the side-car began to leap and bound uncomfortably, Billy muttered an expletive and checked their speed, and she realised that they had reached the last stage of their journey and were bumping over the farm-track which led up to the door of the cottage. A minute later cycle and side-car came to a standstill, and he flung himself out of the saddle and came round to help her out.

"You go in," he said awkwardly. "They won't want me. I'll stay here and keep a look-out for Mortimer's dog-cart."

A sudden inspiration came to her.

"No, don't stay here," she said quickly. "Go round to the back entrance and we'll get away by the other road. If we drive back the same way we came we shall inevitably meet Sir Francis."

"Right you are." And as she lifted the old-fashioned knocker on the door, he started propelling the machine slowly across a jungle of rough scrubby grass and bracken which lay to one side of the cottage, intercepting the two roads it adjoined.

Receiving no reply to her first rap, Herrick lifted the knocker again, at the same time trying the handle of the door. It yielded beneath her fingers and she stumbled into the little hall and stood hesitating just inside the threshold. The murmur of voices, a man's and a woman's, came from a room on her left. Evidently no one had heard her knocking at the door, not even Mrs. Muffet.

Time was passing. Some premonition of danger quickened within her. She crossed swiftly to the room whence came the sound of voices and threw open the door.

"Jem! . . . Carol!" The words left her lips with impetuous urgency. "Sir Francis is on his way here!"

They were sitting by the fire, having coffee together, as she entered. On a white-clothed table lay the remains of supper, a very simple supper such as a man might have ordered for himself alone—cold meat and salad, some fruit and cheese. To one side of the table stood a half-empty Cona coffee machine.

Herrick took in the scene at a glance. Her mind seemed to be working with peculiar clarity, and in a sudden flash she divined the whole situation, guessed pretty accurately what had occurred. The absence of any answer to her knock, the simple supper, both premised that Mrs. Muffet must be out. . . . While Carol, driven by her longing to see Jem once again before he went away, had come to the cottage un-invited, unexpected. And Jem had let her stay—snatched at a few last hours together. What man who loved as he did would have acted otherwise—sent her wisely and sensibly home?

"Sir Francis is on his way here!"

At the sound of Herrick's voice, sharp with anxiety, Jem and Carol both sprang to their feet.

"Francis—coming here!"

The words stammered from Carol's lips. Her face went white and she looked round the room with terri-fied, hunted eyes like some trapped wild thing seeking for escape. Jem slipped a hasty arm round her shoulders or she would have fallen.

"Is this true, Herrick?" he asked quickly. "He was away from home—not coming back till to-morrow, Carol said."

"I know—I know," answered Herrick. "But listen!" And in a few hurried words she told him of Billy's discovery and all that had occurred.

"So Carol must go home at once," she wound up. "Sir Francis mustn't find her here."

"But how can I go?" Carol demanded shrilly. "Jem

was going to drive me home later. But his pony isn't even harnessed yet——" She broke off, her mouth working painfully.

Jem's face wore the stunned, desperate expression of a man who knows himself weaponless, utterly helpless to shield the woman he loves from approaching danger.

"You can't stay here," said Herrick imperatively to Carol. "You must go back with Billy." As she spoke she began tearing off the thick motoring coat she had been wearing. "Quick! He's waiting round at the back door."

"But what about you?" protested Carol distractedly. "We can't both ride in the side-car."

"I'll stay here—Jem can take me back afterwards. But you must go at once."

"Oh, I can't—I can't do that——"

Herrick turned urgently to Beresford, thrusting her coat into his hands.

"Make her go, Jem!" she implored. "For God's sake, make her go at once!"

He nodded and began helping Carol into the heavy motor-coat. She yielded passively, like someone moving in a dream.

"You must go, dear," he said firmly and steadily. "It's the one possible chance."

"And hurry—hurry!" urged Herrick. She felt as though she could scream with the tension. To her strained senses the beat of her own pulses sounded like the beat of horses' hoofs—relentless, pursuing hoofs.

She cast a swift glance round the room and uttered an exclamation of dismay. Carol's own light walking-coat and hat and gloves lay on a chair. Snatching them up, she bundled them into Jem's arms.

"Quick—oh, do be quick!" she entreated.

A moment later they were all three outside, where the engine of the motor-bike was throbbing like a live thing panting to be gone. Herrick exchanged a few swift, incisive words with Billy and picked up the basket which contained the puppy, holding it while Jem lifted Carol bodily into the side-car, then thrusting it hastily on to her lap.

"Don't worry, either of you," said Billy's boyish voice imperturbably. "I'll get her safely home. The kitchenmaid was wrong. Carol was dining with Mim at Windycroft—and don't any of you forget it."

The machine moved forward, lurching over the uneven road, and, as it disappeared into the darkness, Jem hurried off into his stable-yard and ordered Joe Westcott to harness and put in the pony as quickly as possible. Then he and Herrick turned back into the cottage together.

CHAPTER XXVI

THE UNEXPECTED HAPPENS

I CAN'T ever thank you enough. You've been an absolute brick, Herrick."

Jem's voice was not quite steady as, back once more in the little living-room of the cottage, he and Herrick faced each other rather breathlessly.

"And you've been—a trifle foolish, you and Carol," she answered, though there was an indulgent smile in her eyes. "Whatever made you do it—run such a risk?"

"We'd no idea that there *was* any risk," he said. "Otherwise, I should have taken her straight back to Mortlake the moment she arrived. You see, Mortimer wasn't expected home for two days or more, so it really seemed perfectly safe. . . . We've not had a moment alone together for weeks—he's seen to that. And—well, we probably shan't see each other again for as many years. . . ."

He broke off. His face was haggard, and she could guess what the decision to leave St. Heriot—leave England—had cost him.

"We're trying to run straight," he added simply.

Impulsively she held out her hand to him, and he gripped it closely.

"I know," she said, her voice glowing. "It's—it's splendid of you."

His mouth twisted wryly.

"It's a 'splendidness' I'd not be guilty of but for one thing." She looked her question and he continued: "I expect you know. Carol's told me at last . . . the reason why nothing will induce her to leave Mortimer, the bargain she made with him. Otherwise——"

"Otherwise?"

"Why, I'd think it right, not wrong, to take her away from him. There's no sanctity in a marriage such as theirs. God never joined Francis Mortimer and Carol together."

"No," assented Herrick. "She's paying for the—mistakes her father made. I wonder why we all have to pay so—so terribly for what other people do?"

Jem smiled rather sadly.

"Because life's a game of consequences, I suppose—the most serious game of consequences in the world, only we none of us ever realise it until it's too late."

She drew her hand out of his, all at once recollecting that, while they talked, time was flying.

"There'll be some further 'consequences' if I don't go home soon," she said. "Do you think your man's got the pony-trap ready for us yet?"

Jem came back to the necessities of the moment with a start. Thanks to a relieved sense of accomplishment, of safety achieved for Carol, both he and Herrick had been waiting without undue impatience whilst his pony was harnessed in readiness for him to drive her back to Windycraft. And while they waited the conversation had led them into sudden depths. Now, once more, the question of time came sharply uppermost.

"I'll go and hurry him up," said Jem. "Though,

after all we've actually only been waiting a very few minutes," he added reassuringly.

He disappeared, to return again with a slight cloud of anxiety on his face.

"These country bumpkins are the limit!" he exclaimed irritably. "There's Joe been all this time hunting for fresh candles for the carriage lamps. 'Couldn't think where he'd put them,' the careless fool! And now he's broken a bit of the harness and is patching it up with a string. I'm going back to help put the cob in— we really can't lose any more time. I'll come and tell you the minute we're ready."

He disappeared once more, and, left alone, Herrick for the first time began to feel some concern on her own behalf. Carol was safe—that was the principal thing. But she had no wish herself to be discovered by Sir Francis at the cottage, and she walked up and down the room restlessly, too impatient to sit still. She was amazed when, after what seemed an eternity of time, she looked at the clock to find that barely two minutes had elapsed since Jem had left her in order to hasten the progress of matters in the stable.

Another sixty seconds crawled by, and she wandered out into the hall and so to the back door, whence she could glimpse a light moving hither and thither across the stable-yard to her left. She discerned Jem pulling the pony-trap out through the doorway of the shed where it was kept, and Joe Westcott leading the pony with one hand and swinging a lantern in the other. The next moment, there came a clash of breaking glass and the lantern had slipped from his heedless grasp and fallen clattering on to the cobbles that paved the yard. Followed a shout as the pony reared suddenly jerking its bridle out of the man's hand, then the clattering of hoofs as it galloped past Herrick and headed down the road, Joe in futile pursuit.

An angry ejaculation broke from Beresford, and he came running across the yard, swearing volubly at the man's carelessness.

"What are we to do now?" asked Herrick, calm with the stoical calmness of despair.

"Wait. That's all we can do," he answered grimly. "But don't worry," he went on, perceiving that her face had grown rather white. "The cob won't run far. He was only startled. He'll come trotting back into the stable-yard in a minute. But it's too cold for you out here; come into the sitting-room again."

He shepherded her back once more and proceeded to poke up the dying fire. And then, just as it leapt into new life, came a sharp, imperative rat-tat at the front door. Followed immediately the sound of its opening, then hasty steps across the hall, and in the same instant Sir Francis's tall, lean figure appeared in the open doorway of the room. Behind him loomed another figure, and Herrick, petrified with dismay, found herself staring with horror-stricken eyes at Mac Kenyon. He met her gaze, and his expression became all at once hard and impenetrable.

Mortimer looked round the room with swift, suspicious eyes, rather as though he expected to discover Carol hiding behind a chair or sofa. Then his glance fastened on Jem's face.

"Where is my wife?" he snapped, and Herrick was

disagreeably reminded of the motion of a venomous snake darting its head forward to strike.

Jem rose to the occasion.

"How should I know?" he said coolly. "At home, presumably."

"I don't believe it," retorted Sir Francis, his eyes narrowing malignantly. "I'm not to be bluffed as easily as that. I happen to know for a fact that she came here. Where is she now?"

"I'm afraid I can give you no information as to where she is," returned Beresford. "She's certainly not here."

"Do you expect me to take your bare word for that?" Sir Francis laughed scornfully. "Well, I don't." He made a sudden lunge at the curtains which had been drawn across the windows, and dragged them apart. Jem's fists clenched.

"Look here," he began in a dangerous voice. "She's not behind the curtains, and I tell you she's not in this house. Leave the place alone!"

At this juncture, Herrick, who had been standing in stunned and stricken silence, stepped impulsively forward.

"It's perfectly true, Sir Francis," she said. "Carol isn't here."

Mortimer wheeled round on her, unveiled dislike in his glance.

"And what are *you* doing here, pray?" he asked in soft, oily tones. "My friend Kenyon will be interested to know that, I'm sure."

It was as though, baulked of the cruel triumph he

had hoped to gain over his wife, he must needs sink his poisonous fangs into whatever other victim presented itself. For an imperceptible fraction of time Herrick hesitated, her eyes tragically seeking Mac's for any sign of understanding. But there was none. It seemed as though he deliberately avoided looking at her, and his face remained hard and inflexible, rigid as though hewn out of granite. Then, realising that if Carol were to be saved, there must be no vacillating on either her own part or on Jem's, she answered Sir Francis's question.

"I should think that that's self-evident," she said quietly, and pointed to the table with its remains of a supper laid for two.

Mortimer's gimlet glance raked the table avidly, then a slow, malicious smile twisted his long, loose lips.

"O-ho! I see. A little *tête-à-tête* supper. Very nice— *ve*-ry nice indeed. Eh, Kenyon?"

Still Kenyon did not look in Herrick's direction. Instead, his eyes, a frozen steely grey, rested first on Jem's face, then on that of Sir Francis himself.

"At least," he said coolly, "Miss Waylen's presence, alone here, will have convinced you that you were misinformed about my sister's movements, Mortimer. I never supposed that you would find her at Two Ways Cottage. You dragged me here, as I expected, on a false errand."

Sir Francis smoothed his chin with two bony fingers.

"But not an altogether fruitless one," he submitted, with a sneer. "You've increased your knowledge somewhat, haven't you?" He paused, then added contemplatively: "Mr. Beresford seems to be a man of catholic tastes."

The two-edged thrust went home. A positive fury of wrath woke in Mac's eyes and he made a sudden savage gesture—a gesture checked almost instantaneously by an iron will. For the moment he conveyed a curious suggestion of arrested movement.

But Jem made no effort to control his anger. Sir Francis's bitter gibe found his nerves raw-edged with strain. His arm shot out and his strong fingers gripped the older man by the collar, shaking him as a terrier shakes a rat.

"It's only your age which saves you from the thrashing you deserve, you swine!" he said hoarsely. "But you'll get out of my house—and get out quick!"

For once in his life Sir Francis had no choice but to obey. The impulse of the muscular arm propelling him was a force he could not reckon with, and Jem ran him swiftly out of the room, across the hall, and almost flung him through the open doorway into the arms of Humphreys, who stood waiting outside with the dog-cart. Then, closing the house-door, he leaned against it for a little space, breathing heavily, trying to get himself in hand again. Finally, he came slowly back into the sitting-room. As he entered, doggedly prepared to meet whatever was the next outcome of this night's doings, Mac strode past him, pausing only to say cuttingly:

"Doubtless you'll see Herrick to her home—when she wishes it."

Jem swung round.

"Damn it! Come back, Kenyon!" he called sharply.

But Mac had already reached the door and as he made a movement to follow him Herrick sprang forward and caught him by the arm.

"No, let him go!" she said imperiously. Her face was ash-white, her eyes brilliant. "Let him go. Mac and I have finished with each other."

CHAPTER XXVII

A QUESTION OF LOYALTY

"I HAVE no explanation to offer." Herrick spoke
very quietly, her words dropping into the silence
with the finality of pebbles into a pool.

It was the day after their unexpected encounter at
Two Ways Cottage, and she and Mac were standing
facing one another in her little sitting-room at Windycroft—the room in which they had once come to a
rather wonderful comprehension of each other's love.
And now it looked very much as if that same room
would see the snapping asunder of every link which
bound them together.

"But there must be an explanation." Mac's manner implied a kind of dogged patience, a stubborn intention to get to the root of things. "And I'm entitled
to demand it."

She shrugged her shoulders.

"Well, if it comes to a matter of explanation:
What were *you* doing at Jem's cottage?" she countered.
"Did you come to spy on me?"

Her eyes blazed.

"You know very well I did not," he returned, in a
voice of intense anger. "I had no idea, when I came
with Mortimer, that I should find—you—there."

"Then whom did you expect to find? Carol? Were

you helping him to spy on her?" she demanded recklessly.

With an obvious effort he controlled himself.

"No," he said deliberately. "I went with Mortimer
for my own reasons—to be on hand in case she had
really been foolish enough to go there."

"What made you think she might have gone?" asked
Herrick, with curiosity. All along she had been puzzled to understand how Mac came to be at the cottage
in Sir Francis's company.

His face darkened. He could recall every word of
the brief interview which had taken place betwixt his
brother-in-law and himself the previous evening, when
the former had called at Greenwood on his way from
the station.

"My wife's here, isn't she?" Mortimer had asked
with surface amiability. "I thought I'd look in as I
was passing to see if she was ready to go home. She
might drive back with me."

And Mac, naturally enough, had replied that Carol
was not there. Instantly a look of animal triumph had
leapt into Sir Francis's eyes. That was the answer he
had expected.

"Not? Then I shall know where to find her—that
saintly sister of yours! She'll be with Beresford—at his
cottage."

"You lie!" The denial had sprung furiously from
Mac's lips.

"So I lie, do I?" Once more Sir Francis was his
usual suave self. "Then, if you feel so certain of her
innocence, come with me—and find out for yourself.
Or are you afraid?"

"Certainly I'll come with you." And he had gone, hoping that if Carol had actually been guilty of such madness his presence might help to minimise the consequences, restrain to some extent her husband's fury.

In a few curt words he answered Herrick's question, making quite clear the circumstances which had brought him to the cottage.

"It was a pity you came," she commented listlessly.

She felt curiously detached. She knew, somehow, that what she had said to Jem was the truth—she and Mac had finished with each other. This was the end. He would never forgive her for going, as he thought, to supper at Jem's cottage—anger and jealousy and bitter distrust fought together within him, and only by telling him the whole truth of yesterday's happenings could she ever clear herself in his eyes.

And she had no intention of doing that. Whatever happened, the fact that Carol was at Two Ways Cottage last night must be kept secret. In the circumstances, her going there, if it were ever known, would lay her open to an unbearable suspicion—a suspicion to which her hasty flight, at which they had all connived, only added colour. Mac would have no forgiveness for his sister, if the truth were revealed, and Sir Francis would revenge himself upon her by various methods of his own which would make her life insupportable.

No, there was no alternative but silence. Carol must be kept out of it, whatever the consequences. Herrick realised that. And she realised, too, that by one of the curious ironies of fate, the very fact of an ensuing break between herself and Mac would be the strongest plank in support of Carol's innocence. It would absolutely convince Sir Francis that she, and not his wife, had been Jem's guest yesterday evening. But above and beyond all else, Herrick's unswerving sense of loyalty closed her lips utterly and forever. You cannot go to a friend's rescue, pull her out of dangerous quicksands, and then, when you find that helping her has involved you in unlooked-for difficulties, thrust her back into the quicksands and save yourself at her expense.

" 'It was a pity I came'!" Mac repeated her words with bitterness. "Yes, it was a pity—a thousand pities —if I was to keep my belief and trust in you."

"Haven't you lost it—rather easily?"

"Easily! Good God! Do you call it 'easily,' when a man finds the woman he loves in another man's house —supping with him—alone?"

"You needn't have jumped immediately to the worst conclusion."

"The least conclusion I can draw is that you like him—that he means something in your life. More, presumably, than I do—since you consider him first."

"Why should you think that?" asked Herrick quietly, lifting grave eyes to his. "You know who is the only woman that counts in Jem's life."

"Perhaps," returned Mac harshly, "perhaps I've been misled. Some men have room for more than one woman in their lives."

She shrank suddenly away from him. This was indeed the end to all things between them. It was incredible to her that Mac should think what he evidently did think. She could not know of the little happenings which throughout the long hours of the night had been tormenting his memory, adding substance to the suspicion which her presence in Jem's cottage had aroused. Happenings slight enough in themselves, but which, considered in conjunction with the astounding discovery of last evening, had all at once taken on a disproportionate importance—a word here or there, indicative of the sympathetic understanding which existed between herself and Jem, a laughing reference to some joke they had shared together, an exchange of glances. Above all, Jem's horror on the occasion when her horse had bolted with her. Trifles, all of them, just the small-change of good comradeship, yet now distorted in Mac's mind into the semblance of essentials, connoting a more far-reaching sentiment.

"Some men have room for more than one woman in their lives." Mac's bitter speech cut into Herrick's consciousness like a knife, and she flung back at him an equal bitterness:

"You, apparently, have no room for even one woman in yours."

"Not for a woman of your sort, who will play with one or two—given the opportunity, perhaps with three or four men at the same time," he answered implacably. "I ask one thing from the woman I love—loyalty. And that you evidently couldn't give me."

Her lips curled a little.

"And there's no forgiveness of sins with you, any more than there is with any other man. . . . Oh, Mac!" with a sudden broken, tortured note in her voice. "You spoke very differently the other day in the garden at Greenwood."

"I was speaking of something different—of the weaknesses and temptations which come to us all in differing degrees. But loyalty, to me, means something essential. It's the core of the soul, and if the core is rotten, it's the end of everything. It must be."

He spoke inflexibly, and suddenly out of the past something leapt at her, something he had once said in the early stages of their friendship, when she was only gradually and imperceptibly coming to know him: *"Disloyalty—a double game—is the only thing I can never forgive."* And he thought her guilty of the one sin he counted unforgivable.

Her hands went out to him involuntarily.

"Then—then it's all over between us, Mac?" Her voice shook a little. The pride which had upheld her was weakening beneath the fierce pain of realisation.

He looked at her, and something like supplication pierced through the cool contempt which had veiled all other emotion.

"An explanation . . . I've asked you . . . is there no explanation?" he said, his voice tense.

Her hands dropped to her sides.

"None," she answered. The brief monosyllable faded desolately into the silence, and for a moment the man and woman stood staring haggardly into each other's eyes, the masks of pride and indifference wrenched suddenly from their faces.

"So—so you don't love me any more," she said at last, in a curious little cracked voice.

His hands clenched slowly. It seemed as if only some tremendous effort of will kept him where he stood, a pace away from her.

"God! Not love you!" he said under his breath. The inner agony of disillusion and farewell broke through the restraint he had been forcing on himself and he went on hoarsely: "Not love you? Do you think I shall ever cease to love you? Life would be a very easy thing if a man could stop caring when he chooses! . . . But he can't. I can't. I shall love you as long as I live. But I won't marry you."

"And you'd never—forgive me?" she asked very low. "You couldn't, I suppose?"

"I could forgive you. But, don't you see, I could never trust you again?"

"Yes, I see," she said tonelessly. "I see that."

For a moment he stood looking at her in silence, a kind of desperation in his eyes, his love and his bitter distrust of her battling one against the other. Then, still in silence, he turned to leave the room.

A stifled cry broke from her as his fingers closed round the handle of the door, and she made a half stumbling step towards him. But he did not look back. Quietly, inexorably, he opened the door and went out, shutting it behind him.

For a moment she remained standing just where he had left her, her gaze fastened on the blankness of that closed door. Outside, the birds were twittering in the budding trees. The sunlight streamed in happily through the window, making a pool of gold about her feet. The sunlight . . . which had always mocked her. . . . With a little choked-back sob she caught at the chimneypiece, and, leaning her arms against it, hid her face. . . .

CHAPTER XXVIII

"BY MUTUAL AGREEMENT"

I DON'T see how you can expect me to stand quietly
and watch you and Mac smash up your lives when
a word from me would put matters straight."

Thus Lady Bridget indignantly. Three days had
elapsed since the unlucky happenings at Two Ways
Cottage, and during that time she had made repeated
and futile efforts to persuade Herrick into enlightening
Mac as to the true circumstances.

"Mim, you're *on your honour* not to speak." It
was a rather shadowy-eyed and white-faced Herrick
who made answer. After all, you cannot with your
own hand destroy the entire fabric of your happiness
in life without paying for the proceeding in frayed
nerves and sleeplessness and an apathetic aversion
to meal-times. But although the last three days had
taken their physical toll of her, she was still in spirit
her own indomitable self.

"You wouldn't have been let into the secret at all,"
she went on, "but for Billy's brilliant idea that we
should all swear Carol had been dining here that night.
If we'd known Sir Francis was going to catch me alone
at the cottage," she added, with a wry smile, "there'd
have been no need for that scheme. And my being
found at Two Ways would have boshed it anyhow,

as even Sir Francis couldn't be expected to swallow the story that I was having supper with Jem while Carol dined with you!"

"Billy's idea was quite a good one," said Lady Bridget, a gleam of humour in her eyes. "And of course we'd all have stood for it, if it had been necessary, in order to get Carol out of a scrape. But I can't stand for your making a burnt-offering of yourself on her account."

"There's nothing else for it," returned Herrick wearily. "You know what it would mean for Carol if Sir Francis ever discovered she'd been to the cottage . . . I'll be quite honest with you, Mim. I didn't *intend* to 'make a burnt-offering' of myself in the first instance. It just happened. I—somehow I thought Mac would understand, guess that we were shielding Carol," she finished wistfully.

"A man who is jealous—or a woman, either, for that matter—never 'understands,'" said Lady Bridget. "Jealousy is the most blinding thing in the world."

"I suppose it is. But I never dreamed that Mac would distrust me. It—it was horrible of him!" she added, with a sudden flare of passion. "If he hadn't," she went on, dropping back once more into the kind of wistful apathy of her former attitude, "if he had only asked me, then and there, what I was doing at the cottage—where Carol was—it would have been so easy to tell him all about it. Instead of that, he just assumed—at once—that I wasn't playing straight by him."

"Let me tell him that you were," begged Mim.

"You—you'd forgive him for distrusting you, wouldn't you?"

Herrick reflected. Then a faint, rather sad little smile curved her lips.

"Would I?" she said slowly. "Yes, I suppose I would—in time. Because I love him. And I don't think you can help forgiving people you love." She was silent a moment, then went on: "You see, Mim, I think, in a way, all this—all that's happened—is just part of my inheritance. If—if I hadn't told Mac that I'd got bad blood in my veins, he might not have suspected me so easily. I don't mean that he said to himself in so many words: 'One of her parents was a rotter, so she's probably the same.' But that unconsciously it affected him—made him more ready to think the worst. I'm sometimes even afraid, myself, of the taint in my blood—of doing something thoroughly rotten one day."

"Don't be absurd, dear child." Lady Bridget spoke hastily. "You think too much about poor Quin's misdoings. Anyway"—with a very tender smile—"no matter what happened in the past, it's wiped out now. No woman who could do the plucky and splendid thing you've done need ever be afraid of her own nature. I've no belief in heredity to that extent."

Herrick flushed a little shyly.

"Thank you, Mim darling. But really, I couldn't have done anything else. And you won't say anything to Mac? You'll promise? Because I couldn't bear to take my happiness at that price—making Carol pay for it. I should feel so—so mean about it that it wouldn't even *be* happiness. Besides, I don't think I could forgive Mac quite yet. He must trust me without that. So you'll promise?"

"Very well," agreed Lady Bridget reluctantly. "I promise."

Herrick had an almost equally hard fight to ensure Billy's silence. He could hardly be restrained from rushing over to Greenwood and giving Mac a full, true, and particular account of the proceedings at Two Ways Cottage.

"It's ridiculous of you," he protested hotly, when Herrick insisted upon his secrecy. "And I think Jem's a dirty sweep to let any woman bear the whole brunt of the thing like this."

She smiled.

"Jem, my dear, isn't a 'dirty sweep' at all. He's just natural man. He's got two women to consider in the matter, and of course he considers the woman he's in love with first, and last, and all the time. He'd be a sweep if he didn't. Supposing it was a case of Barbara or me, what would *you* do? Which of us would you try to keep out of the mess?"

Billy grinned unwillingly.

"You've got me there. But still, why don't *you* tell Mac—privately? There's no reason why that old swine of a Mortimer need ever know."

"I don't tell Mac for several reasons," she answered coolly. "One: That if he knew, he himself would be furious with Carol—for reasons you don't know of, Billy boy. Two: That if Sir Francis ever taunted him afterwards with my having been at Jem's cottage, Mac would simply shove the truth down his throat—if he knew it—and then Carol would have to pay the piper. And three: If Mac can't trust me without you and Mim rushing to tell him that he's no reason to *dis*trust me, then I don't think his trust is worth having. So that's that."

"You women are queer creatures," commented Billy, regarding her with puzzled green eyes.

"We are," she agreed with promptitude. "And it would take a good deal more than you to understand us. I don't think," she added rather ruefully, "that we even understand ourselves."

So she had her own way and securely sealed the mouths of the only two people who could have cleared her in Mac's eyes. As far as Carol was concerned, she was left in complete ignorance of the fact that her husband had discovered Herrick at the cottage. She did not see Jem again before he shut up his home and departed, and when he came to say good-bye to his friends at Windycroft, Herrick cautioned him, if he should write to her, to say nothing about the matter.

"Don't ever let Carol know that Sir Francis found me at your cottage," she said. "It would only worry her. And we may as well save her from any worries that we can."

"But Mortimer will probably tell her himself," replied Jem.

She smiled and shook her head.

"I think not. You don't suppose he's going to give himself away to her as having spied upon her in vain, do you? That would be presenting her with too much of a whip-hand. No, I think Sir Francis will keep very quiet on the subject of what happened the other night. He didn't make exactly a triumphant exit, did he?"

A brief, reminiscent smile crossed Jem's face. Then it clouded over again.

"I haven't seen Mac since," he said rather wistfully. "He's gone down to Dartmoor, I hear. Is it all right between you two?"

And because the man beside her was going away into the desert of loneliness in distant lands, carrying a heavy enough burden with him and carrying it bravely, Herrick would not add one tiniest atom to that burden. So she looked him tranquilly in the eyes and answered quietly:

"Quite all right, Jem." A lie which the Recording Angel surely entered on the credit and not the debit side of her account.

Beresford accepted it quite simply.

"And you'll be her pal?" he continued urgently, his thoughts really only concentrated on the one woman in his world. "Help her as much as you can when I'm gone, Herrick?"

"Always," she answered steadfastly.

So Jem went his way into the wilderness and his place in the life of St. Heriot knew him no more.

Carol came over to Windycroft the day following his departure. She had been kept practically a prisoner until then by the sudden illness of her husband. He had returned home from Two Ways Cottage a sick man. The intense inner excitement he had undergone that night, owing to his malignant desire to entrap his wife in suspicious circumstances, followed by his bitter disappointment at his non-success, had tried a heart already weakened by constant drug-taking. And the forthright treatment he had suffered at Beresford's hands had shaken him badly. He had reached Mortlake Hall almost speechless, gasping for breath, and Humphreys and the butler had together lifted him out of the dog-cart and carried him up to bed. Carol, horrified by his appearance, had hurriedly summoned the doctor, and in perfect good faith had answered in the negative the latter's question as to whether Sir Francis had suffered a shock of any kind. The doctor was frankly puzzled, and accordingly Humphreys was interrogated, to see if he could throw any light upon his master's condition. Had there been an accident on the return journey from the station? Or any trouble with the horse which might have alarmed Sir Francis?

"Not as I knows of," had been the surly answer. The only thing to be commended in Humphreys' unbalanced make-up was his fixed idea of loyalty to his employer. Sir Francis had gasped out, as they quitted Two Ways Cottage: "You know nothing of all this, remember." And Humphreys doggedly remembered that he knew nothing and remained supremely uncommunicative.

The doctor, Lincoln by name, had only been established at St. Heriot about a year, and how much or how little knowledge he possessed of the relations existing between Mortimer and his wife it would have been difficult to say. He was a lean, rather cynical-looking young man, of few words and no graciousness of manner, and, although he was acknowledged to be clever at his job, he was not personally popular in the neighbourhood—except amongst a few desperately poor patients who had good reason to know that the blunt, taciturn doctor could be amazingly kind and sympathetic on occasion.

However that might be, his manner to Carol was entirely non-committal when he informed her that her husband's health must be regarded as more or less precarious.

"I don't mean that there is any immediate danger," he added coolly. "He will most certainly recover from this attack. But his heart is not in a good condition. And"—he looked at her with sudden directness—"as you are aware, he drugs. I've told him frankly that if he doesn't wish to curtail his life he must give up drug-taking."

All of which Carol recounted to Herrick when at length she found herself free to go over to Windy-croft.

"We can none of us imagine what could have upset him that night," she said. "If"—with a faint smile—"he had discovered me at Jem's cottage, I can quite imagine his flying into such a violent rage that it might have brought on this attack. The only thing I can suppose is that the disappointment of *not* finding me there annoyed him almost as much. Only I can't very well tell the doctor that!"

Then, dismissing the subject of Sir Francis's illness, she came to the real object of her visit, which was to try to discover the true reason for the breaking-off of her brother's engagement. As Herrick felt convinced he would, Mac had remained absolutely silent concerning the fact that he had found her at Two Ways Cottage. All he had done was to write to his sister, from the lonely farmstead on Dartmoor whither he had betaken himself, informing her that his engagement had come to an end "by mutual agreement."

"I'm not going to pretend—it wouldn't be any use pretending to *you*, even if I wanted to," he had written, "that it hasn't been a bad knock, but it's better to have discovered that we're not suited to each other now rather than after marriage." And Carol, with the sure, unerring instinct which twinship seems to confer, knew perfectly well that the few brief lines hid an anguish of pain—pain which had driven him to seek the loneliness and silence of the Moor wherein to face and fight it down.

"Is it true that you've agreed together to break it off?" she demanded of Herrick. And Herrick had answered that it was quite true.

"We've found out that we neither of us want to marry the other—now," she said. And nothing that Carol could say or do would move her to further confidence.

"Some day," she hazarded, "we may be able to be friends again. And it's better to be good friends than bad lovers."

And with that Carol had to be content.

But as the days slipped by, Mim's keen eyes, closely watching the girl she so much loved—child of the man who still lived in her heart—could discern an increasing alteration in her. She was rarely outwardly depressed. At times, even, she seemed almost as gay and bright as she had been wont to be, but there was something superficial about her gaiety—like the lightly ruffled surface of a mountain tarn whose depths are still and dark with some tragic secret which they hold.

And when the news filtered through the village that Kenyon was shortly expected back at Greenwood, it seemed as though the strain became more than she could bear. There was a look of suspense in her eyes, a nervous sense of tension about her, as though she dreaded his coming, and at last Lady Bridget proposed that she and Billy and Herrick should all run up to town for a few days. She felt that a change, a definite break of some sort, before Herrick and Mac met again, would go far towards giving the girl back her poise. This waiting day by day for his return, wondering when it would take place, dreading the possibility of some sudden, unexpected meeting with him, was, as Mim mentally phrased it, "wearing her to fiddlestrings." She determined to take her away, and keep her away until Mac's return to St. Heriot was an accomplished fact. Meanwhile, all that London could offer her by way of distraction should be used to prevent her from brooding over the past.

"Spring always gives me that 'new frock' feeling very badly," Mim declared, therefore, one morning at breakfast. "What do you say to a few days in London, Herrick, and let us both have an orgy of new clothes? You and I and Billy could amuse ourselves quite well in town for a little while, I think."

Perhaps Herrick divined the kindly purpose which lay behind the innocently suggested plan. Be that as it may, she grasped at it eagerly. Here, at St. Heriot, there was too much time for remembering, too many places packed with sweet or bitter memories of Mac.

Fields and woods over which they had hunted together; leafy country lanes whither they had ridden homeward, side by side; her own little sitting-room where they had found love together—and lost it. And there was Jem's cottage, now blankly closed and shuttered—that, too, had held some of the most wonderful and some of the most terrible moments of her life. While that glimpse of the red roof at Greenwood, which you could catch as you drove by, once tinged with all the glamour and romance of the home that would one day be hers—hers and Mac's—now seemed only to mock her every time she passed it.

Here, at St. Heriot, with its long, tranquil country days, there was no means of thrusting the man she loved out of her mind, whereas in London she would be doing, not thinking. Amid the amusements and distractions of the big city she would be able, at least for a little space, to keep her thoughts at bay, to adjust herself to a new attitude towards life and love. And when they came home again, she would *know* that Mac was back once more at Greenwood—there would be no sickening tension of waiting and wondering which day might bring him. She would be prepared, ready for any chance meeting that might occur —armoured against the future.

So the trip to London was speedily decided upon, and, once there, Herrick found herself caught up and swept along in a whirl of gaiety which left her well nigh breathless, and so tired, when night came, that she slept out of sheer physical weariness. Mim and Billy between them seemed determined that every minute of the day should be filled, and their efforts, albeit from a totally different motive, were reinforced by those of Gair Severn.

He made his first appearance on the scene only two days after Herrick's arrival in town. As Lady Bridget remarked with rather rueful amusement to Billy: "He would! Gair has the instinct for turning up at the psychological moment for his own ends developed to a high state of proficiency. Or if his instinct happens to be off duty, then his luck steps in."

On this particular occasion he had come across Herrick at the Savoy one evening, whither Billy had taken her to dine and dance. He himself had been dining in the grill-room with a recently acquired acquaintance, and after dinner they had both strolled down into the foyer and had stood for a few minutes watching the dancers who thronged the floor below. All at once Gair espied Billy and Herrick fox-trotting together, and his involuntary exclamation of surprise drew an amused inquiry from the man with him.

"Just spotted some people I know," he explained, indicating Herrick and her partner. "I shall go down and pinch a few dances from young Rivington when this one's finished." And a characteristic gleam of Puckish amusement crossed his face at the thought of Billy's probable resentment of his intrusion.

The two men remained talking together until the dance was ended, then Severn bade the other goodnight and made his way to the table at which Billy and Herrick were sitting. There was a light of triumph in his eyes as he joined them, greeting them as though perfectly certain of his welcome, and in a few minutes he and Herrick were dancing together, while Billy was left to the doubtful enjoyment of a solitary cigarette. Gair was an exceptionally good dancer, and Herrick was far too fond of dancing for its own sake not to appreciate this to the full, so, forgetting her many disagreements with him in the past, she surrendered herself to the enjoyment of the smooth, rhythmic motion as they swept round the floor. For a few moments they danced in silence, and she was so absorbed in the sheer delight of their rapid movement that she almost started when at last he addressed her.

"I'd no idea you were in town," he said. "I shall have a bone to pick with Barbara for keeping me in ignorance. It was very bad staff work on her part," he added, laughing down at her.

"It was rather a sudden decision of ours—to come to London," she answered. "Mim and I were suddenly afflicted with the 'clothes' hunger. That's how it happened."

"And what did Kenyon say to your flying off like that? I shouldn't have allowed it, had I been in his shoes."

Herrick stiffened a little. But Severn was bound to hear ultimately of her broken engagement; he might as well know soon as late.

"My comings and goings don't concern Mac—any longer," she said.

She could feel his body jerk, sense the faintest pause in the rhythm of the dance. Then they moved smoothly on once more.

"What does that mean?" he asked composedly.

"It means that our engagement is broken off."

A look of something that resembled relief gleamed for an instant in his eyes, to be immediately masked by his customary expression of dare-devil assurance.

"Quarrelled, have you? It's just as well. It will"— smiling challengingly down at her—"save me the disagreeable business of intervening. I should have had to engineer a quarrel between you if you hadn't managed one for yourselves."

Herrick's head went up.

"Nothing *you* could have said would have influenced either of us," she replied contemptuously.

The dance was coming to an end, the music ceased, and for a moment she and Severn stood facing each other on the rapidly emptying floor.

"Wouldn't it?" he said softly, and there was a curious note in his lowered voice, a note of absolute conviction. "There you are vastly mistaken. You seem to forget what I once told you—that I never give up. Never."

She made no answer beyond a disdainful shrug of slim shoulders as she turned to leave the floor in the wake of the other dancers, and he glanced obliquely at her with a faint, enigmatic smile as he walked beside her.

But for once that arrogant note in his voice seemed to have fallen on deaf ears. If it had done nothing else, her break with Mac had at least freed her from Severn's domination. She had suffered so much that it seemed to her there was nothing further she could suffer. Gair could no longer come betwixt her and the man she loved—Mac's own decision had already set

them immeasurably apart, and there was no way in
which another man could widen the gulf between them.
Nothing could make any appreciable difference now.
There was neither good nor bad ahead of her—only
a long vista of drab monotony painted on a background of pain.

CHAPTER XXIX

CAROL INTERVENES

GOD bless you, my very dear. Whenever you feel lonely, try to remember that I'm still somewhere on this old planet, loving you all the time. And that I shall be waiting for you always—as long as life lasts, and after."

Carol folded up Jem's letter, written just before he sailed, and locked it carefully away. She did not know when she might receive another from him. He had told her that he would never risk writing to her direct from wherever he eventually pitched his camp, lest Sir Francis's cunning eyes should note the foreign stamp. If ever a letter came to her, it would come in a plain type-written envelope, as uninteresting and inconspicuous in appearance as a bill from a shop, and would be sent under cover to Mrs. Muffet, who would post it in England.

The letter brought its meed of comfort, for Carol had been feeling unbearably lonely the last few days. Not merely had she had to contend against the unutterable blank of Jem's absence—for, even though she did not see him very often, it had been something to know that he was only a mile or so distant at Two Ways Cottage—but the departure of Mac to Devonshire and of the Windycroft household to London had left her still more solitary. And her husband's illness had added to her burden. He was recovering now and had been allowed to come downstairs again, and Sir Francis in the rôle of convalescent was even more demanding and exigeant than usual. Moreover, he was in a peculiarly disagreeable mood—a mood which she found it difficult to understand. Frequently he shot at her a sharp, barbed speech containing a veiled innuendo which she could neither place nor refute, and sometimes, when he was supposedly reading, she was aware that from behind his book or paper he was covertly watching her beneath half-closed lids, his narrowed eyes sparkling with a kind of malignant triumph, as though he were in possession of some secret hold over her which he was not going to divulge until it suited him.

She had barely bestowed Jem's letter in a place of safety when a servant came to her room, bringing a message from Sir Francis to the effect that he was dressed and downstairs and would be glad if her ladyship would join him. She knew what that meant— an hour's reading aloud to him from the morning paper. Gathering up her other letters in her hand, she proceeded to obey the summons and found him waiting for her in his study.

"Good-morning, my dear." He implanted a long, deliberate kiss on her shrinking lips. "And how is my charming wife this morning? A trifle peeky-looking, surely." He held her away from him, his bony hands on her shoulders, and scrutinised her face unmercifully. "You must take more care of yourself, I think. At your age a woman shouldn't begin to lose her looks."

"Am I losing them?" she answered indifferently. She was so used to these suavely uttered taunts of his that they had long since ceased to hurt her. She only felt utterably weary in his company, as though in some way he sapped her of all vitality.

He let his hands fall slowly away from her, and she gave a little involuntary shrug of repugnance. She loathed his very touch.

"Crying for the moon is conducive to wrinkles," he said sententiously. "Never forget that the moon is out of reach—quite."

She made no answer but glanced towards the newspapers which lay neatly folded on the table.

"Do you want me to read to you?" she asked.

"All in good time, all in good time. I see you've had some correspondence this morning."

She looked down at the letters she was still holding in her hand.

"Yes," she replied evenly. "A note from Mac to say he is back at Greenwood, and a couple of bills."

"There is a fourth envelope there."

"From Herrick Waylen. They are staying in London for a few days longer." She answered like a child repeating a lesson.

Sir Francis nodded appreciatively.

"Lady Bridget is a wise woman. Best thing she could do to keep the girl out of the way for a bit after she'd made such a fool of that trusting brother of yours."

Carol flushed indignantly and opened her mouth to reply but Sir Francis went on smoothly.

"And rather a fool of you, too, my dear. You thought Beresford was your own particular property until that little hussy from Paris tripped you up and proved he was no more faithful to you than he need be."

For a moment she was almost too angry to speak. Then she whirled round, her habitual fear of him momentarily submerged in a gust of contempt.

"That is a lie," she said in a low, vehement voice. "And you know it. You can say what you like to me—I can't stop you. But you shall not take away the character of my friends."

Sir Francis eyed her with malicious enjoyment.

"I shouldn't think Miss Waylen has much—er—reputation left to take away—after her visit to Beresford's cottage," he said urbanely.

Carol shrank back, her eyes dilating. For a moment all the blood in her body seemed to rush to her heart, thudding violently there. Then it raced away again, leaving her suddenly weak and nerveless. She felt as though her knees were going to give way beneath her.

" 'Her visit to Beresford's cottage?' " she repeated with an effort. "I don't understand you."

"No?" Sir Francis appeared to be inwardly amused. "Do you mean to say she never confided in you? Well, well, so much for women's friendship! Tch! Tch!" He clicked his tongue against his teeth as though shocked and incredulous.

"Confided in me?" Again Carol repeated his words. It flashed across the back of her mind that there was something parrot-like about this dreadful repetition. "What was there to confide?"

"The reason why her engagement was broken off, of course. I suppose you'll pretend not to know that, either?"

"I don't know it," she answered, doggedly.

"Dear me! There seems to have been a positive conspiracy to keep you in the dark," he commented with mock amazement. He strolled across the room and looked negligently out of the window as though, as far as he was concerned, the subject were ended. Carol followed him.

"To keep me in the dark about what?"

He looked round at her, his eyes snapping venomously beneath their pouched lids, and his answer flashed out like a swiftly drawn rapier.

"About what happened at Two Ways Cottage one night."

She caught her breath. A dreadful foreboding filled her mind. What did he know? How much? And what did he mean when he spoke of Herrick's visit to the cottage? At all hazards she must find out—make sure.

"Tell me—what happened," she said in a stifled voice.

He told her with the satisfaction of one enjoying a particularly luscious morsel—in words that did not bear repeating, damning Herrick utterly and omitting to describe his own involuntary exit from the cottage.

"That's why your brother broke off his engagement," he concluded. "Any man would do the same in similar circumstances."

"Did he tell you that was why?"

"No, he did not. Your brother and I are not precisely on——what shall I say?——confidential terms. But now you know what occurred"——he regarded her derisively——"can you think of any other reason?"

She could not. The whole thing was as clear as daylight to her now. It was as though scales had dropped from her eyes and all that had been puzzling and obscure had suddenly become transparently plain and intelligible. Herrick had saved her, and in saving her lost everything herself.

A wave of indescribable emotion surged through her. The pluck and self-sacrificing loyalty of it! She felt that nothing in the world was too great to lay upon the altar of such a friendship, and in that moment Carol, baited and badgered as she had been into a nervous, shrinking woman, lost all fear and rose to the heights that were within her. Quietly, and with a curious aloof dignity, she turned to her husband.

"You are quite mistaken," she said. "And Mac, too, is mistaken. Herrick did not come to the cottage that night on her own account. *I* was there." She lifted her head and faced Sir Francis composedly. "I went there to say good-bye to Jem, and Herrick only came to warn me that you were following me——that"——with sudden scorn——"you hoped to catch me there."

"Ah-h!" An ejaculation of triumph broke from Sir Francis. "So at last I've forced you into confessing the truth. I thought I should——I thought I should!" He chuckled, and there was something indescribably horrible and macabre about the sound. It was like the bestial chuckling of a madman. Carol shuddered, but forced herself into speech.

"Then you knew I had been there—all the time?"
He nodded complacently.

"I was quite sure of it. Humphreys watched you go.
And the next morning—long before your friend Beresford was awake—he found the tyre-marks of young
Rivington's motor-cycle and side-car outside the cottage. We left nothing to chance, Humphreys and I."

Carol flung him a glance of contempt.

"I suppose you planned it all—pretended you were
going to stay away longer than you did on purpose."

"I thought, if you felt yourself quite free of my
supervision, that you'd probably do something foolish
—commit yourself in some way."

"And so you set Humphreys on to spy on me?"

Again Sir Francis nodded with a self-satisfied smile.

"Humphreys is an invaluable servant," he remarked
placidly.

"Invaluable, I should think," retorted Carol. "The
only thing I can't understand is why you've let matters
go on as they were for so long—allowing Herrick to
take the blame. It can have been no particular satisfaction to you that her engagement was broken off."

"There you are greatly mistaken. It was a very
particular satisfaction to me. Miss Waylen had exceeded her privileges. She chose to interfere in my
private and personal concerns, and I permit no one to
do that with impunity. She deserved to be punished—
and she got her deserts."

Carol regarded him with frank disgust. With every
word he uttered the man was revealing the vileness of
his nature. She felt as though she had been exploring

some fetid, stagnant pool which hid unnamable corruption beneath the slimy smoothness of its surface.

"I suppose," she said slowly, "that as long as you hurt somebody, revenged yourself on someone, it didn't matter much to you who suffered."

"You underrate my abilities," he replied. "There is such a thing as killing two birds with one stone. Miss Waylen has had her lesson, I trust, and will, in future, probably refrain from interfering in my affairs. As for you"——he smiled sardonically——"I knew I could snap the trap-door down on you whenever I chose. You'd never let that precious brother of yours suffer if you could help it—so you were bound to give yourself away sooner or later."

"You're right. Mac shall not suffer one instant longer." Carol's blue eyes were wide-open, ablaze with honest anger, and she faced her husband unafraid. "I'm going—now at once—to tell him the truth. To clear Herrick. And then you can do what you choose with me. Divorce me, if you like—I wish to God you would!"

Sir Francis's eyes flickered evilly a moment. Then:

"I'm sure you do, my dear," he said blandly. "But I'm not such a fool. There are other—and more amusing—ways of punishing unfaithful wives."

Despite her new-found courage, she shuddered a little at the horrible menace in his voice. Then across her troubled consciousness flashed a sentence from Jem's letter: "Remember I'm still somewhere on this old planet, loving you all the time." It was like the clasp of a friendly hand—clean, and true, and loyal in the midst of this welter of malice and deceit and cruelty. She met the malevolence of her husband's glance unwaveringly.

"I have never been unfaithful to you," she said levelly. "And you know it as well as I do. Nor need you try to frighten me. I don't think I shall ever be afraid of you again."

She turned and left the room, calmly and deliberately, and for some reason, obscure even to himself, Sir Francis made no effort to prevent her. Perhaps sheer amazement held him motionless and silent. Or perhaps it was the cool courage of her—courage, which is always the most baffling weapon to apply to a bully.

Half an hour later found her at Greenwood, pouring out her story brokenly and a trifle incoherently to Mac—for it was a far more difficult task to confess the truth to him, who had so suffered through his ignorance of it, and whom she loved so much, than it had been to fling it defiantly at her husband. But she got it out at last, somehow, in a tumble of disjointed words and phrases, and knew from Mac's face, from the sudden, still look on it, that he had understood, grasped the whole significance of the happenings at Two Ways Cottage.

"Do say you forgive me, Mac," she pleaded distractedly, terrified by that strangely withdrawn expression which he wore.

And at that the mask-like stillness of his face broke up and a faint smile curved his mouth.

"There's not a great deal to forgive you for," he said gently. "You couldn't know what happened after you left the cottage."

"I thought you'd be so angry at my going there at all," she faltered, half incredulous at the grave kindliness with which he had accepted her confession. "I was afraid you'd think it—disloyal."

A curious expression came into his eyes.

"Perhaps I should have been angry—once," he replied slowly. "But I'm beginning to learn that sometimes one loyalty conflicts with another."

For a while they talked together quietly, but she did not stay very long with him. Instinctively she divined his need to be alone. She ventured only one question as regards the future.

"And Herrick? You'll write to her, Mac?"

"Yes," he answered briefly. "I shall write."

And so it came about that the next morning a letter in a familiar handwriting lay on Herrick's plate at breakfast time. She felt her heart give a jerk, was conscious of the swiftly veiled glances of Mim and Billy—of all the eagerness and sympathy hidden behind the veil. Silently she slipped the letter into her pocket. Not even under those kind eyes could she bear to read it—risk meeting its contents. Later, alone in her room at the hotel, she opened it, and a little smothered cry broke from her as her eyes flew along the beloved characters. Somehow, even the way the loved one crosses his T's has a particular charm of its own.

"Herrick, can you ever forgive me?" ran the letter, its very brevity vibrating against her heart. "Carol has told me all about that night at Two Ways Cottage. I can never forgive myself."

For all her pride, she did not find it difficult to forgive him. As she had told Mim, you can't help forgiving people that you love. And during the interminable days which had elapsed since she and Mac had parted, she had had bitter times to think, to realise how terribly easy it is for either man or woman to destroy their whole life's happiness on an ungoverned impulse, and to learn of what little value pride is against love. She had recognised, too, that if the cases had been reversed, she might equally have doubted Mac. It is so difficult to know at what angle a certain circumstance may strike you until you are actually confronted with it.

A note, even briefer than Kenyon's own, went on its way to Greenwood.

"We return the day after to-morrow. Come and see me.

HERRICK."

CHAPTER XXX

THE MILLS OF GOD

HERRICK woke the following morning to a thrill of eager anticipation. To-morrow was here and the next day she would be back once more at Windycroft. It was really only a matter of hours now until she should see Mac, and then together they would bridge over the dark gulf of misunderstanding and distrust which had set them apart.

She jumped lightly out of bed. Spring was in the air, and spring was in her heart. Even the conventional hotel bedroom, flooded with the morning sunlight, took on a new aspect, and as Herrick splashed joyfully in her bath she could hardly believe that a day and a night could have so transformed the world. She sang while she dressed, humming away in a happy, husky little pipe of a voice as she moved about her room, and pictured to herself Mac reading the brief missive she had sent him, so non-committal in its wording and yet conveying to the man who received it all he wished—everything she wanted him to know.

For some reason, best explained by the peculiar intricacies of the feminine mind, she had only given Lady Bridget a very partial confidence.

"I've had a letter from Mac," she told her briefly.

324

"He wants to see me, so I've replied that he may come when we get back."

"Is that all, dear?" asked Mim. She had not quite understood the girl's varying moods of late.

"That's all at present," Herrick had answered, with a funny little smile.

Perhaps it was some superstitious fear of anticipating her happiness, of putting it into words before it was actually assured, that held her silent, lest the listening gods should overhear and mockingly snatch it from her. But, nevertheless, it continued to bubble up inside her, and when, soon after lunch, Gair Severn called for her—they had planned to go out somewhere together—she went to meet him with so radiant a face that Lady Bridget wondered within herself if she had possibly mistaken the direction in which the girl's happiness really lay. She said as much to Billy as he and she set off for a matinée performance at the theatre, leaving Herrick and her visitor in undisputed possession of the hotel sitting-room.

"I'm really puzzled, now, to know which of the two Herrick likes best—Mac or Gair Severn," she confessed, as the taxi they had taken threaded its way through the traffic.

Billy's nice green eyes grew round with astonishment.

"Why, Mac, of course. Surely there's no question about that," he answered. "She was sick and sorry enough when their engagement came to an end."

"I know she was—at the time. But there *is* such a thing as love coming to an end—if it's hurt badly enough, and, once that's happened, not all the king's

horses nor all the king's men can make it live again.
. . . And there's also such a thing as being caught at
the rebound."

"Darling old thing, your thoughts nip around so
fast that I can't keep pace with them," said Billy
patiently. "Do you mind explaining a little more?"

"Well, it seems to me it's possible that Mac's distrusting Herrick over the Two Ways Cottage affair
was just the one bit more, so to speak, than she could
stand—finished her as far as he was concerned. And
then, plump at the right moment, the other man comes
on the scene—Gair, in this case. He's quite an attractive sinner, you know—and not altogether a sinner,
either! And Herrick has been about with him here,
there, and everywhere since we came up to town."

"'M. He's seen to that," observed Billy rather
ruefully. On more than one occasion Severn had ridden
him off, as it were, and taken possession of Herrick,
much in the same way as he had once been wont to
push him aside when he wanted Barbara's companionship.

"Herrick had seemed quite pleased to have him with
her," suggested Lady Bridget mildly. "I really think"
—smiling—"we must hold ourselves prepared for any
eventuality, Bill."

"You don't mean that you think she'd ever *marry*
Severn?" he demanded incredulously. "Why, he's such
a—oh, I don't know!" he ended lamely.

"I don't think the idea's altogether 'off the map,'
as you would say," responded his mother. "After all,
Gair's rather an endearing rascal—and women always
have a soft corner in their hearts for a scapegrace."

Lady Bridget secretly owned to a very soft corner for Severn. "And if a woman has had a smash-up with one man, she almost invariably ends by marrying his diametrical opposite." At this juncture the taxi pulled up at the entrance to the theatre, and the conversation came automatically to an end.

Meanwhile, in the Rivingtons' sitting-room at the hotel, the two people who had supplied its principal topic had greeted each other with a cordiality that seemed to give some support to Lady Bridget's theory.

"Well," inquired Severn blithely, when they had shaken hands, "how shall we amuse ourselves this afternoon?"

"Oh, I don't mind one bit," replied Herrick—quite truthfully. Nothing really seemed to matter to-day. She was merely waiting, living for to-morrow, and to-day meant no more to her than so many hours to be got through with as little boredom as possible. A picture gallery, a tea-dance, even a Punch and Judy show— each and all she would have welcomed with the same negligent good-humour. It was all one to her, and she was in the mood to be mildly entertained by almost anything Gair cared to suggest. "What have you thought of? I feel too amiable to quarrel with you over it, whatever it is."

She smiled as she spoke, and something in the way she smiled, some unconscious revelation of an inner source of happiness that hovered round her lips, arrested his attention. His blue eyes raked her face with a sudden scrutiny.

"You seem unusually pleased with life to-day," he remarked. "One might almost think you and Kenyon had made up your quarrel. Have you?" he added abruptly.

She flushed warmly at the direct question, hesitated a moment, then met his glance with a half nervous, half deprecating frankness.

"We haven't yet. But we're going to," she said simply. It was better, she decided swiftly, that he should know what impended—realise once and for all that it was useless his harbouring false hopes.

They were sitting together by the window, and, as she spoke, it seemed to her that his whole figure suddently tautened as if he were bracing himself for some tremendous effort.

"Have you seen him then—seen Kenyon?" he demanded sharply.

"No." Against her will, she felt impelled to tell him what had happened. She could sense his demand to know so strongly that it was as though he were deliberately imposing his will upon hers. "No. But he has written to me. The—foolish thing we quarrelled over has been explained. It was just a misunderstanding."

"I'm sorry," he said bluntly.

"That isn't very nice of you, Gair. It would be more friendly if you tried to be a little glad—for my sake. Couldn't you be?" she added on a note of appeal.

He brushed her words aside almost violently.

"Haven't I told you before that friendship doesn't enter into it between you and me? I'm *not* your 'friend.' *I* don't want to be. I'm the man who wants to marry you—and I intend to."

Herrick felt her temper rising.

"It's ridiculous to talk like that," she replied with

spirit. "You can't make a woman marry you if she doesn't want to."

"Can't you? I think in some cases you can."

"This isn't one of them."

"Yes, it is. Herrick"—his voice softened to an unexpected warmth of tenderness. "I don't want to force you—to compel you. I'd ever so much rather not. That was why I was so glad when I knew your engagement was broken off. It seemed to give me a chance to win you other ways——"

"No," she interrupted. "You never had a chance, Gair. Believe me—never."

The sudden impulsive vehemence of her answer seemed to rouse the devil in him. When next he spoke all the tenderness had gone out of his voice. It was arrogant as of old—triumphantly, savagely arrogant.

"Then I've my chance—*now*," he said, speaking very deliberately and watching her intently while he spoke. "I happen to know who your father was. Kenyon doesn't. Do you think he'd marry you if he did—if I told him the truth about you?"

It was like a thunder-bolt out of a clear sky—like some hammer-blow of fate aimed at her with an unerring hand. She shrank back, white to the lips. Then, with a tremendous effort, gathered herself together to resist. Severn himself, in his heart, paid her unwilling homage for the pluck with which she faced him.

"Mac wouldn't mind if you did tell him," she said, her straight, steady glance defying him. "*I* have already told him, as much as he would hear. And he simply *does not care* what my father did."

For a moment Gair was silent. Almost it seemed

as if a flash of involuntary pity showed itself in his eyes as they rested on the slight young figure of this girl so gamely confronting the fate which had dogged her long enough and now threatened to bring her house of happiness—scarcely yet regained—in ruins about her feet. Then the pity died out. He had recognised the flaw in her defence and snatched at it. "Perhaps he might not care—in the abstract. But did you ever tell him that your father was—Quintin Lindris?" He laid a significant stress on the last two words.

"No . . . no," she said uncertainly, obviously shaken. "But I don't see what difference that makes—whether his name happened to be Quintin Landris or John Brown. It was what he did that mattered."

"It makes all the difference in the world, in this case."

"But why—why?" she repeated. Without being able to divine the wherefore, she was beginning to be conscious of an increasing fear. She felt as though there were still something—something terrible and calamitous, something of which she was in ignorance—waiting to leap at her out of the chaos which was Destiny.

Severn looked away for an instant out of the window to where the roofs across the road glinted in the afternoon sunlight. When his eyes came back to her face they held a curious look of concentration—definite, relentless.

"It makes all the difference in the world whether your father happened to be Quintin Lindris—or some other swindler," he said slowly. "Because it was Quintin Lindris who ruined Kenyon's father."

"Mac's father?" The words broke from her halt-ingly, incredulously. Then, because it seemed too hideous to be true: "You're lying!"

He shook his head.

"No. I'm not lying. Your father swindled old Kenyon out of every penny he possessed. He lost his entire fortune in the Lindris speculations. He'd been warned by a friend, but he believed Lindris in spite of the warning—and paid for his belief. He was only saved from blowing out his brains because he happened to die first—a few minutes before he would have pulled the trigger. It all came out in the papers at the time."

"Oh, no—no!" gasped Herrick.

She felt as though she were going mad. The whole horror of it rushed over her—the endless, insupportable tragedy. First Mac's father, ruined, and dead from shock; then his mother, fading out of existence because all that had meant love and happiness had been torn from her; and, last of all, Carol, by her despairing, unavailing effort to save that beloved life, trapped into the martyrdom of wifehood to Sir Francis. Three lives wrecked and made utterly desolate—the three lives most precious to the man she loved. And it was her father who had done this thing!

And now the mills of God were grinding out the last grains of ultimate and inevitable consequence.

Herrick passed her hand across her forehead and drew it away wet. Tiny beads of moisture rimmed her mouth, and her face had taken on a curious ashen pallor. Her eyes looked blank—stunned out of all expression.

"What are you going to do?" she said lifelessly.

"That depends upon you," answered Severn. "I hate to use such a weapon, but I'd go to any length to stop your marrying Kenyon. When he knows whose child you are, he won't want to marry you any longer."

She woke to sudden, shuddering life.

"You don't mean you'll tell him?" she cried, aghast.

He bent his head. A shamed determination blazed at her out of his eyes.

"Unless you'll marry me, I will. If you won't marry me, at least you shall never marry Kenyon."

She made no answer—only stared at him dumbly. He winced at the stark, naked agony in her face.

"Herrick——" He made a stumbling step towards her. "For God's sake don't look like that! Only say you'll marry me, and I swear Kenyon shall never know a word about your father. I hate to force you. Why on earth can't you say you'll marry me and spare us both any more of this? If——"

"Hush!" She made a little gesture, so bleak, so anguished, that it silenced him. "Let me understand. If I marry you, you'll keep silent about my father. If I won't, you'll tell Mac. Is that it?"

"Yes. But, if you will, I swear to God I'll make you happy," he urged desperately.

"Happy?" She smiled—a small, chill smile as though he were babbling foolishly of something that had no existence either in this world or the next. It checked the sudden passion which had been rising in his voice and he waited in sullen silence until she spoke again.

"Otherwise, you will tell Mac." Almost it seemed as

though she were communing with herself, had forgotten his presence.

"Yes. Otherwise I tell him," he said doggedly.

Again a heavy silence fell between them. Her gloves lay on a chair beside her. She had tossed them down there when she had first entered the room, ready dressed to go out. They caught her eye and she stooped and picked them up, smoothing them out meticulously between her fingers.

"You must give me a little time to make my choice, Gair," she said at last, without looking at him. "I can't decide here and now."

"When, then?" he asked hoarsely.

She paused.

"To-morrow morning—before I leave London."

She turned to leave the room, but before she was half-way across it she halted and looked back at him with a kind of detached curiosity in her eyes.

"Tell me—I forgot to ask you—how did you find out that I was the daughter of Quintin Lindris?" Her intonation was as casual, as indifferent, as though she had asked him where he bought his cigarettes.

Severn answered her explicitly.

"A man named Dereham—Rex Dereham—told me. He and I were dining together that first night when I met you and Billy at the Savoy. He saw you dancing."

Rex! So it was Rex, the man who had robbed her of her first girlish happiness, who had now slain all joy in life for her forever. It seemed curious, she reflected dully, when she found herself once more alone in her

own room, that Fate should twice use the same instru-
ment in order to accomplish her destruction. It made
her feel as though she had been travelling in a circle,
and now that she had come round again to the same
place where she started the same thing had happened
automatically a second time, the same blow been delivered at her happiness. Only on this occasion the blow
was immeasurably harder, more completely shatter-
ing. Fate had made a good job of the matter this time.

And Rex—had the cruelty of it all never struck
him? He was not cruel by nature, as she remembered
him, only rather weak and conventional. Probably he
had never intended to injure her as he had done by
enlightening Severn in regard to her identity. People
inflicted suffering on each other so lightly, so thought-
lessly—just for the sake of imparting a piece of gossipy
information, sometimes. She would give Rex the
benefit of the doubt; he had not intentionally done her
this grievous harm.

And then the thought of Rex passed out of her
mind and the problem of the choice which she was
called upon to make rose up before her and filled her
whole horizon. That Gair was prepared to keep his
word and tell Mac the facts she did not doubt, and
she had to think what was the best thing to do—not
for herself, but for the man she loved. There was
no question of any "best" for herself. Whatever
happened, once Mac knew the truth, whether she
married him or whether they parted finally and irrevocably, her whole life must henceforth be maimed and
shadowed by her father's sin.

Once she had thought she was going to escape her

destined heritage. But she knew, now, that there was no escape. She had thought that some similar tragic happening lay in Kenyon's past as in her own, and that they were equal in the burden which they each had to bear, that his father, too, had sinned. And now she knew that the only sin of which Mac's father had been guilty was that he had trusted her own father too blindly—had disregarded the warnings he had received. *That* was what Mac had meant when he told her that his father had been "unwise"—unwise over money matters. Oh, what a miserable fool she had been to so misunderstand, to have jumped so easily to the wrong conclusion—building her house of love on a foundation of sand!

Well, everything was quite clear now—terribly, hideously clear. She had only got to decide what to do . . . what to do . . . Oh, God! What *was* she to do? . . .

Plunged into the uttermost depths of an agony and despair that was almost more than she could endure, torn this way and that to arrive at some decision, she lost all count of time, and when at last she came to herself again the sun was dipping westward, its rays slanting rosily across the roofs opposite. But out of those hours of a suffering so intense that she felt physically weak and exhausted had come a clear, irrefutable knowledge of what she must do. She must marry Gair, and so save Mac from what, if she became his wife, could only end in misery and disaster.

Rex had once said he could not make her, the daughter of a swindler and a thief, the mother of his children. Still less was she fit to be the mother of Mac's children. She recognised it clearly. His children could not—*must* not be born from the stock of the man who was morally responsible for the death of Mac's own father and mother and for the tragedy of his sister's life.

And it must be she who would make the decision. She felt convinced that even if Gair told Mac the truth the latter would still insist upon marrying her —partly out of a sense of honour, and partly because, now that he knew how he had misjudged her, he would be so eager—so blindly eager—to prove his love, to atone for his distrust, that for the time being he would triumphantly refuse to let any other consideration enter in.

For the time being! But what would happen afterwards? Later, when there might be children, and Mac realised that his sons were the children's children of a swindler and a suicide, of the man who had ruined the lives of his own father and mother and sister? Herrick felt as though all the horror of their future together were unrolled before her. She could look forward and see how the shadow of her father's sin would slowly and inevitably spread itself over the whole of their married life like a blight.

Mac, however much he might fight against it, would be always sensible of the disgrace attaching to her parentage, of the taint in his children's blood, secretly living in constant dread of some manifestation of it. Above all, he would be conscious of a corroding sense of disloyalty to his own kith and kin in having married the woman whose father had wrecked their lives, and out of these things there would gradually be born an inalienable sense of antagonism towards his wife—an antagonism that might even extend itself to her children. Ultimately it must eat into all their happiness, poison it at its very source.

And it was she who must save Mac from this— save him from his very love for her—she who must take the choice out of his hands. This was the one good thing she could do in the world—the one reparation she could make for the evil which her father had wrought. And she could accomplish it by marrying Gair Severn. That would effectually cure Mac of his love for her, she reflected desolately, since he had always been jealous and suspicious of her friendship with Gair. And some day, when the smart and sting of the wound she had dealt him had softened with time, he would find some other woman who would make up to him for all the pain she had so unwittingly brought into his life.

Herrick slipped into Lady Bridget's room that evening just as the latter was dressing for dinner.

"I've something to tell you, Mim," she said. Her eyes were very bright, and a little rouge and lipstick, skillfully applied, completely concealed the pallor of her face. "Gair came here this afternoon to ask me to marry him."

Lady Bridget smiled.

"He's done that several times before, hasn't he?" she inquired with some amusement.

Herrick smiled back brilliantly.

"Yes, it's been rather chronic with him. He's coming to-morrow for my answer."

"What will it be? Have you made up your mind?"

Followed an infinitesimal pause. Then:

"It will be—yes," said Herrick.

CHAPTER XXXI

HERRICK'S DECISION

FOUR o'clock of an afternoon, and across the scented garden silence broke a man's clear utterance.

"I've come for my answer. Is it—absolution?"

Mac spoke quietly, but there was a clipped tenseness about his voice which held its own significance. Herrick stood very still by the sundial where he had found her, her arms full of the flowers she had been gathering for the house. The faint elusive scent of early pinks, the warmer perfume of wallflower and lilac, filled the air, and across the sheaf of sweetness she held clasped in her arms she stared with dry, aching eyes at the man who had spoken.

This was her cue—those few tensely uttered words, and now she must take it up and dash that look of eager hope, of supreme love only waiting for forgiveness, from his face.

Four o'clock! And at ten that very morning she had promised away her life into another's keeping—had told Gair Severn that she would be his wife. Afterwards, when the hurry and bustle of leaving London were over and the train was bearing her swiftly back to St. Heriot, her thoughts had been preoccupied with this very moment which had now arrived.

There was only one way of accomplishing her purpose. Mac must be made to believe that it was by her own will, her own choice, that she was marrying Gair. He would never have believed it if they had once made up their quarrel, bridged over the bitter misunderstanding which had separated them. But they had not bridged it yet—and it was for her to show him clearly that it never could be bridged. He must be convinced that her love for him had not been able to withstand the blow which his distrust of her had dealt it—made to believe that understanding had come too late. Only in this way would he let her go to Gair unhindered. The few non-committal words of the brief note she had sent him revealed nothing—pledged her to nothing, and now the letter she had penned with such an uprush of surpassing joy was to become the sword by which she cut herself asunder from that very happiness.

"Is it—absolution?"

Herrick lifted her head and her voice was perfectly steady as she gave him back his answer. She had rehearsed it mentally so many times.

"No, Mac, it isn't," she said. "I've thought it all over, and I don't feel that I can marry you now."

He fell back a step, almost as though she had dealt him a physical blow, and stared at her with eyes that held a desperate incredulity.

"Do you mean that?" he demanded hoarsely. "That you can't forgive me?"

"I don't mean it quite like that. I—I can forgive you—I could be friends again. But"—she shook her head—"but I don't want to marry you any longer."

"Friends! I'm not asking for friendship." It was

the echo of Gair's own words, she thought—horribly, ironically like. "Do you mean," he went on rapidly, "do you mean to say your love has been killed so easily? Or is it pride? I did distrust you—I know it, but I think many a man in my place would have done the same. And God knows I've paid for it—suffered for it. If I could wipe out that night at Two Ways Cottage with ten years of my life, I'd do it. . . ."

"Yes, if you could. Only one can't wipe out things, Mac." A sudden anguished recognition of the bitter truth of what she spoke drove at her. "That's just what one can't do—wipe out things!"

He could not know the inner thought which prompted that desolate cry, but the pain in her voice brought him quickly to her side.

"Won't you let me try, beloved?" He spoke with a passionate vehemence that almost broke through her defences. "Won't you give me the chance to *try* to wipe it out? Between us . . . Herrick . . ."

He would have swept her into his arms, but she drew sharply aside, lifting her hands instinctively to ward him off, and the flowers she had been holding spilled themselves about their feet. Her courage was going from her, her will weakening because of his dear nearness. The sound of his beloved, unhappy voice clamoured against her heart. She must finish with the matter—finish it while she still had the strength to carry out her purpose.

"No," she said, her voice flat and hard by reason of the compulsion she was putting on herself. "No. It's too late. I—I've changed my mind. I'm going to marry Gair Severn."

"God!"

There was a new and terrible note in his voice—an awakened note. Hitherto he had been fighting what he had expected to have to fight—a woman's hurt pride, love that had been wounded and bruised. But now, in so many words, calmly and without an atom of compunction, the woman he worshipped was telling him that she had promised herself to another man. So it wasn't either hurt pride or injured love that was dictating her refusal to marry him, as he had supposed. The plain truth was that he had been superseded—her love for him had been so light and fickle a thing that it had perished. His face hardened.

"I see," he said. Then, bitterly: "You've consoled yourself very quickly, haven't you? Surely, it would have been a little more—decent—to have waited, ever a few weeks, before so openly transferring your affections."

She shrank away from the savage contempt in his voice, and, unconsciously to herself, the agony she was enduring showed itself in her eyes. He was shaken by it, wondering, even now, whether he had misjudged her, whether, hurt and miserable at his treatment of her, she had not been over-persuaded into this engagement to Gair Severn.

"I can't believe it's true," he said. "It isn't you to do this thing, Herrick. You've allowed Severn to dominate you—while you were in London, while you were angry with me." He laid his hands on her shoulders, forcing her to face him. "Tell me—and if you answer yes this time, then I'll accept it as the truth: Do you really—honestly—want to marry him?"

With an effort she compelled herself to meet his eyes. This was the moment when she must play up, act to the utmost limit of her capability

"I honestly want to marry him," she said steadily, and there was that in her voice which carried utter conviction to the man beside her. "I couldn't be happy if I didn't." And she knew that she was speaking the sheerest truth, although truth from a standpoint which Kenyon could not possibly divine. "I'm—I'm sorry, Mac, but I can't marry you, that's all."

"It's enough," he said. And without another word he turned and left her.

She listened till his footsteps had died away. Then she stooped and, gathering up the flowers she had let fall, made her way slowly back to the house.

During the weeks that followed Lady Bridget tried very hard to elucidate the truth, to discover if there were any ulterior reason behind Herrick's engagement to Severn. She wanted so badly to make sure of the happiness of the girl she loved, and she found her elusively uncommunicative.

"You don't think you've been too precipitate?" she asked her one day tentatively. "Don't let a foolish pride spoil your life—if that's the only reason you've sent Mac away."

Herrick smiled.

"Are you suggesting that I should break off my engagement with Gair, now, and give Mac another trial, Mim?" she replied, with a little cool, derisive note in her voice. "One can't *keep on* chopping and changing, you know!"

"It's better to keep on chopping and changing than to make a mistake and marry the wrong man—a mistake which is going to last you for the rest of your life," returned Mim practically. "Look here, Herrick, if it's that, and you're afraid to dismiss Gair, let me do it for you. I know he's rather an impossible person to deal with, but I'm not afraid to tackle him—or anyone else—if it means your happiness."

Herrick flung her arms impulsively round the older woman's neck.

"Mim, you're the biggest angel on the face of the earth," she said warmly. "I believe you'd go to the stake or be cut up in little pieces if you thought it would be doing a good turn to someone else. But you needn't immolate yourself on any altar for me. I know now that it would have been a mistake if I'd made it up with Mac. You—you can't really make it up with people when once you've distrusted them— or they've distrusted you." She was surprised at the convincing ease with which she could lie. "And I'd rather—now—marry Gair than anyone else." That, at least, she reflected, was the truth.

Meanwhile Severn spent a great deal of time at the Rectory and was pressing for an early marriage. And now that he had gained his own way he was his old self once more, by turns whimsical and charming and imperious—and always a passionate and demanding lover.

"I swear I'll make you happy, Herrick," he told her one day. "Although I know you don't believe it. Honestly"—and there was something new and unaccustomed in his face as he spoke—a rare gravity in the dare-devil blue eyes, an odd, unwonted tenderness in the curve of his lips. "Honestly, I hated using the pressure I did. I'd far rather have won you without that. But you shall forget it all some day—when I've taught you to love me. As I will."

And Herrick had answered quietly:

"I shall never forget it. I've promised to marry you—but I've never promised to love you." With Gair, alone out of all the world in these days, was she able to be really herself—to be utterly and uncompromisingly truthful.

To Lady Bridget fell the task of trying to console Carol, who was miserably overwhelmed at the trend of events. She had felt so sure, after she had told Mac the true story of what occurred at Two Ways Cottage, that her brother and Herrick would make up their differences, that the news of the latter's engagement to Severn had come upon her as a blow—the harder to withstand because so entirely unexpected.

"I feel as if it's been all my fault—mine and Jem's," she declared wretchedly. "If I hadn't played the fool and gone to the cottage that night, none of this would have happened."

"No, my dear," answered Lady Bridget. "I'm afraid it's Mac's own fault. He has hurt Herrick beyond bearing—that's all. And Gair took the opportunity it gave him."

"I would never have believed that Herrick could be so unforgiving," declared Carol, bitter for her brother's lost happiness.

Lady Bridget sighed. She herself could not quite understand Herrick, but she upheld her with unwavering staunchness.

"You must try not to be too hard on her," she answered. "Remember, Gair has a curious gift of fascination for women. Even I—old as I am"—with a smile—"can recognise that in him. He's been terribly persistent, and I suppose at last he's carried Herrick off her feet."

"He's not good enough for her," protested Carol, swinging to the opposite side of the compass, torn betwixt her love for Herrick and her love for her brother.

"Very few men are good enough for the women they marry," replied Mim tranquilly. "I don't think even your adored Mac would be quite good enough for Herrick. As for Gair, he's headstrong and selfish. But"—her eyes twinkling—"those are not very uncommon faults with men. They're just like grown-up children—think they ought to have all they want in this world. I suppose that's why we women try to give it them."

So Carol took her way home, sore at heart, since hers was not a nature ever to acquire the humorous, tolerant, and tender philosophy which carried Mim through life. And in the hall she encountered Dr. Lincoln, whom a second, albeit less alarming heart attack had summoned once again to Sir Francis's sickbed, whither the latter had betaken himself with all speed when he felt the first symptoms.

The doctor shook hands, and there was a reflective look in his rather unfathomable eyes as he scanned

Carol's tired and wistful features. With a gesture he indicated an adjoining sitting-room, and followed her into it.

"It's his heart," he said simply. "It won't stand very much more of the drug he takes—or very much excitement of any nature. I've warned him again. . . . And I think it my duty to warn you. I give him a year —eighteen months at the outside."

He made no profession of sympathy, but stared with apparent absorption into the crown of his hat. When he had finished speaking he raised his eyes once more to her face and their expression was as inscrutable as usual.

"Good afternoon, Lady Mortimer."

And whether he knew, or did not know, all that his pronouncement held of ultimate happiness and freedom for the woman standing beside him, quietly listening, it was impossible to tell.

CHAPTER XXXII

THE DOORS OF HAPPINESS

TIME either flies or crawls, but, whichever it does, it is invariably the exact antithesis of what we want it to do. In moments of happiness, when we would so gladly prolong each one into a hundredfold its length, it rushes past us like the wind, whereas each pain-filled second stretches itself into a small eternity.

To Herrick, inwardly dreading the day fixed for her marriage with Gair Severn, the time seemed positively to flash by. Morning had hardly dawned when evening came treading almost on its heels, then a few brief hours of darkness and it was morning again. And so the race went on until she woke to her last day of freedom, to the day whose morrow would make her Severn's wife.

It had been settled that the wedding should take place in London, as quietly as possible. This had been Herrick's stipulation, and nothing would move her from it. She felt that it would be more than she could endure to be married in the little grey church at St. Heriot, set so peacefully amid the country woods and fields, the church where she and Mac had been wont to worship Sunday after Sunday, and where she had dreamed that they two would be made man and wife— more than she could bear to see Alec Fane, with his kind, discerning eyes, waiting for her at God's altar, hear his familiar voice, with its underlying note of tender friendship, pronounce those solemn words which would forever cut her off from any hope of happiness. No, she had taken up her burden, the burden which her father's sins had laid upon her, and she would carry it to the end, but she would at least omit those refinements of torture which a wedding at St. Heriot would entail.

So it had been arranged that, accompanied by Lady Bridget and Billy, she should go up to town the day before that appointed for the ceremony, and then be quietly married in her travelling dress at one of the churches in London—a church which held no memories, no dreams.

And now the actual day of departure had arrived. Overnight, Herrick had been busily occupied in finishing the packing of her trunks and in either destroying or throwing away the litter of odds and ends—old letters, trinkets, valueless trifles of all sorts—which everyone seems prone to accumulate. There had been one or two things over which she had hesitated, which she would like to have kept. A small—very small—packet of letters, brief little notes that Mac had had occasion to write her at one time or another, the programme of a concert at Tanborough to which they had gone together one afternoon, a four-leaved clover he had picked for her one day and given her, saying laughingly: "Don't lose your luck!" But she had lost her luck so completely that there was no use in keeping the symbols of it any longer, and so these few poor little relics went their way along with the other rubbish.

She had been very Spartan in her clearance, and now, on this final morning, as she glanced round her sitting-room to see if anything had been forgotten, the room, denuded of its familiar touches, had a curiously bare and unlived-in appearance. She wandered over to the window and looked drearily out across the park. The lake, gleaming in the valley below, sparkled up at her in the sunshine; a mist of young green clothed the trees. Spring everywhere—spring with its prophecy of summer, its promise of fulfilment. She felt her eyes suddenly wet and drew her hand across them quickly.

"Don't be mawkish!" she apostrophised herself, and turned abruptly from the window to find Lady Bridget standing on the threshold of the room. She came in quietly and closed the door behind her.

"How bare it looks without all your own little knick-knacks about," she said, looking round the room regretfully. "Herrick child, I don't know what I shall do without you."

"I hope you'll ask me to stay, sometimes," suggested Herrick, smiling determinedly.

Lady Bridget regarded her with soft eyes.

"There's not much doubt about that," she said. "Meanwhile——" She hesitated, fingering a letter she held in her hand.

Herrick felt her breath catch suddenly in her throat. Was the letter for her? She could not see the handwriting, but something, some wild, irrepressible hope woke in her heart. Was it a last word—some last word of kindliness, of farewell—from Mac?

"Is that for me?" she asked with dry lips, glancing towards the letter.

"Yes," said Lady Bridget. "It's for you. It's from your father. He wanted it to be given to you on your twenty-first birthday, or on your wedding-eve if you were married before then."

A curious sense of unreality took hold of Herrick at the thought of receiving a letter from a man who had been dead more than three, nearly four years.

"From my father?" she repeated wonderingly.

Lady Bridget nodded.

"He sent it to me just before he died, and I've kept it for you ever since. Once"—with a faint smile—"I thought I should have to keep it always. I thought I should never find you."

She slipped the letter into the girl's hand and left the room, to read again, as she had read it many a time during the years when she had been secretly searching for Lindris's daughter, another letter, written by the same dead hand, which had accompanied the sealed envelope she had just given to Herrick.

"By the time you get this, Bridget," it ran, "I shall be well out of harm's way. I can't grumble. I've had a good run for my money, and if I've come a cropper at the last fence it was only to be expected. If you ride hell for leather, hell generally gets you sooner or later. So I'm clearing off to the place which issues no return tickets, and the only thing that worries me is—Herrick. People are always inclined to ask rather a lot of you 'for the sake of old times'—and that's just what I'm going to do. Do you remember the kiddy —a small brat of five when you last saw her? She'll be left high and dry when I'm gone, with nary a soul in this world to look after her. (Even if I elected to stay in it, I couldn't help her one jot, as the scope of my activities would be a trifle circumscribed! In any case, a father in gaol is hardly an asset to any young woman.) So will you, out of the kindness of that big heart of yours—for it was always a big heart, Bridget—give her a helping hand at the start? Somehow I know you will, and I'm going out secure in that knowledge.

"Give the enclosed packet to the child when she is twenty-one. Or, if she should marry before then, give it her on her wedding-eve. It's the only wedding-present I can give her—and it's costing me more than you'd think to give it her at all."

Very quietly Lady Bridget re-read for the hundredth time this last letter from the one man she had really loved—written to her a few minutes before he took his own way out of life, with the means of a swift exit from the world in which there was no longer any place for him lying beside him on the desk. She had carried out his last behest, found—and loved —the child he had left behind him. Her lips moved as though she were speaking to someone who was near at hand, who could hear what she said.

"I've done what you wanted, Quin—kept her safe."

She alone guessed what it must have cost Quintin Lindris to write that letter—consigning the care of his child to someone else. Probably that had been the bitterest drop in the cup he had brewed for his own drinking. For Lindris had always been imbued with a passionate love for children. It had been the one entirely beautiful trait in a character that was otherwise warped and marred. For him, the longing to have a child of his own had been the desire of his life.

"Think of the marvel of it, Bridget," he had said to her once, in the young, far-away days when they had believed that all their lives would be spent together. "To have a little chap belonging to one—like oneself, like the woman one worships, born of love. Oh, I think it must be the most wonderful thing in the world to have a child of one's own!"

And although that first dream of his—when she herself had been the dream-woman, the dream-mother in it—had never come quite true, another, later love had come into his life for the woman whom he had eventually married—Dorothy Vaughan, whose first husband, after leading her a dog's life, had finally been killed in a French railway accident, leaving her practically penniless.

It was then, during one of his sojournings abroad, that Lindris had met her, and her frail beauty and tragic plight had appealed to him so instantly and deeply that he had fallen in love and married her as soon as possible. Lady Bridget did not meet her until they returned to England, two years later, accompanied by a girl-baby, frail and tiny like its mother. The "little chap" Lindris had longed for had not materialised, but his adoration of the small Herrick was so intense that the father-love in the man appeared completely satisfied.

Afterwards, when a swift and sudden illness had robbed him of the fragile woman he had grown to worship, it seemed as though the whole of his love had thenceforth centred itself in her child, and the two became all in all to each other. And now that child was reading his last letter to her, reading between its scribbled lines how devotedly—albeit selfishly and wrong-headedly—he had loved her.

Enclosed with the letter was an old signet ring which her mother had always worn, together with one or two legal-looking papers and a birth certificate. These Herrick laid on one side for later perusal, and, unfolding her father's letter, began to read it. At the first few lines, an expression of bewilderment crossed her face, then she bent over the closely-written sheets, absorbed in their contents.

"Herrick, little old pal," ran the letter, "I wonder if when you have read this to the end, you will be able to find it in your heart to forgive me, will still try to think of me as the good comrade I always wanted to be to you. I hope so, for, whatever else this letter takes from you of our memories together, the memory of our comradeship one with the other remains true and real. This you can still believe— that I loved you as much and as completely as any father could love his child. Even though I was not in reality your father. That's the whole reason of this letter—to tell you that there was no actual blood-relationship between us.

"You were Dorothy's child, not mine. You came into the world three months after your father died, and because he never even saw you—never touched or kissed you—it seemed to me to make you more utterly and completely her child. Her child, not his. And I loved you at first just *because* you were hers. So I made you mine, and you were never told that I was not your actual father. And later on, as you grew up, I loved you so much for yourself that I could never have endured that you should know you were not really mine. I thought of you as mine—loved you as mine.

"It was an easy enough deception to carry through. You weren't ten weeks old when Dorothy and I were married, and when we returned to England, a couple of years afterwards, there was no reason for anyone to suspect that you were not my very own child. And you were such a wee mite of a thing for your age that no one did suspect.

"But now I've made such a holy hash of things that the only choice ahead of me is prison or death, and there's no question which I shall take. I can't leave you a sixpence, my dear—I've nothing to leave. But there's still one gift I can give you—the knowledge that you are not the child of a swindler. A clean sheet, little Herrick—that's my last gift to you. Probably you'll think I ought to have let you know the truth long before you will receive this—not deliberately delayed your learning it. I suppose I ought. But somehow I can't bring myself to do it. I've a selfish fancy to remain a little longer in your heart just as I used to be. I wonder if you'll understand how much I hate your ever knowing that I'm not really your father, that you're not Dorothy's child—and *mine?*

I don't suppose you will. I've faced most things in life, and now I'm facing death, but somehow I couldn't face this. I suppose we've all got our breaking-point somewhere, and that's mine. Anyway, even if you don't quite understand, try and forgive me."

At first, when Herrick had finished reading the letter, she felt stunned—too stupefied to realise its far-reaching significance. Mechanically she examined the birth certificate and other papers which had accompanied it, although she felt no need of further proof. The letter itself rang with stark truth.

One thought overwhelmed all others: The man whom she had always regarded as her father was *not* her father, was, indeed, no relation whatsoever. Her first swift consciousness was one of loss. She felt curiously bereft. Her father had constituted everything of kith and kin that she had ever known—her recollection of her mother was too vague to count—and now the relationship which had been interwoven with the whole of her life had been suddenly wrenched from her.

That was her first reaction to the contents of the letter. She picked it up and her glance wandered bewilderedly over it once more. And all at once three words seemed to leap at her from its pages, bringing with them a sudden realisation of its whole import— its wonderful and glorious import: *"A clean sheet."*

A clean sheet! Why, that meant—that meant that she was no longer an outcast, no longer to be branded as the daughter of a swindler and a suicide! She was

herself—free, with no bitter heritage to carry. There
would be no more need to fear the future, to be afraid
of the taint in her blood. There *was* no taint—no
handicap. And with that realisation came the knowledge that there was no longer any barrier betwixt her
and the man she loved—nothing to keep them apart.
The doors of happiness had been suddenly flung open
to her—wide open. She could pass through them into a
clean and goodly world—pass through and find love
waiting for her.

It was somewhat a tremulous and shaken Herrick
who presently carried her news to Lady Bridget. But,
beneath the ebb and flow of the conflicting emotions
that stirred within her, the pluck and directness which
had upheld her when life had seemed to hold nothing
but pain governed her still. She was determined that
no false pride, no vacillation should spoil the sweetness
and fullness and beauty of life now that it had been
so amazingly given back to her.

"I'm going to send a note over to Greenwood, now
at once, asking Mac to come to me," she told Mim
steadily. "And I shall telegraph to Gair, telling him
I can't marry him. I'll write to him as well, explaining
why."

And Lady Bridget, whose own life and marriage
had been so woefully arranged for her by her parents,
smiled a thought wistfully, yet with an unselfish gladness in her heart, at the frank, sure way in which this
child of a later, freer generation handled her own
affairs—coolly, on the actual verge of a marriage in
which love had no part, brushing aside the conven-

tions which might have held her to it and forging straight ahead in search of happiness with the man she loved.

To Herrick no other course was possible, or even conceivable. Her love for Mac swept all other considerations away. Long ago she had forgiven him the one thing for which he had needed forgiveness—his distrust of her, just as now, in her new-found freedom, she could find it in her heart to forgive her father for jealously guarding his secret so long—even though, by so doing, he had bequeathed her such unhappiness. He could not know, had not stopped to think, how much his selfish secrecy might cost her, she argued, and what she had once told Mim in regard to Mac held true also in regard to the man she had never ceased to love as father—"You can't help forgiving people you love."

There was only one thing which puzzled and bewildered her, for which she could find no explanation— no key to the enigma. And this she confided to Mac when the first glorious ecstasy of reunion had melted into the sure stability of mutual understanding.

"It's so difficult to understand the why and wherefore of things," she said uncertainly. "The whole of this time I've been fighting against something that was only imaginary—breaking you and myself against a wall which didn't really exist. It all seems to have been so useless—so purposeless."

And Mac, standing hand in hand with her, both of them children of Time peering into the dim and hidden alleys of Eternity, kindled to a brief vision of the ultimate unfolding.

"Your pluck was the same as if what you believed to be true had been actually the truth," he said slowly. "I think that's what counts in life. Don't you see, beloved, it's just the fact that you put up such a splendid fight which makes you—*you*."

THE END

There Are Two Sides to Everything—

—including the wrapper which covers every Grosset & Dunlap book. When you feel in the mood for a good romance, refer to the carefully selected list of modern fiction comprising most of the successes by prominent writers of the day which is printed on the back of every Grosset & Dunlap book wrapper.

You will find more than five hundred titles to choose from—books for every mood and every taste and every pocketbook.

Don't forget the other side, but in case the wrapper is lost, write to the publishers for a complete catalog.

THE NOVELS OF TEMPLE BAILEY

THE BLUE WINDOW

The heroine, Hildegarde, finds herself transplanted from the middle western farm to the gay social whirl of the East. She is almost swept off her feet, but in the end she proves true blue.

PEACOCK FEATHERS

The eternal conflict between wealth and love. Jerry, the idealist who is poor, loves Mimi, a beautiful, spoiled society girl.

THE DIM LANTERN

The romance of little Jane Barnes who is loved by two men.

THE GAY COCKADE

Unusual short stories where Miss Bailey shows her keen knowledge of character and environment, and how romance comes to different people.

THE TRUMPETER SWAN

Randy Paine comes back from France to the monotony of every-day affairs. But the girl he loves shows him the beauty in the common place.

THE TIN SOLDIER

A man who wishes to serve his country, but is bound by a tie he cannot in honor break—that's Derry. A girl who loves him, shares his humiliation and helps him to win—that's Jean. Their love is the story.

MISTRESS ANNE

A girl in Maryland teaches school, and believes that work is worthy service. Two men come to the little community; one is weak, the other strong, and both need Anne.

CONTRARY MARY

An old-fashioned love story that is nevertheless modern.

GLORY OF YOUTH

A novel that deals with a question, old and yet ever new—how far should an engagement of marriage bind two persons who discover they no longer love.

THE NOVELS OF
GRACE LIVINGSTON HILL

GROSSET & DUNLAP, *Publishers*, NEW YORK

MARGARET PEDLER'S NOVELS

TO-MORROW'S TANGLE

The game of love is fraught with danger. To win in the finest sense, it must be played fairly.

RED ASHES

A gripping story of a doctor who failed in a crucial operation---and had only himself to blame. Could the woman he loved forgive him?

THE BARBARIAN LOVER

A love story based on the creed that the only important things between birth and death are the courage to face life and the love to sweeten it.

THE MOON OUT OF REACH

Nan Davenant's problem is one that many a girl has faced---her own happiness or her father's bond.

THE HOUSE OF DREAMS-COME-TRUE

How a man and a woman fulfilled a Gypsy's strange prophecy.

THE HERMIT OF FAR END

How love made its way into a walled-in house and a walled-in heart.

THE LAMP OF FATE

The story of a woman who tried to take all and give nothing.

THE SPLENDID FOLLY

Do you believe that husbands and wives should have no secrets from each other?

THE VISION OF DESIRE

An absorbing romance written with all that sense of feminine tenderness that has given the novels of Margaret Pedler their universal appeal.

WAVES OF DESTINY

Each of these stories has the sharp impact of an emotional crisis---the compressed quality of one of Margaret Pedler's widely popular novels.

GROSSET & DUNLAP, *Publishers*, NEW YORK

RUBY M. AYRES' NOVELS

May be had wherever books are sold.   Ask for Grosset & Dunlap's list.

THE MAN THE WOMEN LOVED

THE LITTL'ST LOVER

CANDLE LIGHT

THE MAN WITHOUT A HEART

THE ROMANCE OF A ROGUE

RICHARD CHATTERTON

A BACHELOR HUSBAND

THE SCAR

THE MARRIAGE OF BARRY WICKLOW

THE UPHILL ROAD

WINDS OF THE WORLD

THE SECOND HONEYMOON

THE PHANTOM LOVER

GROSSET & DUNLAP, *Publishers*, NEW YORK

GEORGE W. OGDEN'S WESTERN NOVELS

THE BARON OF DIAMOND TAIL

The Elk Mountain Cattle Co. had not paid a dividend in years: so Edgar Barrett, fresh from the navy, was sent West to see what was wrong at the ranch. The tale of this tenderfoot outwitting the buckaroos at their own play will sweep you into the action of this salient western novel.

THE BONDBOY

Joe Newbolt, bound out by force of family conditions to work for a number of years, is accused of murder and circumstances are against him. His mouth is sealed; he cannot, as a gentleman, utter the words that would clear him. A dramatic, romantic tale of intense interest.

CLAIM NUMBER ONE

Dr. Warren Slavens drew claim number one, which entitled him to first choice of rich lands on an Indian reservation in Wyoming. It meant a fortune; but before he established his ownership he had a hard battle with crooks and politicians.

THE DUKE OF CHIMNEY BUTTE

When Jerry Lambert, "the Duke," attempts to safeguard the cattle ranch of Vesta Philbrook from thieving neighbors, his work is appallingly handicapped because of Grace Kerr, one of the chief agitators, and a deadly enemy of Vesta's. A stirring tale of brave deeds, gun-play and a love that shines above all.

THE FLOCKMASTER OF POISON CREEK

John Mackenzie trod the trail from Jasper to the great sheep country where fortunes were being made by the flock-masters. Shepherding was not a peaceful pursuit in those bygone days. Adventure met him at every turn—there is a girl of course—men fight their best fights for a woman—it is an epic of the sheeplands.

THE LAND OF LAST CHANCE

Jim Timberlake and Capt. David Scott waited with restless thousands on the Oklahoma line for the signal to dash across the border. How the city of Victory arose overnight on the plains, how people savagely defended their claims against the "sooners;" how good men and bad played politics, makes a strong story of growth and American initiative.

TRAIL'S END

Ascalon was the end of the trail for thirsty cowboys who gave vent to their pent-up feelings without restraint. Calvin Morgan was not concerned with its wickedness until Seth Craddock's malevolence directed itself against him. He did not emerge from the maelstrom until he had obliterated every vestige of lawlessness, and assured himself of the safety of a certain dark-eyed girl.

GROSSET & DUNLAP, Publishers, NEW YORK